A fight for her rights. A job she can't quit. And a man who makes her burn . . .

It's not Shannon Calhoun's first rodeo. She's supposed to be running the show. But since her father's will landed her in a wretched cubicle, typing out press releases for her own family's company, she's been trapped in a job with no prospects, no control—and barely any cash.

When her old flame Billy Pagan turns up with a hundred rude questions and a thousand-dollar suit, Shannon isn't sure if the heat she feels is from humiliation, fury, or desire. But whatever else has happened, the chemistry between them has only intensified.

Long before he became Houston's best defense attorney, Billy had a thing for the spoiled rich girl who got away. But now that Shannon is hustling to save the family business, she's more irresistible than ever. Too bad about the murder investigation and the fraud that's going to bring the company crashing down around her.

Unless, of course, his Texas princess actually pulls off the save of a lifetime. With Billy's negotiating skills and Shannon's determination, the hardest part might be keeping the business away from the pleasure . . .

Books by Gerry Bartlett

Texas Fire
Texas Heat

Published by Kensington Publishing Corporation

Texas Pride

The Texas Heat Series

Gerry Bartlett

LYRICAL PRESS
Kensington Publishing Corp.
www.kensingtonbooks.com

Lyrical Press books are published by
Kensington Publishing Corp. 119 West 40th Street New York, NY 10018

All Kensington titles, imprints, and distributed lines are available at special quantity discounts for bulk purchases for sales promotion, premiums, fundraising, and educational or institutional use.

Special book excerpts or customized printings can also be created to fit specific needs. For details, write or phone the office of the Kensington Special Sales Manager:
Kensington Publishing Corp.
119 West 40th Street
New York, NY 10018
Attn. Special Sales Department. Phone: 1-800-221-2647.

Kensington and the K logo Reg. U.S. Pat. & TM Off.
LYRICAL PRESS Reg. U.S. Pat. & TM Off.
Lyrical Press and the L logo are trademarks of Kensington Publishing Corp.

First Electronic Edition: October 2017
eISBN-13: 978-1-60183-986-2
eISBN-10: 1-60183-986-3

First Electronic Edition: October 2017
eISBN-13: 978-1-60183-987-9
eISBN-10: 1-60183-987-1

Printed in the United States of America

This book is dedicated to Jackolyn Landry, a strong Texas woman.
Love you, Aunt Jackie!

Dear Reader,

Yes, I'm from Texas, born and raised. I still live here and love to write about the Lone Star State. The oil industry is a big part of it. Many native Texans have their own stories to share about big oil. If only my father-in-law hadn't left the oil fields back in the day to become a plumber...

Houston, in particular, rises and falls on the price of oil. I drive past pumping oil wells and refineries all the time on my way to the big city to shop. Fortunes are won and lost daily here and the social scene thrives because of the oil rich. Of course, the closest I get to the business is when I fill my tank at the gas pump. I hope you enjoy this peek inside Calhoun Petroleum. (You know it's my own creation, don't you?)

Another figment of my imagination is the Indian tribe in *Texas Pride*. I based it very loosely on the Alabama-Coushatta Indians who live in the piney woods near Lake Livingston, Texas. The reservation is beautiful and the tribe recently opened a casino. No, they don't serve alcohol--I added that bit to fit my story. Everything about my hero Billy Pagan is fictional and my writer's mind added details about the Tribe as well. Apologies in advance if I accidentally offended anyone.

I hope you enjoy the third book in the *Texas Heat* series. Shannon is the eldest of the three Calhoun sisters. As a romance writer, I took a vow to always give my characters a happily ever after, even though how they get there may not be easy. I hope you enjoy Shannon's journey.

Gerry Bartlett

Chapter 1

"This is my desk? In this cubicle? You have got to be kidding." Shannon Calhoun threw her purse on top of the scarred wood. "My family's name is on this company. Honey, I didn't put on my Prada pumps for this."

The woman who'd walked her here from personnel didn't bother to hide her smirk.

"They're such lovely Prada pumps too." A middle-aged woman in a fashionable black suit leaned over the partition that supposedly gave the cube some privacy. "Run along, Marge. I've got this."

"Are you sure, Ms. Wilson?" The woman from personnel, Marge, seemed reluctant to leave.

"She said to run along. You afraid to miss the fireworks?" Shannon smiled and apparently she still had what it took to make underlings like Marge get the message. She ran.

"Look around the room, Ms. Calhoun." Ms. Wilson gestured with a well-manicured hand. "See anyone else here?"

Shannon stepped out into the aisle. Her footsteps echoed as she walked between the rows of cubes. Clean desktops, neatly shoved in rolling chairs. The whole place had the air of a ghost town.

"Where is everybody?" Shannon faced the dragon in good shoes.

"Laid off. It seems public relations isn't exactly a top priority in a company that's foundering. I've been told your father left a will that puts you to work—hopefully you will earn your keep since Calhoun Petroleum can't afford any dead wood. Follow me." Wilson turned and strode toward the end of the aisle and a closed office door.

Shannon swallowed. Reality? It had been hitting her hard ever since her daddy had died. First there'd been the reading of his will and a surprise half-sister. On top of that, the price of oil had taken a plunge that had the entire industry in a tailspin. Their family's personal issues piled on to make it seem like Calhoun Petroleum was destined for bankruptcy unless she and her siblings could work a miracle.

She followed the stylish woman rocking her own designer outfit and straightened her shoulders. She had to make good in this job. Wilson threw open the door just as Shannon noticed that it read Caroline Wilson, Vice President of Public Relations on the nameplate. Huh.

"Time to get to work. I read your resume. Thank God you have a degree in marketing and seem to have been quite active in local charity work." She handed Shannon a stapled pack of papers.

"Yes. I've been on the board of several worthwhile causes." Shannon noticed that while Wilson sat behind her desk, she didn't offer her a chair. "I'm really involved with the rodeo committees, for the scholarships they give. And then there's the ballet and the medical center—"

"Fine, fine. So you have contacts. That will help when you start making phone calls. Because here's what I need for you to do." Wilson nodded toward the papers Shannon now held. "Calhoun Petroleum has been very generous over the years with various charities."

"I know. It's good for our image." Shannon glanced at the top page and actually got excited. The gala for the Cancer Society. That was one of her favorites. *Of course* she'd be glad to go and represent the company. Maybe a new ball gown could go on an expense account.

"Your job today is to call every one of those organizations and regretfully decline their invitations to buy a table or sponsor the event. We can't afford to give generously this year, as much as we'd love to participate. Blah, blah, blah." Wilson sat behind her desk, her smile fixed as she leaned back. The window wall behind her had a breathtaking view of the city. "The Ballet Ball is coming up soon. Get right on that one. They'll have to scramble to find another underwriter."

Shannon struggled for breath. This couldn't be. It was so humiliating. Her entire social life existed because she was on charity boards, helped raise funds, wrote checks.

"Is there a problem, Ms. Calhoun? I put the contact person's name and telephone number right there on the list. Your background should help you smooth the waters, so to speak. The social season is about to start. Time's a wasting. As I said, it's very late for us to notify that we are pulling out." Wilson leaned forward. "And we *are* pulling out."

"No! You can't be serious. Everyone will know Calhoun is in trouble. It's a PR nightmare." Shannon glanced at the first name on the list. "Reconsider the Ballet Ball! If we cut funding, they might not be able to bring in their guest dancer, a soloist for *Swan Lake* this year."

"The PR nightmare would be if our check bounced." Wilson picked up her phone. "Now I suggest you hop to it. If you have any more concerns about the funding, take it up with your sister, the new CFO—I believe her office is two floors up."

Shannon clutched the papers and stalked off to her assigned hole. Impossible. It had been bad enough going through human resources. She may have made a scene when she'd realized what her pay was going to be. But it was ridiculous.

She sat in the chair and stared at the list. She knew some of these contact people personally and just couldn't do it.

Two floors up.

Her newly discovered half-sister Cassidy had proved to be a valuable ally and was a whiz with numbers. Surely she would understand that this was the wrong move. Bad publicity. Shannon grabbed her cell and her list and headed for the elevator.

* * * *

Cassidy's floor was certainly not a ghost town. It bustled with activity. Of course. This was where they figured out the money. Her sister even had an assistant who guarded her door.

"Holly, I have to see her. This is very important company business." Shannon's feet were starting to hurt. She'd never given these beautiful shoes this much of a workout.

"She's in a meeting, Shannon." Holly Rogers gestured to a couch then smiled. "They should be done soon. If you wait, I'll let her know you need to see her. First day on the job?"

"Yes." Shannon sat. She was tempted to ease out of the right shoe but toughed it out. Her right foot had always been slightly bigger than her left. "I don't seem to have a secretary or assistant or anyone to help me."

"I remember seeing the memo. Public relations took a hard hit in the layoffs." Holly held up a hand when her phone buzzed. "Excuse me." She answered the phone.

Shannon studied Cassidy's layout. Big office, name on the door. But she couldn't be too jealous. Cass had a business degree and banking experience. She'd already impressed the board of directors with the way she'd started work early and jumped in with some solutions when they'd found out Calhoun Petroleum was on shaky ground for a number of reasons. She was bucking to be named CEO in their father's place. Since no one with sense would want to board this sinking ship, Shannon bet she got the job. Then she'd be moved up another two floors to Daddy's office.

Shannon hadn't even known about her father's first marriage and daughter until that crazy will had been read a few weeks ago. Now she was glad Cass had turned out to be smart and was doing what she could to save the company that was their inheritance. She was nice too. In her place, Shannon wasn't sure she wouldn't be bitter if she'd been left to grow up poor when the rest of the Calhouns had lived in luxury just a few miles away.

And then there was what had happened once Cass had started working at Calhoun's headquarters. She'd been attacked in the parking garage. More than once. Then finally in her office here.

Shannon shuddered. When they'd found out who wanted Cass out of the way, it had been the worst shock ever. All the chaos had led to Shannon starting work weeks late. But she was here now. She wanted to make it up to Cass. Show her that she was behind her and wanted to help the company turn around. But dropping the charities was not the way. Hopefully she'd listen.

"Shannon?" Holly stood in front of her. "Cass says to come on in. She's meeting with the lawyer and wants you to hear what they're discussing. Family business."

"Oh, right." Shannon jumped up. That "family business" concerned her father and his shady dealings when he'd started Calhoun Petroleum. It was an even bigger problem than the low price of oil these days.

Holly opened Cassidy's office door. "Here she is, Cass."

Shannon stepped inside, assuming it would be the same lawyer who'd taken care of her father's will. But no. Instead, it was the man who was best known in Houston as the one to call when you were in trouble with the law. Criminal law.

"Billy Pagan? Well, hell. We must really be in deep shit if Cass called you to help us." Shannon ignored his hand, which he'd held out to her, and collapsed into a chair.

"You are. In deep shit." William P. Pagan took the chair next to her. "Nice to see you again, Shannon. You look very"—he swept his gaze over her, starting at her feet and lingering at various spots until he got to her newly highlighted hair—"professional."

"Why, thank you, Billy. That's very polite of you to notice." Shannon looked him over too. Custom-tailored suit in black that matched his hair and brows. He was in great shape, his broad shoulders set off by the way that jacket fit so perfectly. He had a silk tie in red that looked perfect against a white shirt that made his bronze skin glow. She wondered if a salesman had helped him put the outfit together or a new girlfriend. Not that she cared.

"Cassidy, are we thinking that what Daddy did was *criminal* behavior? Is that why you called in Billy?" Shannon tore her gaze away from Billy when she realized he was smiling at her.

Cassidy moved out from behind her desk and pulled up a chair. It still gave Shannon a start that her new sister with her dark hair and stubborn chin looked so much like their late father. "I wasn't sure. I wanted an opinion and Mason thought Billy might be a little more comfortable with this type of case than his brother."

Dylan MacKenzie was the lawyer handling their father's estate and the will. He was also an expert in oil and gas issues. His brother Mason was their evaluator who had to make sure they followed the terms laid out in that will as they worked in the company for the next year, or lose their inheritance. Shannon hated how complicated it had all become. Cassidy had fallen hard for Mason so she seemed to be in her element, running the company and living with Mason now. The way things were shaking out made Shannon wonder if she was going to find herself left out when the year was over.

"Dylan and I go way back. Went to law school together. But Shannon knows that." Billy leaned toward Cass which meant his shoulder brushed Shannon's. "He's perfect for the kind of paper pushing he does day in and day out, like your daddy's will. But if you need to get down and dirty, I'm your man." He actually winked at Shannon. "Shan knows what I mean."

"Back off, Billy." Shannon could smell his cologne. It was so damned subtle. She knew he'd never actually spray on something. He used a special soap. Oh, shit, she should not be remembering him in the shower. He had a masculine body, solid, strong and with moves…

"Shannon, I've told him what we're up against. Shown him the papers my mother gave me." Cassidy touched Shannon's arm. "I know it's upsetting, but the amount of money it will take to make this right is staggering."

"Daddy forged signatures, tricked little old ladies out of their oil rights. Maybe we *should* suffer now because of what he did." Shannon blinked as tears filled her eyes. The idea that her father, who she'd put on something of a pedestal, had been a crook was still hard to take.

"It's not only your family who will suffer, Shannon. There are stockholders who will too. Me among them. We owe it to them to keep the damage to the company to a minimum." Billy was taking this seriously now. "Some of the people Cassidy notified have already hired lawyers of their own. What we don't want is this turning into a class action suit." Billy patted her hand. "Hiring me puts them on notice that Calhoun isn't going to lay down and roll over. I have a reputation…"

"You sure do." Shannon frowned when he took her hand. She wrestled it away from him. "You represent criminals. So hiring you is almost like we're admitting we're just as dirty as the motorcycle gang that shot up that diner in East Texas or that creep who killed his mother and put her in the freezer."

"Not true. I won those cases because the boy who put his mother in the freezer had suffered decades of abuse at her hands. And the gang thing was provoked. By stereotyping. Or I guess we should call it profiling. The police overreacted when they saw the Harleys in the parking lot and went in guns drawn. The whole thing got out of hand. But that's not why I'm here." Billy glanced at her hand. "Calhoun Petroleum spent decades earning money legally. With an unblemished record. Just because your daddy cut a few corners early in his career doesn't mean we should give up everything he worked for after that."

"A few corners?" Shannon poked him in his expensive tie. "You sound like you're talking to a jury. I saw those papers. Daddy, with help from my mama, started this company based on theft and deception. How are you going to spin that, lawyer man?"

"He's not the only one who's going to be spinning the truth." Cassidy had been observing their interaction and frowned. "I hope you can get along with each other because the public relations aspect of this is going to be your responsibility, Shannon. I don't want Caroline Wilson involved."

"It'll be a nightmare. I just hope we can settle things quietly." Shannon turned her back on Billy. "As for PR, that's why I'm here." Shannon handed her sister the papers. "Look at this. Ms. Wilson told me I'm supposed to cancel all these charitable obligations that Calhoun has always honored. Pull our sponsorships. Talk about bad public relations! It's a mistake."

"Wilson's doing what I told her to do, Shannon. We can't be generous with others when we're barely staying afloat." Cass shook her head. "Sorry, but you'll have to make these calls if that's what she told you to do. It's your new job.'"

"Let me see that list." Billy tugged it from her hand before Shannon had a chance to stop him. "The ballet? Not really my thing but I remember you loved it. Cancer Society, definitely. You remember my mother died of ovarian cancer, Shan."

This time Shannon touched *him*. She did remember. "What are you saying, Billy?"

"Let me go through this list with you. I can pick up some or most of these sponsorships." He smiled, that rakish twist of his lips that always pulled her in, before she realized they were so not right for each other.

"Really? You'd take over the financial obligations?" Shannon thought for a moment. "That's a lot of money."

"Honey, I've made a butt load of money." He flipped the page then glanced at her, his bright blue eyes twinkling. "Since you've obviously been following my career, I guess you know that."

"I've not, I mean…" Shannon glanced at Cassidy, but she'd moved back to her chair and was intent on her computer, meeting over.

"I have a condition, though. If I take over these things., especially the symphony and the ballet thing." He stood and pulled her to her feet.

"What?" Shannon backed up a step. Typical Billy, in her space. Not letting her breathe.

"You have to be my date for these events. On my arm, looking beautiful. I can talk to the press, have for years. But it's not my favorite thing. You can be the mouthpiece." His eyes lingered on her mouth.

"That's ridiculous." Shannon licked her lips and he grinned.

"No, it's not. You can play up the PR angle for Calhoun. Explain that it's a joint effort, the Pagan and Calhoun sponsorship. Obviously, my image needs polishing since I've had some negative press lately. This will help, giving to charities. We'll be partners. My money, but Calhoun gets half the credit. You can spin it any way you want when you make your calls."

"Seriously? It will be all your money?" Shannon realized Cass had stopped working long enough to listen. "Calhoun can't afford to kick in."

"That's okay." He stroked a hand down her arm. "Nothing adds polish like a beautiful woman on your arm, especially one of those Calhoun women. You can tell the press what a good guy I am, Shan. So…giving."

"Strictly business, Billy, or it's no deal." Shannon stepped out of reach. Why, oh why did his touch bring back so many memories? Nights in his bed. The way he could make her feel. They always had chemistry, but that wasn't enough.

"We'll see." He smiled. "See you, Cassidy. Let me know when you have those figures ready. And be sure Holly sends me the names of any lawyers hired by the people suing Calhoun." He grabbed Shannon's elbow. "Now it's lunchtime. I'm thinking sushi. You like stuff like that. There's a place just a block from here. We can go over the list of charities and I'll put the dates of those events on my calendar. Strictly a business lunch. Are you game?"

Shannon glanced at her phone. It wasn't quite eleven o'clock. Lunchtime? But he'd thrown her a lifeline. Now she wouldn't have to call those people. She nodded then waved at her sister before she let him guide her out to the elevators. She had just time to wish for her purse and lipstick before the doors opened. Oh boy, was she going down.

* * * *

William P. Pagan sat across from Shannon Calhoun and figured he had to be the dumbest son of a bitch on the planet. This whole move was going to cost him over a million dollars when all was said and done. For what? To have a half dozen dates with a woman who didn't want him? Goddamn it.

The truth? He wanted *her*. This was all about proving to her once and for all that they belonged together. He'd come up hard, poor, and working angles all his life. God had blessed him with a brain that saw everything, and he knew how to use what he saw to his advantage. This charity thing? An opportunity he could not resist. A scholarship to college got him where he needed to be to make the right connections, and he'd quickly figured out who those were. Dylan MacKenzie had been one of them. He and Dylan had become fast friends and that son of an important family in Houston had opened many doors for him after law school. Dylan chose the paper pushing; Billy had always known that his flair for the dramatic needed to play out in a courtroom. Lucky for him, unlucky for his clients, the rich also needed a good criminal lawyer. Dylan had come through for him with referrals when he was getting started. Now he was sitting pretty. He could afford to blow a cool million on a strategy to get Shannon back in his bed and into his life.

He didn't know why he still wanted her. God knows, she'd hurt him when she'd dumped him on his ass the first time. Yet they kept circling each other. Had tried again over the years, three or four times. It seemed like whenever they got close to making it work, she'd run. Because he couldn't keep his mouth shut about her drinking. Yeah, he'd fallen for a party girl, the last thing he should want with his family history. And yet the beautiful, fascinating Shannon Calhoun kept pulling him in. He'd go along for the ride until he couldn't stand it and would ask her to give up the booze. She called it controlling. And, boy, did she hate anyone who tried to control her.

He'd known as soon as he'd heard about the Calhoun crisis that she would be taking it hard. She had worshiped her daddy. So far they'd been successful in keeping it quiet. Dylan had asked Billy to look into it or he wouldn't know a thing about it. But if they didn't get this problem under control, Shannon and her family could lose everything. Maybe once, when the pain of losing her had been fresh, Billy had wanted her to suffer. But he'd gotten over it. Grown up. Now, he just wanted to help. And to see if maybe she was finally ready to make it work between them. Was it too late for them to reconnect?

"If you're going to polish up that image, Billy, you need to quit taking on clients like Rupert Billingsley." Shannon ate the olive out of her martini.

"He didn't kill his wife, Shan. I'll prove it." Billy shook his head when the waiter hovered.

"But he could have hired it done. I saw the story online. And everyone who knew the couple heard them fighting. I almost felt sorry for him. Evelyn was a bitch." Shannon looked around. "I could use another drink."

"Nope. You have to go back to work. As for my case? Can't talk about it. But it doesn't matter if Evelyn was a bitch or not. Rupert is innocent. I don't take on clients I don't believe in." He called for the check. "You're a working girl. I think you have a boss now, right?"

Shannon made a face. "Ms. Wilson. Dragon Lady. You think they'll dock my tiny pay if I'm late getting back from lunch?" She sighed. "You should see my desk, Billy. I don't even have an office. And my paycheck? I spend more than that a week on cocktails and manicures."

"Cassidy said your father wanted you to work for a year in the company. To prove you could stick with something to gain your inheritance. Surely you can put up with anything for a year." Billy handed the waiter cash to cover the bill.

"A year is a long time." She rested her head on her hand. "I have to live at home too. Which I've figured out is actually a good thing. Free room and board. And a car and gas are provided, along with housekeeping."

"There you go then." Billy stood. "We'd better get you back."

Shannon got up, holding onto the table when she wobbled on those high heels of hers. "Why are you doing this, Billy? Helping Calhoun? I know you have a busy law practice."

He looked her over. She had a natural grace and he remembered she'd done ballet for years before going off to college. Her blonde hair had a bunch of colors in it that seemed to catch the light when she ran her hands carelessly through it before she picked up her papers and her phone. She looked up at him through her lashes, her gray blue eyes gleaming. Shannon worked the angles too and he admired the way she usually saw right through him. Yep, just like she was seeing right through him now.

"You know why." He pulled her in, ignoring the chatter and clatter of the lunch crowd around them. "How long are we going to pretend there's still not this thing between us?"

"Ah, Billy." She ran her fingernails over his jaw. "This thing is bad for both of us. That's why we don't need to start up again." She let her thumb drift over his lips and he got so hard he ached.

"No other woman does it for me like you, Shannon." He felt the bump of a waiter at his back and came to his senses. "We need to get out of here."

"Back to work." She smiled and led the way through the tangle of tables to the glass door then out to the sidewalk. "Thanks for lunch."

"I'll walk you." Billy really wanted to pull her in, kiss that mouth that had lost its lipstick when she'd devoured her lunch. Shannon had always had a healthy appetite. For everything.

"No, you go do your lawyerly thing. I have phone calls to make. And you don't need to show up in my office and meet my boss. She'll think I was out on a date." Shannon touched his chest. "You should wear a blue tie, to match your eyes." And with that she was on her way.

Billy watched the sway of her hips in a narrow black skirt that hugged her butt. Her legs in those high heels made him remember the way they'd wrapped around him, holding him in. She was stronger than she looked. He needed to remember *that*.

Chapter 2

"I guess you saw his noisy motorcycle out front." Mai Murakami, Billy's paralegal and invaluable assistant, greeted him at the door with her hands on her hips as soon as he hit the office. "Of course, Albert just barged in without an appointment. One of his 'emergencies.'"

"That's not good news." Billy glanced at his watch while she reached for her purse which matched the designer suit she wore. Mai always looked professional but today even Billy could tell she was going all out. She had a perfect figure, though she didn't come up to the middle of his chest.

"I'm late for lunch, but I wasn't about to leave him here by himself." She glanced back at Billy's open office door. "But if you need me…"

"Go. I'll take care of this." Billy patted her shoulder. "Sorry I'm so late. You look great. Hot date?"

"No. Just my great aunt Iku." Mai gave him a pained smile. "I'd have cancelled if I could. The closer I get to thirty, the more hell-bent she is on finding me a husband. I'm afraid a candidate may be waiting at the restaurant."

"Tell her you and I are destined to be together, baby doll. And that you'll never love another man." The booming voice made her jump. "Also promise her that any man she tries to fix you up with will never live to make it down the aisle. I'll see to that."

Billy turned and bumped fists with the giant of a man in black leathers who stood in the doorway to his office. "Slash, talk like that is what gets you in trouble. I just heard you threaten some poor sap."

"Albert, it is that kind of conversation that makes me afraid to date you." Mai stalked to the door. She turned and gave the giant a tiny smile. "Eight o'clock. And you pick me up in a car, not on the back of that loud motorcycle. Are we clear this time?"

"Yes, ma'am." Albert Madison, also known as Slash to the members of his motorcycle gang, grinned like he'd won the lottery. "I have tickets to that acrobatic thing you like."

"Good. And wear a suit." She looked him up and down. "Made of cloth." She swished out the door.

"God, I love that woman." Albert followed Billy into his office. "By the time she gets through with me, you won't know me, Billy."

"You're changing for her." Billy settled behind his desk. He had a thick file with Albert's name on it. Because of his motorcycle gang. He was a good guy behind his gruff exterior. None of the charges had stuck. Because Albert had a lot of money and had hired Billy, the best criminal lawyer in town. Billy wouldn't have taken him on as a client if it was dirty money. No, Slash had invested in local real estate. The man had a nose for areas of Houston that were due for restoration and trendy upscale development. His motorcycle "club" was a group of men, many of them veterans with anger issues, who loved their loud motorcycles and long rides. They'd organized when it became obvious that law enforcement didn't like to see them coming.

"I'm trying to change, but it ain't easy. Had a run-in with the law last weekend." He held up a hand when Billy started to speak. "No, I didn't call you because it didn't go that far. Just wanted to give you a heads-up now. We were on the road going east. Drove through a little town. You know the kind. Speed slows from seventy to thirty-five so quick you have to hit the brakes. So we all slowed down. Not one of us was doing over the speed limit. Patrol stopped us anyway."

"Anything happen?" Billy leaned forward. "You have some guys that like to carry things they shouldn't."

"You think I don't know that? I've told them to ditch the drugs they don't have legitimate prescriptions for. Get the fucking permits for the guns. I'm getting some pushback on my 'rules' for the rides." He stood and walked around to examine the bookcases lining one wall. "PTSD is a bitch. A few need weed to chill. I get it. Still, we gave the cop no reason to search anyone. None. But he made every one of us show our driver's licenses. Wouldn't you know that dumb ass Jaime Reyes had let his expire? Then the law starts looking at him funny. Because he's Latino. Well, what do you know? Cop asks to see his green card." Albert picked up a trophy Billy had won in a golf tournament and held it in one fist. "Why the hell should he have a green card when he was born in Pasadena fucking Texas?"

"I have a feeling I know where this is going." Billy got up and wrenched his trophy from Albert's fist. "Don't bend that. I suck at golf. I only got that because I was in a foursome with friends who can putt." He put it back on the shelf. "So what happened?"

"We moved in, surrounded the asshole cop and Jaime. Let the fucker know that when you're born American and have served your country, you sure as hell don't carry no green card." Albert's English was getting rougher and his face redder. He was six-five, red-haired, and his face flushed easily.

"I have a feeling the cop was calling for backup about then." Billy eased Albert into a chair. He pulled a bottle of water out of his mini-fridge and tossed it to him. "Calm down. Obviously, it ended all right or I'd have spent the weekend dealing with this."

Albert drained the bottle then handed the empty back to Billy. He took a steadying breath and pulled the tie from his hair to shake it out. "It still makes me so damned mad, Bill. The prejudice. You know?"

"Yeah. I know." Billy sat in the chair next to him. The gang Albert ran was diverse and the stronger for it. He'd always liked Albert for his world view on racial matters.

"Anyway, backup came and who should show up but a Latino cop." Albert chuckled. "I tell you, it did my heart good to see that white cop's face. He picked up his walkie, like he was going to call in someone else and that other cop gave him such a look. He just strolled up to Jaime and they started jabbering in Spanish. Seems a few questions about parents and grandparents and everything was cool. Both cops backed off and we were free to go on our way. Jaime got a warning to get that license taken care of, that's all."

"Good. So why are you here?" Billy sat back and relaxed.

"To see Mai, of course." Albert laughed. "I made up an excuse, but I really just wanted to ask her out. She's been playing hard or next to impossible to get. Her family wants her to marry a man with a Japanese background." He looked around the office. "You got something stronger than water in that fridge?"

"Sure. Beer?" Billy got up and opened the mini-fridge built into the bookcase. "Corona okay?"

"That'll hit the spot. Join me." Albert took a cold bottle gratefully and popped the top. "You know Mai's family would shit a brick before they'd accept me. But she's enough of a rebel that it just might suit her to bring me into the fold, so to speak." He took a deep swallow.

"Don't steal my assistant, Albert. She keeps this place running." Billy sipped his beer. Not a good idea since he had a lot of work ahead of him today. But maybe it was a good idea to talk to Albert about this. "How did you get her to give you a shot? You two are very different."

"I've been wearing her down. I had to find out what she liked. That acrobatic troop. Cirque de whatever. Heard her on the phone with her sister. So I bought the tickets. Then there's the fact that her auntie's fixing her up with guys who are bound to be, no offense, lawyers, doctors, straight arrows. I'm different. You may not know it, but women like Mai get sick of the same old, same old." Albert grinned and finished his beer. "Women all secretly want a bad boy." He unzipped his jacket sleeve and stretched out his arm covered in tattoos. "I've literally got danger written all over me."

Billy laughed. Sure enough, there was "Danger" in bold letters up one forearm. Bad boy. He'd been one before he'd realized that he needed to clean up his act if he wanted to make something of himself and fit in with the society folks who could afford to pay well for his legal services. Now he was so groomed and sanitized he could hardly remember what it was like to be the wild teenager who'd made girls scream when he drove up into their yards and whisked them away for a night of what they'd called naughty pleasure. He had a sudden brainstorm—and here was someone who could help, sitting right beside him.

"Hey, Albert. I'll let you borrow my Beemer for your date tonight if you'll let me ride your Harley. What do you say? Just for one night." And a plan was put into motion. He had to swear on a stack of bibles he'd treat Slash's Harley right or he'd be lawyering for his gang *pro bono* for years to come, but it would be worth it.

* * * *

"I don't see how linking Calhoun Petroleum with that lawyer is going to help the company's image, Shannon." Caroline Wilson had decided that she was the boss and she wasn't going to call her underling Ms. Calhoun. It apparently grated on her last nerve. As did the announcement that they were partnering with Billy Pagan on the charitable donations.

"We don't have a choice, Ms. Wilson." Shannon stood in front of the woman's desk. She hadn't been invited to sit. She thought about collapsing in the chair next to her anyway, but she was determined to play this game to win. "Cassidy approved it. Mr. Pagan is willing to front the money to save our pride, if you want to call it that. It is unbelievably generous of him."

"Are you sure he won't let it leak that he's all the money behind this?" Wilson frowned. "What an embarrassment that would be. Do you trust him? Should we get something in writing? A nondisclosure?"

"Since he's acting as our in-house counsel at the moment, I don't know how I could ask him for such a thing." Shannon gave up and sat. God, her feet were killing her. "Look. He's a family friend." Yes, that was the way she was spinning his offer. "He's doing this as a favor. Because he realizes that his own image, as a lawyer who has represented some pretty shady characters, could use some polish. Donating to local charities is good public relations for him as well as for us. He's promised to keep his mouth shut that he's footing all the bills as long as I stay by his side for the events on this list."

"Oh my God! This is a dating scheme." Wilson smirked. "Seriously? You're willing to go out with the man to save the company embarrassment?"

"I'd date a chimpanzee if it would keep us from becoming the town laughing stock." Shannon slammed the papers down on the desk. "In case you aren't paying attention, that's my last name on the company. My father built it from the ground up. If I have to go around with Billy Pagan on my arm at a few charity functions, then that's a no-brainer, Caroline."

She marched—or tried to—back to her cube. Too bad she was limping now. What would happen if she showed up in flats tomorrow? Oh, who cared? She fell into her chair and almost landed on her butt when one of the rollers fell off. Great. She'd obviously been given a piece-of-crap chair to sit in.

The papers on her desk rustled as she tried to straighten them with shaking hands. Had she blown it? Would she be fired on her first day? No big deal. The consequences were merely her entire inheritance. She looked up and realized Caroline was standing in front of her desk.

"I've been giving you attitude." The vice president frowned. "Get up."

"What?" But Shannon struggled out of the wobbly chair anyway.

"Someone's idea of a joke. Friday was a nightmare. Six people laid off. Everyone knew a Calhoun was coming in on Monday while they were out of a job." She walked around and grabbed the chair then rolled it awkwardly over to another cubicle. "This one's better. I'm sorry about that." She tested the new chair, then brought it back and slid it over to Shannon. "Can we start over?"

"I'd like that. I went over your head about the charity thing. I'm sorry." Shannon held on to the chair back. "My inheritance rides on my performance here. If I've screwed up already…" No, her voice did not crack.

"Actually, your idea is perfect. We won't let down the charities and Calhoun is still seen as philanthropic." Caroline smiled. "Mr. Pagan knows a lot of influential people. Yes, most of those have been in trouble with the law, but he got them off. I'd say that just makes him more interesting." She shook her head. "You sure you don't mind going out with him for the cause?"

Shannon sighed. "He won't do this any other way. We have a history. Bad breakups in the past. You'd think he would give up, but he just keeps trying."

"I've seen his picture. You could do much worse." Caroline glanced down the room. "My phone is ringing. Would you believe I don't even have an assistant now? Just you. And I expect you to get busy on those calls this afternoon. Spin it like we're collaborating with Pagan. Full partners. The charities don't have to know we're not kicking in a dime."

"Oh, that's what I planned." Shannon sat and kicked off her shoes. "I'll get right on it."

"He must really, really want you, Shannon." Caroline frowned when her phone rang again. "Rich and handsome. I'd give the man a shot." She hurried down the hall.

Give him a shot? Sure. If she didn't mind letting him order her around like one of his clients. *Don't do this. Don't drink that. You've had enough, Shannon.* She'd be damned if she'd let him boss her around, even if he was paying for the privilege. That would be like… No, she wasn't even going to think it. Her phone rang and she stared at it. Who had this number? But maybe it was public relations business.

"Public relations, Shannon Calhoun speaking."

"Don't you sound professional. Very impressive."

"I *am* very impressive. What do you want, Billy?"

"I think we need to finish going over our calendars. I want to get together tonight."

Shannon thought about it. Did she want to see him again? "We could straighten out our calendars over the phone. Or with an email. Let me give you my address."

"That's so impersonal. There are things we need to discuss. Dress codes, stuff like that. I wouldn't want to embarrass you, Shannon, by wearing the wrong thing to an event."

"Seriously, Billy? You've been going to social gatherings for years now. And embarrassing me didn't used to worry you." She remembered being hauled out of a party when he'd decided she'd had too much to drink. Billy had a caveman mentality. She needed to remember *that*. Of course, when they'd got back to his place… No, some things were best left in the past.

"I'm trying to change. I could use your help." He actually sounded sincere. Of course, she knew he could turn that sincerity on and off, like he did in front of a jury.

"I'm really tired, Billy. It would have to be casual."

"Exactly what I had in mind. I'll pick you up at seven. We'll catch dinner and coordinate our plans. Is that okay?"

The very fact that he'd tacked on a question was progress. "Since you asked instead of told, yeah."

"Perfect. I'll see you at your house. Casual. Wear jeans. I have a surprise for you." Then he hung up.

Shannon frowned at the phone. Didn't he remember that she hated surprises? *He* loved them, of course. It was just one thing they didn't have in common. Wear jeans. That could mean any number of things, none of them good as far as she was concerned. But jeans meant boots or maybe even, bless them, tennis shoes. She glanced down at the torture shoes under her desk and decided Billy would be surprised at just how casual she could be. She was smiling as she picked up her list and began to dial. She didn't like anyone to surprise her, but surprising him would be something to look forward to all afternoon.

Jeans with strategically placed tears really shouldn't cost more than those without a single hole in them, but the designer label had made this skintight and faded pair ridiculously expensive. It seemed a shame to pair them with the leather running shoes but her feet thanked her for the choice. No way was she dragging out another pair of stilettos. Shannon picked up the phone in her bedroom when it beeped.

"Your date is here, honey." Their housekeeper, Janie Schaumberg, had answered the door.

"Thanks, Janie. I'll be right down."

"Brace yourself. Mr. Pagan has a surprise for you." Janie chuckled.

"What is it? Maybe I should back out." Shannon walked over to the window overlooking the front of the house. She couldn't tell what he'd arrived in though because he'd obviously parked under the portico. "Janie?"

"Come on down, honey. I think you're in for a fun night." She hung up.

Shannon grabbed the cross-body bag where she'd stuffed her driver's license, cell, and lipstick then gave her hair a final pat. She'd decided to just pull it back and tie it with a scarf that coordinated with her bright blue top and matching jacket. No, she wasn't trying to please Billy, though she did know blue was his favorite color. It was also a color that brought out her eyes.

A woman should always look her best, no matter who she was going out with. You never knew who else you'd run into. That was why she fussed with her earrings, changing them at the last minute from studs to silver dangles. Oh, this was ridiculous. She had no reason to be so worked up about a casual dinner with Billy Pagan. But a surprise? Her stomach knotted as she finally threw open her bedroom door and headed down the stairs.

He stood at the bottom, a helmet in his hand. What the hell?

"Billy, that looks like a motorcycle helmet." Shannon frowned as she reached the last step, staying there before joining him in the entry.

"It is. I picked up one with a shield. Wouldn't want you to be bothered by the wind or, God forbid, insects." He grinned. "Try it on for size."

"Since when do you ride a motorcycle?" She ignored his outstretched hand. They were eye-to-eye as long as she stayed on this step. Otherwise he'd be taller, above her, making her look up and feel small and feminine to his big and masculine. She didn't hate that feeling, but it wasn't something she liked about herself, that tendency to let him overpower her with his strength.

"I borrowed it for our date. I thought it would be fun for a change. What do you think?" He grinned. "Come on, Shan, let's do something a little wild. A little adventurous. Are you up for it?" He settled the helmet gently on her head and fastened the strap under her chin. His smile shined in his eyes too, as if his enjoyment of life, of being with her, was going to make for a great evening if she would just loosen up and go along.

"Billy…"

"Of course if you're afraid to get on the back of a motorcycle, I can call a cab." He was daring her to be Shannon the wet blanket, throwing cold water on his plans. Well, maybe she'd surprise him for a change.

"Afraid? Not on your life." She grabbed his hand. "Let's go!"

He took her elbow and showed her to the door, throwing it open so she could see the enormous Harley parked at the bottom of the front steps.

She pushed past him. "I haven't been on the back of a motorcycle in years. Tell me you're a good driver." She glanced back at him. He was grinning. Of course. He'd manipulated her. Damn it. Well, so what? She was going with it. It was a beautiful night and this looked like fun. She needed to cut loose. Her life had been nothing but dreary disappointments lately.

"I took a few practice runs on my way over here. It's a powerful machine. I admit it took me a few minutes to get the feel of it. It had been a while for me."

"Who does it belong to?" She ran down the steps and touched the shiny chrome. "It's beautiful."

"A client who also works as my investigator. It's his baby. So you'd better believe I'll drive carefully." Billy showed her where to sit behind the driver's seat. "Watch for the tailpipe. I'm glad you have on jeans but those holes may give you trouble."

"They're not anywhere the pipe will touch me." Shannon grinned, liking the way the bike felt between her legs. "Didn't you notice? I have rips in very strategic places."

"Oh, I noticed." He winked. "I'm on my best behavior, Shan, in case *you* didn't notice." He picked up a second helmet that he'd left on the seat and slipped it on. "But that can change in a heartbeat." He stared at her for a long moment. "We're starting over. I hope you'll let me do that. Start fresh with you."

"Billy." Shannon held onto the leather seat. When they took off, she'd have to hold onto him. Hold his waist and maybe lean against his firm back. She'd be able to inhale his male scent, so familiar, making her remember… "I want to think that could happen, but…"

"I know. We have history. I made mistakes." He smiled sadly. "I hope you'll admit that you did too." He dragged his leg over the bike and settled into the seat. "Brace yourself. This hog is loud." He turned the key.

Mistakes? She wasn't touching that one. And could they really start fresh when there were so many things she couldn't forget? Shannon grabbed him when the roar felt like it was going to blow out her eardrums.

He revved the motor then yelled at her to hold tight as he eased them down the driveway. The house where her inheritance forced her to live had been her late father's dream home. It was in the middle of sedate River Oaks, the mansion-filled neighborhood where the rich in Houston lived. The loud motorcycle was no doubt drawing attention and frowns from everyone on the quiet street as Billy drove them toward one of Houston's many freeways.

Zipping down the highway once they hit an interstate was exhilarating. Billy seemed to know what he was doing and didn't take chances. Yes, it was a little terrifying when large trucks zipped past them. But then many people in small cars honked and waved, some of them men with obvious Harley envy. By the time Billy pulled up in front of a popular Cajun restaurant and parked, Shannon was windblown and thirsty but hooked.

"What did you think?" He was grinning as he helped her climb off.

"I loved it. Now buy me a drink." She handed him her helmet and glanced at the restaurant. "I hope they make a good martini here."

"Will you humor me? Remember why we keep breaking up?" He put his arm around her shoulders and squeezed.

"How could I forget?" Shannon had always enjoyed a party. Billy had been serious and had disapproved of her lifestyle. "What's the deal, Billy?"

He faced her and looked into her eyes, so serious she braced herself. "Billy?"

"Would you mind not drinking? I would really love for us to make this date alcohol-free."

Shannon wanted to kick over that damned bike. Not that she could manage it. Now it started. He wanted to change her. Always had. Hated her drinking. Thought she was an alcoholic. She swallowed, licked dry lips. Suddenly the thought of a martini made her almost desperate. He just stared at her, waiting. Damn him. Why couldn't he ever just accept her as she was?

Chapter 3

"Do you really want to bring that up now? When we were having such a good time?" She stared into his eyes—hers were big, blue and shiny with tears.

"When should I bring it up? After your fourth martini?" Billy hated to do this. Here, in a fucking parking lot. But it was the big thing that had come between them before and he couldn't seem to let it go. He had his reasons. Maybe it was time to lay them out for her.

"You think I can't quit drinking. That's obvious." She looked over her shoulder at the restaurant. "You always make a big deal out of this. What's the matter with having a few drinks to relax?"

"I guess we're really going to do this in the parking lot." He wanted to touch her, needed to touch her. But maybe that wasn't fair. Billy kept his hands fisted by his sides. The memories were always with him, nights when he'd poured his own mom into bed, sloppy drunk. There'd been a couple of those with Shannon too and it had made him sick to his stomach, bringing it all back.

"Let's go inside. Get a table. I won't order a drink yet. We can have tea with our meal." She must have seen something in his face because she grabbed his hand and pulled him toward the door. "Billy, I don't want to ruin this night. I'm not a total bitch."

"I never said you were." He stopped and pulled her to him. "Drinking is *my* issue. I need to explain."

"Inside." She smiled and ran her hand over his cheek. "Seriously, this dust and car exhaust is getting to me." She sneezed. "It's allergy season. Ragweed. Come on." She pulled him toward the door again. "We'll get this talked out. Finally."

Billy let her drag him inside. He should have picked a quieter place.

This was one of those loud music, jumping joints, with the band about to tune up and a space for dancing. It had seemed like a good idea when he'd borrowed the hog. A wild night and his old persona would have loved it. And now he'd ruined the vibe by bringing up his own dark past and the big fat issue hanging between them.

He wanted Shannon. He had since their first go-round. She was beautiful, a fairy princess come to life. She had all the things he'd dreamed of when he'd been working his ass off to become rich and famous. She'd be the best partner a man on the rise could have by his side. Except she loved her drinks. Which pushed a hot button of his so hard he couldn't keep his mouth shut about it.

He asked the hostess to find them a table as far away from the noise as possible, but it was still not easy to be heard over the roar of a happy crowd. They ordered spicy shrimp and hush puppies, iced tea, and a basket of the kind of greasy onion rings that Shannon usually refused to touch. This time she grabbed one immediately and dipped it into the spicy sauce the waitress brought with it.

"Mmm. Delicious. I've never been here before. It's fun. Are we going to dance later?" She tapped her fingers on the table to the tune that the band started. "I have no idea how to dance to that stuff but I figure we can watch and learn."

"You really are in a mood, aren't you?" Billy was mesmerized. In a low-cut top that let him see just enough breast to make him want to slip a hand inside and tease her nipple, Shannon was breathtaking. He dropped a pile of paper napkins in his lap and picked up an onion ring. "Since when do you eat these things?"

"Fried food? Why not? My future is uncertain; the Calhoun billions may be disappearing so I figure I'd better live for the day." She took a bite and closed her eyes in bliss. "And now I'm working for a living. I can take a diet lunch every day if I need to. Which I guess I will." She frowned. "My current wardrobe is going to have to last me a long time."

"Let's hope we can salvage at least some millions for you after your year of working is up." Billy took a sip of his tea. "About the drinking."

"Can we put the talk off until after we eat? Here comes our shrimp. I'm hungry. Sushi never sticks with me." She smiled at the waitress. "Thanks, hon."

"The band will be playing for the next hour. You two should get up and dance after you finish eating." The waitress smiled.

"What if we don't know how?" Shannon picked up a shrimp by its tail.

"We'll have Zydeco instructors on the floor in a little while. Jump up and join in as soon as you're ready. You sure I can't bring either of you a beer or a cocktail?" The waitress glanced at the tea glasses.

"No, we're fine. On the wagon tonight." Billy smiled at Shannon. "And my lady underestimates me. I spent a summer working in New Orleans. I can show her how to dance to this. As soon as we're finished eating."

"You're kidding!" Shannon leaned across the table, kissed Billy on the mouth then sat back and dug into her dinner. "Hurry up and eat. I can't wait to see your moves."

Billy leaned across the table this time. He touched her chin, holding it still just as she was about to take a bite. "Baby, you've seen my moves, remember?" He brushed her hand aside and kissed her then, tasting the spicy Cajun sauce on her tongue and the unique Shannon flavor that he'd never been able to forget. Finally, he rubbed a dot of pepper from her bottom lip with his thumb before settling into his seat again.

"This looks good." He grinned, satisfied with the way her eyes fixed on his face and her shrimp had drifted down to land on the plate again. "Shannon?"

"Hmm?" She licked her lips.

"Eat up. We've got some dancing to do and it's pretty athletic. You'll need your strength." He popped a shrimp into his mouth.

She sighed and looked him over. "And maybe you'll need yours, Billy boy. Think on that." Then she slipped that shrimp into her mouth, her lips caressing it in a way that made Billy painfully hard.

"I'm thinking." He ate with a grim determination. Dancing? He guessed he'd have to go through with it now, but he hoped there was a bigger surprise coming after that. She asked him about New Orleans and he told her about the case he'd helped with there. Laws were different in Louisiana and a client had gotten in trouble during Mardi Gras. It was a shame when good people got taken in by bad. It had been satisfying to help the New Orleans PD blow open a scam that targeted tourists.

"You did a good thing there, Billy. I love New Orleans and have been to Mardi Gras many times. It's pretty wild." She ate her last shrimp and drained her glass of tea.

Billy wiped his greasy fingers on a napkin. "You *would* love that. Which is why I've tried to forget you, Shan."

"Now that's not a nice thing to say." She looked at him through her long lashes. "But I understand. We keep hurting each other. You said I've followed your career. It's true. You've done really well, Billy. Because you were focused. Serious. Business was all you wanted to think about. Of course, wild didn't suit you then." She reached across the table. "Does it now?"

"I'm willing to find out." Billy got up then pulled her to her feet. He smiled at her. "You ready to dance?"

"If you'll show me how." She touched his chest. "You wore a blue shirt. To match your eyes. For me?"

"Everything I've done has been for you, Shannon." Billy slid his arms around her. "You just didn't know it."

"That sounds like the smooth talk of a lawyer." She laughed up at him. "I'm not buying that line for a minute."

"Hey, it was worth a shot." Billy pulled her to the dance floor. She thought he was kidding. Well, maybe he was and maybe he wasn't. The Shannon Calhoun he'd known since college hadn't been his dream girl. But he'd known that inside the wild party girl was a woman he could love forever.

"You can really dance!" Shannon laughed as they finally collapsed into their seats again. Billy looked so damned good to her. He'd left his leather jacket at the table, so she could enjoy the way his T-shirt hugged his broad chest. And those jeans! Well-worn, they'd lovingly cupped his taut butt. More than one woman had watched him steer her around the dance floor, his contagious grin making her throw her head back and laugh with pure joy.

It was almost enough to make her forget how controlling he was. Everyone around them was getting their buzz on. Most of the crowd favored beer. Anything would be better than yet another glass of the sweet iced tea that had already sent her trotting to the ladies' room, twice. She saw that the waitress had refilled their glasses while they were on the dance floor. She took a sip and wrinkled her nose.

"You ready to get out of here?" Billy threw some bills on the table. "I still want to talk."

"Might as well." Shannon knew he was disappointed that she stalked out ahead of him. But her good mood was vanishing. She felt him close behind her, even before his hand landed on her shoulder.

"Slow down." He grabbed the door and held it open. "You're marching out of here like you're mad or something. I thought we were having a good time."

"We were." Shannon stalked over to the huge motorcycle. "But it could have been better. What would have been the harm in having a few drinks, Billy? I don't get it." She snatched the helmet he carried and pulled it on. "I'm not addicted or anything, I just like to relax, enjoy myself."

"And you can't do that without alcohol?" He frowned as he pushed on his own helmet. "Listen to yourself. You're not making sense. I saw you out on that dance floor. You were having fun. And you didn't have a thing to drink other than sweet tea. Are you going to deny that you were relaxed anyway? Seriously, Shannon?"

"Fine. It was fun. *You* were fun. Until you start preaching at me again.

Controlling me." She threw her leg over the leather seat. "Let's go. Take me home. We can talk there."

"I don't think you're in the mood to listen. What I want is an honest conversation. I don't consider it preaching or controlling." He got on the Harley and turned the key. "Hold on."

She wrapped her arms around him when he put the motorcycle in gear and they took off in a spate of gravel. She was disappointed. He'd claimed he had a plan for a great night and now he'd ruined it. She'd pulled her scarf out of her hair and let go on the dance floor, happy to see the Billy she'd loved all those years ago alive and well. Now, just because she wanted to relax with a cocktail, he was turning judgmental again. She couldn't stand it.

It wasn't like he was Mr. Perfect either. What would he do if she asked him to stop working so hard? Lighten up? Yes, he'd taken tonight off, but she knew that was probably rare for him. He'd already told her he'd borrowed the bike they were riding. This night out was him making an effort, trying to be something he wasn't. So he was pushing her to be different too, sober as a freaking judge. How realistic was that? This relationship was doomed. They should face facts.

She looked around and noticed he wasn't taking her home after all. Where were they going? She squeezed him a few times and tried to yell questions at him. But he ignored her. They rode over the Kemah bridge and she recognized Galveston Bay and the boardwalk where a local entrepreneur had created an area of carnival rides and restaurants. Not Billy's usual scene. But then did she know what he liked anymore?

He found a parking place where the bike wouldn't be bothered and turned off the motor.

"What are we doing here?" She pulled off the helmet when he reached out a hand to help her climb off.

"You didn't think we were done, did you?" Billy grinned at her.

She knew she looked a sight with her hair blown wild and her cheeks wind-burned.

"I thought you wanted to talk." She pulled her scarf out of her purse and managed to tie her hair back again. "Yet here we are at another noisy place."

"You obviously aren't in the mood to talk, so I decided to come here." Billy waved toward the colorful area lining the waterway that connected Clear Lake with Galveston Bay.

"And you say you're not controlling." She turned away from him.

"Come on, Shan. I remember that your dad was big into the circus. Maybe you have just a little weakness for a carnival?" Billy pointed to the colorful and well-lit wharf. "Look, there's a roller coaster, a bungee jump over the bay, and some other thrill rides."

Shannon couldn't believe he'd thought of bringing her here. "Daddy took me with him to carnivals when I was little, before he got obsessed with work. We rode rides together. I do love them." She shook her head. "How on earth did you know?"

"I'm not entirely unobservant, Shannon. I think you and your daddy are more alike than you want to admit."

"How do you mean?" Her breath caught. Could she be like Daddy? Was he insulting her? Or complimenting her?

"He had a crazy side to him. Collecting circus memorabilia, taking chances on oil well sites that others wouldn't touch. He was a risk taker. For some reason, you keep that side of yourself under wraps. That fun, crazy Shannon Calhoun is buttoned up unless she's had a few too many drinks." Billy slid his hands around her waist.

"You have no idea why I am the way I am." Shannon resisted the pressure as he tried to pull her closer. She'd grown up tiptoeing around her mother with her volatile moods, her father gone most of the time making deals. She'd learned quickly it was better to be invisible or out of the house.

"I'll give you that. We never have taken the time to really get to know each other." He just kept looking at her, pressing her gently with those big hands.

He managed to get her closer anyway. Damn, the man was strong. Shannon had to admit he had a point. Because feeling his hard body against hers told her why they didn't really know each other. There was this instant chemistry. The craving to sink into his touch and let go.

"Billy."

"I'll let this go for now. But you seem to think it's okay to blame the fun Shannon on the alcohol. But she's the real you, like you were tonight. Why not let her free without the booze?"

"I'm not fun all the time?" She tilted her chin to look up at him, fighting a smile.

"Honey, you used to work at being a pain in my ass. Trying to get me to fit in with your crowd, seeing how far you could push me with your wild behavior. And I let you get away with it." Billy pulled her in tighter, right where she liked to be. Her breasts were against his chest, her hips cradled against what felt like a hard-on. "Tonight I want us to play with clear heads. Are you game?"

"But I like being a pain in your ass." She kissed his chin, then slid out of his arms and turned toward the rides. "Roller coaster first. I just love it when we get to the top and it slows to give you time to dread that rush downhill. Don't you?"

Billy groaned. She had him now and she knew it.

"Honestly, sweetheart? I hate the fucking things. You have no idea what a sacrifice this is going to be."

That got her. She laughed and grabbed his hand, tugging him toward the colored lights trimming the enormous wooden Boardwalk Bullet. There was a line, of course, but it didn't take long before they were strapped in and Billy was praying out loud for rescue. No such luck. He gripped the safety rail until his knuckles were white. Shannon didn't bother to hold on. When they got off, Billy fell to his knees and kissed the ground. She was ready to ride again.

Shannon hated to admit Billy might be on to something. They rode the roller coaster twice before she finally took pity on him. The bungee jump? Well, there was no way she was going to fall for that, she told him. Ha ha. Anyway, she *was* having fun. It impressed her that Billy had gone to so much trouble to get to know her, to please her. By the time he slung his arm around her and walked her toward the parking lot and that ridiculously loud motorcycle, she had to admit she was forgiving him for the booze ban. Then he stopped in his tracks and put her behind him.

"Stay here."

"What is it?" She looked around him. There was a cluster of motorcycles parked next to theirs now and men, big men, standing next to them. A couple of women too.

"Trouble." Billy turned to her. "Maybe you should duck into one of those restaurants, wait for me there."

"Are you kidding? I'm not leaving you to face whatever this is alone. Come on." She grabbed his hand. "I can call the police for you if nothing else." She pulled her cell out of her cross-body bag.

"That's a last resort. Keep the phone out of sight. Let me do the talking." He frowned. "Hey, you can go to the bar in the restaurant, have a drink."

"Damn, you're really desperate to get rid of me." Shannon kissed his frown. "Maybe I should go ahead and hit 911."

"No." He tucked her against his side. "Just follow my lead." He grabbed her hand and stalked over to the motorcycle.

"This is Slash's bike. Who the hell are you?" A huge man with a denim vest and sleeves of tattoos stepped forward from the group.

"I'm Billy Pagan, a friend of Slash. He loaned me his bike for the night. What business is it of yours?" Billy let go of Shannon's hand and put her behind him again. He seemed to swell before her eyes, becoming bigger, mean.

"You sure you didn't steal it? I never heard of him loanin' his bike before." The man looked it over, then raked Billy with a contemptuous gaze.

"You're welcome to call him. Far as I know, he has no beef with the Skeleton Cruisers. So why are you looking into his business?" Billy didn't seem worried that he was outnumbered four to one.

Shannon jumped when the two women with the group sidled over to inspect her. One had on the tightest jeans she'd ever seen and a tube top that was overflowing with breasts with a firm up-thrust that couldn't be natural. Her dark skin was flawless and she had braids woven with colorful beads. She was beautiful. The other woman obviously was as fond of the tattoo parlor as the man talking to Billy. Her T-shirt advertised a popular motorcycle rally in Utah. The shirt was about two sizes too small and straining to contain her double Ds.

"Those are the ugliest fucking shoes I've ever seen," T-shirt woman said. "Where's your pride?"

"I worked all day in Prada heels. My feet fucking hurt." Shannon whirled, ready to start something.

"Give her a break, Goldie." Tube Top pushed her friend back. "Waitress? I feel your pain, sister." She looked down at her own feet. "Get you some gel insoles, girl. Makes all the difference." She grinned. "But men do like those high heels."

"We'd better shut up, Stan's staring a hole in us." Goldie, whose hair was a rather startling shade of gold-blonde, waved them quiet.

"So what do you want?" Billy was getting to the point.

"Tell Slash that one of his crew, the guy who rides that vintage flat head, owes money. He's been playing poker in our clubs and losing. He needs to clean up his debts or collection's going to get ugly." The man put his fist on the handlebar of the bike Billy had borrowed then shoved it over until it hit the ground. "Do I make myself clear?"

"What the fuck, man!" Billy moved toward the jerk, fists raised.

"Don't even try it." The big guy's pals grabbed Billy's arms. "Now pass on that message."

"Messing with Slash's bike was a mistake. This sounds like someone else's problem." Billy strained against the men holding him.

Shannon gasped and moved toward Billy or tried to, but Goldie and Tube Top suddenly grabbed her arms, holding her still.

"Slash knows how the clubs work. He needs to keep his men in line." The man rested his boot on the fallen bike, pressing down hard on the tailpipe. "You're on our turf. Next time, watch where you ride alone."

"Watch it yourself, you dumb fuck. You trying to start a war?" Billy glanced back at Shannon. "I'll pass on your message. Tell your women to leave mine alone."

The leader laughed. "But it would be fun to watch a cat fight."

Shannon stomped Goldie's foot and sent an elbow into Tube Top's soft stomach. They hadn't been expecting it and she got free. "Billy!" She ran to him. "Let him go! I called 911 when we saw you waiting, assholes."

"Shannon, get back." Billy shot her a warning look. "The Cruisers were just leaving."

"You called the cops?" The leader signaled his men who released Billy. "We're out of here. Deliver the message, Pagan." The big man pulled a card out of his vest. "Here's where we can be reached. I wrote the amount of the debt on the back. That little shit is not welcome in our game rooms. He comes anywhere near one, he gets a beat down. Is that clear enough for you? Or do we need to make our point another way?" His hard eyes travelled over Billy then raked the bike. "I have a feeling Slash wouldn't give a shit if we touched you, but when he sees his bike, he's going to know we mean business."

"I'll carry the message. Now move along. My lady and I are leaving before the cops get here." Billy smiled. "Of course, maybe you want to have a talk with them."

Shannon looked back at the two women. "Thanks for the fashion advice." She took her helmet from Billy, relieved that no one tried to stop them, and pulled it on. "Come on, let's go."

Billy had managed to get the bike up and was frowning at the bent tailpipe and a scrape along one fender. He gave the group around them hard looks.

"Get on the damned bike, Billy." Shannon shoved his helmet at him and got on the back. To her relief, he did just that as the rest of the bikers backed out of the way to watch them leave the parking lot. They hadn't gone far when Billy pulled into a convenience store parking lot and jumped off the motorcycle.

"Shit! Come here, Shannon." He pulled her off the bike and into his arms. "Are you crazy? Taunting those bikers?"

Shannon pulled off her helmet and stared up at him. She let her lips tremble then couldn't help herself, she laughed out loud. "Billy, I've never been so insulted in my life. Those women disrespected my fashion sense."

"Laugh all you want, woman, but we could have been in real trouble." He had pulled off his own helmet and kissed her hard. "I give up. I wanted to show you I still have a wild side but I'm too conventional now. All I could think about when I was talking to those assholes was that I never should have brought you where someone could hurt you."

"Stop it. I'm fine. Nothing happened, except I may have a bruised wrist.

Goldie is strong. I was going to run to your defense and she kept trying to hold me back." Shannon held up her hand and Billy examined it in the light from the parking lot.

"You're kidding. You were going to help me fight off the enforcer from the Skeleton Cruisers and his three thugs?" Billy kissed her wrist. "What a woman."

"Hey, we were in a public parking lot. I didn't think it could go too far. I saw a security guard cruising the area and figured he'd be around soon. You know I lied about calling the cops." Shannon took a breath. Adrenaline still spiked through her. Danger, excitement from the rides, and Billy pressed against her body had her stirred up. She was tempted to make a reckless decision.

No, she needed to take her time with Billy. Rushing into something wasn't smart. He might look like a hot, dangerous biker right now, but he still wanted to make decisions for her and she had to remember that.

"Take me home, Billy. We both have work tomorrow, you know." She saw his mouth droop with disappointment that the evening was going to end.

"I do know." He started to say something when his phone rang. When he saw the number, he frowned. "I've got to take this. Sorry."

"No, I get it. You're always on call for your clients." She stepped away so he could have privacy. Good. She needed to cool down. Because she was so very tempted to kiss Billy and let their chemistry make her decision for her. Again.

"Shit. I've got to go." He pulled on his helmet. "I'm sorry, Shan. I'll take you home."

"It's okay. I had a good time." She smiled and touched his cheek. "And, look, I'm stone-cold sober." She shook her head and climbed on the back of the bike. He was solemn, not even cracking a smile as he started the engine. Whatever the call was about, it was serious. Of course, he was a criminal lawyer. Someone might have landed in jail.

Shannon sighed and leaned against him. She could think of a dozen reasons why starting things with Billy again was a bad idea. But holding him as they drove through the night, it was easy to forget them. He still wanted her, even after all the mess they'd been through. There was something very seductive about that. Very seductive.

Chapter 4

Billy thought he'd done a decent job of hiding how that phone call had him tied in knots while he was with Shannon. Now he had to arrive at the county jail on the back of Albert's motorcycle since he hadn't planned to get his car back until morning.

When he climbed off the bike, he got some looks from the cops clustered in front of the glass doors of the massive jail near downtown Houston. It was time for a shift change so there were more men standing around than usual. A few he recognized.

"Pagan." A sheriff's deputy stepped into his path. "Not your usual ride. Where's the rest of your gang?" He nudged one of his buddies and they cracked up.

Billy knew better than to start something. He just smiled. "Even lawyers like to cut loose now and then. But the bike isn't mine. I'm sure Slash would take it really hard if something were to happen to it here."

"Yeah, I bet he would." The deputy eyed the bike. "I'm a veteran too. Slash is all right, though some of his crew needs a firmer hand. I'll make sure nobody touches the bike, though it looks like somebody already did." He frowned at the dent in the tailpipe. "Good luck in there. I heard she's been making quite a lot of noise."

Billy winced. "Thanks for the warning." He'd been afraid of that ever since the phone call. Now he knew his connection to the perp was common knowledge. Shit. When the deputy stepped out of his way, Billy headed on inside and passed through the metal detectors after emptying his pockets. He knew this place too well. By the time he got to the women's lockup, his stomach was churning. Damn it. Tonight of all nights, when he'd been feeling so good, she'd pulled this.

"Sally Marie Winthrop." He gave the name to the clerk and showed his identification. "I'm her lawyer." He sat and waited while they sent for her. The smells and the sounds were always the same. It wasn't a place he wanted to ever visit, much less come to see a woman he knew and was supposed to love. He heard his name called and headed for the room the clerk indicated. He found Sally slumped at a table. What the hell was she doing in an orange jumpsuit? It didn't suit her and was a bad sign. Her dark hair was matted and she looked like she'd washed off her usual makeup. When she raised her face, he could see her eyes were bloodshot.

"Billy, sweetheart, you've got to get me out of here." She didn't bother saying thanks for coming. Of course. He was always going to be there for her. He'd promised his mother on her deathbed to take care of Sally.

"Aunt Sally, I'll do my best." He sat across from her and took her shaking hand. His mother's sister. If ever there was a reason for him to hate drinking, it sat right here. Sally was only forty-six years old, his mother's baby sister because of what his grandmother called a "change of life" accident. She looked closer to Gran's eighty-four.

"They won't let me smoke in here. Nazis. And this is all a big lie. I only had a few belts. Was driving home from bingo when that cop pulled me over. I know I wasn't going over the speed limit. Didn't do a damned thing to make him stop me." She squeezed his hand. "He made me get out of the car when he saw I was driving on a suspended license."

"You still had a couple of months to go on that last DUI, Sally. The arrest report says you were weaving and hit a construction cone." Billy dropped her hand and sat back. How the hell was he going to get her out of jail this time? Third strike and it was a miracle this was only the third time she'd been caught driving when drunk. At least she hadn't hurt anyone. Yet.

"I can't just sit at home, Billy. I go crazy. The bingo hall is only a few blocks away." She ran a hand through her hair and seemed surprised when it got tangled and she had to jerk it free. A few dark strands came with it and she cursed. "Look at me. The guards were so mean. Just because I threw up when I got here. Ruined my outfit. They gave me no privacy. Stuck me naked under a shower. The water was cold, Billy." She started crying, big heaving sobs.

"Sally, honey." Billy got up and walked around to hug her thin shoulders. His heart broke for her. But, damn it, why the hell couldn't she pull herself together? He stopped when a thought struck him. "Gran wasn't with you, was she?"

"No. It's her night for *Dancing with the Stars*. She likes bingo but you couldn't blast her out of her recliner on a Monday night when that show's on. She bitched at me for driving but I got the car keys anyway." Sally wiped her eyes and grabbed a tissue from the box on the table to blow her nose. "She'd hid them in a coffee can." She snorted. "Like I didn't know that trick."

"It's her car, Sal. And she was only doing what I told her to do. You weren't supposed to drive. If you want to get out, call a cab or Uber." Billy sat across from her again. Damn it, what now? He'd paid for her to dry out after the last DUI and yet here she was again, reeking of alcohol. A couple of drinks? Not if the way she smelled was any indication.

"I can't afford to pay for a ride. Renee was supposed to pick me up, but she forgot." She grabbed another tissue. "She's got a new boyfriend. Me? I've got nothing, Billy. Can you blame me for wanting to have a little fun?"

"I blame you for getting behind the wheel after you drank too much. You could have killed someone, Sally. Then what? You want that on your conscience?" Billy leaned forward, sick of what had become a familiar scenario. "I've a good mind to leave you in here. Let you sweat this shit out of your system in jail."

"No, you can't. I'm sick. The doctor said so." She reached for his hand again. Her skin had a yellow cast he recognized. Her liver was failing. Her doctor in rehab last time had warned them she had cirrhosis. She was flirting with the need for a liver transplant. Except she wasn't a good candidate. Not if she wouldn't stop drinking.

"You've got to get me out of here, Billy. I'll go to rehab again. I swear it. And never drink again. But I can't do jail. The women in here are hard. You should see the way they look at me. Mean eyes." She leaned against him. "I'm scared."

"You got yourself into this situation, Sally. It won't be easy to get you out this time. I saw you failed the field test for sobriety." He didn't take drunk driving clients as a matter of principle. Family was the sad exception.

"I explained why I couldn't stand on one leg to that cop. Inner ear problems. Would he listen? No. I told you. I only had a few drinks. And they were weak. That bingo parlor waters down the booze and charges an arm and a leg for it." She stared at him, pleading.

"You're drunk. I doubt you weigh more than one-twenty soaking wet. Three drinks and you're over the limit, Sally. Honest to God, I can smell the alcohol on you from here. If that's from three weak drinks, I'm Superman." He leaned back, looking away from her welling eyes. "Face facts. You can't drive. I'm taking the car keys this time."

"Who will take Mama to her doctor appointments? The grocery store? You know how she likes to shop and pick out her produce." Sally swayed in her chair.

"Gran can drive, you can't. But I'll make sure she gets where she needs to go. If you're in rehab, what difference will it make? First we need to see if I can keep you out of jail. The only good thing going for you as far as this infraction is concerned is that you were close to home and no one got hurt." Billy looked around the dingy conference room. "And that you're one of hundreds of DUIs on the Harris County rolls each month. If I can work a deal for rehab and community service, a judge will be glad to get you off his over-crowded docket."

"I love you, Billy. Your mama would be so proud of you." Sally dissolved into tears again then noisy gulps and sobs.

Billy hardened his heart. Sally had made a mistake bringing up his mama. He'd worked his ass off to become successful so he could rise above a life where three generations crowded into a run-down two-bedroom house, living on food stamps and charity. He'd made it too late to help his mother, who'd died early from her own alcoholism and the cancer that had taken her fast at the end.

As he saw Sally being led away by a hard-eyed guard, Billy realized this was just one more chapter and verse of what he'd lived with all his life and what would probably be in his future. Maybe he was being selfish, asking anyone to take on the misery his family represented. Shannon certainly had no idea what kind of baggage he brought with him.

He had plenty of time to think while he worked his way through red tape during the rest of a long night. Wait for a judge, file a paper, wait for a court time—it was a game he'd played many times—but it was necessary so he could get Sally out of lockup and into rehab.

Of all the women in the world, why did he think he had to have Shannon Calhoun, a party girl who thought she couldn't have fun without a drink in her hand? Maybe *he* was the sick one. Why was he drawn to a woman with the same problems he'd resented since he'd been old enough to understand them?

She didn't drink tonight. That thought made him unclench his fists a little. He was so crazed about this issue, he was going to drive Shannon away if he wasn't careful. Was that what he wanted? It had happened before. He'd make demands and she'd run like hell. Who could blame her? He sure didn't let anyone dictate to him. Shit.

If he didn't get his shit together and soon, he was going to lose her. And this time, he didn't think he'd get another chance.

Chapter 5

"Happy Birthday, sis."

Shannon threw her ugly tennis shoes across the living room at the shadowy figure sitting in the dark. "Ethan! You scared the shit out of me. What are you doing lurking like that?"

"Couldn't sleep. I came down here for a night cap. Want one?" He got up and walked over to the built-in bar next to the bookcase and snapped on a light. Ethan had her father's dark hair and stocky build. The youngest of the Calhoun kids, he was handsome and should have looked relaxed at this time of night. Instead, she saw worry lines between his dark brows.

"What?" Shannon realized her mouth was watering. Oh, God, did she have a drinking problem after all? "No, just water. I have to get up early and go to work tomorrow. So do you."

"Yeah. How'd your first day go?" Her brother poured water into a crystal tumbler and handed it to her then splashed some bourbon into his own glass before settling into his chair again. "Sit. Tell your little bro all about it."

"I survived." Shannon studied him. Was he all right? Maybe he was just as bummed about working as she was. Except he got to use his computer skills, something he was really into. "My feet hurt and my new boss clearly resents having to take on a Calhoun. How about you?"

"The same. Except at least I didn't feel the need to put on high heels." He laughed and sipped his drink. "Believe it or not, my boss Amanda is hot. She's older, of course, has been with the company for years, but a real brain. I think I can learn a thing or two from her. We were actually getting along until Cass barged in and hit her with the news that I was on a 'special project' for the family and couldn't do anything else. That didn't go over well. Now Amanda treats me like I have leprosy."

"Tough luck. But she can't know what you're doing for us. You have to find all those people our daddy defrauded *and* keep it a secret, or we'll be sunk before we can even try to make things right." Shannon drank her water—ugh, it had no taste or zing—and fell into a chair across from him. Flats tomorrow. "How's it going?"

"Too well. So far I've found eighty-five people or their descendants who we owe a ton of money. It'll be up to your pal Billy Pagan to figure out how to get them to sign off on a settlement that won't put us into bankruptcy. That was him I saw riding away on a hog a few minutes ago, wasn't it? I didn't take him for the biker type."

"You'd be surprised." Shannon leaned back. "He took me to a carnival. We rode a roller coaster." She sighed. "I love those things."

"You and Daddy. I never got it, wanting to be scared until you screamed or barfed." Ethan stood and stretched. "After midnight, sis, so now you're thirty. Ancient." He laughed and walked over to kiss her cheek. "Big plans for tonight? With the company in trouble I'm afraid those awesome birthday party days are over."

"You don't have to tell me." She got up and gave him a hug. "It's really bad, isn't it?"

"Millions of dollars so far and I hit a real pothole today in my research." He rubbed his forehead and, for a moment, Shannon wondered if he was going to cry. "Shan, you know where the Patagi Indian reservation is located?"

"Vaguely. Is it in Louisiana?" What fresh hell was this? Surely their daddy hadn't cheated them too.

"No. Livingston. East Texas. There's oil around there, of course. East Texas is full of it." He ran his hand through his hair, making it stand on end. "I swear to God, if Daddy were here now, I'd knock him on his ass. Why did he pull this fraud crap when there were good, honest ways to make a buck in the early days of wildcatting? There were plenty of decent leases available without having to forge signatures, lie to folks, do all the underhanded things Daddy did to take advantage of people who didn't understand what in the hell they were giving away when they signed his bogus contracts."

"There have been a lot of problems lately in other parts of the country with pipelines crossing Tribal lands. None in Texas that I know of. You sure we even found oil there?" Shannon looked longingly at the bar. A drink would relax this coil of tension that was beginning to knot at the base of her neck. No wonder Ethan couldn't sleep. No, she'd made it this far tonight without drinking. It would be stupid to cave into a craving now. She'd show Billy Pagan she could resist the call. But Ethan. She worried about her brother as he polished off his drink and headed back to the bar.

"We found it all right. Nine wells are still pumping. Good, producing wells. But there's something strange about the numbers. Like maybe he put in more wells than they know about or is doing slant drilling." Ethan picked up the decanter. "You know this is new to me, Shan. I'm still learning the lingo. All I see are figures that don't add up. Wouldn't surprise me if Daddy didn't pull a fast one. I did enough research to know that these Indians are very particular about the environment. I'm scared the extra wells Daddy authorized go against Tribal policy. We're sending them royalties, but it's not nearly enough as far as I can see. I'm surprised they haven't snapped to it before now." He started to refill his glass but Shannon slapped her hand over it.

"I hope you're wrong. But it's not *our* fault." She couldn't believe she was the one sliding the bourbon out of her brother's reach. "We can't clean up Daddy's mess overnight, you know." She hooked an arm through his. "Come on, bro. I'm tired and I'm sure you are too."

"Tired." He yawned and leaned against her. "Yeah. Staring at a computer screen all day when it's not gaming is harder than I thought it would be."

Shannon laid her head on his shoulder. "You're doing great. I'm proud of you. Mason can help you if you need him. Or let Billy take a look at what you've found. He's a genius at problem solving."

"He'd better be." Ethan let her take his empty glass and set it on the bar. "Thanks for listening, sis. It's just that what we owe keeps getting bigger and there seems to be no end in sight. Talk to Cassidy. She actually gave out her email address in the letters she's sent so far. Now she's getting hate mail from those people." He pushed away from her and looked her in the eyes. In the dim glow of the outside security light, she could barely make out his face.

"More threats?" She'd hoped they were done with that.

"Not how you mean. More like the kind that could cost us money. People are bitter. Wouldn't you be if you'd been cheated like they were? Some of them were left to live in poverty while here we are in a fucking mansion, enjoying money they see as rightfully theirs." His shoulders slumped. "No, we didn't do it, Daddy did. But I still feel guilty as hell."

"Stop it. We didn't know about any of this." Shannon grabbed him and shook him.

"Doesn't matter." He wobbled and held her hands. "Face it, Shan. We're on the Titanic here. If Billy is willing to marry you, grab him. I know he's loaded from the high-profile cases he's won. He may be your life jacket."

"Oh, please. Like I'd do that to him. Or give up on Calhoun Petroleum so easily." She steered her brother, who was more than a little drunk, to the elevator. "This is the booze talking. You need to hang in there. Remember, we've got Cassidy and Megan to help with this. Just do your research and let's see where we can go once we have all the facts." She punched the button to open the elevator then got them both inside. Ethan fell against the back wall.

"You don't sound like yourself. All serious and logical. What's happened to you?" He stared at her and blinked. "You're sober. And you've been with Billy Pagan. Hmm. Guess you got laid." He wagged a finger in her face. "No wonder I'm depressed. Maybe I need a woman."

"There you go. This weekend go out with your buddies and meet someone. Hook up and ease some of this tension." Shannon grabbed his arm when the doors opened on the second floor and helped him to his room.

"Ah, the wisdom of old age." He dodged her pop on his arm, then kissed her cheek before he staggered into his room. "Thanks, Shan."

After he fell on his bed, she took pity, pulling off his shoes then throwing a cover over him before closing his door. She still felt a little wired after the night she'd had, but seven came early and she needed sleep. By the time she climbed into her own bed, she'd figured out one thing—she might resent Billy for his high-handed tactics, but he was there when she needed him, there for her family too. She didn't doubt she could drop some of these problems, including the one with the Indians, into his lap and he'd help her deal with them.

She fell asleep wishing he were with her, his body warm against hers. Of course, then she wouldn't be sleeping, would she?

The mental hospital where Shannon's mother was staying by court order had strict rules, but her mother had managed to order a birthday present for Shannon—a beautiful red dress for the Ballet Ball. Shannon left her a thank you message and found out her mother was only allowed visitors once a month. It would be strictly supervised and there was a list of rules online. The next opportunity was weeks away.

It was a stark reminder that this was no fancy rich person's facility but a mental hospital, her mother's punishment for trying to kill Cassidy. Cass had agreed to drop charges as a favor to her new brother and sisters, but the judge had overruled the arrangement with the DA and insisted on a harsher punishment, years in the facility. Even the family had to admit it was more than fair.

Shannon had just settled at her desk in the office with a list of more people to call when a delivery arrived. The woman set a beautiful cut crystal vase on the corner of her desk. "Shannon Calhoun?"

"Yes." Shannon admired the cymbidium orchids and exquisite arrangement of lavender and pink calla lilies. There were other exotic flowers as well, dazzling her.

"Happy birthday." The woman handed her a card, smiled, then hurried away toward the elevators.

Shannon opened the small envelope and stared down at the printed signature inside the birthday card. *Dinner tonight? Yours always, Billy.*" He hadn't signed his name because he knew she wouldn't be able to read it. She reached for the phone. His cell went straight to voice mail. Did that mean he was already in court? She called his office.

"He's in a meeting in his office, Shannon. There's yelling so I shouldn't disturb him." Mai sighed. "I guess you know what happened to Albert's motorcycle."

"Yes, I was there. Billy defended it, but he was outnumbered." Shannon leaned over to smell the arrangement. It was like inhaling an island breeze.

"Albert is furious. But he'll get over it."

"Would you tell Billy I got his flowers? They're absolutely gorgeous. I've never seen an arrangement like this before. Tell him yes, I can't wait to see him tonight. I don't know how he knew it was my birthday today."

"So he didn't send you roses? He did something different?" Mai sounded surprised. "I got red roses from Albert. Not that I'm complaining, but he could use some imagination."

"I'll text you a picture of these flowers. I can't believe them. Oh, here comes my boss. I've got to go. Give me your cell number." Shannon wrote it down, hung up, then took a quick picture and sent the text to Mai's phone.

"What's this? Special occasion?" Caroline Wilson leaned over to smell the arrangement. "You really rate with someone."

"Guess so." Shannon grinned. "It's my birthday. Turning thirty."

"I remember that birthday. It's a tough one. This would take some pain out of it for me." Caroline nodded. "Your sister called me. You need to figure out our phone system here, Shannon. Apparently she called you first and you didn't pick up. Guess you were on the other line and didn't see the flash that showed you had another call."

"Oh." Shannon glanced at the phone. Her brother would call it a dinosaur. Now she noticed there was a blinking light with *message* printed underneath it. "I had no idea."

"Well, here's her extension. Dial it. I don't want to be used as a messenger, Shannon. So figure things out here." She stomped back to her office.

"Great." Shannon picked up the receiver and decided to see if she could listen to her message first. God, she had over a dozen in her mailbox and finally slammed down the receiver midway through the list. She needed a notepad if she was going to call back all those people. Hopefully she hadn't erased any of them. She took a breath then dialed the four-digit extension on the paper. Nothing happened.

"Well, hell." So she got up and took the elevator up to her sister's office. Holly greeted her with a smile.

"Happy birthday. Cass has been trying to reach you." Holly reached for her own phone.

"Wait! Holly, can you tell me how to call someone's extension? I was going to return Cass's call but when I dialed, nothing happened." Shannon felt like such a fool.

Holly smiled and gestured for her to come around her desk. "I can't believe no one has taken the time to explain our system. It's archaic but we don't have the money for an upgrade right now. Watch and learn." She quickly went through a tutorial. Luckily she was great with simple explanations and Shannon knew she wouldn't forget what to do.

"You're a treasure. I hope my sister appreciates you."

"She does." Cass came out of her office and gave Shannon a hug. "I hope I can take you to lunch today. Happy birthday!"

"I'd love that. Thanks." Shannon took a few moments to catch up on news. Cass was sporting a new engagement ring and planning her wedding to Mason MacKenzie.

Business came first though and Cass waved her away when Holly called her to the phone. Shannon headed back down to her office with a smile. Lunch at a fancy place, Cass had made that clear. And dinner tonight with Billy. Maybe turning thirty wasn't going to be the depressing disaster she'd thought it would be.

* * * *

Billy let Albert rant and rave long enough to get it out of his system then he had to get ready to go to court.

"I'll have the bike repaired. Tell me where to take it or you do it and send me the bill."

"The fucking Cruisers should pay for it. Showing muscle like that. They didn't hurt your girl, did they? I swear to God—" Albert's face was red and he looked like he was about to hit the wall with his fist.

"Chill, Albert. I think she liked the excitement, if you want to know the truth. I was the one who was about to stroke out over it." Billy gathered up the files he'd need. God, but he was tired. Was he going to be sharp enough to do his client any good? At least this was only a preliminary hearing. He hoped the evidence would be insufficient and he could demand the charges be dropped. If that didn't work, a date would be set and then they'd have months to prepare because of a crowded docket. No big deal.

"Who was claiming my guy has gambling debts?" Albert paced the office, his bulk filling the place.

"He didn't give a name but I'm sure you know him. The enforcer for the Skeleton Cruisers." Billy handed Albert the business card with the club name on it then rubbed his eyes. He needed some drops or something. Mai usually had them in her first aid kit in her desk. He opened the outer door.

"I know the son of a bitch. What was he thinking coming to you with club business in public like that?" Albert followed him out and leaned against a corner of Mai's desk.

"Eye drops?" Billy stuffed what he needed into his leather briefcase.

"Sure, boss. Get off my desk, Albert." Mai pulled open a bottom drawer and found a squeeze bottle. "You need sleep, Billy."

"Hah! Got lucky, didn't you?" Albert had obeyed Mai instantly. "I have to jump through more hoops. Like those fucking acrobats we saw last night."

"Language, Albert."

"Excuse me, Mai. Like those motherfucking acrobats." Albert grinned. "Someday you'll realize you can't change me completely, doll. It's my edge you find so fascinating."

She got up and stalked around the desk. "And it is *my* edge you find so sexy." She had a ruler in her hand and whacked his arm. "Foul mouths don't kiss these lips, mister."

"Ow!"

Billy finished dousing his eyes with the drops and grabbed a tissue. Fascinating. He could feel the tension between these two from here.

"I think he's sleeping where he stands. Maybe you should drive him over to the courthouse, Albert." Mai's soft hand touched his. "Billy, wake up."

Billy shook himself and grabbed his suit jacket. "Good idea. Drive me over in my car, Al. I'll take a cab back. You're right. I shouldn't drive. But I wasn't up all night with Shannon. Don't I wish. Aunt Sally caught a DUI, Mai. You'll see her new charges on my desk. Put it with the rest of her file."

"Oh, shit." Mai covered her mouth with one hand.

"Did I just hear a bad word come out of that sweet pink mouth?" Albert hooted then took Billy's car keys. "We will discuss this when I get back, woman. Come on, Bill, let's go. I'll pull the car around front." He stomped out of the office ahead of Billy.

"I'm sorry about Aunt Sally." Mai followed him to the door.

"Me too." Billy leaned against the frame and tried to find some energy. "I hope this is the last time. I got her into Caruthers about seven this morning. The way the courts are backed up, I'm hoping to make a plea deal that will keep her out of jail. Caruthers is supposed to be excellent. Maybe this time they can get her off the booze for good." He rubbed his eyes again. "She's killing herself, Mai. Just like…" He couldn't say it.

"Oh, Billy. You try so hard. This time, it will work. You'll see." She patted his back then handed him the briefcase he'd almost left on her desk.

"Oh, will you call and get Gran's car out of impound? Pay the fee out of petty cash. Call one of Sean's drivers to deliver it to her. You can bet she's freaking out. What day is today? She may have a doctor's appointment." He blinked to clear his eyes. "I should call her." He pulled out his cell and stared at it, then walked toward his office.

"I'll do it. Leave Grandmother to me." Mai steered him back to the door again.

"Thanks. I may owe you a raise." He frowned at his cell, not sure why it was in his hand then stuck it in his pocket again.

"You do." She smiled and gently kept pushing him to the elevator and hit the down button. "Focus. It takes thirty minutes to get to the courthouse. Take a power nap in the car. It will help."

"Good idea. I'll tell Slash you ordered it." He grinned and kissed her cheek, feeling a little loopy. "You ever going to put him out of his misery?"

"Maybe. I know him well enough to realize he doesn't appreciate anything he doesn't have to work for. Sound familiar?" She raised a dark eyebrow.

"Seriously? I have to endure a little analysis this morning on top of everything else?" But Billy did think about it on his way to the car. Yeah, maybe that was part of Shannon's appeal. She had never been easy. Fun. When had he just relaxed and enjoyed an evening like he had with Shannon last night? Thanks to her housekeeper, he'd found out her birthday was today too. So tonight he'd see her again. A bright spot to look forward to. It was almost enough to give him a second wind. Almost.

Once in the courthouse, things went from bad to worse. He couldn't concentrate and his client was pissed. Billingsley was paying him an outrageous sum. So far it had kept him out of lockup. Now it was supposed to get the charges dismissed at this preliminary hearing. The prosecution had circumstantial evidence and, if Billy had been on top of his game, he might have had some of it thrown out then and there. But he had to admit, a thirty-minute power nap had done nothing to sharpen his wits.

The housekeeper's testimony was hearsay, but the judge liked it and allowed it. More witnesses to what amounted to gossip made an impression on the judge and Rupert Billingsley was painted as a man who'd been abused until no one was surprised that he'd "snapped."

"What the hell's the matter with you, Pagan?" The man collared him next to the elevator. "You didn't even cross-examine that lying old bat."

"Which one, Rupert?" Billy knew he'd made a mistake the minute the words came out of his mouth.

Rupert looked around then shoved Billy into the men's room. "What the fuck are you trying to pull? Did her kids get to you? Are they paying you to tank this defense?"

"Why ask me that? You think Evelyn's kids will get her estate if you're found guilty of her murder?" Billy pushed back, not liking Rupert's hands on him. He also didn't like that he'd blown it in the courtroom.

"Of course I do. You need to bring that in. I wouldn't put it past either Dinah or Sherman to have hired a hitman and then pinned this on me for that very reason. They aren't exactly loving children."

"Let me look at her will. I thought she left them a portion of her estate." Billy walked over to the sink and washed his face. He had been about to apologize, but now he realized he should just keep his trap shut and listen.

Rupert was checking to make sure they were alone, going from stall to stall. It was something Billy should have done immediately.

"Yeah, why didn't you already look at it? And she was changing her will. They were going to be left out in the new one. Sound like motive to you?" He grabbed Billy's tie and yanked him closer. "Don't fuck with me again, Pagan, or you'll be sorry." He let Billy go, then left the bathroom, the door slamming behind him.

Billy took a steadying breath. He'd been so sure that Rupert was a victim himself. This was the first time he'd seen a violent side of a man he'd been convinced had been abused by a domineering wife. The murder had looked like a robbery gone bad. Rupert had claimed to have been tied up in a bathroom while Evelyn had been shot to death in front of her safe where her jewels were kept.

Detectives hadn't bought his story. The gun, registered to Rupert, was found at the scene and had been wiped clean of fingerprints. He claimed the intruder must have found it, used it, then dropped it beside the body. Details like the disarmed alarm and the fact that Rupert hadn't called for help had convinced the district attorney of his guilt. Now Billy was seeing what he'd failed to see before. Shit. Could he have agreed to defend a guilty man? He prided himself on only taking cases where he was on the right side of the law. Yes, he made deals for his aunt, but that was the only exception. No matter how hard he tried, he couldn't shake the hold she had on him—especially when he hadn't been able to help his mother. But more than anything, he wanted to use the law to help the innocent. Make sure mistakes were corrected. The Calhoun mess was complicated, but he'd be helping people on both sides of that issue—the people Conrad had robbed would get restitution, and the many employees and stockholders depending on the company would come out with something. Those were his goals. He'd have to be on his toes to manage both.

He picked up his briefcase from the floor and ran his hand through his hair. Rupert's threat didn't bother him. He could take care of himself. But he'd be damned if he'd help a murderer walk free. He needed more information and he knew just who to call.

Chapter 6

"I got your message to dress up, but you know that left me with way too many options." Shannon settled into his car and looked at him. He was elegant in his custom-tailored tux. My, how he'd changed since she'd first met him all those years ago. "You look good enough to eat."

"Careful now." His grin went wicked. "But thanks. I'm trying to impress a girl. You look perfect." He leaned across the console to kiss her, careful not to ruin her lipstick. "I knew you'd figure it out." He eyed the edge of her plunging neckline. "You always fit in wherever you go."

"A little black dress. Hard to go wrong with one. So where is it this time?" She shivered as she captured his warm fingers before he could touch her and held his hand. "Stop teasing me. I'm not starting the night in your bed or we'll never go anywhere else."

He laughed and sat back. "Now that was quite a compliment. Dinner first. We have the private wine room at Theodore's. Then they're doing a new ballet this week and I've arranged for us to see the dress rehearsal tonight. I figured you'd like that."

"Are you kidding me?" This time she forgot all about her makeup as she leaned over and kissed his smile. "How did you manage that?"

"I handled something for the stage manager's son a while back when he was falsely accused of a hate crime. He loves me now. They've been rehearsing all week so when I told him a special lady loved the ballet, he said to come on. They'll be there late so we can sit wherever we want and enjoy watching the last run-through."

"I have a feeling the ballet's not your favorite thing. Janie reminded me of that just this morning." Shannon straightened his bow tie then sat back.

"She showed me the birthday cake she baked for you. I told her we'd try it when I brought you home. *If* I brought you home." He finally put the car in gear.

"You're being optimistic." She smiled. "I think Janie likes you. Even though she's not so keen on the fact that rich people use lawyers like you to get off when they shouldn't." Shannon saw him frown. "Sorry if that touched a nerve."

"Rich people use me when they're innocent. I don't know what anyone else does. But this is your night. Sit back and relax. You know I can't talk about my cases anyway. Except for the one your family is involved in. And we sure don't want to get into that on your birthday." He drove down the tree-lined streets toward the tony restaurant where he'd obviously made a reservation.

Shannon knew the exclusive wine room was usually booked solid. Had he used another grateful client connection? It was becoming obvious to her that the years since she and Billy had been together had been very good to him.

"You know, I owe you an apology."

"What for?" He glanced at her, suddenly serious. He always took her seriously.

"Our first go-round I wasn't very kind to you. I didn't understand your work ethic and wanted you to act like one of my rich boyfriends, always available." She started to look away but realized that was being cowardly. She needed to watch him.

"Yeah, I knew that. In college, I was drowning in debt, trying to stay in school and working two jobs. I wanted to give you everything. I was crazy about you. But I had this goal for my future. If I didn't achieve it, you wouldn't have wanted me anyway." His hands tightened on the steering wheel. "I can be obsessive. It's a fault that I can't seem to get past. When I set my mind to something, get out of my way."

"Yes, I know. That's why you're so successful." Shannon touched one of his tight hands. "There's nothing wrong with being driven."

"But I drove you away." He opened his fist and clasped her hand. "I regretted it. We were young. A mature man would have figured out a way to manage both your wishes and the other pressures. Or at least tried to open up, explain things so you could understand why I couldn't be there for you."

"My wishes for you to drop everything and come when I called? And do you really think I'd have been interested in your explanations back then?" Shannon realized her laugh had a bitter edge. God. Turning thirty was making her see just what a selfish bitch she'd been in the past. Past? How about five minutes ago? "Billy, I was, am, a spoiled brat. I had no concept of what it was like to have to work for what I wanted. Daddy gave me everything. I didn't even have to study hard, majoring in fun and games."

He lifted her hand to his lips. "You're smart, Shannon. Don't put yourself down like that."

"Thanks." She smiled, wondering why he insisted on pursuing her. "You said we could start over. Fresh. I'm willing to try."

He smiled. "That's enough for me."

"You're crazy, you know that? You have no idea what you're taking on. My mother is insane and my daddy was a crook. You may end up having to bail me out someday or visit me in an asylum."

"It'll be my pleasure." He pulled into the parking lot, then leaned over to kiss her.

It was a sweet but deep and satisfying kiss that made her sigh into his mouth and hold onto his hard middle. She shivered, terrified that she'd screw it up. She drew one hand up to cup his firm chin when he finally lifted his head.

He smiled down at her. "Will you be mad if I tell you I'm starved? No lunch. And that restaurant has the best damned steak you'll ever put in your mouth."

Shannon laughed and pulled a handkerchief from his pocket. He always carried one because his grandmother had trained him to do it. He'd even done it in college which had made her friends laugh at him. She wiped away the lipstick from his face. "Let's go. I'm hungry too. Even though Cassidy bought me an absolutely decadent lunch today, including dessert."

"Wasn't that nice of her?" He opened his door as the valet opened the passenger side door for her.

Shannon pulled down the vanity mirror and quickly fixed her face then got out of the car. "Cass is amazing. A financial whiz."

"So you think Cassidy can help save the company?" Billy handed his keys to the valet.

"She's doing her best. Of course, Mason is a great advisor. None of us knows a thing about the oil industry. Daddy deliberately kept us in the dark. Now I think it's because of how he'd started the company." Shannon looked around. She had to be more careful. This was a deeply shameful thing for the family.

"It doesn't hurt that Mason seems to have fallen hard for Cassidy." Billy smiled when the maître' d greeted him by name and hurried to escort them to the private room where their table waited.

"This isn't how this room usually looks. It's beautiful." Shannon stopped in the doorway. There were dozens of white flowers and candles decorating the room usually tricked out as a wine cellar. It was a magical transformation.

"I wanted it to be special for you." Billy took her elbow and guided her to a velvet chair at a small table set for two. There was a bottle of fine champagne in a silver bucket next to it. A waiter appeared from a discreet side door to show Billy the label then opened the bottle.

"Champagne?" Shannon couldn't stop smiling.

"Did you think I was going to deny you the bubbly on your birthday?" Billy sat across from her and smiled.

"It had crossed my mind." She laughed when the cork popped. "Sorry, but I love that sound." She took the glass the waiter handed her then waited while he filled one for Billy before he left them alone.

"A toast." Billy touched his crystal flute to hers. "To the most beautiful woman I've ever seen. Happy birthday."

"Thank you." Shannon sipped and savored the tingle of the tiny bubbles. She'd barely made a dent in the champagne before a waiter appeared with the first course.

"Have you been stalking me? How did you know all my favorites?" Shannon was almost too full after they'd worked their way through five courses, from a hearts of palm salad to chocolate mousse.

"I pay attention. And I called Janie." He grinned when her empty dish was whisked away.

"This was perfect." Shannon toyed with her glass. She had a pleasant buzz. To her surprise, they hadn't even bothered to finish the bottle of champagne. "You seemed to find plenty of beautiful women to escort when we weren't dating."

"And you always had one of your rich Romeos hanging onto you." He stood and held out his hand. "We'd better get going if we want to see any part of that ballet rehearsal."

"Maybe I'm not so eager now." Shannon let him wrap her silk jacket around her shoulders, then turned in his arms as they waited for the valet to bring his car around.

"No way. I went to some trouble to arrange the ballet thing." He beat the valet to the handle and opened the car door.

"I admit I'd like to see the visiting prima ballerina from New York. Her solo is supposed to be spectacular." Shannon settled into the leather seat and watched him walk around the car. She was too happy. There was something wrong here. She'd never let herself trust a man like this before.

Old doubts hit her as he drove them downtown. He'd get tired of her. Men always did. Or she'd get bored. Turning thirty had rattled her, made her worry that time was running out. That she'd never find a mate, settle down, have a family. Honestly, though, did she really want that? Billy certainly did. He'd mentioned kids once, long ago. He deserved a couple of them. Little League, the whole domestic bliss thing. But where would that fit in with his busy schedule? Her father had missed every one of her ballet recitals growing up, always putting business first. Would Billy do the same? Staying driven even after it was clear he was already on top of the heap?

By the time they'd parked and he'd talked a security guard into letting him leave his car in front of the auditorium, she was in full panic mode.

She took his hand and stepped into the fantasy world of the ballet. But reality kept creeping in, making her heart race and her breath catch. He leaned forward in his seat, pointing out the mechanics of the set, pretending to like the way the dancers moved gracefully across the stage. He had even arranged for her to meet the ballerina, an icon in the dancing world. When she handed Shannon an autographed pair of her shoes, it was all she could do not to cry.

Off and on—mostly off—then two days together. This was moving too fast. All this special treatment was very seductive and he was looking way too good to her. But soon he'd remember the Shannon who didn't measure up to his strict standards. She shivered and he slipped her jacket over her shoulders before they headed to his car.

"Great night," she murmured, sighing inwardly. "Thank you."

Billy had become an expert at reading people. He'd done it in the courtroom for a decade. He knew when a witness was jumpy. Shannon wasn't on the stand, but she was anxious about something. Was he pushing her too hard? Coming on too strong? She was showing signs of bolting, like a fugitive.

No, hell no. He was going to have to take drastic action. He'd been studying her—yes, they'd been apart for a long time. But it didn't mean he hadn't kept tabs on her. She'd worked her way through the no-account playboys in her set and he'd held his breath. She'd come close a time or two to settling for the smooth lines of the major players.

He didn't blame the guys who'd come after her. She was everything a man could want—beautiful, smart and accomplished. She could enter a room and charm everyone in it. A man could make a dazzling career with a woman like that at his side. Yeah, he knew that. Had known it from the get-go. But it was more than a cold business decision that made him determined to have Shannon Calhoun. It was the undeniable spark between them. The thing that made him watch for her every time he went to one of those social things that his business required, the high society gigs she lived and breathed for.

She had a grace and sophistication that part of him craved. He always had to be tough and it was damned exhausting. He needed a soft place to fall and in his mind, it was Shannon he pictured beside him when he finally relaxed the relentless pace he'd set for himself. A different man might find other women more impressive. Prettier, funnier, curvier. Didn't matter. None of them did it for him like Shannon did.

So he'd arranged for this thing with the ballet. Saw her face light up and watched her carefully. She said what he'd expected. Clutched those nasty toe shoes to her little black dress like they were platinum and even teared up when the famous ballerina signed them. He got it. If a certain basketball great had signed a ball and handed it him, he might have teared up too. He liked seeing her happy. Her smile when she turned to thank him, made him feel ten feet tall. He wanted to make her smile like that all the time. For him; because of him.

Once they were in his car again, he hoped the evening wasn't over. He turned to her as he put the car in gear. "Shannon…"

"Billy, maybe I should go home now. To my house. Work tomorrow, you know. It's late." She gestured at the clock on his dash.

"Really?" He reached over and touched her bare knee. He did love the way the dress she wore hugged her curves and kept sliding up her legs.

"I'm tired." She yawned and leaned back in her seat. "I know you must be. You told me over dinner that you were up all night with your aunt and her problems."

"I took a nap this afternoon. Found a second wind. But if you come home with me, we could sleep. I'd love to wake up with you in my arms." He grinned. "I'm pretty good in the morning. Remember?"

"Hmm." She held his hand on her thigh. "I do remember."

Was she softening? Billy stopped at a light. This was where he would turn left or right. Her house or his.

"Make a decision. I won't push it." His body was screaming at him to push and push hard.

"This was a perfect evening. You made it wonderful." She nodded. "I'd love to fall asleep in your arms. But I can't."

He just resisted pounding the steering wheel. "I guess that means you're not ready. And maybe we should do things differently this time around. Okay." He made the left turn and eased off the accelerator, no longer in a hurry.

"You seem to have picked up a lot of favors since you started your law practice." She watched him drive.

"Yeah. It's a good way to do business. You never know when you'll need one. Like tonight. That sure came in handy. And the restaurant owner. I had to pull a few strings to get the wine room at the last minute."

* * * *

"It was worth it. I've never had such a perfect meal." She sighed. "We're here. Thank you again for such a great night."

"Your birthday's almost over and I haven't given you your present yet." He parked and pulled out a wrapped box.

It was small. Jewelry? She stared at him across the dark car.

"We should have done this during dinner." He handed it to her.

"Why didn't we?" She slid the ribbon off the box and tore off the paper. Inside was an old velvet jewelry box, the kind with an attached lid.

"This means something special. I wanted it to be just the two of us when you opened it." He grabbed her hand before she could snap open the box. "Maybe I should explain."

"You're nervous. What is this, Billy?" Shannon studied his face. "Is it a family heirloom? Or a piece of estate jewelry? I love things like that. Pieces with history."

"Oh, hell. Just open it and then I'll explain." He let go of her hand.

She flipped up the lid and saw a short gold chain with an enameled charm in the middle. Lifting it, she could see that it was a bracelet. The charm was obviously Indian, a two-headed bird of some kind. "It's beautiful."

"It's the symbol of my great grandfather's tribe, the Patagi. Those are twin birds. They represent our right to choose between good and evil. Gramps chose to leave the Tribe. Later in life, he had this made for my great grandmother. He made peace with the Tribal Council but never went back to the reservation to live."

"But surely this should stay with your grandmother, or your aunt." Shannon laid it on her wrist. It would fit perfectly and was obviously high-quality gold with very fine enamel work.

"Gran can't wear it. Her arthritis makes it hard for her to work a clasp like that. She sure won't give it to my aunt. She's furious with her. Has been for a while. So she gave it to me some time ago and told me to give it to someone special." Billy pulled her closer, his hands on her shoulders. "That's you, Shannon. It's not a commitment or anything like that, so don't freak out. If you don't want to wear it, I'll understand. I've noticed you don't wear much jewelry except to your fancy shindigs."

Shannon stared at him. Not a commitment. Of course not. But it obviously meant a lot to him and accepting it would be a step toward healing things between them. She just hoped he didn't regret giving her such an important family piece.

"I love it. I'll be proud to wear it every day." She held out her wrist. "Put it on for me."

Billy fastened the clasp securely. "I had a jeweler add a safety chain. My grandmother lost it for a while then found it in a sofa cushion when I was just a kid. So she put it away. It's the only valuable piece the family managed to keep after my great grandfather lost everything in the Great Depression."

"I want to know more about the symbol."

He kissed the inside of her wrist. "Yeah, there's a lot to that symbol. I'll tell you about it when I'm not so dead tired."

"Of course." Shannon leaned over to kiss his lips. "Thank you, Billy. This is the best birthday I've had in a long time."

* * * *

"I owe you an apology, Rupert." Billy pulled up a chair and gestured for his client to sit. Billingsley wasn't having it, pacing the floor in front of Billy's desk.

"You think?" Rupert stopped in his tracks and glared at him.

"I blew it in the courthouse. I need to try to make things right."

"Can you?" The man's face was red and he finally slumped into the chair. "Fuck. I'm scared, Pagan. I can't handle jail. That was the longest night of my life. Terrifying." He kept staring daggers at Billy. "Tell me right now if those two demon spawns got to you. If they paid you to blow that hearing, I swear to God…" His hands fisted. "I'll pay you double whatever they offered you."

"Listen, Rupert. I'm on your payroll, no one else's. And I resent you thinking that I could be bribed. I was tired after a sleepless night helping another client so my game was off. Won't happen again." Billy wondered if he should let this one go. His first meeting with Billingsley had made him think the man might be innocent. Getting him off would be bringing justice to a wrongly accused man.

"I'm sorry, okay? But I'm sure those bastards are setting me up. If you can't prove they're behind Evie's murder, I'm doomed!" Rupert dropped his face into his hands.

"Hey, calm down. You mean Dinah and Sherman Greene?" Billy had done a little background work on the players in the case. "Why would they want to kill Evelyn? Their own mother?"

"Stop right there." Rupert sat up and wiped his eyes. "Sherman keeps calling her 'Mother' but Evelyn was their stepmother, big difference. When Evelyn married L.J. Greene, his two children from wife number one went nuts. After he died, it only got worse because Evie inherited a big chunk of stock in his real estate conglomerate, Greenespace. Sherman and Dinah Greene run it now, but Evelyn wasn't happy with them. She had a seat on the board of directors. Was threatening to start a war, get the other board members together and replace those two sharks. She suspected they were skimming. Had even begun working on the other board members to start an investigation."

"Now that's a motive for murder. You should have told me this right away, Rupert. I'll get my investigator to look into that, and all the financial angles." Billy dropped a hand on Rupert's shoulder. He really seemed broken up over his wife's death. If this was an act, he deserved an award. "But what if this was just a robbery gone bad?" Billy dropped into the matching chair and picked up his tablet. "The police zeroed in on you quickly. Why?"

"Don't get me started. Maria, our housekeeper. She called those fucking Greenes right after she called 911. So they were there almost as soon as the cops were. Naturally they started screaming 'Murderer' at me right away." Rupert's eyes filled again. "I'm pretty sure they slipped Maria money every month to spy on Evie and me." He took a watery breath. "We couldn't fire her. She'd been with Evelyn for decades. Knew things Evie didn't want spread around."

"Are you sure you're not being paranoid, man?"

"No, listen to me!" Rupert gripped his arm. "Those bastards, even Maria, never believed that I loved Evelyn, truly loved her. Evie was nineteen years older than I was. Which is a lot, I know. But I didn't care about that. Yes, she could be mean to me, but that was her way. I could take it."

"You sure? At the hearing, the housekeeper made it sound like Evelyn was abusive." Billy knew he wouldn't have stayed five minutes in a relationship like that. Couldn't imagine Shannon ever calling him the ugly nicknames the housekeeper had said Evelyn routinely used for Rupert, even in front of others. Shithead had been one of the kindest.

"Maria exaggerated. And Evelyn liked her little jokes." He sobbed and looked away from Billy. "I loved her. Maybe that makes me a sick puppy, but I didn't mind the name calling, or the way she treated me in public." He took a deep breath. "Because in private, she was all mine." He sniffled and Billy had to bring out his handkerchief. "Oh, God, I can't believe she's gone."

Billy waved it away when Rupert offered him the handkerchief back.

This wasn't the first crying client he'd dealt with and wouldn't be the last. "Okay, I believe you."

He laid his hand on Billy's knee. "Evelyn and I had a perfect setup. She even brought in cute guys to liven up our sex life. What did I really have to complain about?"

Billy patted Rupert's hand. "Sounds to me like you had everything just the way you wanted it. It's a compelling argument. Not sure how a Texas jury will like hearing about your lifestyle, but let's hope it doesn't come to trial." He studied the man who couldn't have hit thirty yet. Conservative Texans didn't want to hear about role-playing sex games, even within the sanctity of marriage. And they sure wouldn't believe this handsome younger man hadn't knocked off his older wife to get his freedom, not without hard proof.

"Oh, honey, you don't have to tell me that." Here came the waterworks again. "Dinah and Sherman were convinced I was the Devil incarnate, once Maria let them know what kind of games Evelyn and I played. They even staged an intervention, if you can believe it. Evie laughed in their faces. Called them uptight prudes. You can bet that didn't go over big." Rupert sighed.

"Did they ever try to have Evelyn declared incompetent?" Billy figured a talk with Evelyn's lawyer might give him some insight.

"Oh, sure. But it wouldn't wash. She was practically running Greenespace, L.J.'s real estate holdings, at the time. She had too many witnesses that were willing to swear she was perfectly sane." He blotted his red nose. "We were two consenting adults, Billy. No one should care what we do in the privacy of our own home. Right?"

"If any of this gets out, the tabloids would have a field day." Billy stood, ready to move on. "Now let me get into this. Do some more research. Again, I'm really sorry about that fuck-up in the courtroom. Luckily it won't be up to that judge, but a carefully selected jury when or if this comes to trial. I'm hiring a private investigator to dig into this"

"I can pay for whatever you need. Evelyn was very generous with me over the years. I have my own money now." Rupert frowned. "Which made Sherman and Dinah Greene insane, of course."

Billy got up. "Try to relax and stay the hell away from those people. Okay?"

"Oh, never fear. I'm terrified of them. If they think I might get off and inherit even part of Evelyn's estate? What's to keep them from taking me out next?" Rupert shuddered then stood. "Thanks, Billy. I was sure you'd gone over to their side for a while there in the courtroom. I thought you were sleeping on the job." He laughed. "I just about wet my pants."

"I don't blame you. I promise that will never happen again." Billy walked him to the door. "I'll work to find evidence to prove your innocence." He fixed Rupert with a probing stare. "You sure I won't also find evidence that you had a little something on the side? Trust me, the prosecution is looking for that hard, right now."

"No, hell no. I wouldn't dare. It would void my prenup. Besides, I told you. Evelyn satisfied all my needs. All I had to do was tell her what I wanted and she provided." Rupert reached out and straightened Billy's tie. "Understand?"

"Yep. I'm sorry, buddy. Sounds like you had just the kind of marriage you wanted." Billy shook his head when Rupert offered him the handkerchief back again. "Keep it. I have dozens. I'll let you know what I find out." He smiled as he stepped back. "You stay safe and, I'm sure I don't need to say this, celibate, until we come to trial."

"I get it." Rupert winced then straightened his own tie. "I want you to know, though, that I haven't forgotten what happened at that court appearance." His eyes hardened and he threw back his shoulders. "I expect the best defense my money can buy, Pagan. If I get even a hint that you're favoring the other side?" He leaned closer, close enough to whisper in Billy's ear. "Well, I'm not such a cream puff that I don't know where to find my own muscle, sweetheart." He patted Billy's arm, a little harder than necessary, then tossed an air kiss at Mai before he walked out the door.

"He's certainly calmed down." Mai looked up from her computer.

"Maybe, maybe not. Can't say I blame him. I really blew it at his hearing. Call Albert for me? I need to talk to him." Billy walked back into his office and closed the door. Rupert Billingsley. Cream puff? Not exactly. But some instinct that he'd learned to trust told him he still represented a man who was innocent. Of murder at least.

He sat at his desk and focused on paperwork. He had several cases that needed his attention. And then there was the biggie—Calhoun Petroleum. He was going to head over there right after lunch. Bonus? He'd get to see Shannon. He tackled a mountain of paperwork then answered the phone. He'd made Billingsley happy but now he had to try to clear him. Making things right. It was why he'd gotten into the law.

* * * *

"What do you mean? Conrad did something funny with the Tribe too?" Billy couldn't believe it. As if he didn't have enough shit to shovel, here was one more thing staring him in the face.

"The numbers don't add up, Billy." Ethan Calhoun handed him a computer printout. "Your Tribe wasn't on the list of people my father may have cheated, but I can't reconcile the payments they're getting with the output from their wells."

"I know the Tribe gets oil royalties. Have for decades." Billy frowned down at the printout. "Why are you suspicious?"

Ethan sat at his work station and began hitting keys on his computer. "Take a look."

"What do you want me to see?" Billy stepped behind him.

It was odd, taking Ethan seriously. He'd known him since he'd been dating Shannon the first time. At fourteen, Ethan had always been in trouble, trying to get his sister's attention by doing stupid tricks like splashing her hair or tossing towels into the pool. Now he was all business, wearing a polo shirt with the Calhoun logo and khakis.

"There's a section on the Tribe's website that mentions the nine oil wells that provide important revenue for the Tribe." Ethan scrolled down so Billy could read the text. "But I've got a map here that shows more wells than that. And figures that indicate there were nine at first, but now…" He glanced at Billy. "You might want to take a look at what actually is there. You on speaking terms with the Tribal Council?"

"Yeah. We're good." Billy stepped back from the computer and took a breath. "Let me see that map."

"I haven't been to the area, but I guess it's in the piney woods around Lake Livingston. The Big Thicket." Ethan got up and went to a table where there were stacks of huge maps and plats. He rummaged through them until he finally picked one and laid it on top. "Here. Look at this."

"You should go. It's beautiful. Only a little over an hour from Houston. They have campgrounds around the lake with cabins they rent out, a nice restaurant and now the casino. It should take off when the people here discover it." Billy frowned down at the map. Yes, he could see the largest lake and then the reservation's land and several smaller lakes. "These marks are the wells?"

"I think they are. I'm still learning how to read this shit. But the money coming in from the wells and what was going out to rights owners is what I'm supposed to reconcile." Ethan frowned. "Daddy signed the leases with them when he started the company thirty years ago. That, at least, seems on the up and up. But the section he had permission to drill is here." Ethan stabbed the map with his finger. "Notice anything?"

"Yeah." Billy sighed. "The wells are creeping across the line to a place where the chief might object. The Tribe is really interested in protecting its natural resources, especially the lakes. If there is any fracking going on, pollution might also be an issue." He frowned. "Who drew these maps?"

"Engineers, I guess. I'm trying to keep this in the family, you know. I don't want to show them to anybody else. It would be great if this is just a mapping error. We sure as hell don't want to get crossways with the Indians. That could involve the federal government, couldn't it?"

"Of course. The Department of Indian Affairs. But let's see if we can handle this without that complication." Billy shook his head. "Have you got any aerial maps?"

"No. But we should have them. I guess Daddy didn't want them. Might catch him in the act." Ethan's shoulders slumped. "I hate this. Finding out Daddy was a damned thief. It was so unnecessary."

"Maybe he didn't think so, Ethan." Billy gripped the younger man's shoulder. "You have no idea how much it costs to run a big place like this. To keep on top of the oil business. Maybe your father had pressures you know nothing about. I see it every day in my law practice. A man can cave in to that kind of stress, do the wrong things for the right reasons."

"So says a lawyer." Ethan managed a smile. "Thanks for being on our side." He glanced back at his computer. "So what should I do now?"

"Let me make the next move. I want to check out the placement and number of those wells myself. Talk to the Chief. I'll let you know what I find out." Billy held out his hand. "Hang in there, Ethan. Looks like you're doing a fine job. You're right. Keep this in the family. If word gets out, Calhoun stock will take a nosedive. That hurts us all, including those we owe money."

"Guess you've got some of our stock too." Ethan gripped his hand. "Sorry about that."

"It was a good investment and paid a decent dividend so I've never regretted it. Now let's make certain I don't lose a bundle on either bet." Billy smiled. "And now I'm heading to Shannon's office. You know where it is?"

Ethan laughed and gave him directions. As Billy walked to the elevator, he realized he was still a little worried about boring her, his party girl. Could they really have a future together if he had to rein in his natural caution? The part of himself that liked to make plans and see well down the road? No wonder Shannon teased him about being too serious. But one of them had to plan ahead, worry about the future. He liked knowing what was around the next corner. Maybe Shannon would learn to like that too. If she didn't, well... Spontaneity wasn't a bad word. Just a scary one to a man who alphabetized his DVDs.

* * * *

"What do you mean, you have an airplane?"

"You really don't know me at all, do you? I may not like roller coasters, but I love to fly. I took lessons, got my pilot's license and bought a sweet little plane, a vintage Cessna." Billy laughed at what must have been her shocked look.

"Why an old plane? I'd think you'd want brand new, everything right off the lot and up-to-date." She stood. Where was this going?

"I've had it worked over. It's in great shape. It's a fine little plane. And we need to take it up. On company business." He glanced down to where Caroline Wilson was eyeing them through her open door. "I'll square it with your boss."

"Wait. What are you going to tell her? Explain this 'company business.'" Shannon didn't like the way he was taking over, as usual. "Tell me everything."

"Ethan showed me what's going on with the reservation and the wells there. We need to investigate. The Big Thicket isn't called that because you can get there easily. It's a pine tree jungle. Impossible to navigate unless you're really familiar with the roads and the winding paths that even the deer get lost following. I want to see it from the air, count how many rigs are actually pumping on the Tribe's property."

"That sounds like a good idea. Why do you need me?" Shannon didn't know why she even asked the question. She'd love to go up in a plane. It was just one more thrill ride for her. Billy as a pilot. She'd always pictured him with his nose in dusty law books. This was an unexpected side of him she liked. The adventurous side.

"I need you as navigator and recorder. I have a map that we'll use for comparison. Then we'll hit the reservation and talk to the Chief. Find out what anyone there might have noticed." He grinned. "Plus I want to show you off."

"When are we going?" She still had work to do. Caroline had piled on the assignments since she was now a staff of one. There were also more of those phone calls to the charities. She explained that to Billy.

"How about tomorrow morning? I have work of my own. Calhoun is an important client, but not my only one. And I need to check on my aunt." He leaned in for a kiss. "Dinner tonight?"

"Sounds good. Before or after you see your aunt?" She knew his Aunt Sally was in rehab now but not where he'd arranged for her to stay.

"Would you ride out there with me?" He named a facility outside of town, looking surprisingly uncertain for self-assured Billy Pagan.

"You need moral support?" Shannon really had no desire to visit a rehab facility. Was it part of his effort to make her give up alcohol? She'd be damned if she'd be scared sober. But maybe she was being paranoid. He'd told her over her birthday dinner about his aunt and her DUI. That had clearly shaken him. She could afford to support him with a ride along.

"Call it what you want, it's quite a drive and I'm not looking forward to it. I don't expect you to go in to see her, just keep me company on the trip. You can wait in the car. I promise I won't stay long, just touch base and make sure she's taking this DUI seriously. We have a hearing next week where we'll see if the deal I worked out with the DA will satisfy the judge."

"Okay, I'll ride with you. You can tell me what else you've been up to, besides earning your pilot's license." Shannon walked him to the elevator. "I'll handle my boss about tomorrow. She knows family business has to come first. Mason told her that."

"I love it when you're ballsy." He smiled down at her and pulled her close just as the elevator arrived. "I'll pick you up at your house about seven tonight. Pack a suitcase. We can leave from my place in the morning."

"Hmm. That sounds like more than just dinner tonight." She ran her hands through his thick hair. "Just promise me you're an excellent pilot."

He kissed her cheek. "I would never take you up if I wasn't absolutely sure I could get us both down safely. You have my word."

"All right then. See you later." Shannon watched him until the elevator doors closed then marched down to inform her boss that she was going to be gone the next day. It didn't go over well. But what could she do?

"I don't suppose I'm allowed to know the nature of this 'family business.'" Caroline tapped the stack of papers on her desk.

"I'm sorry, but no. Let me just say it has to do with the terms of my father's will. Very complicated." Shannon smiled to take the sting out of that. "I'll be with our lawyer tomorrow dealing with one of those complications."

"You and Mr. Pagan seem close." Caroline wasn't smiling. "Convenient, isn't it?"

"It is. I've known him a long time. It's reassuring." Shannon knew there was no point in getting into her relationship with Billy now.

"Whatever you say." Caroline picked up a memo, clearly dismissing her.

"Listen, I'm truly sorry, Caroline, for bailing on you like this. But I'm finishing the calls to the charities this afternoon. And they've all been very understanding. The Calhoun-Pagan sponsorship is getting good buzz. I'll prepare a press release and have it on your desk for your approval in the next hour."

"Fine. I'm eager to see it." Caroline frowned as her phone rang. "About time I saw a work product from you." She waved Shannon away and answered her phone.

Shannon sighed and headed back to her cube. So much for trying to make peace. She couldn't blame Caroline for being bent out of shape when her only help kept disappearing. Didn't matter. What did matter was making things right with the people her father had defrauded. She looked down at her wrist and that gleam of gold. Twin birds and the choice between good and evil. Her father had chosen badly too often. She prayed that the rig count would prove there was nothing wrong at the reservation. Maybe this time her father had actually done the right thing. Because, while Billy had excellent reasons to stay on Calhoun's side, his heritage would pull him the other way. She really didn't want him to have to choose between her and Tribal loyalties.

Chapter 7

"Mai called me. Said you had some business to discuss." Albert stood in the doorway, as usual not bothering to let Mai announce him.

"Come in. Sit." Billy told him what he needed for the Billingsley investigation then leaned back. "Think you can handle that? I can email you what information I have."

"Yeah. Greenespace. They have holdings all over Houston and in the suburbs—apartment buildings, strip centers, even a couple of major office buildings. I own stock in that company. Pays a good dividend." Albert started working his phone. "Stock price is down since Evelyn Greene was whacked. Not surprising. She was a solid board member."

"Is this a conflict of interest for you?" Billy tapped his desk. "I need you to be impartial. Rupert thinks Sherman and Dinah Greene wanted Evelyn dead."

"No conflict. I want justice. So I'll be looking at all the money trails." Albert walked over to quietly shut the door between Billy's office and Mai's. "Be aware, you could be stirring up a hornet's nest if these folks did it and get wind you're on to them. Billingsley should be in a safe place. Might need a bodyguard. I could set that up."

"Security? Not a bad idea. I'll talk to him about it. He's staying in a hotel. His house is a crime scene." Billy made a note to speak to Rupert.

Albert glanced toward the door leading to where Mai held court. "Glad I heard from you. I was going to call you anyway, about something else."

"If it's about my assistant, leave me out of it. Mai handles her own affairs." Billy grinned. He knew Albert had it bad. He recognized the symptoms. He was suffering from them too. All he could think about was when he could see Shannon again, touch her, taste her. Shit. Albert had said something and he'd missed it. "What?"

"I said that little turd, Simon Davis, needs to sell one of his bikes. You interested?" Albert roamed the carpet. "That Skeleton Crew is going to come after him again and I've a good mind to let them have him. But a debt is a debt. He needs to pay up and stop playing poker in their game rooms."

"Tell me about the bike." Billy got up and opened the refrigerator. He got a water for himself and offered Albert a beer. His own Harley. Yeah. It had been great being on the road again and Shannon had gotten into it.

Albert rattled off statistics, model and year as well as upgrades. "He won it in a game a few years ago. I checked. He's got the clear title. Maybe if he has to give up something he loves, it'll teach him a hard lesson. Get this shit under control."

"Don't know about that, but I want to see it, check it out personally." He followed Albert to the elevator since apparently Simon was waiting outside with the bike, hoping for a quick sale.

"What are you boys up to? Albert?" Mai got up from her desk. "It's not lunchtime."

"He's showing me a bike, Mai." Billy grinned when she looked horrified.

"You get my boss killed, Albert, and we are done." She stomped around the desk and met them at the elevator.

"I've told you, baby doll, riding is very safe. It's the driver who makes the difference." Albert grabbed her hand as she was about to stab him with a red fingernail. "Bill, back me up. You're a safe and sane rider, right? I sure as shit wouldn't have loaned him my bike otherwise, sweet pea."

"He's right. Relax, Mai." He heard the bell that signaled the elevator's arrival. "I'll be back in a few minutes. Hold down the fort."

"I'll see you later." Albert pulled her in for a kiss then jumped into the car, laughing as the doors closed before she could say a word.

"You really think she's the woman for you? She hates motorcycles." Billy punched the button for the lobby.

"All talk. You should see her on the back of my ride with the wind in her hair. The woman loves it." Albert slapped Billy on the back. "Now Simon's got the title in his pocket. He'll try to jack up the price. The man has had a run of bad luck lately. But that's not on you. Blue Book on this baby isn't as high as he's asking. Negotiate if you like it. You hear me?"

"Loud and clear." Billy followed him out to the street. The vintage Harley made his heart beat faster the moment he saw it. It gleamed red with chrome just where it should be. It had obviously been lovingly restored and kept in mint condition. He had to have it. After a ride to the closest freeway and back, he'd have paid double what Simon asked for it. But he knew he needed to keep Albert's respect. So he negotiated a decent price and pulled out his checkbook.

"No. Cash. Can we go straight to your bank? I have to give those cocksuckers cash." Simon stroked the leather seat of his Harley like it was a favorite pet. "I'm sure going to miss Gertrude."

"Gertrude?" Billy pushed Simon's hand out of the way and got on again. He should have left his suit coat upstairs. He knew he looked stupid—an uptight lawyer on a big bike—but this felt perfect. He was going to have to make time for more fun in his life. Work less, play more. With Shannon. The idea made him smile.

"Named after my granny. She loaned me the money to buy my first bike." Simon actually wiped away a tear. "I get it. Going back for another game when I was on a losing streak was stupid. And I have my suspicions. Don't know how, but I think their fuckin' game was rigged."

"Quit your bitchin', Simon." Albert was having none of it. "You okay with cash, Bill?"

"Sure. Leave the bike here and we can go in my car to the bank." He pocketed the key, not about to let this deal get away. "You can sign the title there."

"Sure. Whatever. Get this over with." Simon stumbled as they walked to Billy's car while he took one last look at the bike.

"As a lawyer, I'm going to advise you to give the person who holds your debt a cashier's check. You don't want to carry it all in cash. Too risky." Billy unlocked his car parked in front of the building. "What do you think, Albert?"

"Listen to him, Simon." Albert grabbed Simon's arm. "In fact, I'm going with you to that game room to hand over the check. I have a few words to say to those fucking Cruisers. And I wouldn't put it past you to stop somewhere and get in another game. Maybe lose it before you ever pay your debt. You hear me?"

"Quit treating me like a fucking kid, Slash." Simon jerked his arm, trying to get free. But the wiry man was no match physically for the huge leader of the bike club.

"Not a kid, but an addict." Billy had to add his two cents. "I've lived with addicts all my life. I know one when I see one."

"Shut the fuck up." Simon glared at him. "I can quit gambling any time. What do you know about it?"

"More than I want to. But if you're so sure you can, then quit. Show me, show Slash here how you can stop gambling. But clear your debts first." Billy looked back at that flame red motorcycle. God, it was a beauty. "You just lost a bike you loved. That's proof that gambling has cost you. Time to give it a rest."

"You're right about that at least." Simon looked down to where Slash still held his arm. "Let me go. The check is a good idea, you as a witness too. Then the motherfuckers can't say I didn't pay them."

"Now you're thinking." Slash let him go.

"Yeah. Thanks, Slash." Simon held out his hand and shook the biker's. "Thanks for buying the bike too, uh, Bill. It's a sweet ride. Take care of it."

"I will, Simon. I promise." Billy shook his hand then got in his car. He'd just bought a vintage Harley. He was filling up his garage and had to think about that. But inside the bank, the deal almost went sideways.

"Wait!" Simon stared at the cash Billy had withdrawn and licked his lips. The title sat on the bank officer's desk, ready for his signature.

"Wait for what?" Albert walked over to see what was going on.

"Maybe instead of selling Gertrude, we could work out a loan, Bill." Simon reached for the pile of money but Billy slapped a hand down on top of it.

"What the fuck, Simon?" Albert dropped a hand on the biker's shoulder.

"Listen. I've got a tip. A sure thing this weekend. On the Cowboys' game. Great odds. I could win enough to clear all my debts." Simon tried to shrug away from Albert. Wasn't happening.

"I'm not in the loan business. Janice, will you give us a minute?" Billy smiled at the woman who'd been waiting to witness their transaction. She nodded and walked away to speak to the teller holding his cashier's check. Give up gambling? That had lasted maybe five minutes.

Albert put his face close to Simon's. "Listen, you little fuck. A deal is a deal. If there was a sure thing, you wouldn't be in this bind, would you?"

Billy shook his head. "Give it up, Albert. I'm sure you can find another bike for me. Let's get out of here." He waved at Janice. "Thanks for your help. Guess I won't be needing that check after all."

Albert nodded and let Simon go. "Yeah, I can find you another bike, Bill. I can think of two off the top of my head."

"Wait!" Simon stood there, his fists clenching and unclenching, his eyes darting around the room before fixing on that pile of cash under Billy's hand.

For a moment Billy thought Simon was going to do something stupid. The bank's security guard had moved closer, obviously picking up on the vibe too.

"I have clients coming later. Quit wasting my time." Billy grabbed the title. "You selling this bike or not?"

Simon snatched it out of his hand, seized a pen and scribbled his name. "There. It's yours. Now let's get out of here." He glanced at the guard, who'd put his hand on his gun.

Billy gestured and Janice hurried over with the check. Obviously, she'd been listening to them. "All right." He slipped the cash into the bank envelope with the cashier's check. "Thanks, Janice." Then he followed the men outside. On the sidewalk he handed the envelope to Simon. The title went into his inside jacket pocket.

"When my luck turns, I'll be back for that bike." Simon started counting the cash.

"The hell you say." Billy grabbed Simon's T-shirt, pulling until they were nose to nose. Shit, had the man lost his toothbrush when he'd lost his mind?

"Hey." Simon tried to jerk loose but Billy wouldn't release him.

"I own that bike now. You're not getting it back."

Albert stayed out of it, standing so that no one inside the bank could see them.

"I'll pay you double." Simon held onto the money with one hand while trying to pry off Billy's fist with the other. "Come on, man, have a heart. You're rich. Wear nice threads, drive a fancy car. It was just a run of bad luck." His voice sounded like the whine of petulant child.

"You make your own luck, asshole. I learned that a long time ago." Billy wanted to shake him until his rotten teeth fell out of his empty head. "You lost that bike. Get used to it." He glanced at Albert, who nodded grimly. "I've got to go. Can you two get a ride from here?"

"Oh, yeah. Take off." Albert smiled. "I've got this."

Billy finally let go of Simon and stalked to his car. Fuck. Way to take the joy out of his purchase. He forced himself to calm down while he drove back to his office. When he got there, he made a decision. He had a little time. He called Mai and told her he would be back in an hour. Then, after he locked his suit coat in the trunk of his car, he took the key out of his pocket and put on the helmet Simon had thrown in as part of the deal.

He sat astride Gertrude—she needed a new name—and started the engine, savoring the roar of the powerful engine. It was no crotch rocket but better. He *was* rich now. The Harley suited him in every way—rare, in perfect condition and, yep, a little flashy in red and chrome. The ride cleared his head, reminded him why he'd wanted the bike in the first place. He felt young and free, something he'd never been, not even when he'd first met Shannon and fallen for her. Thank God he'd learned a few things since then. He'd gone into this deal with his eyes wide open, determined not to be screwed over. He drove into his own garage and dialed Uber for a ride back to his car. Eyes open. He'd have to remember that.

* * * *

"We have to stop by my grandmother's first. She has a suitcase full of stuff to take to Sally." Billy glanced at Shannon, sitting in the passenger seat of his car. He'd thought about surprising her by riding up on that new Harley, but his grandmother had called and blown up that idea.

"Sure. I'd like to meet your grandmother. Is she going to be upset that I'm wearing her bracelet?" Shannon played with the gold chain on her wrist.

"Shouldn't be. She gave it to me and told me to let my heart guide me." He stopped at a red light then leaned over to kiss her. "That's what I did."

"Okay. I just hope you're right." She looked out the window. "Interesting part of town. I've never been here before."

"I'll just bet you haven't. Interesting? It's scary for a girl like you. Stay out of it unless it's broad daylight or you're with me." Billy gunned the motor as soon as the light turned green. In this neighborhood, you didn't want to make another driver mad by being slow off the mark. Road rage ended up with shots fired. "I've tried to get Gran to move, but she won't budge. It's close to her church, the bingo parlor and, most important, her beauty salon." He laughed. "Don't be surprised at her hair color. It can change from month to month."

"Really? I assumed she would either be gray or have dark hair like yours." Shannon turned to face him.

"Nope. She says she'll never let her gray show. She has an adventurous side, at least when it comes to her looks. Wait and see." Billy turned a corner and studied the street with fresh eyes. Burglar bars on most houses. Peeling paint and patched roofs. His grandmother's house was in excellent repair because he made sure of it. The frame house had a well-tended flowerbed lining the sidewalk and the flowers that he'd never bothered to learn the names of were in full bloom.

Shannon grinned when he stopped the car in front of the house. "The garden is incredible. Your grandmother must have a green thumb."

"She's ashamed of me because I hire a yard crew. I don't have time to do anything with flowers. Don't care either." He got out and walked around to open the car door for Shannon. Of course, his grandmother had been watching for them and stood in the open front door. She came out onto the wide porch, a smile on her face.

"Billy! Who's that with you?" She let the door made of iron bars clang shut behind her and walked down the porch steps.

"Gran, this is Shannon Calhoun. I think I've mentioned her a time or two in the past." Billy held Shannon's hand while hitting the lock button on his key fob. He never left his car unlocked around here. "Shannon, my grandmother, Diana Pagan." He almost laughed when Shannon tried not to stare at the older woman. "Gran, orange hair? Is that for Halloween?"

He pulled Shannon up the sidewalk, not about to say anything about the orange-flowered top, dangly earrings, and stretch pants Gran wore. Typical outfit for his grandmother who was into bright colors, comfort, and staying cool. The thermometer had hit close to ninety today so naturally Gran wore short sleeves that showed off her arms, tanned from hours spent tending her garden. He thought she looked good for a woman in her mid-eighties. She applied makeup every day, this month favoring green eyeshadow and orange-looking spots of color on her cheeks. Went with her color scheme, of course.

Billy glanced at Shannon in her black pantsuit with the white blouse. Gran probably considered the look boring. He thought she looked perfect, professional and beautiful, though it wouldn't hurt if she'd let her hair down and unbuttoned a few of those buttons so he could see some cleavage.

"Halloween, fall, I was in the mood, Billy." She took Shannon's hand then pulled her wrist up to study the bracelet. "Well, look what we have here. I recognize this." She pursed her lips which wore lipstick a shade even brighter than her hair. "Billy, boy, you gave her this?"

"Yes, Gran." He kept his arm around Shannon. "Can we go inside? I figure it's only a matter of time before we have a drive-by shooting in this neighborhood."

"Oh, stop. We're perfectly safe. I make those gang boys and girls cookies. We have an understanding." She slapped his chest then turned and walked back toward the house. "Come. I have some iced tea made if you're thirsty." She stopped in front of the door then turned. "Sorry, Shannon, but I won't have liquor in my house."

"Oh, that's good. I mean, I don't need a drink. Billy and I are fine. Right, Billy?" Shannon looked like she wanted to bolt back to the car.

"Of course we're fine. We just need to get Sally's suitcase and head out to the facility. It's a long drive. We can't stay but a minute." Billy held open the door and followed both of them inside. He tried to see it through Shannon's eyes. Small, tidy, but so classless. If he was being judged by this room where he'd spent all the years he was growing up, then he'd get a D minus. At least the vinyl recliners were now leather thanks to his gifts at Christmas and birthdays. And the TV was a big screen and the latest technology. But Gran wouldn't let him replace the worn linoleum or upgrade the kitchen, clearly visible through the open doorway. She liked the tiny house the way it was. Though the central air conditioning and heat had been happily accepted.

"Oh, are we interrupting your show?" Shannon gestured toward the TV. "Our housekeeper watches *Wheel of Fortune* every night. How are you at the puzzles?"

Well, she'd always been good with people and that question at least coaxed a smile out of Gran. Soon the two were in deep discussion on the advisability of buying a vowel.

"Hey, we do need to get on the road. Don't you DVR these shows, Gran? I showed you how." Billy stepped between the two women.

"Yes, yes. Come into Sally's room, Billy. She called just before *Wheel* started and asked me to put a few more things into the suitcase. That girl! Thinks she's at a fancy hotel, not there to work on her problem." Gran led the way down the hall. "Shannon, you stay here and see if you can get the puzzle."

Billy followed his grandmother. Once they were in Sally's bedroom, Gran grabbed his arm.

"What the hell are you thinking, boy?" She glared up at him, her eyes bright, her mouth quivering.

"Wait. What?" Billy felt her fingernails, painted a surprising purple, dig into his skin.

"Shannon Calhoun. You think I don't remember what you went through with her all those years ago? She broke your heart, Billy mine. I know you loved her. She was your first serious girlfriend." She shook his arm. "Grow up! Think! You told me she had a drinking problem back then. That never goes away. Have you learned nothing from the mess your family has made?"

"Stop it. Keep your voice down." Though Billy knew Shannon probably couldn't hear them. Gran kept the TV loud enough that he'd heard it from the curb when they'd got out of the car. "She's different now. We're both older, wiser." And he'd obviously talked too much when Shannon had broken his heart in college.

"Pah! You lust for her. I know how men are. I lived with one for almost fifty years. Thinking with what's in your pants, not what's in your head. I'm ashamed of you." She turned away in disgust and threw open the closet door. She pulled out a silk blouse and pair of black pants and folded them carefully. "She will break your heart again."

"I didn't come here for your blessing, Gran." Billy waited for her to put the clothes into the suitcase and snap it shut. "I'm sorry if you're unhappy, but I'm a man who can make my own decisions. Shannon is who I want. Get used to it." He grabbed the suitcase and marched out of the room and down the hall.

"Mrs. Pagan, the puzzle was 'It takes two to tango.'" Shannon was smiling as they entered the room. She took Billy's arm. "Billy and I will be going to the Ballet Ball soon. Can you tango, Billy?"

"I've had a few lessons. You'll have to wait and see." Billy struggled to school his face, hoping Shannon couldn't see how furious he was with his grandmother. Damn it to hell. Why had Gran brought up that ancient history? He'd never felt such pain as when Shannon had dumped him in college. So he'd vented to his mother and grandmother about it. But his grandmother was an elephant when it came to remembering things her only grandchild had said and done. He sure hadn't told her about the other times he and Shannon had tried to make things work and failed.

"Tango lessons? I can't believe it. You just keep surprising me." Shannon's happiness made her glow. "Mrs. Pagan, I know you must be proud of Billy and the success he's become."

"Sometimes." Gran stood stiffly, not smiling. "Billy, you said you were in a hurry, but do you have time to air up a tire for me? That right front looks low. There's a warning light on the dashboard that keeps saying I need air. Fancy car." She glanced at Shannon. "Billy bought it for me, Shannon. He's such a good man. But so busy with his law practice." She shrugged. "If you can't do it, Billy, maybe one of the boys on the corner will take care of it for me."

"One of those gang members?" He shook his head. "Stay away from them, Gran. It should just take a minute. The air pumper in the garage?"

"Sure is. But I just hate to use it. It hurts my knees when I bend down, you know." She sat in her recliner. "Thanks, Billy."

Shannon smiled at Billy. "I'll wait here." She sat tentatively in the matching recliner. "It's almost time for the prize puzzle, Mrs. Pagan. I love to see them win a trip." The front door clanged when Billy left. Shannon saw his grandmother's face change, all pretense of friendliness gone.

"Cut it out, Shannon Calhoun. You're not charming me by pretending you give a damn about *Wheel of Fortune*." Billy's grandmother pulled herself to her feet and stood in front of her. Her bright blue eyes blazed. "Stand up, girl."

"What?" Of course, Shannon stood, then winced when Mrs. Pagan grabbed her arm and jerked her toward the door. They were on the porch before she knew where they were going.

"Listen to me, Shannon Calhoun." For a small woman, Billy's grandmother had a firm and painful grip. "You hurt Billy so bad all those years ago I thought he'd never get over it."

"I'm sorry." Shannon gently tried to pry off those lethal fingernails. "You mean when we were in college? I was young and stupid then."

"No excuse!" The woman darted a look toward her driveway. They could hear the sound of her car engine starting then what must be her air pumper going. "Stay away from him. He deserves a nice girl, a decent woman who knows how to treat him right." Her eyes filled and she knuckled a tear off one cheek, smearing her blush. "Damn it, I mean what I say. You hurt my boy again and I'll send one of those pups on the corner after you." She nodded toward the half dozen boys and girls who were smoking and laughing a few doors down.

"I'm sorry, Mrs. Pagan, but I don't want to hurt Billy. He's a fine man. I want things between us to work this time." Shannon jumped when Mrs. Pagan dragged her down the steps and whistled. The boys on the corner looked their way. She nodded and they gave her a thumbs-up.

"You see that? Those boys will do me a favor. They've marked you now. Know your face. You hurt my boy and you will be very sorry." She let Shannon go when they saw Billy stride down the driveway toward them.

"Got all the tires at the right pressure, Gran." He looked surprised to see them outside.

"Thanks, sweetie. I figured you two were ready to hit the road."

"Yes, of course." He stepped inside and got the suitcase then looked from one to the other. "Ladies? Everything all right?"

"What do you think?" His grandmother had followed him up the steps and held on to the iron door. "Let me know how Sally is doing out there." She kissed his cheek then stepped inside, clearly ready for them to leave. "I think I'll start the program over, I missed too much."

"Goodbye, Mrs. Pagan." Shannon didn't even try to smile.

Gran let the door slam shut. "Run along."

"Lock this door, Gran. Don't forget." Billy stared at her through the burglar bars. Obviously, the chill in the air was impossible to miss.

"In a minute. Let me figure out how to rewind this thing." She was punching buttons on her remote control. "Damned technology. Why is it so complicated?"

"You can do it." Billy used his own key to lock the burglar bars.

Shannon stopped him as he was opening the passenger door on the car. "She hates me."

"She worries about me and remembers our old breakup." Billy kissed her quickly. "I took it hard back then. That's all. She doesn't want me hurt again."

"She made that clear." Shannon put her arms around him, deciding that telling him about the threat would do no one any good.

"Give her time. She'll come around." Billy held her for a moment then obviously noticed the sketchy-looking group of teens eyeing his ride. "Get in the car. We should get out of here."

"Yes, they don't look like they're interested in cookies." Shannon hurriedly got in and they were soon on the road again. "She needs to move out of that neighborhood." And away from potential hit men. She shivered. Crazy to think that Billy's granny with the orange hair could be dangerous. But she'd sounded so deadly serious.

"I've tried. She won't go." Billy picked up her hand. "I just hope she settles down. I'd like her approval but don't have to have it."

"I caught the dig about alcohol too. I know that's a sore subject for her." Shannon sighed and looked out the window. "I'm not going to turn into a teetotaler, Billy. I enjoy a cocktail occasionally. More than one, as you've noticed."

"I know that. You know I drink too. But I don't do it around Gran. It makes her crazy." He rubbed the chain where it lay on her wrist.

"Fine. As long as we're clear. You don't lay down rules for me and I won't lay down rules for you." She turned to face him.

"Is that how relationships work?" He seemed to really want to know.

"I don't have a clue." She turned her hand over so she could grip his. "I suck at relationships. Haven't had much practice at them, if you want to know the truth."

"Yeah, me either." Billy smiled. "So we'll figure this out together."

* * * *

"Billy, you've got to get me out of here." Sally looked better but her hands shook as she lit another cigarette from the butt of the one she'd just finished.

"The district attorney is willing to let you get by with community service and probation if you spend six months in this facility, Sally. Not a day less. So getting out of here isn't an option. Unless it's straight to jail." Billy sat back, not crazy about breathing her second-hand smoke. He hadn't mentioned the big fine he'd have to pay for her. What was the point?

"What kind of a deal is that?" She glared at him. "I thought you were a hot-shot lawyer. You telling me that was the best you could do?"

"It was your third strike, Sally. You're lucky he doesn't throw in house arrest after your release from here." Billy wondered if hell would freeze over before he got a thank you from his aunt. "You want to hire another lawyer? Feel free. Of course then you'd have to pay. Or go with a public defender."

"You know I don't have any money." Her lips trembled. "You want me to suffer, don't you? I know how you feel about drinking and driving. You make no secret of it."

"You're right. I hate it. I hope you've thanked God that no one was hurt this time." Billy leaned forward. "And it's not just driving drunk. I hate what alcohol has done to this family. Grandma is sick over your latest shitstorm. My mama broke Gran's heart first, now you're doing your damnedest to break it again."

"The counselors here tell us it's a disease, Billy. We can't help ourselves." She sniffled.

"Here come the waterworks. Part of the cure is staying here and doing what they tell you. Six months will pass quickly. Think how much better this is than jail. If you're lucky, you'll come out of here cured of the 'disease.' Please, use what they can do for you here. It's supposed to be one of the best. Let them help you." Billy looked around the room where they'd met. It was decorated like an expensive living room. Gran had begged him to find a decent place for Sally and he'd done it. One of his clients had used this palace for the privileged for her son when he'd been facing the same kind of jam Sally was in.

"It *is* nice for a kind of prison. The sheets are high thread count and the meals are actually tasty. I've already gained three pounds." She mopped at her cheeks with a tissue from a fancy gilded box on the wooden coffee table. "Don't think I don't know this is costing you plenty, sweetheart."

"Don't worry about that. It'll be worth it if you work the program. Come out clean and sober. For yourself. And for Gran. She's been through enough." Billy shifted in his seat, eager to get out of there.

"I'll do it. I swear I will. As payback for sticking me in such a nice place." Sally smiled coyly and brushed back her straight black hair that was clean and had obviously been freshly styled. "I'm sorry I snapped at you. It's the withdrawal, I guess. You know how it is." She frowned. "No, I guess you don't. You never had to fight the demons your mama and I did."

"Hang in there, Sally. Do what they tell you. This place is supposed to work wonders." Billy patted her hand. Demons? He didn't believe in them. He believed in counting on yourself to make things happen.

"It must have a great reputation. You won't believe who else is in here." She stubbed out her cigarette and leaned closer. Her eyes lit up and she got excited as she threw out a name. When he looked at her blankly, she hit him on the arm. "Oh, come on. Surely you know her. You have all those famous clients. She's on that reality show. The one they filmed right here in Houston."

Billy let her rattle on, pretending to be interested. Sally had always loved celebrity gossip and she was happy to have some to share. He glanced at his watch and realized Shannon was probably getting antsy in the car.

"Well, then, make some new friends. Obviously, money didn't keep her from having the same kind of problems. You can bond over them. Maybe she'll be in your therapy group." He stood. "I've got to go."

"Tell Ma to come see me. Maybe you could spot her some cash so she could buy me some nice lounging outfits. So I'd fit in with this crowd." She stood and hugged him. "I do appreciate what you're doing for me, Billy. You're a good boy."

"Not a boy now, Sally. A man who has to work hard to pay for this fancy rehab. So don't worry so much about how you look here, worry about getting off the sauce." Billy did hold onto her for an extra minute. "Gran needs you to get well. Understand?"

"Yeah, yeah. Tough talk." She smiled up at him. "But I remember years ago. You were always my little guy. You take care of your family. It's one of your best qualities." She patted his cheek. "Come back soon, Billy. I love you."

Billy just shook his head. He couldn't say it. She'd hurt him too many times. So he pulled back and strode out of the room, glad to see that security was tight. There were surveillance cameras everywhere and it took showing identification and passing through a well-manned guard station to get in and out of the place.

"She okay?" Shannon looked up from her phone when he got in the car.

"She's dealing with things." Billy leaned over and kissed her. "I appreciate your coming with me. Sorry I took so long."

"No problem. I had some e-mails to catch up on." She smiled at him. "You look down. Guess seeing someone you love in a place like this will do that to you."

"Yeah. So let's get out of here." He leaned back and took a moment before he started the car. "I'm starving. What do you think about picking up some takeout and eating at my place? I'd like to get an early start tomorrow." Billy looked down at that gleaming gold bracelet on her wrist. "That sound like a plan you can live with?"

Shannon squeezed his fingers. "Perfect. Tell me what you're in the mood for, and I'll text the order so it'll be ready by the time we get there to pick it up." She hit an app on her phone with her thumb, proving she could operate it one-handed. "Chinese? Pizza? Name your poison."

"Surprise me." Billy realized he honestly didn't care as long as this woman was sharing it with him. He was sick of dark and gloomy thoughts. She hadn't mentioned needing a bottle of wine to go with dinner. Hadn't shown signs of alcohol dependency at all since he'd made such an issue of it. Obviously, this was his hang-up and he needed to lighten up.

Shannon was busy typing into her phone, a mischievous smile on her face.

"What are you up to?" Billy tried to get a look at the screen.

"Never mind. Drive. I've got a delicious dinner planned. Take your usual route home. We pick up dinner about five blocks from your house, on Westheimer." She laughed and shut down her phone.

"I can think of at least four decent restaurants along there that I wouldn't mind getting food from. Good call." He put the car in gear. "You're in a fine mood. Something happen at work today?"

"My boss actually praised my 'work product,' as she called my press release." Shannon leaned back as he drove them toward the nearby freeway. "I consider that a major triumph."

"It is. Caroline Wilson looks like the type who isn't easy to please." Billy wasn't surprised Shannon had handled her assignment well. He was just sorry she had to prove herself like that. "Tell me about the work product." He listened as Shannon talked about her press release. He was impressed. "You really have the hang of this. If you want to leave Calhoun after your year there, you could work for me. We're always dealing with the press, trying to get good spin for our clients when we're at trial."

"I thought juries weren't supposed to read about a trial or watch the news once they're picked to serve." She leaned against the passenger door, her beautiful face mysterious in the lights from the dashboard.

"That's the law. But before a trial, there can be lots of press with a high-profile client. If we can plant a story that puts our client in a positive light, we'll do it." He put the car on cruise control and reached for her hand. "Anyone notice your bracelet today?"

"Of course." She smiled. "It's unusual. And, like you said, not like me to wear something of this type. My brother noticed at breakfast. He asked me if we were serious. I think he has visions of a lawyer in the family as a good thing. You know he has a history of skirting the law."

"Kid stuff. Unless there's something I don't know. I remember he did a little joy riding in one of your dad's exotic cars and the old man called the cops himself."

"Daddy about had a cow when Ethan drove his vintage Lamborghini across the lawn and into the neighborhood at the tender age of thirteen. Ethan didn't quite know how to shift gears and you could hear the transmission protest from blocks away."

"I'd have pressed charges myself." Billy laughed. "Dylan MacKenzie told me your dad's car collection is being auctioned off. That he didn't want any of his kids to have even one of those cars."

"You can imagine how that made Ethan feel." Shannon sat up suddenly. "Look! It's a pack of motorcycles. But not the Skeleton Cruisers."

"No. Check out the back of their vests. That's a Galveston group—the Gulls and Dolls. Quite a few women riders among them. They seem to be headed south toward their home turf." Billy realized he hadn't told her about his purchase today. She'd see it soon enough in his garage. "Would you like a bike of your own?"

"I don't know. I haven't thought about it. It was fun riding behind you." She studied him. "Maybe. I'd have to try it. The women on those bikes look powerful. In control. That appeals."

"I'll just bet it does." He laughed and stayed back from the bikes which were clustered together, driving carefully. Yeah, he could see Shannon on her own bike. It was something to think about.

"So what did you tell Ethan? When he asked if we were serious?" Billy let go of her hand when traffic slowed and he had to change lanes.

"I plead the fifth." Shannon laughed. "You should see your face."

"Do you even know what the fifth amendment means?" Billy could hear his teeth grind. Why couldn't Shannon just say *Hell, yes, we're serious*?

"I have a vague idea. If I tell you my answer, it might come back to bite me later." She grinned at him. "Does that fit fifth amendment parameters?"

"Quit trying to weasel out of this, woman." He cursed when traffic snarled again and required all of his attention. Damned Houston freeways. An idiot cut him off and he blasted his horn.

"Hey, relax." Shannon leaned over and laid a hand on his thigh. "Serious about you, us? Yes. And it scares the hell out of me."

Billy breathed then covered her hand with his. "That makes two of us."

Chapter 8

Shannon loved the look on Billy's face when she told him where to pick up their dinner. Cheeseburgers, fries, and onion rings. Of course she knew what he liked. She'd made a study of the male of the species since she'd hit puberty. It didn't take her long to figure out men and what they wanted. There was a difference in her relationship with Billy though. Before, she'd been calculating. Figuring out the angles when she was with a man. This time wanting to please him seemed natural.

"Check out what I bought today." Billy hit the garage door opener.

"You're kidding." Shannon couldn't miss the gleaming chrome and red Harley parked where she'd imagined putting her own car. "That's sudden."

"The deal fell into my lap. I couldn't resist." He hopped out of the car and reached into the back seat for the food bags. "Let's eat, then maybe we can go for a ride."

"It's a beauty." Shannon straddled the leather seat. She'd made pantsuits her work uniform since she'd sworn off stilettos except when going out at night. Okay, so the machine was big and a little intimidating. But a few lessons and she could see herself like those women on the freeway, in formation, hitting the highway.

"Uh, it's mine." Billy's hand on her shoulder jolted her out of the daydream. "But you can ride behind me."

"Maybe I want one of my own." She grinned at him. "Come inside. Let me show you how I can rev a motor."

"Now you're not playing fair." He helped her off the bike when her pant leg got caught on some fancy thing sticking out of the side.

"Seriously, Billy. Maybe I'll save my money, buy one for myself. How much does a bike like this cost?" Shannon realized she'd never had to pay for wheels in her life. What did that say about her upbringing? It had been so different from Billy's. Seeing that tiny house where he'd been raised had made her very aware of the fact that they might both be native Houstonians, but her Houston and his couldn't be more different. She couldn't imagine his childhood. Glad she didn't have to. The fact that he was now rich and successful just made her admire him more.

"You don't want to know." He picked up a rag and polished the chrome bumper where she'd left a fingerprint.

"Yes, I do." Her mouth fell open when he told her what he'd paid for the vintage Harley. "You're exaggerating."

"Not at all. It's in mint condition and a rare model. The guy kept it in great shape and just had the engine rebuilt. I got a good deal." He glanced at his BMW. "You really don't have a clue what any of the things you and I drive cost, do you?"

"Let's drop this for now. Obviously, I've been living in an ivory tower all my life. We need to pray that we salvage the company so I can continue with my sweet and very secure lifestyle." Shannon grabbed the bag with the French fries and popped one in her mouth. "We need to eat these while they're hot. Come on."

"Salvaging the company is just one part of the equation. You've got to prove you can work successfully at Calhoun for the next year. If your boss tells Mason MacKenzie you're not cutting it, then that could be a problem." Billy unlocked the back door and held it open for her.

"I'm not worried. PR is coming naturally to me. Yes, it's changed since I got out of college. Now everything's online. Social media is where it's at." She dropped her bag on the granite countertop and opened a cabinet to pull out two plates. "Ethan started teaching me about the latest in that stuff right after we found out about the will."

"That's great, Shannon. That you're confident." He pulled out their cheeseburgers, two for him, one for her, and began dividing the fries and onion rings. "You ordered enough for an army."

"I know you have a big appetite." She pulled out two sodas. "I figure leftovers won't be a problem. Midnight snacks, maybe."

"I plan to be sleeping at midnight." Billy popped a fry in his mouth. "With you curled up by my side."

"I like the sound of that." She really did. The thought of being spooned next to his big body made her warm all over. She carried their plates to the dining room table set with placemats and silverware. "I'd like to meet your housekeeper. She's taking good care of you."

"She'd like to meet you too." Billy laughed as he brought in the drinks and settled across from her. "She'll inspect you to see if she thinks you're worthy."

"Should I be worried?" Shannon looked around then got up again. "I hope *she* hasn't heard about our history."

"No, of course not. Now where are you going?" He grabbed her hand.

"Ketchup. I can't eat fries without it." She headed to the fridge where she'd seen a large bottle in the door. They were settling into domestic bliss with frightening speed. She stared into the orderly refrigerator and got lost in thought for a moment, jumping when he dropped his hands on her shoulders.

"Earth to Shannon. Ketchup's right here." He reached past her and snagged the jumbo bottle. "Not enough mustard." He grabbed that too. "You okay?"

"Yeah, sure." She looked down at that bracelet, a family heirloom. "Maybe I should go home after dinner. Ethan was going to tell me about online ads. I should know that stuff."

"Seems like he'd be tired of computers after working with them all day. But you can always call and see if he's up for it, after we eat." Billy studied her, frowning.

The kitchen light was harsh, and Shannon wished she'd had time to do more after work than just throw things in a bag and run a brush through her hair.

"You have candles? We need ambiance." She pulled open a drawer. "Nope. Batteries and a flashlight."

"Ambiance for a hamburger dinner?" He steered her back into the dining room, shoving the ketchup and mustard under his arm. "I have dimmers." He turned the knob on the wall and the room darkened. "Is that better?"

"Yes. I should have freshened my makeup after work. I look a sight." She sat , then hopped up again. "Napkins!"

"Here. There are plenty in the sack." Billy had picked up the burger bag while in the kitchen and dumped a wad of paper napkins in the center of the table. "Would you relax? What's up?"

"Everything's moving too fast, Billy. That's what's up. Look at us. We're too comfortable. Like we've been together for years. Can you believe it?" She picked up a fork then realized that was ridiculous. She never ate a hamburger with anything but her hands. Fries either. So she grabbed the burger then realized she was shaking. Stupid.

"I've waited years to be with you again. Comfortable? I should hope so." He looked at her burger leaking juice, pickles, and lettuce onto her plate. "Don't freak out about it, baby. Relish it. Soak it up." He walked around the table and put his arms around her. "That's what I'm doing. I want us to make it work this time. I see you trying. I appreciate it." He pressed a warm kiss behind her ear, his strength seeping into her.

To hell with eating. She dropped the mess on her plate and wiped her fingers on the napkins. Standing up, she fell into his arms. "I don't do this, Billy. Commit. If you've been paying attention, you know that the past few years I've been wandering from man to man, thing to thing, trying to figure out what the crap I should do with my life."

"Do?" He held onto her gently, yet with a firmness that left her with little doubt that he didn't want to release her. "You do plenty, Shannon. Smile and light up my life. Talk to me and make me forget the shit I have to shovel daily. Use that clever gift you have to make people believe in the many causes you've helped fund ever since I've known you—cancer, the ballet, the museums in town, even daycare for the homeless." He laughed when she stiffened. "Oh, yeah, I have been paying close attention. You talked your daddy into funding that daycare center at the Star of Hope mission, didn't you? Now the homeless parents can look for work without worrying about their kids. I know that wasn't Conrad Calhoun's idea."

"It seemed logical. I don't know why no one else had thought of it." She sighed as she leaned against his wide chest. Why was she in such a state? Because men usually tired of her when they realized that behind her charm was a shallow woman who had nothing real to offer them? She knew the signs well. That's when she ran, dumping them before they could drop the hammer on her.

Billy thought she was something now, but how long before he realized she was less? Less than those supercharged females he usually dated with real careers who could whip out a PowerPoint, persuade a jury, or run a company? Women who hadn't had everything handed to them all their lives—cars, blank checks, killer wardrobes. Billy had made something great of himself despite coming from that scary neighborhood and a home smaller than her pool house. She knew better than to say any of that out loud. To remind him of what a loser she was.

"Stop thinking, Shan. Feel. I don't want anyone but you. It's been that way since the first moment I saw you. Call it an obsession, if you want to. It might be that. I've always been driven. Determined." He stroked a firm hand over her back. "I tried to move on from you. That didn't work. You were always there, waiting. The gold standard I used that made other women come up short."

"Now that's scary, Billy. I'm not—" She stopped when his finger touched her lips.

"You are." His blue eyes burned with an intensity that could make even the most stubborn juror decide to vote in his favor. Because she knew he meant what he said and spoke from his heart. How strange that he wanted her, out of all the women who would be happy to be his. And what Billy Pagan wanted, he got. But he wanted a Shannon he'd created in his mind. A fantasy woman who didn't drink and would make him proud to stand beside her.

She shivered. Could she measure up? Be that for him? She inhaled the spicy scent of his masculinity. God, how she'd missed him. She wanted to be worthy. To be the paragon he'd painted in, yes, his obsessed mind. She needed this man. He made her better. Without him... Well, it didn't take a genius to see that she couldn't go on like she had been—drinking too much, partying like she'd be young and free forever. It would soon become pathetic. And had already become lonely. With Billy, she'd never be lonely. Was she strong enough to pull this off? To become the woman he wanted her to be?

She pulled his face down for a kiss. "I give up. You want me? You've got me. Now our supper is getting cold. I hate limp fries."

"And you've got me." He held her for a moment longer. "Too bad you don't like raw onions though. I notice neither of us got them on those burgers."

"I don't like them first- or secondhand, counselor. Will you give them up for me?"

"You bet your sweet ass I will." He kissed her slow and deep.

She sighed when she finally pushed him away to sit again, pretty sure those fries were stone-cold now and she couldn't have cared less. He was laughing as he walked around the table and settled into his chair. She reached for the bottle of ketchup and their hands collided. Laughing, they took turns, easy as they ate and talked about tomorrow. She deliberately let her worries go. It would be fine. Whatever problems they encountered they'd handle together. That's what couples did.

But when they hit the sheets, she was determined to show Billy just how much she cared in another way.

* * * *

Shannon laughed up at Billy when he tossed her on his new bed. He stripped off his shirt then dumped his boots on the floor. She was busy with the button on her pants when he stopped her.

"Let me." He dropped to the floor and pulled her legs toward him so that he knelt between them. "I liked you better in those jeans you wore when we rode the Harley. They looked painted on. How the hell did you squeeze into them?"

"I had to go commando that night." She ran her hands through his hair.

"Shit, Shannon. If I'd known, it would have made me crazy." He peeled off the pants, so hard against his own zipper, he hurt.

She rose on her elbows so she could watch him. "Why, Billy, you're flushed."

"I've been waiting a while for this." He hooked his fingers into the tiny black panties he'd exposed and eased them down along with her pants.

"You look good kneeling down there, William." Her smile got wicked. "Any plans?"

"You'd better believe it." He traced a circle around her navel with his lips.

"You know what that does to me." She moaned and flopped back on the bed.

"I'm just getting started." He tossed her pants aside. "This is new. I've seen strippers with more down here."

"Don't talk to me about strippers." She was up again, laughing as he wiggled his eyebrows at her. "But do you like?"

"Baby, I love." He ran his hands over her thighs then eased them apart. "Is this something you like?" He pressed an open-mouthed kiss there, diving deep. Her gasp told him he'd hit the target. She called his name and grabbed his hair when he slid his hands under her hips and found just the right angle to give her the pleasure she deserved.

"Billy! God!" She shuddered, her orgasm making her toss her head while she almost tore hair from his head. "Please, come inside me."

He stood then and shucked his own pants, digging a condom out of his pocket with shaking hands. She still wore her prim white blouse. But her eyes were unfocused now, her hair spread out around her head. She reached for him, pulling him to her.

"Kiss me, Billy. I want to feel your body against mine." She ripped open her buttons and he saw she wore a work of art over her perfect breasts.

"Shannon, you make me crazy." Billy fell on her, careful not to put his weight where it might hurt her. He touched the pink and beige lace that barely covered her, exploring the edge of the bra with his tongue. Shannon was having none of that and unhooked the front to fling it open. Her ripe pink nipples begged for his mouth and he tasted first one, then the other. Sweet, so sweet. He wanted to tell her how he felt. Take his time and slow down. Just look at her flushed cheeks and kiss her long and slow.

But Shannon was restless, her hands everywhere. "I need you, Billy. I ache for you." She wrapped her legs around him and guided him to her. In a strong move, she forced the issue, pushing up her hips until he was suddenly inside. Oh, yeah, this was where he wanted, needed, to be. They moved together, giving and taking, seeking that elusive perfection that he knew they could reach. She held onto his chest, her fingers finding his nipples and pinching them hard. Billy grabbed her thighs and pulled them up until she cried out.

She'd tried to rush their lovemaking. Was she trying to control things? To get back at him because of the drinking thing? Damn it, he shouldn't be able to think at all right now. He was inside the woman he wanted, holding her in his arms. He should be able to turn off the lawyer in him who always calculated the winning and losing side. Why couldn't he just *feel*?

He moved, watching the way her cheeks flushed and her eyes half-closed even while they stayed on his. Right or wrong, he loved Shannon. As he leaned down to kiss her again, he sensed desperation in both of them. They wanted to make it work this time. But it never had before. No matter who took the blame, it never had before.

He pulled back then rolled them so she could take the driver's seat. She threw her hair over her shoulders, perfect, mesmerizing. She rode him, pulling his hands to her breasts. He wanted to tell her how he felt but words might ruin this. He pulled her down to kiss her again, sick of his own cynicism.

So he just let his body do the talking, holding onto her and rising to meet her. Good, they were so damned good together. When she fell on him, kissing him like she couldn't get enough again, he finally let himself go and felt her tremors in response. Complete and together, at last. When they fell apart to lay side by side, he felt as close to her as he'd ever let himself get to anyone.

* * * *

Shannon ran her hands over Billy's body, gleaming under the light from the lamp beside the bed. "You are amazing."

He smiled as she sat up and traced a path across his chest and down his stomach. He had such a great body.

"No, that was you." He captured her hand then kissed her before she sighed and settled back beside him.

"I guess we should go to sleep. I want a well-rested pilot." She snuggled into his side. "Did you set an alarm?"

"No need. I doubt I'll sleep more than a few hours anyway." He yawned until his jaw cracked. "That's what usually happens. Insomnia. It's a beast."

"Wake me if you want some company." She pulled up the sheet, shivering as his air conditioning cycled on. "Are we going to have a problem with the temperature around here? I'm freezing."

"I like it cold. Pull up the comforter if you need to." He reached for it instead, tucking it around her while keeping his body barely covered by the sheet. "I run hot, always have. Warm enough?"

"Perfect." Shannon ran a hand over his chest, not surprised that he'd already calmed down. He captured her hand and held it over his heart which was beating strong and steady. "Good night."

"Not good, great." He sighed and closed his eyes. "Sweet dreams."

Shannon sighed. It was something her mother had said to her, before she'd lost touch with reality. That had been years ago. Missy had become impossible to live with not long after Shannon had met Billy at her birthday party. Her parents had put on a good show for the crowd, but their marriage had already been on its last legs. An acrimonious divorce had made headlines in the Houston gossip columns, though Missy's mental illness had never been mentioned. Instead, Conrad had taken the blame, showing up at charity functions with beautiful women on his arm.

"You're tense. What are you thinking?" Billy squeezed her hand.

"Stupid ancient history. Nothing to do with us." She wiggled her fingers and turned over, spooning her backside against Billy. "Relax. Sleep. Tired pilots make mistakes. You don't want that to happen."

He rolled to his side, pulling her in so that they fit perfectly together. "You're right about that. So let the past go. Think about the future. Us. Flying high over the piney woods together. It's beautiful. You'll see."

Shannon drifted off to sleep listening to Billy describing the land around the reservation. Tall trees, a vast lake. She let all her worries go and imagined them together flying high. Billy was trying hard to be all about fun this time around. She decided there was nothing wrong with that. Nothing at all.

* * * *

"Well, you do seem to know what you're doing." Shannon finally relaxed and enjoyed the ride. It was a perfect fall day with hardly a cloud in the sky. The Big Thicket lived up to its name as they flew over, making it seem like a wilderness yet closer to Houston than she'd realized.

"I should hope so." He grinned at her. "Having fun?"

"Yes. This is better than a roller coaster." She laughed when he made the plane dip and rise then dip again. "Okay, you can stop that." Billy had impressed her when they'd arrived at the private airport outside of town. The plane looked new, though he claimed it was decades old. He examined it from end to end and supervised the fueling himself. He told the airport manager they'd be doing a round trip, over the reservation and back.

"Thanks. I notice you didn't say anything when I described our trip as sightseeing. No one needs to know our real business."

"Agreed." She had the map they'd use next to her, waiting for Billy to tell her when she should spread it out to check the well sites. This was actually exciting. Like they were doing detective work.

Billy glanced at his cell phone which was never far from his side. "Damn, it's a text from Albert. I told Mai I was going to be out of pocket today. I should have forwarded all my calls to her." He nodded at the controls next to him. "Take the wheel. Just hold it steady while I deal with this."

"Are you kidding me? I can't fly a plane." Shannon grabbed the wheel when he picked up his phone. "Billy! Ignore that. Take the controls back." The plane's nose dipped and she held on but didn't know what to do. Left, right, back, forward?

"Pull the wheel toward you a little. It's fine. You're doing fine. I need to answer this. It's important." He was busy thumbing in a response.

"It's not fine. I think those trees down there are closer than they were." Shannon jerked the wheel when there was a sudden noise. "Did you hear that? It was a gunshot. I swear it was."

"Probably hunters. Deer season hasn't started yet, but you can bag turkeys or wild hogs now." He put down the phone and took back the wheel then glanced out the window. "You're right, though, we are lower. Did you pull back on the wheel like I said?"

"Of course I did. I'm not an idiot. We went up at first but now we're going down. What's wrong, Billy?" Shannon glanced at the instruments, but they meant nothing to her. Another bang. Definitely a gunshot. The plane shuddered this time. "I think someone's shooting at us. Are we over the reservation yet?"

"No, we're about fifteen minutes away." Billy frowned at the instrument panel. "Shit. You're right. Someone's shooting at us. Son of a bitch hit the fuel tank. We're leaking gas. What the hell?" He looked over the side. "Not a good place to land."

"Land? We can't land on pine trees. We'll be stuck like hors d'oeuvres on a toothpick."

"Nice image, Shannon." Billy picked up his radio. "Mayday, mayday." He rattled off the plane number. "We're losing altitude. Our fuel tank has been hit by random gunfire and we have to make an emergency landing." He looked at his instruments and told whoever was listening his coordinates. When he clicked off, he waited but no one answered.

"Shouldn't someone say something? Answer your call?" Shannon stared out the window. They kept dropping, losing altitude rapidly. She could see treetops closing in and the occasional grassy area, but where the hell were the houses?

"It's as if there's a frequency jammer at work. Which makes no sense. Who out here would use one of those? Look!" Billy shouted. "There's a clearing and what looks like a crude dirt road. Hang on, I'm trying for it." He kept doing things on the control panel and the engine coughed. Then he aimed the nose of the plane toward what did look like a wide path with enough space between the trees to work as a makeshift runway.

"Oh, God, Billy!" She held on to the arm rests as the ground came rushing at them.

"Shannon, tighten your seatbelt. Hang on to the armrests, put your face in your lap, and say your prayers." Billy was concentrating on doing whatever pilots do to land. His hands flew over the instrument panel, then he gripped the steering wheel.

"Don't you dare crash this thing and kill us both." Then Shannon bent over until that seatbelt dug into her stomach. She did pray. The plane hit the ground hard, bounced, then hit again before it rolled and shuddered to a stop.

"Holy shit, we made it." He sounded surprised. "Now sit up slowly. You're not going to believe what's out there."

"You saved us!" She did sit up in time to see Billy dig under his seat and pull out his pistol. He stuck it in the back of his pants under his shirt while he unlatched his seatbelt.

"Not so sure. I'd say stay here but I don't think that's an option."

Shannon looked outside. They were surrounded. Men and women had come out of the woods that lined the crude runway. And they all carried guns. Most were rifles. There were even some of those semi-automatics like terrorists favored.

"Billy! What is this? Where are we?" Shannon reached for him.

"Beats the hell out of me." He grabbed her hand. "I had no idea anyone lived so close to the reservation. Play it cool. Let's see what happens."

"Get out." The plane door was jerked open. A tall man in camouflage gestured with his rifle. "Hands in the air. Move it."

"Easy now. What in the hell happened here? Did you think we were game birds or something?" Billy tried for a genial laugh but it didn't work. "Someone here must have made a mistake. We were on our way to the Indian reservation and the casino. For a little gambling." Billy kept his hands up as he jumped out of the plane. He reached back to help Shannon climb out then frowned at the place where there were bullet holes in the metal and at the gas pooling under the plane's fuselage. "Hell of a shot if this was an accident. Surely no one here meant to take us down."

"Shut up." The man shoved Billy against the plane and quickly found his gun. He tossed it to one of the other men. "I'm not buying your story. On the way to the reservation? When they don't have an airport?" He scanned the crowd around him and there were nods and mutters. "You were flying low, like maybe you were trying to see something you shouldn't." He poked Billy in the stomach with his rifle barrel. "The government send you?"

"What?" Billy raised his chin and shoved the rifle away. He was about the same height as the man who seemed to be in charge. "Watch it. I told you, we're on our way to play the slot machines. We were going to land in Huntsville, rent a car. Not that it's any of your business."

"That makes no sense at all. Not when you could just drive in from Houston." The man watched Shannon who had moved closer to Billy and grabbed his hand. "I don't like this. Not at all. Charlie, look in the cockpit."

"You got it, Will." A man jumped into the plane and then shouted. "Check this out!" He came out with the map and powerful binoculars Shannon had planned to use when they got over the well sites. "I'll be damned. There's a camera with a telephoto lens too. Government spies all right."

"Give me that map." The man he'd called Will handed his rifle off to another guy and took the map. He frowned as he studied it. "This is a Calhoun Petroleum map. You two working with them?"

"Yes. You got us." Shannon stepped forward, ignoring the way Billy tried to hold her back. "We're thinking of drilling some new wells. Is this your land? We might be interested in buying the mineral rights if you own them. There's money to be made, real money." She felt Billy at her back, his hands on her shoulders. "Now that the price of oil is up, we're buying again. I can get the contracts to you right away, offer excellent terms."

"Contracts!" He spit on the ground. "Money trails. The government loves those." The man scanned her designer jeans and the snap front Western shirt she realized was showing too much cleavage thanks to Billy's wandering hands when they'd climbed into the plane earlier. "You don't look like any oilman I've ever seen before." He frowned. "She leave a purse in there, Charlie?"

"Yeah, right here." Charlie was back in the cockpit, rummaging around. "Check her identification."

"Well, lookee here. Seems we pulled down a Ms. Shannon Calhoun." Charlie stuck his head out of the plane. "If we were in the kidnapping business, reckon we could ask for a good chunk of change for the gal. Backs up her story though."

"Ransom? Kidnapping? How would that help us stay off the grid, numbnut?" Will stomped over to the cockpit and pulled Charlie out by his shirtfront. "We'd have Feds crawling up our ass for sure then, wouldn't we?" He threw Charlie to the ground and looked like he wanted to kick him but held back. Instead, he glared at Shannon and Billy. "Trouble has landed here, folks. What the hell do we do now?"

"While you two are arguing about it, we're stuck here. You damaged my plane and broke all kinds of laws, shooting a plane out of the sky. Federal laws." Billy stepped in front of Shannon, like he wanted to take his chances against the group, armed or not.

"We don't recognize federal laws." A woman strode into the clearing and there was a murmur from the crowd.

"Darlin', I was just about to tell him that." Will swept off his dark green cap and placed it over his heart. "What do you want me to do with 'em?"

"Who was the dumbass who shot them down?" The woman wore a long denim skirt, boots, and a loose dark green T-shirt. She had a gun belt around her narrow hips and looked like she would be happy to draw down on whoever answered her. "Well?" She swept the crowd with a hard gaze. "Look at me, Exiles!"

"Maggie, we don't know who took the shot. But we all got spooked. The man was flying low, like he was spying on our camp. Maybe count our numbers and report to someone. We had the jammer on but that doesn't mean he couldn't have sent out a call somehow." Will looked like he wanted to put his arm around her, but didn't quite have the nerve. He held both their cell phones and caught the plane's radio receiver when Charlie, who'd dusted himself off and crawled back into the cockpit, ripped it out and tossed it to him.

"Get that plane covered up right now. It won't take long for these people to be reported missing. Planes can't just disappear nowadays. If it's got a black box, put it through a shredder, whatever it takes to make it quit working." She tapped her foot, staring at Shannon and Billy appraisingly. "Will, you and Jack take these two to my cabin and tie them up while I think on the matter."

Maggie turned and stared at the group that seemed frozen in place. "Get a move on, people. Find a big tarp, cover it with branches. Or shove the plane into the trees. I don't care how you do it, but make it disappear. You hear me?"

"Right. Someone could fly over and see it. Then we'll be overrun with government types." Charlie was out and organizing, determined to redeem himself. It made Shannon wonder if he was the one who'd shot them down in the first place.

When a man grabbed Shannon's arm, Billy lunged at him. It took two other burly guys in camouflage to hold him back.

"Hey, it's okay. I'll come with you. Leave him alone." Shannon hated the way they slammed Billy against the side of the plane again.

"Don't touch her, assholes." Billy struggled against them.

"Billy, calm down. You know they don't want to kill us. It'll bring down all kinds of government problems for them." Shannon looked down at her arm where the man gripped her tightly. "Ransom isn't out of the question, you know. Calhoun Petroleum is worth billions. You can buy a lot of government forgiveness with money."

"The government lies." Maggie walked up and slapped Shannon so hard her ears rang. "Quit trying to confuse my people. We don't deal in ransom. If we decide to get rid of you, it'll be because we don't have any use for you. Understand?"

Shannon bit her lip, the pain in her cheek shocking. She couldn't speak so she just nodded. Billy was going nuts, trying to get to her. She looked back at him and shook her head. If this woman got really mad, would she draw her gun? Shannon didn't want to test her. It was a short walk before they came to a hut that had been built to blend into its surroundings under a stand of pine trees. Shannon was sure it couldn't be spotted from the air. Once inside, she and Billy were tied up in chairs across the room from each other.

"What were you doing spying on our camp?" A man who one of the others called Jack stepped up to Billy. "We don't like people getting too close to our place. Looking down on us."

"I told you. I was just going from Houston to the reservation. You weren't on my radar." Billy glanced at Shannon. "I sure wouldn't bring my lady along if I was intent on spying, now would I?"

"So you say." Jack looked at Maggie. "But we know that it can be the woman who calls the shots, don't we, sis?"

"In a perfect world, we'd be ruling it." Maggie sat in the only cushioned chair in the room. She propped her boots on a wooden footstool. "Now here's what we know. You obviously do have a link to Calhoun Petroleum. And the reservation is near here. We don't mess with them. As far as we know, they don't have any idea we're here. That's the way we like it. The reservation is under federal government control. That's poison to us. In case you haven't figured that out by now." She studied her fingernails. They were plain, neatly trimmed, on delicate fingers. "We are exiles from the institutions the United States tries to impose on us. We will not bow down to their control or interference."

"Then I don't know why in the hell you parked yourselves so close to a place where they have an interest." Billy seemed determined to bait her. Shannon wished she could get her hand free enough to slap it over his mouth.

"Figured it was the last place the Feds would look. So far it's worked out." She smiled with a flash of straight white teeth. "Most of us here quit paying income tax a long time ago. It's a matter of principle. The Feds don't like that. We say tough shit. We sure don't salute their flag or accept their laws. So we stay off the grid to keep our freedom." She leaned back and crossed one ankle over the other. "Hide and seek. It keeps us on our toes."

"I get it. You let us leave and we'll never tell anyone we saw you. I'm not crazy about the Feds either. Why should we work just to give them a cut of our hard-earned money?" Shannon glanced at Billy. Easy for her to say, but he was out a very expensive plane. How did that work with his insurance company? He was also called "an officer of the court," sworn to uphold the law. He'd turn these people in as soon as they hit civilization.

Maggie laughed. "As if someone with the name Calhoun ever had to work a day in her life." She shook her head. "I'm not buying your act, Shannon Calhoun." Maggie held up a card. "You're awfully quiet, William P. Pagan. We got this from the cockpit. Your pilot's license. Reckon you're a bit peeved about the loss of your plane. Shame about that."

"Peeved? You could say that. I'm not too happy about the way you treated me and the fact that you fucking hit my woman." His face flushed red and he strained against the ropes that held him. "No one hurts Shannon and gets away with it."

"I think I just did." Maggie shook her head. "You have a temper. But I like the protective instinct. Shannon, he's a keeper. He carries a gun too. We believe in the right to bear arms. Too bad it didn't help him here." She smiled. "You were outgunned, weren't you, Pagan? Funny name."

"Don't taunt him, Maggie." Shannon hated to see Billy so worked up. Her face still throbbed from that slap and if he could see a handprint on her cheek? Well, he was obviously livid. Protective? She loved it, but she wasn't going to let that instinct get him killed.

"Maggie, a lot of people knew where we were going today. People in the company. Okay, so we weren't going to gamble, we were flying over the reservation to count oil wells. They're close to here. We filed a flight plan. People are expecting us back at the airport outside of Houston by a certain time. Your jammers might have kept our mayday from going out, but we can't just disappear. You really want search planes flying over here? Government planes?" Shannon took a breath. Was Maggie even listening? She'd picked up Shannon's purse and was going through her makeup bag.

She thought about mentioning Billy's Indian connection but decided to hold back that information.

"I don't think you'd last long in a camp like this, Shannon Calhoun. Look at all the makeup. Just for a simple flight over a few oil wells? That is if what you say is true." Maggie glanced at her then held up a tube of moisturizer. "But I like this. I'll keep it. I get too much sun out here."

"Maggie, listen to me. Billy is a lawyer. He has important court dates he can't miss. If he disappears, you'll have a lot of government types hunting for him."

"Give it up, Shannon. Maggie isn't listening. She's clearly not only off the grid, she's off her rocker," Billy snarled as he swayed the chair he was tied to toward the woman. "Your people fucked up. Now you don't know what to do with us and that's a fact."

"Shut up. I could kill you both and bury you in the middle of the Big Thicket where no one would ever find you. I've done it before when people came along who disturbed our peace." Maggie stood and walked over to face him. She kicked over his chair so that Billy landed on his back. "A lawyer? I hate fucking lawyers. They love to use the law to tie us in knots."

"Billy!" Shannon thought for a moment that he'd hit his head and Maggie had knocked him out. Then he thrust out his feet, catching Maggie on the shin. She cursed and jumped back.

"You must have a death wish." She pulled her gun and walked around the room. "You think I won't kill you? Try me." She jumped when the door opened.

"Maggie! Someone is coming."

Chapter 9

Maggie and the rest of her crew ran out of the hut. That left Billy on the floor and Shannon sitting in her chair. Tied up.

"She's going to kill us." Shannon's voice shook.

"No. We're getting out of here." Billy had been working on his knots since the asshole who'd put him there had made sure the rope was tight enough to cut off the circulation to his hands. Damn it. Thumping, coming closer. He turned his head to see Shannon determinedly rocking her chair across the wooden floor.

"You're right. We can't let that bitch win." She kept coming.

"Careful. You don't want to fall over. I can tell you, it hurts." Billy realized the one thing his fall had done for him was loosen the ropes on his feet. He concentrated on those, kicking to see if he could get them free.

"I got lucky. The guy who put me in my chair probably thought I'd just sit here and wait to be rescued. I'm sure my knots aren't as tight as yours. I heard him say he hoped your hands turned blue. Then there was this nail sticking out of the post next to me... Anyway, I've almost got my hands loose." She looked down at him, her eyes bright with tears. "*Are* you hurt? I wanted to tear that woman's hair out."

"When she slapped you, I wanted to kill her." Billy could see the faint print of the woman's fingers on Shannon's cheek. Kill? Oh, yes, and the hard way. "What do you mean there was a nail? Shannon!"

"Got it!" Her hands came out from behind her back, one wrist streaked with blood. "Hah! That sexist pig. Will obviously thought this little gal wouldn't risk her manicure trying to get loose." She leaned over and untied her feet then shook out her hands before going to work on Billy's ropes.

"You're amazing!" He grabbed her wrist as soon as she had him loose. "Damn it, Shannon, that nail tore a hole in you."

"I'll live." Before he could stop her, she grabbed a clean bandanna and wrapped it around the wound while he was still untying his feet.

When he was finally free, Billy jumped up and kissed her. "You may have just saved our lives, woman. Shit, did I just sound sexist too?" He wished he had time to hold her for a minute. Her hands were a mess, with broken fingernails and the wrist that wasn't wrapped rubbed raw.

"We'll discuss it later. Now what?" She looked around the room. "I don't see any weapons. And what do you bet there are guards outside?"

"Let me see what's here." Billy rummaged in the pile of blankets in the corner. Of course, they'd taken his cell phone but he did have one bit of luck. He tossed a blanket to Shannon and pocketed the small knife. It wasn't much, but at least he didn't feel completely helpless.

She grabbed her purse and looked inside. "They got my cell too, but this is something." She held up a nail file.

"You're right about that. Bring it." He watched her sling the strap across her body. "Stay behind me and let's see if they left a guard." The hut had one window but it was too damned small. Shannon could climb out, but he doubted he'd make it through with his bulky shoulders. He eased open the door and saw a group of people on the far side of the clearing. Apparently, a messenger had arrived. There was a lot of talk and loud arguing. Discussing their fate? No one was looking their way so they needed to move right now.

"Billy?" Shannon stayed close behind him.

"Come on." He grabbed her hand and pulled her out and around the back of the hut, quietly shutting the door behind them. With luck, these nut jobs wouldn't discover they were gone for a while. They ran through the trees, careful to make as little noise as possible. Billy stopped when he heard Shannon gasp for breath.

"We have to keep going. I don't know if they've got any decent trackers, but try not to break a branch if you can help it. Step where I step. We have to stay quiet." He brushed his fingers across her glistening forehead. It was still hot and the trees were dense. Spiky palmettos had slapped at them and vines hung down, catching their hair, thorns painful when they found bare skin. She hadn't complained, constantly surprising him. "It'll get cooler when the sun goes down so don't lose that blanket. You want me to carry it for you?" He had one too, tied around his waist.

"No, I've got it. You're good at this," she whispered, holding his hand when he helped her over a fallen tree. "How, city boy?"

"Summers spent on the reservation. Some boys join Scouts. I played Cowboys and Indians, and the Indians always won." He thought he heard a noise. "Move. Quiet now. I'm glad you wore boots."

Shannon frowned down at them. "Cute cowboy boots. Not made for walking. I'll try not to slow you down."

"You look great, always do." He squinted up at the sky. They needed to head toward the lake on the reservation. He could see just enough of the sun to be sure he was headed in the right direction. He also thought he could smell water. Wishful thinking when they'd had a drought all summer?

Dogs barking. Bad news if they had their scent. But they hadn't left any clothing behind, had they? He didn't have time to think about that, pulling Shannon along into a shallow ditch with a miracle—a bit of water that would mask their smell if the dogs did have something of theirs. The rocky ditch made for tough walking that challenged even him. Shannon kept up and he turned several times to give her a smile of encouragement.

After an eternity, the dogs' barking got fainter then disappeared entirely.

* * * *

Mosquitos buzzed and bit. She bled from a dozen scratches, but Shannon was determined not to slow them down. She inhaled the incredible smell. Pine and fresh air. Her feet killed her, but she had to ignore them. And then there was her throbbing wrist. When had she last had a tetanus shot? Couldn't think about any of that now. This was a run for her life, *their* lives. The baying dogs finally disappeared, and she wondered if they could actually be winning this race.

She stumbled over a tree trunk and fell hard. Oh, God, please don't let her ruin this for both of them. She lay there, struggling to catch her breath. Billy knelt beside her, murmuring, checking to see if she was hurt.

"I'm fine. Give me a minute," she croaked. She sat up carefully and did a body check. No new damage, just the aches and pains she'd already catalogued. Man, was she tempted to pull off those cute boots. But there was no way she'd walk barefoot over this ground. Something rustled in the brush. Critters, maybe even a snake. That got her on her feet so fast she almost knocked over Billy.

There was a shout nearby that pushed her into a sprint. This time she pulled Billy. He was too worried about her. She wasn't a damned prima donna. If he thought she was a delicate flower, he could think again. Didn't he know ballerinas had to be strong? If he could have seen her as a teenager at ballet camp, he'd have learned a thing or two. She'd fallen a million times and had to get up fast under the eagle eye of Madame Olga. Landing on pine needles was nothing compared to the hard wooden floor of a dance studio. Of course, her lifestyle lately would make anyone go soft. Good thing she still got in the occasional dance class. Now she'd show Billy she was tougher than she looked or die trying.

She pulled the dull brown blanket around her shoulders, pretty sure her bright red blouse had given away their location. Billy's hand landed on her back, a pat of approval.

They hadn't gone far when Billy stopped and pointed. There was a clearing and a garden. Rows of well-tended plants were obviously thriving.

"Is that what I think it is?" Shannon struggled to catch her breath.

"Cash crop, though they might smoke their own dope instead of selling it." Billy stayed close, talking so quietly she had to strain to hear him over her own labored breathing. He looked behind them. "No wonder they don't want us to escape. They're not going to like leaving this behind." A gun shot rang out and a branch exploded next to his shoulder. "Shit. Run!"

Shannon leaped over a fallen tree then ran flat out. Billy stayed on her heels as they zigzagged through the brush. Two more gunshots snapped leaves over their heads. Of course, they'd posted guards next to their marijuana. How long would they keep chasing them? Raked by more thorns, slapped by palmetto, Shannon had never been so miserable. But she kept running, her thighs burning, her feet screaming, too terrified to slow down.

Another gunshot. Billy grunted and she almost tripped when she looked back to make sure he hadn't been hit. He shook his head, plucking a branch of leaves from his head. A near miss. Dear God.

It was dusk by the time she finally staggered to a stop. Shannon didn't think she could walk another step. The only sounds she heard besides her own wheezes were birds singing and running water. Peaceful sounds. *Keep going.* She'd lifted one of her aching feet when Billy grabbed her arms.

"Shannon, wait. Look over there."

"What?" She turned her head and saw a creek. Or maybe it was a river or bayou. She couldn't tell the difference. What she knew about nature could fill a tweet on Twitter. Good thing Billy had spent summers learning survival. Besides dance, her camp had included such critical skills as makeup and manners, the things a woman should know to be a graceful hostess and beautiful asset when she married Mr. Right one day. She swayed on feet that hurt so bad she fought tears. Useless, she was useless here.

Billy studied her, his face reflecting his concern. "Hey, are you okay?" He put his hands on her shoulders. "Shannon?"

She firmed her stance, refusing to fall into his arms. "Water. What does it mean?"

"It's a good sign. We've come a long way. I don't hear any people or dogs behind us. Haven't for a long time. I hope that creek means we're close to Lake TomTom. It's on the reservation. I think we can stop and rest." Billy slipped the blanket off her shoulders and threw it down in the clearing next to the water. "Sit. Take off your boots. You've been limping."

"Yes. Blisters." She wasn't going to cry. No way. But the idea of taking off those boots…

"Baby, let me." He helped her sit then reached for one of her boots.

"No!" She brushed away his hand. "I have to do it. They're hard to get on and off. Custom made. If you pull wrong, you could cause more damage to my foot. I'll wiggle it off." She smiled and touched his cheek. "Thanks, though. Check the water. If it's cool, once they're off I'd love to stick my feet in there."

"Sure." He walked to the edge and washed his hands, then his face. "It's great." He drank a handful of it, something Shannon didn't think she could do. "It's fine. Quit frowning. I don't think it'll kill you."

"You don't think." She began working off the first boot, trying not to scream at the pain. Yes, these were custom made and had always been fine for her days as a Houston Livestock Show and Rodeo volunteer. Of course, she hadn't demanded much of them. She'd mostly ridden a golf cart around the huge parking lot at NRG stadium where the rodeo was held every February. She directed other volunteers because she liked the scholarship programs the rodeo provided. As a perk, she scored free tickets to the performances.

"Hey, Billy, you like country music? I can get us into the shows at the rodeo." She figured talking about music might take her mind off the pain as she wrenched off the first boot. Oh, yes, she had a blister the size and color of a strawberry. Damn, now was not the time to think about food. She was starving.

"Not really my thing. But the rodeo usually books a few rock groups, hip-hop. Maybe we can find music we both like." He frowned when he came over and saw her foot. "Look at you. That must have hurt like hell."

"Don't look. My feet are hideous." She started on the other boot. "Not heavy metal, I hope. I can tolerate almost anything but that."

"If I can sit through the opera and ballet, you can sit through my noise, lady. How do you feel about football? I have season tickets to the Texans, the Longhorn games too. In Austin." He watched her work on that boot.

"Football? I like watching men in tight pants. Then there are the hotdogs." She winced as the second boot came off. "Austin. Sure. It would be fun to go to games and spend the weekend. I've discovered some great shops there."

"All right then. Football and shopping while we're in Austin. I can live with that." He waited until she dropped her other boot then picked her up and carried her to a flat rock where she could sit and dip both feet into the cool water. "How's that?"

"Heaven." She sighed. It did feel good. "Seriously? We're going to have to learn to deal with each other's tastes? I guess this relationship is going to be all about compromise."

"Guess so. We didn't try that the first few times, did we? Compromise is what mature people do when they want to make things work." He smiled as he sat beside her and pulled off his own shoes and socks. He'd worn sensible boots and his feet looked a little pink but had no sign of real damage. He stuck them in the water too. "Maybe if we both try, we can do this thing."

Shannon thought about that. Working on a relationship. That was new. Could she do it? Long term?

"Hey, you're tired, I'm tired. And hungry." Billy put his arm around her, obviously willing to let the relationship talk go for now.

"Me too." She leaned against him. "What are we going to do about it? I hope it's not foraging for nuts and berries."

"I could catch a fish, cook it over a fire. But the crazy anti-government people might smell our smoke and come after us again." He pulled her closer. "Of course, so could someone at the reservation. We might be getting close. If this creek is the one I think it is. I explored these woods as a kid, learning survival skills from my cousin Jacob."

"Seriously?" Shannon couldn't imagine walking another mile right now, but close? "Maybe you should go on without me. I can wait here, soaking my feet."

"I'm not leaving you, Shannon." He held her tighter.

"I could hide. Wrap myself in the blanket in the brush. Wait for you." She loved his protective instinct but hated how helpless she felt in the woods. Give her a cause and she'd raise funds all day long. She could even knock out a pretty good press release. But out here in nature? Billy had impressed her with how he'd seemed to know just by looking up at the sky which way to go. And he could move so quietly.

Okay, maybe she deserved a little credit today. She'd been good at the quiet thing, thanks to her ballet training. And she'd pushed through some serious pain to keep going. She watched him scanning the area, his eyes intent. She didn't ask him how he'd catch a fish or start a fire, pretty sure he'd figure out both things and do them efficiently with nothing but a nail file and a pocket knife. She told him as much.

"I'm glad you have so much confidence in me, babe." He smiled and kissed her cheek. "But I have a better idea. You don't weigh much. Leave the boots and hop on my back. I'll carry you. I think if I follow this creek, we'll hit the reservation in about an hour or so. If I'm wrong, then I'll light a fire. We should be close enough by then to alert someone to come find us. They don't like anyone making a fire in these woods. Not unless it's in an authorized campground. We've been under drought conditions for months now."

"Carry me? I won't tell you my weight, but it's too much!" She could see that he'd made up his mind though when he pulled his feet out of the water and dried them on the blanket. He had on his socks and shoes before she could talk him out of it.

"Why won't you tell me your weight?" He was grinning as he gently dried her feet.

"Mama always says that a woman who will tell you her weight, will tell anything." She gave in and hopped on his back when he turned around. He settled her legs around his waist.

"Then I guess I'd better trust you. Since you're so good at keeping secrets." He nodded. "Put your arms around my shoulders."

"Are you sure you want to do this? I'm not a lightweight." She squirmed, trying to get comfortable without strangling him. She spared a glance for her boots. No, she didn't know what her car cost, but she sure as shooting knew what those custom-made cowboy boots with the red leather inserts had run, down to the penny. She'd had to wait months for them too. Oh, well, it wasn't as if she didn't have five other pairs of pretty boots in her closet. And what did that say about her spoiled existence to date?

"Hang on, we're off." Billy strode along the creek bank, sure-footed and seemingly as confident as always about where they were going. "With luck, we'll run into some signs that this creek feeds into the lake. That's what I'm counting on."

"If I'm too much for you, just say so." Shannon leaned against him, absorbing his warmth and glad that she'd given this man a chance to come back into her life.

"Hey, this feels like one of those CrossFit workouts." He chuckled. "You ever try one of those? Carrying you is nothing compared to some of the things they make you do to get you to sweat."

"I prefer dance routines for my workouts. I still do some ballet classes, though I don't even try for *en pointe* any more. I like working out to music though." Shannon closed her eyes. He'd sped up and watching the trees go by was making her woozy.

"You like exercise machines? I never did show you my workout room. You can use it. Anytime."

Billy kept talking quietly but Shannon dozed off, lulled to sleep by the rhythm of his steps and the low rumble of his voice. Impossible but she was comfortable, even lost in the woods. She didn't *feel* lost though, not as long as she was with Billy Pagan.

* * * *

She woke up when he stopped and slid her off his back and onto her feet.

"I give up. This is the longest, crookedest damned creek I ever saw. I guess I got turned around and we're not where I thought we were. Jacob would be ashamed of me." He spread out a blanket and sat on it, holding out his hand.

"You sure it's safe?" Shannon looked around the small clearing. "What if those Exiles see it?"

"I know from exploring these woods as a kid that the creeks run toward the lakes. We've walked for hours. They wouldn't have put their crazy camp anywhere near the lake at the reservation." Billy was breathing hard.

"How far did you carry me?" Shannon felt guilty that she'd actually slept while he'd been walking. It must have been a long way too. It was full dark now and the night was barely illuminated by a rising sliver of a moon. She looked around, trying to adjust her vision to the dim light.

"Don't worry about it." He leaned his head on his knees. "As soon as I catch my breath, I'll gather some branches and make that fire."

"I can do that." Branches. Yes, there were a few nearby that had fallen from the trees. Shannon picked her way over to them and dragged them closer to the blanket.

"Honey, let them go. I'll take care of it. I know your feet hurt." He did take out that little pocket knife, though, and started stripping leaves off the branches she'd brought him.

"And your feet don't?" She spotted another branch, this one bigger, and heaved it into the growing pile. "You're not used to walking so far in that kind of shoe either, are you?"

"No. You're right. They hurt like a son of a bitch." He hacked at the bigger branch. "Try to find some small twigs. We have enough big pieces. Feel them. If they bend and don't break, they're too green. Dry and brittle is better for our purpose."

Shannon got right on that, testing all the small pieces of wood she found. She was limping of course. Her feet *were* killing her. She dumped a small pile of what she figured would be his kindling next to him.

"That's enough for now." He got up and gathered some stones. He made them into a circle, their wood inside it.

"How are you going to start a fire? I don't even have a book of matches and I haven't noticed you carrying a lighter." She collapsed on the blanket and watched him build a pyramid of wood.

"One of my cousins taught me how to start a fire the old-fashioned way, by rubbing sticks together. It takes time and patience." He glanced at her. "I'm not feeling a whole lot of patience right now because I want to get you the hell out of here, but I hope I can remember what he taught me." He picked a flat rock and put straw on it, then started twirling a stick between his palms. She heard him murmuring.

"What are you saying?" She leaned closer.

"Jacob swore that chanting made the fire start faster. It couldn't hurt. It also takes your mind off the fact that this is painful on your palms." He grinned ruefully. "You think I'm nuts?"

"No, anything to help. It's getting chilly too. A fire would feel good as long as it doesn't bring the bad guys down on us. Tell me the chant. I'll do it with you." She grabbed the blanket from around his waist. Unreal that he'd kept it on during that endless walk. It had cushioned her. He was so caring it made her eyes sting.

"I promise the bad guys are long gone. Ready?" He had to repeat the unfamiliar words three times before she got it. Then they said them together. He rubbed the sticks against one another frantically. Their chant got louder and quicker too. Suddenly there was a spark and the straw caught.

Shannon heard herself squeal. "Wow! You did it!"

"Feed some of those small twigs into the flames or it will go out. Easy now. Blow gently on it too." He kept rubbing his sticks. Flickering would come and go.

Shannon grabbed a few dry leaves and poked them close to a spark. To her amazement, they did catch fire. She gave it a few careful puffs of air. It made a nice little blaze. "Now what?"

"We have to get the fire from this stone to our pile of wood." He added more twigs to the burning mound they'd already created. "I'm going to make a torch to light our bonfire. I hope we're close enough to the reservation so the smoke and smell will drift over there and someone will alert the fire patrol."

"There's a patrol?" Shannon watched him cut a strip from the blanket then use it to tie some short branches to a long one. He lit them, then carried the torch carefully to their bigger pile of wood. She clapped when it caught immediately. If she was good for nothing else, at least she could serve as cheerleader. "You did it!"

"Yeah. Now we have to keep watch over it. These woods are too damned dry. One stray spark could cause a forest fire that would be devastating to the region, not to mention anyone who gets in its way. The drought is killing the local trees and drying up the lakes and creeks. Notice how we can see the rocks in the bottom of the one we've been following? I remember when all the creeks around here were overflowing their banks."

"I've heard about the drought on the news. And devastating fires in other parts of Texas." Shannon watched the fire. What would they do if the fire spread? Throw dirt on it? Too bad they had nothing to carry water in. Billy's shoes? Not enough to do any good. They sure couldn't outrun a forest fire.

"That's why they have fire patrols. We've been praying for rain, but a stray lightning strike or careless camper could start a fire that would be hard to stop." He walked around the fire, pushing a few more sticks inside the rock ring. "There's very little breeze this time of night but they're very vigilant." He finally settled back on the blanket and gestured for her to join him. "Relax. There's water nearby. If we see there's a problem, we can soak our blankets in the creek and put out the fire with them."

"Oh, the blankets." Shannon finally breathed a sigh of relief and hobbled over to his side. Walking barefoot over the rocky terrain was no treat. Every burr and sharp rock had seemed to be out to get her.

"Now we sit and wait. I could try to catch a fish but it's really too dark to see one." He glanced at the creek. "You sure you don't have any food in that purse of yours?"

"I have sugarless gum and breath mints. Pick your poison." She pulled her small bag off her shoulder and dug into it.

"The gum. Maybe chewing will fool my stomach into thinking that food is on the way." He took the gum, stuck the wrapper in his pocket then chewed with a groan. "Spearmint. Delicious." He leaned back and held out his arms. "Come here and keep me company."

"We can't accidentally go to sleep, Billy. The fire." Shannon could see sparks floating up into the night sky. The crackle of the flames worried her. How could he just lay back like this was no big deal?

"I'm watching it." He'd wadded up the extra blanket to make a pillow for his head. "Come here."

"Thanks for carrying me. You know I fell asleep, don't you?" She did finally snuggle next to him.

"It was pretty obvious when you drooled down my neck."

"Did not!" She shoved away from him.

"I didn't mind." He laughed and pulled her in with a hand around her waist. "It showed that you trusted me enough to relax completely." He rubbed her back. "I am so damned tired. If I close my eyes for a few minutes, will you watch the fire?"

"Oh. You trust *me* to do that?" She glanced at that fire again. It was a big responsibility. But he'd walked miles with her on his back. "Sure. I don't dare lie down though. If I get too comfortable, I might fall asleep too. I'll stay sitting up."

"Good. I'm glad you're taking it seriously." His yawn was loud and contagious. "Just a quick nap, then I'll be good as new."

Shannon fought her own urge to yawn. No, she got up and walked around, stepping carefully over those pebbles and rocks determined to cut her feet. It seemed like a good idea to gather more dry sticks. The fire might be dangerous, but they didn't want it to die out. She poked them in near the bottom, jumping when a log shifted and crashed. A glance at Billy reassured her that he'd slept through that. He needed that sleep desperately.

She scanned their surroundings again and felt better. Nothing stirred and the trees weren't close enough to catch fire. At least she didn't think so.

She settled on the blanket again and tried to enjoy the novel experience of camping out. Yeah, that's what they were doing. Too bad the peppermint she'd chewed hadn't satisfied the nagging hunger that made her feel slightly nauseated. But the fire smelled good and so did the pine and fresh water nearby. The next thing she knew she was nodding off. Oh, hell no. She pinched herself, which didn't do a thing but add a bruise to her other aches and pains.

Finally, she got up and stuck her feet back in the water. It felt pretty cold now that it was dark. She shivered, wishing she had the blanket under Billy's head around her shoulders. She'd just peeled off the bandanna to wash the nasty cut on her wrist when she heard a buzzing sound coming from down the creek. It kept getting louder. A motor.

"Billy! Wake up. Someone's coming." She jumped up and poked him, not surprised when he was on his feet immediately, grabbing his makeshift torch in one hand and the pocket knife in the other. He looked like a warrior, ready to defend them.

"Who? Where? Get behind me." He frowned when she didn't cower there. Instead, she picked up a big stick that hadn't made it into the fire yet and moved next to him.

"Coming from down the creek. Do you hear it? A motor. Maybe a four-wheeler." She waved her stick. "Didn't you say the reservation is in that direction?"

"I hope to hell it is. I admit that the last few miles I was staggering. If this creek made a turn on us, I might not have noticed." He thrust the torch into the fire and lit it. "Please get behind me, in case these aren't friendlies."

He looked down at her. "I'm sorry, baby. I never should have brought you along on this flyover. Ethan and I could have come. Or I could have brought Albert."

"You think I'm blaming you for this?" She pulled his head down to kiss him. "Stop it. Who could have foreseen a forest full of tax evaders? Now let's hope these are some of your relatives from the reservation coming to rescue us. Whoever it is, I am not blaming you."

He stared down the creek. "If it's the Indians, then they'll be mad as hell. Lighting a fire next to their beloved forest? Brace yourself, babe. We may be facing a pissed off Indian Chief."

Two four-wheelers came charging at them out of the darkness, their headlights blinding them long before it became obvious that the men on them were from the reservation. They wore jackets with the Opako Casino logo Shannon recognized. Of course, she'd done research on the Patagi Indians and their reservation as soon as she'd started seeing Billy again. Their new casino was getting advertising time on local TV stations now. The logo was colorful and easy to remember—a passion flower, bright purple and beautiful.

"It's one of my cousins and his posse," Billy murmured as they stood their ground. The vehicles halted a few feet away on the bank of the creek.

"What the hell? Billy?" The man riding the first vehicle parked and marched toward them. He pulled Billy into a hug and pounded his back. "Thank God you're alive. But I never expected that the idiot setting a fire in our woods would be someone I knew and taught better." He turned to the men in the second, larger vehicle and issued orders. They got to work, pulling out buckets and going to the creek to fill them.

"Shannon, this is my cousin Jacob Johnson, the man who taught me how to start a fire. Jacob, my girlfriend, Shannon Calhoun." Billy caught the flashlight Jacob tossed at him and thrust his torch into the creek where it died in a sizzle.

"Ms. Calhoun? Welcome to our home. Billy Pagan is a special friend to the Tribe. So now you will be special to us as well. I don't know what happened to Billy's plane, but it's obvious you have had to make your way through our woods. I'm sure you wish to find a comfortable place to rest. We will leave as soon as I'm certain these woods are safe from the fire."

"Yes, thank you, Mr. Johnson." Shannon shook his hand. "It's a pleasure to meet you. What you taught Billy certainly came in handy tonight. I'm sorry if the fire causes problems for you. We needed a way to signal for help."

"We're hungry and exhausted. It's been a hell of a day." Billy kept his arm around her. "Shannon's right. We had to get your attention. We've been running since about ten o'clock this morning. Did you know you've got a nest of crazies living on the edge of the reservation? They fucking shot my plane out of the sky."

"You're kidding me. We assumed you had engine trouble and made an emergency landing somewhere between Houston and here." Jacob stepped over to the fire and kicked dirt over a stray ember. He turned to his crew. "You guys make sure there's not a spark left."

"Not kidding." Billy wished he could sit on that blanket again, his legs felt like they weighed a thousand pounds. But he tried not to show weakness around Jacob, who was a respected member of the tribe, a mentor, and a man he had looked up to all his life.

Shannon smiled and squeezed his waist. "Billy was wonderful. He used the survival skills you taught him to help us escape from those people who shot down our plane. I'm sure they would have killed us if he hadn't gotten us away from them."

"You were amazing, Shannon. You should have seen her, Jacob, running for miles in boots not meant for it. And she's the one who got us untied when we were held prisoner." Billy kissed her on the cheek. She had dirt on one cheek and a leaf in her hair, but she'd never looked more beautiful to him.

Jacob slapped Billy on the back. "Brave and beautiful. You got lucky, cuz."

"Don't I know it. Now we have to alert the authorities. Those people are probably already breaking camp since we escaped. We don't want them to get away. They had frequency jammers, Jacob. I couldn't even call for help when the plane started going down."

"You will have to help us pin down their location." Jacob looked serious. "It's bad to have people like that so close to our home."

"I will try to show you on a map. But don't go near there. Not without reinforcements. They're armed and dangerous."

"I hear you. First we go to headquarters and check in. The old man has been beside himself. You have several search parties looking for you. Even a biker gang rode in and has been running trails looking for signs of your downed plane." Jacob walked over to inspect the fire's remains. "How did you start this fire?"

"The old way. Just as you taught me." Billy looked down at his blistered palms. "It wasn't easy."

"I'll just bet. But good practice. Now you know why we were so hard on you back then." Jacob smiled at Shannon. "I see you lost your shoes. That had to have been rough walking."

"He carried me for miles." Shannon leaned against Billy. "Can you believe it?"

"A man takes care of his woman. I believe it." Jacob pulled out a cell phone. "I'd better get the word out that we found you. I'm sure Ms. Calhoun has family worried about her too."

"Oh, I hope not." Shannon clutched Billy's arm. "Billy? Do you think they put on the news that we were missing? I'd hate for everyone to get worked up about this."

"Your names were withheld for the first twenty-four hours. Until the wreckage is found, that's standard procedure. The only thing on the news was that a small plane was reported missing. No details." Jacob stopped before he called. "Of course, we were notified because the airport knew you were flying over the reservation. When we heard you were with a beautiful lady, we hoped you two had just taken off for a Las Vegas wedding or something." He grunted when Billy punched his arm.

"This isn't a time for jokes." Billy heard the crew working on the fire chuckle.

"The airport where you were expected to return tried to contact you when you were late. Then they put out the word to all local authorities that the plane was missing. A search was started immediately. They had your contact information so someone called your office. It was your secretary who called us since this is where you were headed. She called other people too, including those bikers I mentioned." He smiled. "A good crew. Their leader knows what he's doing."

"Albert." Billy turned to Shannon. "Mai would have called Calhoun headquarters too. I told her you were going with me. So you'd better call your family."

"Let me call the Chief, then you can use my phone." Jacob made a quick call.

"I bet they were frantic. At least we were missing for hours, not days. Though it feels like forever." Shannon sighed then took the phone Jacob handed her. "This is ridiculous. I can only remember one phone number, my home phone. It's too easy to just program numbers into my cell and forget them." She punched it in.

Billy heard her talking to her housekeeper. He took the phone next and called Mai. When she burst into tears then ranted in Japanese, he was speechless. "Mai, honey, calm down. I'm fine. Just sore feet and a lost plane. Call Albert, will you? I don't have any numbers here. My cousin says he's been leading a search for me." He listened to her scream in English this time. "Yes, I love you too." He grinned and glanced at Shannon. "Got to go. Call my grandmother too, okay? Thanks." He ended the call.

"Your secretary obviously cares about you." Shannon sighed. "I need to meet her."

"Yes, you do." Billy picked her up and carried her to the back seat of Jacob's ATV. "She'll love you." He put his arm around her when Jacob started the motor.

"Any chance we're going where we can get a bite to eat? I'm starving." Shannon pressed a hand to her stomach.

"There's a great restaurant at the casino. I promise you it will be our first stop." Billy was lying. He knew they'd have to see the Chief first. But that news would freak Shannon out.

"But I don't have shoes!" She made a stab at pushing her hair out of her eyes. "And look at me. I think I have pine needles in my hair."

"Trust me. They will serve you however you look." Billy tapped Jacob on the shoulder. "Ready to go?"

"Yeah. The old man is happy. You've been a favorite of his ever since you won the dance competition as a junior."

"What's this?" Shannon's eyes widened. "Dance?"

"At the Children's Powwow. It's held every January." Jacob just had to share that as he turned the wheel and headed back toward the reservation. "You should see Billy do the Grass Dance. Killer." He nodded toward the blanket they'd left by the creek. "The guys will stay for a while, make sure that fire doesn't come back to life, and gather up your things."

"Thanks. Thanks for finding us too, cuz." Billy clapped him on the shoulder, though he could have gone all night without that slip about the dancing. Now Shannon was pelting him with questions. Of course, dancing was her thing. But she'd never seen anything like the Grass Dance. He'd have to bring her out here for that in January. Future plans. He was glad he could relax and imagine them now. He leaned back and kept his arm around her.

The vehicle bumped along the creek bank and he wished Shannon had on a seatbelt. But then she liked roller coasters and this felt like one after the hellish day they'd had. He was beat. And he still had to face the Chief. The old man didn't always approve of him these days because of some of the clients he took on. He'd be unhappy about that fire too. It had served its purpose and that was what counted. They were safe. Any problems they'd have to deal with at the reservation were nothing compared to armed crazies in the woods. Or at least that's what he told himself.

Chapter 10

"A fire in the woods. That was the best you could do?" The chief stalked around the room, clearly unhappy.

"I didn't want Shannon to spend the night out there. We were watching the fire and had a plan for what to do if it endangered the forest."

"Oh, you had a plan." He stopped in front of Billy and finally gestured to a chair. "Sit. You look ready to collapse. How far did you walk? Jacob said you carried the woman part of the way."

"She was no burden. Light as a feather." Billy smiled and sat. Thank God. He'd showered and thrown on a T-shirt from the gift shop but he'd had no choice but to put on those damned shoes and socks again. He was throwing them away as soon as he got home. His feet burned.

"Where is this woman who has obviously captured your heart?" The chief settled into his chair, one designed to give him presence in the room. It had a tall back carved with the passion flower and was painted to match the casino logo Billy had seen everywhere.

"I left her in the cabin. Thank you for that. She wanted a long shower and to wash her hair. Naomi arranged for her to have clean clothes and some shoes. Her boots are still in the woods. They weren't made for long walks." Billy had encouraged her to stay in the cabin, promising Shannon he'd come back for her and take her to the restaurant after his meeting with his uncle, the chief. He didn't have to be a mind reader to know she wasn't eager to meet any more of his relatives while barefoot and with leaves in her hair.

"Jacob says she's one of the Calhoun family. Related to Conrad Calhoun?" The chief tapped the armrest with his right hand. "We had an arrangement with the company to drill oil wells. It has provided us with a fine revenue stream."

"Yes, I know. That's one reason we were flying over the woods. We wanted to check the well sites." Billy knew he couldn't lie to the chief ,but he had a conflict of interest here. Calhoun Petroleum was planning to make good on what it owed the people Conrad had defrauded. Would it be unethical to hint at the real reason he'd done his flyover? Of course it would. Damn it.

"Is there a problem?" The chief was nobody's fool. He leaned forward. "Why the sudden need to check the sites? From the air?"

Billy managed a laugh. "I was showing off my plane. Shannon hadn't been up with me before. And her brother is doing an audit. He wanted to verify some numbers. The company wants to be fair. Since Conrad died, it's only natural the family has to check out things."

"Verification? Are the numbers off? In our favor? Or will we owe Calhoun money?" The chief picked up his cell phone. It was never far from his right hand. He had someone on speed dial. "Daniel, get in here."

"Daniel? Is he your accountant now?" Another cousin. Billy felt like he was backed into a corner. If he said too much, he was breeching client confidentiality. He was also tied to this tribe. He didn't want them cheated.

"Of course. When you start talking numbers, I bring in an expert."

A door opened and Daniel Mathis strode in. "What's up, Chief? Hey, Billy." He held out his hand. "Glad to see you're alive. Everyone here was worried."

"You wouldn't believe what we ran into." Billy was all for a subject change. "I already told Jacob. There are tax evaders camping out close to the reservation, trying to stay off the grid. I'm sure they've been killing wildlife and living off the land. Saw a patch of marijuana growing near what I think is tribal lands too. I hope someone has called in the Feds."

"Taken care of, William." The chief obviously knew exactly what he was doing but let him get away with it. "Jacob put a man on that immediately. And at first light a group of our best trackers will retrace your steps and find this campsite, stake it out." He frowned. "So close. We've been focused on other things. The casino, of course."

"They were hiding in plain sight. It was their strategy. They assumed the Feds wouldn't look for them so close to the boundary of a federally governed property. But I would be surprised if they didn't stray into Tribal lands while they were there. You should check the borders." Billy knew keeping the integrity of the land was important to the tribe.

"Yes, it will be done. We will pick up the litter you left behind too. You said your Shannon left her boots next to the creek?"

"Yes, sir. Couldn't be helped." Billy refused to stare down at the floor like he had when he'd made a mistake as a boy. "I couldn't carry everything on my back."

"Understood." The chief turned to Daniel. "You will need to look over our royalties from the wells that Calhoun Petroleum has drilled on our land. There seems to be a question about the numbers." He stood and Billy jumped to his feet as well. "Obviously, you cannot say more, William. You are their lawyer and have an obligation to the oil company. I remember how you helped us with the casino and dealing with the state of Texas. You have never sent us a bill for that and kept your silence when questioned about it later." He clapped Billy on the shoulder. "I respect your integrity."

"Thank you, sir." Billy hoped that meant he was dismissed. "If you don't mind, Shannon and I haven't eaten since dawn. I promised her dinner at the restaurant."

"A fine idea. And you will spend the night. Someone will drive you home tomorrow. After we find your airplane." The chief turned to Daniel. "Perhaps we can wait to investigate the Calhoun numbers. For a few days, at least. If there is a problem, it would be inhospitable to William's lady to stir up something that could turn into a difficult situation while she is on the grounds."

"Thank you, sir." Billy was startled when the chief embraced him. "I will bring her to meet you right after dinner."

"I look forward to it." The chief was smiling. "Now go. Eat. You look thin and exhausted."

Billy hid a smile. Only the chief, who had at least fifty pounds on him, would call him "thin." He nodded then bolted out of the room. The cabin where he and Shannon were staying was down a road that required a golf cart to get there. He drove past the lake and took a moment to just relax and appreciate the calm of being safe and at a place that always had given him peace.

He found her in the bathroom, putting on makeup from the collection in her purse.

"Ready to eat?" He slipped his arms around her waist. He liked the way she filled out the Opako Casino T-shirt. She still wore her own jeans but she had leather flip flops on her feet.

"Yes!" She finished putting on lipstick then turned to him. "Your cousin Jacob's wife has been wonderful. She brought me a hairdryer, shampoo, conditioner, even shoes!" Shannon leaned into him. "But I'm going commando. No underwear for sale in the gift shop and I couldn't bear to put on my dirty underthings."

"Really. Let me check this out." Billy slid his hand under her shirt and found a warm, round breast. "Yep, just the way I like it. Unrestrained." He grinned. "I'm commando too. Should make it fun when we hit the sheets tonight."

"Are we staying here?" She picked up a tissue and wiped off her lipstick.

"What are you doing?" He got his answer when she gave him a hungry kiss. Finally, she pulled back.

"I can't tell you how much I admire what you did today." She leaned her head against his chest. "I'm sure you're exhausted."

"Tired but not *too* tired." He grinned and kissed her again. "After dinner, I'll show you. And yes, we're staying here. Someone can drive us home tomorrow." He breathed in sweet, clean woman. "The chief is sending out a search party early in the morning. For your boots and my plane." Billy finally let her go.

"You're kidding!" She looked up at him. "I'm not sure I could ever wear those damned boots again."

"The chief considers them litter. You'll get them back whether you want them or not." Billy grinned. "Now put on some more lipstick and let's go eat. I need my strength. All this talk about going commando has got me thinking about sex. But I'll be damned if I can imagine doing a thing about it without some food in my belly."

"Right." She picked up her lipstick and quickly proved she had her beauty routine down pat. "Let's go."

"I have to warn you, we may have company in the restaurant." Billy held open the cabin door.

"Some of your relatives?" She grabbed his hand and they rode toward the large building with *Opako Gaming* above the wide porch.

"You'll see. The restaurant is inside the casino." Billy nodded to the security guard who held open the door when they got to the entrance. He was glad Shannon wasn't limping as he steered her inside. She hadn't commented about the full parking lot or noticed the group of bikes along the side. The noise hit them as they stepped inside.

* * * *

"I hope we're going to eat, not gamble." She couldn't miss the dozens of slot machines in front of them.

"Sure. Look right. There's the restaurant. Handy for gamblers who want to take a break." He steered her to the hostess station which was deserted.

"Billy!" His name became a roar as men poured out of the back room, their beer glasses held in a toast. One man came forward and wrapped

Billy in a bear hug.

Shannon stopped in her tracks. "Bikers!"

"Yep." Billy grinned. "Brace yourself."

"Brother! We were afraid you'd crashed and died on us." The huge man with red hair and a sunburned face wiped his eyes then turned to look at Shannon. "Ma'am."

"Shannon, this is Albert Madison, also known as Slash. He's the leader of this band of bike riders, the Blue Star Brothers. Shannon Calhoun, Albert." Billy poked Albert on his brawny shoulder. "Man, I heard you guys helped search for us. Thanks." He gripped his hand.

"It's what we do when someone we respect is in trouble." He turned to look at his crew, about two dozen strong. "Your tribe was on it as well. We like it here."

"Blue Stars? Did all these men serve in combat? Is that how you named your club?" Shannon studied the patches on his blue jean vest. "Thank you for your service."

"You're welcome." He nodded. "We're all vets and most of us came home with some harsh souvenirs. Bud there has a prosthetic leg, more than a few of us have scars inside and out. Almost all of us suffer from PTSD. Riding together is a kind of therapy for us." He scanned the group of men clustered in the doorway and his eyes narrowed. "Where the fuck is Simon?" His shout made the room go silent.

"Guess." A man with a leather glove that must have covered his own prosthesis stood and gestured toward the slot machines a few yards away. "You want me to take a couple of guys and pull him out of there?"

"Let him go. I'm not his keeper." Albert led the way to a corner table. "You two sit. You look like you've had a rough day and night."

"Thanks, Albert." Shannon smiled when he held out a chair for her. "Honestly, Billy was a hero. You wouldn't believe how well he knew the woods. He started a fire with sticks!" She reached across the table to take Billy's hand. "Even carried me on his back."

"I'll be damned." Albert grinned and waved over a waitress. "Dinner is on me. No arguments. Order whatever you want. Not much of a wine list but I'm sending over a bottle of their best champagne."

"Thank you!" Shannon scanned the menu and told the waitress what she wanted. Billy told her to make it two.

Albert seemed to approve. "Bill, we need to talk business. But tomorrow is soon enough. Me and the guys are about finished eating. We'll leave you two in peace." He handed the waitress a platinum card. "You put their meal on this. I'll be in the casino with my crew. Can you just close out our tab when these two are finished and bring me the bill later, over there?"

"Yes, sir." She giggled when he slipped what must have been a large bill into her hand. "Anything you want."

"We've booked some cabins and will stay over. Some of the guys have been drinkin' steady since we heard you were found safe. I won't let them ride under the influence. Then there's the casino. Guess the ones that want to will try their luck." Albert picked up Shannon's hand and bowed over it. "A pleasure, ma'am. We think a lot of Bill here." He pulled two cell phones out of his vest pocket. "Bill, Mai asked me to get these for you and Shannon. Since my lady couldn't reach you on yours, she figured it was toast and had it disconnected. Ms. Calhoun, here you go. Your brother downloaded your numbers on it for you and had your old one turned off too."

"Already? This is amazing." Shannon couldn't believe it. She took the phone, one of the latest models, and turned it on. Sure enough, there was her contact list. "How?"

"When Mai gets going, there's no stopping her. She figured out who would know what you'd need and took care of it. Apparently, your brother is a techie. I spoke to him myself. He claimed you didn't even keep your phone locked." Albert stood tall, his chest puffed out like he knew he'd just made hero status in her eyes.

Shannon jumped up and hugged him. "Thanks, Albert! He's right. I never bothered to lock it. And I always knew Ethan could do anything with phones and computers." She sat back down, eager to call her brother and thank him right away.

"Mai has my password of course. I appreciate this, Albert." Billy was checking out his new phone.

"No problem. Thank Mai." Albert turned to face the room and raised his voice. "Let's hit it, guys. Leave these people to their dinner." There was a lot of noise as chairs were pushed back and glasses drained then slammed down on the tables. Albert nodded then clapped Billy on the back.

"Talk to you in the morning, bro." He strode toward the casino, his men in his wake.

"Wow. Just wow. Sorry, but I have to do this. I didn't realize how lost I was without my phone until I didn't have it." Shannon stroked the silver case then found Ethan in her contacts and called him to let him know where she was. She gave him a quick summary of what had happened.

Her brother seemed embarrassed when she thanked him for the third time and changed the subject. "Did you get a chance to check out those wells?"

"Not even close." Shannon glanced at Billy who was on his own phone. She heard him say *Gran*. Good. Leaving his assistant to notify his family hadn't been his best move. "I'm not sure how we're going to resolve that problem. Maybe Billy has an idea. We're spending the night here. I guess we could take out a four-wheeler in the morning and try to find the well sites. Maybe somebody here can point us in the right direction. I have to tell you, though, that I've had my fill of the woods for now. I'll let you know what we do."

"Hey, sis. I'm glad you're okay. You scared the shit out of me. I didn't call Megan and clue her in on your disappearance. Figured there was no reason to get her stirred up until we knew what or if…" His voice cracked. "Shit. Daddy's gone, Mama's in the nut house. I'm just happy you had Billy with you."

"Ethan!" Shannon gripped the phone. "I'm fine. Yes, Billy knew those woods, but I helped us get free too. I'm not Conrad Calhoun's daughter for nothing." She sniffed. "Now get back to work. Help save our company. I want to come out of this year with some serious cash. Got it?"

"Got it." He chuckled. "I'll call Cass for you and tell her you'll call her tomorrow."

"I will." Shannon picked up a napkin and blotted her eyes. "Love you, little brother."

"Yeah, me too." He ended the call.

Shannon smelled steak and sighed when a platter was set in front of her. Medium rare steak and baked potato. She dug in.

"Everything okay?" Billy had ended his call and was cutting into his steak. He smiled when the waitress opened the champagne with a pop and poured two glasses.

"Yes." She smiled at their waitress. "Thanks. I think we need a toast." She picked up her glass. A glance at the bottle told her not to expect much but the bubbles called to her and she licked her lips. "To the future. I'm glad we have one."

"I'll drink to that." He touched his glass to hers and sipped. "Pretty sweet. I hope they improve their wine list." He laughed when she wrinkled her nose. "The Tribe had trouble even getting a liquor license. The state really didn't want them to have this casino, you know. They're still fighting it in court. There are a lot of legislators still against gambling in Texas."

"That's too bad. But it looks like it's doing well. The parking lot was full." Shannon enjoyed another bite of a steak which was tender and well-seasoned. "This is delicious."

"Sure is. Just like my great grandfather used to make. When he left the reservation, he had a dream of opening his own restaurant. He did it too, near the city courthouse in downtown Houston. It was a success until the

Great Depression hit. Then no one could afford to eat in restaurants so he had to close."

"Oh, that's too bad." She put another bite in her mouth and let the flavor hit her tongue. It had obviously been grilled over an open fire. It was a Texas specialty and this restaurant did it right.

"After that he got a job working for other people as a short order cook or doing physical labor. He never got to run his own place again but he always cooked for the family." Billy forked up potato loaded with butter, cheese, and sour cream. "He did teach my grandfather how to grill steaks like this and Grandfather passed the secret on to me." He smiled. "I'll have to make a meal for you some time. I like to cook."

"Good thing, because I can't boil water." They both were silent as they ate. By the time they each pushed back from the table and the pecan pie the waitress had insisted they try, Shannon groaned and rubbed her stomach.

"I can't eat another bite." She looked around the empty dining room. "It's a shame this place doesn't draw a bigger crowd. It's not that late. There should be other diners here."

"I don't think anyone knows how good it is. Which is a problem." Billy stretched.

"They should advertise this restaurant. I've seen ads on TV lately for the casino, but none of them mention this place. The prices are reasonable too." Shannon wished she could unbutton her jeans. She'd eaten too much and almost killed that bottle of champagne by herself, even though it wasn't very good. Billy had watched her drink. Several times she'd had to stop herself from asking for that wine list. A cabernet would have been perfect with the steak. A nice red. She noticed he barely touched *his* champagne and sipped water instead.

Was he worried she was going to embarrass him when she got up? Maybe stagger? There was still a good fourth of the bottle left when he tossed his napkin onto his plate. She wanted to refill her glass one more time and polish it off. But then he'd judge her.

She had to let it go. He'd carried her through the woods. Was alcohol that important to her that she'd risk their budding relationship?

"Ready to leave?" She looked away from that damned bottle and picked up her water instead.

"Sure. You know, they could use someone with your marketing expertise to put together an advertising campaign for the restaurant. It's pretty much up to whoever here wants to try their hand at it. There's no budget for any big push." Billy guided her past the noisy slot machines to the door leading outside, ignoring the cocktail waitresses eager to serve the gamblers.

"That's what you call penny wise and pound foolish. You need to spend on things like ads which will more than pay for themselves with increased income when people start coming here to eat. Then they can walk over to play the games in the casino." Shannon stood beside him on the porch. It was a beautiful night. She took a breath and let her frustrations evaporate. Billy wanted what he thought was best for her. She knew that. Had to keep that in mind and stick to her resolve. She didn't *need* alcohol. It was a bad habit. If it wasn't, if she couldn't stop drinking without a twelve step program…then she needed to know that and do something about it.

"Look at the stars." She headed down the steps. "If my feet didn't hurt, I could almost pretend our nightmare had never happened." She whirled around and fell against him.

He pulled her close. "Except you look like you lost a battle with a Palmetto." He ran his hands down her arms, covered with scratches and bug bites. Touched the fresh bandage on her wrist carefully. "Does this hurt?"

"A little. It's covered with an antibiotic cream. I promised Jacob's wife I'd go to my doctor in town for a tetanus shot. I know I'm a mess and the scratches itch like crazy." She wasn't dizzy and proved it by walking a straight line to the golf cart that had brought them here. "See? Full parking lot. So people are discovering the casino." It made her even more determined to get customers inside the restaurant.

"You're frowning. Are you thinking? Worrying?" Billy helped her into the cart then got in the driver's seat and steered toward a large building on the other side of the parking lot.

Shannon could see it was an administration building of some kind, headquarters for the Tribe. It was imposing and had that passion flower over the double doors. Every building in the area looked new and freshly painted.

"Thinking. You should have coupons in the casino. Offer a discount on a meal. Or make a buy one, get one free dinner part of a prize package. There could be cabin and meal deals for your gamblers." She realized he'd stopped on the path. "Where are we? Isn't our cabin the other way?"

"You need to meet the chief. He's waiting." Billy rubbed her back. "I'm sorry to spring this on you, but it's protocol. He's my uncle and he likes to meet any guest I bring up here." He stopped and looked her over.

"Wait, what? The chief is your uncle?" Shannon stared at him.

"Great uncle. Jacob's father. If you're buzzed, though, I'll make your excuses."

"I'm not buzzed, Billy." This giving him the benefit of the doubt was not going to be easy if he thought she couldn't handle a couple of glasses of champagne. "But I look like this." She glanced down at the T-shirt and ripped and filthy jeans. Of course, the chief would probably approve the shirt since it did advertise the casino. Makeup had covered most of the scratches on her face but her arms were a mess. Then there were her broken nails. She'd run her file over them, but the chipped polish couldn't be helped.

Oh, well, the chief knew what they'd been through. She straightened her shoulders. At least Billy had given her time to wash her hair.

"You know you always look beautiful to me." Billy took her hand.

"Thanks, but you seem to be prejudiced. Which I appreciate." She squeezed his fingers. "So he's your uncle. Does that make you part of some kind of Indian royal family?"

Billy laughed. "No, it's a job for life. I expect Jacob will take over. I'm not in the mix."

"I hope Daddy didn't do anything to ruin things with the Tribe." Shannon stopped him before he got to the door. "Maybe…"

"Maybe nothing. I'm committed to your family's company. We'll see what can be done for all the people owed money by Calhoun. No favoritism. That's the way it has to be." He kissed her cheek then wiped it with his thumb. "Sour cream. I couldn't let you go in like that."

"No! I should have brought my purse with me." Shannon put her palms to her face. Maybe she was a little drunk if she'd gotten sloppy with her food.

"Kidding. Relax." He laughed again and guided her inside and down a hall. He knocked on an office door. When a voice bid them enter, he pulled her inside.

"I'm going to kill you later." Shannon pasted on a smile and prepared to meet an Indian chief. Funny. She'd met a prince, several billionaires, and a couple of movie stars, but meeting this guy freaked her out more than any of them. Because it mattered to Billy. Plenty of time to think about what that meant later. She took a shaky breath and held out her hand.

"Shannon Calhoun. Welcome." The deep voice was solemn and Shannon barely kept herself from dipping a curtsy.

* * * *

"That wasn't so bad, was it?" Billy lay sprawled on the bed, naked.

"Meeting the chief?" Shannon liked the way he was so at ease in his body, so masculine. She wanted to fall on him, touch him. But she hadn't forgotten the way he'd teased her just before she'd met the chief or the way he'd made her feel about drinking a few glasses of champagne. "No, not at all. He was charming, though he seemed to want you to be intimidated, the way he quizzed you about my bracelet." Shannon had left on her T-shirt.

She wasn't going to make this easy for Billy.

"I think he was secretly pleased about the bracelet and has a soft spot for beautiful women."

"Margaret is stunning." The chief's wife had greeted them and offered refreshments. It had been easy to refuse gracefully after that wonderful meal. That had turned the conversation to the restaurant and her ideas for stimulating business. The chief had listened to her with interest.

"He also has a soft spot for intelligent women." Billy held out his hand. "You blew him away tonight. I think he wants to offer you a job."

Shannon stayed out of reach. "I have a job. But I'll write up some of my ideas in an email and send them to him. Free of charge."

"Now why would you do that?" He sat up then made a sudden move that had her on the bed and under him. "Value your skills, woman. Don't give them away."

She looked up at him, out of breath from his weight on her. Her T-shirt had ridden up and he'd discovered her bare hip. He was so close she could count his eyelashes, dark and spiky above those bright blue eyes. Reaching up, she smoothed the wrinkle between his brows. God, she'd never forget how he'd carried her through those woods, taking most of the punishment from those thorny vines. Or how proudly he'd stood beside her when he introduced her to the head of his Tribe. Could this man actually love her so much that he'd go all in for her? She shook her head.

"What is it?" He eased up on his elbows. "I know I'm a heavy load. Can you breathe?"

"Barely. But that's not why I'm shaking my head." She took a deep breath. "I just don't get it. Why are you so crazy about me?" Stupid question. What did she expect him to say? He loved her tits and ass? That's what one boyfriend had blurted out in the heat of the moment. At least he'd been honest. Shallow, but honest. Billy was anything but superficial. So she braced herself.

He stared down at her. "You know, I've been asking myself that very question. My grandmother thinks I should be careful around you. You did break my heart years ago."

"Billy!" She lifted her hands to touch his face. "I'm sorry. I hope you know I regret what happened back then. I was young, selfish."

He rolled off her and stared at the ceiling. "You were different from the woman you are now. You threw me away without a thought to what you were doing to me."

"You're right." Shannon sat up and leaned over him. This was a festering wound and talking about it was long overdue. "I was drunk half the time too. No wonder you don't want me to drink around you." She shivered and pulled up the sheet. As usual he had the air conditioner on icy.

"Yeah. That's not the only reason though." He finally met her gaze. "I was working my ass off to better myself. You saw where I came from. I had scholarships, thanks to my Indian blood, but they didn't begin to cover everything. I had to work two jobs and find time to study on top of it." He looked away. "I was always trying to prove I was good enough for you, to fit in with the people in your crowd." He laughed. "What a crock and a total waste of time."

"You shouldn't—" She stopped when he pinned her with a hard stare. Of course, she'd wanted him to fit in back then. Appearance had been everything in college. She'd hated the way he dressed, had even bought him clothes that he'd refused to wear. He'd always been too proud to accept what he called her charity.

"I was young too. Young and stupid. I know that now. Belonging to your crowd meant going to nonstop parties and ending the night falling down drunk." He looked away, his mouth firm. "I'd seen too much drinking at home. I couldn't lose control like that, not even back then."

"No, you wouldn't." Shannon hated who she'd been. But she'd been attracted to dark, brooding Billy Pagan with the electric blue eyes instantly. Had it just been chemistry? She didn't believe that. There'd always been something about him that called to her. He was serious, different. And his intensity had made her want to be more than a silly fool who danced topless beside a pool and played beer pong before the tequila shooters came out. But she'd failed him then. Would she fail him now?

"You finally got tired of my being such a 'downer.' Remember the night we broke up?" He sat up and pushed a pillow behind his back. "I bet you don't. You were wasted."

"You're right. All I remember is that one night we had a big blowup in front of everyone. You didn't seem to care that you embarrassed me. And it wasn't the first time either, Billy. You know, you could take some responsibility for that."

"Okay, you have a point. I have a temper. You were young and wanted to have fun. Maybe I was jealous. I had all these responsibilities, money struggles, and you and your rich friends didn't seem to have anything to worry about."

"If these last few months have shown anything, it's that you don't always know what was going on behind closed doors."

Billy realized he'd never taken the time to see her point of view back then. Yeah, they'd both been immature and impulsive.

"Anyway, after that night, you left and I didn't see you again until we'd both graduated and were back in Houston. You were friends with Dylan MacKenzie so I saw you at parties with him from time to time."

"He was important to my career. I used him." Billy stared down at his hands. "I'm not proud of that, but my connections with your rich friends helped me establish my law practice."

"Cut it out. You like Dylan, I know you do. You two are genuinely friends, right?" She touched his leg.

"Sure. Now. But it started as a calculated move. I couldn't afford to do anything back then that didn't work into my plans for the future. After you dumped me, I was determined to focus solely on success." He smiled at her, a crocodile smile her daddy had called it, cold and merciless. "You gave me that, baby. Motivation to succeed. After that night, the worst of my life, I was on fire to become the best damned lawyer Houston had ever seen. I dreamed of the day you'd need me. Do something heinous and call me from jail." He stared at the ceiling. "Oh, yeah. I had some dark revenge fantasies."

Tears filled her eyes. "Tell me about our last night. I should know."

"Nope. It's history." He shook his head. "Shit. I don't want to go back there. Because when I stopped hurting, I realized I still loved you. That you'd always hold a piece of my heart, broken or not." He reached out and wiped a tear off her cheek. "That's why we kept trying again. But it was never the right time."

Shannon's feelings for Billy had always scared her. He was so sure of himself, while she was never sure of anything. How could she measure up to his impossible standards in the long run? So when she'd seen his disgust, his disapproval of her, she'd hurt him before he could hurt her.

"Now here we are. I've reached the place in my career where I can relax a little. I've made it. I have everything I want except a woman to share it with. And, fuck me, but there's only one woman who will do. And here she is." He pulled her in.

"Are you sure? After what I put you through?" She wrapped her arms around him, a little of the fear that he'd realize she wasn't enough for him still there. No, he kept coming back. That meant something. "I'm older, but am I wiser? I want to be, but I'm only human. Maybe you should run like hell."

"No. We're going to work this time." He studied her, then nodded. "Will you try?"

"Yes, of course. But can you forgive and forget?"

"Forgive? Done. Forget? Never. But that's on me, not on you." He pulled back the sheet and looked down at her bare thighs. "Enough of this. I've been showered, fed, and even rested a little. We should celebrate being alive." He nuzzled her neck. "Held at gunpoint, slapped around, shot at. I never want to see you in danger again."

"Me either." She leaned into the press of his warm lips. It would be easy to just move on. But then…he'd never forget. Well, how could she ask him to? But what she could do was prove to him that she really *had* changed. She couldn't ever revert to that selfish party girl again.

"One more thing." She bit her lip.

"What?" He eased them both down so they were lying side by side. "I have other things on my mind."

"Come on, humor me. We needed this, this dialogue. And I have a question." She hummed with pleasure when he slipped a clever hand under her T-shirt.

"What now?" He pulled the shirt up and off her. "Look at you. Perfect."

"Quit distracting me." The sear of his hot lips over her breasts *was* distracting. "Naomi said something about your last name. Pagan. That the chief wasn't crazy about it. That's when I realized I know nothing about your father. What happened to him?"

"I don't have a father." He laid his palm on her stomach. "Pagan is a name Great Grandfather took when he left the Tribe. Priests called the Indians heathens back in the day. The old ways were 'pagan' rituals that are still practiced today, though there's a church on the reservation grounds and I've attended it all my life. No one will ever erase our heritage. Great Grandfather really didn't like stereotypes. He was a rebel and didn't want to be under federal control or live on a reservation. So he took off as soon as he could."

"I like your last name. It suggests a wild man under your custom-made suits." She ran a fingertip across his muscular chest. "The way you were in command while we were in the woods… I loved it."

"Then we should go out to the woods more often." He groaned when her hand drifted down his body.

"What about your father? Was he a sperm donor?" Shannon didn't know why she was bringing this up now. Not when he'd leaned down to make her body sing with his mouth and hands.

He looked up. "You could call him that. When my mom was in college, she got an internship in Washington, D.C., to work for a legislator. Part of a program to help minorities." He swiped his tongue around her navel. "Mom was smart, tops in her class. But she was away from home for the first time and obviously did something stupid during her summer in D.C.

She would never tell anyone—not even my grandmother—who she had the affair with. But she came home pregnant. Gran always thought it might have been a married man. Someone in the government."

"Wow. That's quite a story. Did she get to finish college?" Shannon gripped his hair when he headed south. "Single mom. That's not an easy road."

"No, she had to drop out. Gran helped with childcare while Mom got a job. She never married. Guess the man in D.C. was either the love of her life or hurt her so badly she swore off men forever. She wouldn't talk about it and rarely dated, though she liked going to bars at night. Guess she found companionship there. Ruined her liver in the process." He shifted Shannon so he was between her legs and began to kiss the inside of her thighs.

She ran her hands through his hair, trying to imagine his life in that tiny house. His family obviously loved him but there were secrets. What would it be like not to know such an important thing? Of course, knowing who your father is, was, could bring you pain. Billy was so smart and successful. Some of his intelligence and drive had to come from the man who'd sired him. Was there a way…? She felt his eyes on her and he'd stopped kissing her.

"Shannon? Let it go. I did, a long time ago." He rested his head on her thigh. "I didn't need a father. I had a stern but loving grandfather and women who spoiled me. Gran was always there to make sure I knew right from wrong." He pulled her legs over his shoulders. "And then there were the Indians."

"Yes. It's obvious that you had lots of people who made sure you turned out to be the man you are today." She smiled. "The man I love."

"There you go." He leaned in, exhaling a puff of warm air that made her shiver. "Now, can we stop talking? Because I can think of much better things to do with my mouth."

She laughed and released his hair. "Oh, go ahead." Shannon lay back, her eyes closing when he showed her just how much better. "Billy!" She moved her hips, the pleasure growing almost unbearably. He held her still when she lost her mind. Then he slid up her body and pressed inside her.

"I love you, William Pagan." She stared up at him, pretty sure she would never feel this way about anyone else, ever again.

"And I love you, Shannon Calhoun." He began to move.

"Will you do the grass dance for me later?" She laughed when he stopped and stared down at her.

"Never in a million years." But he did move faster.

As always, pleasure pushed all other thoughts out of her head in the moment. But later, when he'd finally fallen asleep by her side, Shannon stared at him. He hadn't thrown even a sheet over his gleaming body while she was huddled under a blanket in the chilly cabin.

He'd never answered her. *Why did he love her?* A smart woman would leave it alone. Too bad that, for once, it was her mind that wouldn't be quiet and let her sleep. Was he setting her up for a brutal payback? Revenge for the humiliation and pain she'd dished out all those years ago? She stared at his back, rising and falling with each breath. She knew why he couldn't stand to see her drink. His mother, his aunt. He'd grown up surrounded by alcoholics. And he'd fallen for her, a woman who couldn't seem to have a good time without a drink in her hand. God, it must make him crazy. She moved closer and pressed against him. She didn't want to wake him, just needed to touch him and let his strength seep into her. He didn't play games, did he? Most men who got hurt, wanted to hurt back. And he was a lawyer, expert at manipulating juries into believing whatever story he told them. Guilty or not guilty? She was guilty as sin and deserved to be punished. Loving him and losing him would be unbearable. Oh, God, was she being set up for the worst fall of her life?

Chapter 11

"All right, Albert, what did you find out about Rupert Billingsley?" Billy forked up eggs cooked perfectly and realized the restaurant did deserve more publicity. Two other diners were across the room, out of earshot, so he was confident they couldn't be overheard above the noise from the nearby casino. Early morning gamblers were hard at it already.

"Give me a minute, okay?" Albert held onto his coffee cup like it was the only thing keeping him together. He'd obviously enjoyed the casino himself for quite a while the night before. "I guess it was a mistake to give you a phone. Don't you ever sleep in?"

"It's eight o'clock. Late, as far as I'm concerned." Billy grinned.

Albert leaned back in his chair and it creaked under his weight. "Where's your lady this morning?"

"Still sleeping. We had a rough day yesterday. She needed the rest." Billy took a bite. He'd slipped out of bed only hours after falling asleep beside her. Of course, she'd stirred and tried to get him to come back to bed. He couldn't do it, his restless nature making it impossible. So he'd worked his phone, caught up on e-mails, and finally sent a text to Albert to meet him here so he could get breakfast.

"Come on, man. What did you find out?" He didn't need to think about Shannon, still warm in their bed, or he'd blow off this meeting and head back to the cabin.

"I found out I'm a piss-poor gambler. I'm giving it up." He waved over the waitress and held out his cup. "At least Simon won last night. But that's probably a bad thing." He smiled at the waitress. "The lumberjack special. Thanks." He waited until she had cleared the door into the kitchen. "I liked Shannon." Albert smiled. "Seems like a nice lady."

"Yeah. But we have a history." Billy's gut tightened and he set down his toast. Was he nuts for involving himself with Shannon again? Last night he'd finally let those memories come rushing in. God, but she'd twisted him up inside when she'd tossed him away all those years ago. *Boring. Dull. Uncouth.* Those were the kindest words she'd tossed at him when she'd finally gotten sick of his trying to get her to quit her drinking games and leave a party.

Back then he'd been afraid that the novelty of having a serious boyfriend would wear off for her but, when it had, he'd still been blindsided. *Stupid.* That was the one word she'd screamed that had fit him to a tee. He'd been an idiot for thinking a woman like Shannon Calhoun, from her world of high living and big money, could ever see herself permanently with a man like Billy Pagan. Nope. He'd been a diversion. He'd lasted just a few months before one of the pretty boys with deep pockets had taken his place. A guy who fit in with her people.

He should have seen it coming. Even Dylan had warned him. But he hadn't listened, too dazzled by her beauty and the way she could make everything else in his life seem drab.

It had killed him back then when she'd casually toss aside her bikini top and let those worthless losers look at her, reach for her. He'd wanted to club them all to death and take her away. But he'd known better. Because she would have mocked him for his territorial instincts. Been shocked by his violent urges. Yeah, he had them. And she'd brought them out in him when she'd been her most outrageous. Even yesterday, when that bitch had slapped her, he'd wanted to kill. Didn't matter that it was a woman who'd put a hand on her. Hell, no. You touch Shannon and you're dead meat.

"Bill?" Albert put down his coffee. "Hey, man, I think I'm seeing a little PTSD here. You two really did have a rough time yesterday, didn't you?"

"You could say that." Billy shook his head. "A woman fucking hit Shannon. Slapped her across the face. If I hadn't been tied down, I swear to God…"

"I get it. You want to borrow a bike? And a gun? I'll go with you, right now." Albert jumped to his feet. "We can go after them. I don't have a problem with squaring things. Not when it comes to the women we love."

"No, no, sit down." Billy took a breath. Shit. For a moment, he'd been tempted. But that wasn't his way. He was a man who used the law. "The Feds have already been called. I expect them soon. Let them handle it. I look forward to seeing that whole bunch locked up for a good long time. Plus, I'm not sure where the hell to find them."

"That is a problem." Albert dropped into his chair again and squirted ketchup on the scrambled eggs that were set down in front of him.

"Now, I need to get back to work." Billy forced himself to put his anger aside. "What did you find out about Billingsley?"

"That he has a chunk of Greenespace stock too. He's also named in his dear Evelyn's will."

"Yeah, I knew that. It was in the discovery I got from the DA. Leads to motive." Billy slathered his toast with peach preserves.

"What I bet you didn't get was a copy of Evelyn's new will. One she hadn't signed yet." Albert looked pretty proud of himself.

"How the hell did you find out about that?" Billy dropped his toast. "Never mind. I'm sure I don't want to know."

"You're right. I'm also working on the financials for the two Greenes." Albert smiled as he buttered a biscuit. "They're named in Evelyn's old will, but not the new one. How's that for motive?" He took a bite and chewed. "Damn, that's good." He stuffed the rest of the biscuit into his mouth then attacked his eggs.

"I like it." Billy figured the timing of Evelyn's death was no accident. He could subpoena the new will. Get it into evidence.

"Evelyn must have put the stepkids in the old one right after her late husband died. He'd left her a pile of money and stock in Greenespace. She added Rupert to her will when she married him." Albert looked up when the waitress refilled his coffee cup. "Thanks, darlin'." He ate his eggs until she moved on. "She had her lawyer start work on the new will so she could sign it before she and Rupert were to leave on their big cruise." He had cleaned his plate and sat back with a sigh. "Great food here."

"Yep. Come on, Albert. What else?" Billy knew this would make or break Rupert's motive.

"First, the old will stands since she hadn't signed the new one yet. Which means the Greenes will have enough stock now to control the company. You've got a solid reason to point the finger at them. They'd want to get rid of Evelyn since she was lobbying to remove them from management. Talked to several insiders who verified that she was pushing hard for a clean sweep." Albert wiped his mouth with his napkin.

"The new will?"

"Rupert was still in there. Set to inherit a nice chunk of change." Albert leaned forward. "Here's the kicker. Evelyn had decided to leave the bulk of her estate to the M.D. Anderson Cancer Research Center. Seems she had the big C and her time was running out. I'm sure you can take a look at her autopsy report and confirm that."

"Holy shit. I have it, that report. Didn't look past the gunshot and ballistics." Billy shook his head. He'd been sleepwalking through his cases lately and it showed.

"Poor lady. Had been in remission for years, but this time, when the cancer came back, it was everywhere. The handwriting was on the wall. The person I talked to claimed Evelyn planned to spend her remaining few months travelling. No more chemo or radiation. Just pain meds." Albert frowned at his empty plate. "You think Rupert knew about it?"

"He sure didn't mention that to me." Billy shook his head. Damn. What would *he* do if the woman he loved had been given a death sentence? That cruise would be a great way to spend Evelyn's last days if Rupert loved his wife as he claimed. But if he knew about the new will and resented her giving away her money? "Seems like the Greenes have the strongest motive. So you need to look really hard at those financials. For a payoff to a hitman."

"You have no idea how easy it is to hide shit like that." Albert pulled out his phone. "I can look for cash withdrawals. Unusual phone calls. Offshore accounts and transfers." He glanced at Billy. "What do you think about Rupert?"

"I can't get past the fact that he was right there with the opportunity to take out Evelyn. I was tied up yesterday and I'll be damned if I could get loose—but then again, Shannon worked her way free with a freaking nail sticking out of a wall. He claimed he had a straight razor that he could get to in a drawer in the bathroom. I call that damned convenient." Billy realized he'd finished his breakfast except for one piece of bacon which he popped into his mouth. He chewed and swallowed, but his throat closed. Had Rupert made a fool of him? Killed Evelyn to save her from a slow and painful death? No one had actually seen this "hit man." No one except the grieving husband. The security cameras had been conveniently disabled.

"I do know a few guys who like straight razors." Albert drained his third cup of coffee and signaled the waitress. "You say Shannon got loose first yesterday?"

"Yeah. She tore her wrist on a nail getting her knot untied." Billy managed a smile. "Can you believe it?"

"I'm liking her more and more. But I think you have a problem, Bill. What are you going to do if your client is guilty?" Albert asked for the check.

"Not sure. I don't represent murderers, even if it was a mercy killing." Billy grabbed the check. "This one is on me."

"Thanks." Albert grinned. "I'll keep digging. It would be too bad if Billingsley did take out his sugar mama. Let's hope the Greenes did the deed and I can find the proof. Then you can get Rupert off with a clear conscience."

"Fingers crossed." Billy pulled out a credit card. He stared at it. Hard to believe that the group taking him down hadn't bothered to keep it and the three others in his wallet. But then credit cards made a paper trail. He dug through his wallet. Of course, they'd kept his cash. He added the tip to the credit card receipt then followed Albert out of the restaurant.

"Any word on your plane?" Albert yawned and stretched.

"Not yet. But I'm sure my uncle's trackers will run it down." They both turned when a pair of black SUVs with dark tinted windows drove in to the campground. "What do you bet this is the FBI?"

"No bets on that." They exchanged looks as men in dark suits got out of the two vehicles and slammed the doors. "I'll leave you to your debriefing." Albert ambled away, his steps faster as the men got closer to the restaurant.

"Chicken." Billy walked down the steps to meet the federal agents. The man in the lead pulled off his dark glasses and held out his hand.

"William Pagan?" Of course, the man recognized him. They'd probably looked him up as soon as they'd been contacted about the incident. He was in data bases as a lawyer, a registered voter, hell, even as a man with a driver's license in the state of Texas.

"Yes." Billy shook his hand. "You are?"

The man introduced himself and his fellow agents. "We're here about the people who shot down your plane. Got a call from a Jacob Johnson an hour ago. He found your plane hidden in the woods near a camp that must have belonged to that crew. You want to sit down with us and tell us about the incident?"

"Did Jacob say whether they were still there? Or had they cleared out?"

"No sign of life. Apparently, those folks took off as soon as they realized you and your companion had slipped away from them." The agent gestured toward the Tribal headquarters. "Any chance we can find a room where we can talk? Away from the casino?"

"Sure. Let's go." Billy led the way. He wasn't surprised to be met by a couple of the reservation's security guards at the door. When he explained what he wanted, they found a conference room for him and promised to inform the chief about the situation.

"I've been told you're a lawyer. Do I need to read you your rights?" The agent settled at the head of the table then pulled out a tablet and a pile of file folders.

"I sure as hell hope not. I'm a witness and a victim. Haven't done anything that would warrant a Miranda warning." Billy sat at the opposite end of the table and felt his calm unravel. He took a steadying breath and looked the man in the eyes. "If this is going to become confrontational, I may need to bring in someone from the Tribe to counsel me."

"As to that, do what you want. I'm interested in why you were flying low enough to attract those people's attention. Not that we're upset about that. Sorry for your sake, and Ms. Calhoun's of course, but rousting out this particular group, if they're who we think they are, might be a good thing for us." He pulled out photos from one of the file folders. "Look at these and tell me if you recognize anyone."

"They called themselves Exiles." Billy studied the mug shots. Obviously, these people had been in trouble before. He pointed to a photo of the woman called Maggie.

"I knew it! That's Margaret Lioni." He nodded and one of the agents got on his phone and left the room. "We've been after her and her followers for years. Anyone else?"

Billy recognized a few others, including the woman's brother and that asshole Will who'd held them at gunpoint. "I hope you catch them. But they seemed determined to stay off the grid." He looked up. "Be careful. They're well-armed."

"At least now we've got a fresh trail." The agent gathered the photos and slid them back into the folder.

"What's their beef with the government? No one likes to pay taxes, but that doesn't lead to armed camps and what looked like a militia to me." Billy leaned forward, elbows on the table. "Obviously, they have records."

"Yeah. Margaret, or Maggie as she likes to be called, has been arrested a couple of times during protests. She interprets the Constitution to suit herself. The right to bear arms? She'd take an AK47 into a kindergarten class if she felt like it. You can imagine how that would go over after some of the school shootings we've had."

"Sounds certifiable. Acted like it too." Billy knew he and Shannon had been lucky to escape.

"But brilliant. Has her own law degree." The agent typed on his tablet then settled back.

"Tell me more about her group. She ranted about income tax."

"Yeah, that's one of her hobby horses. The group calls itself Exiles because they claim to have seceded from the United States and say paying income tax is unconstitutional. Want their own country inside Texas which they say was taken away from Mexico illegally." The agent frowned when one of his men rolled his eyes. "Oh, believe me, Maggie Lioni can quote you chapter and verse from history to back up this shit. But she's a bloodthirsty bitch. Armed and extremely dangerous. Didn't you think so, Mr. Pagan?"

"Hell yes. She threatened to kill us. Said she'd done it before. That's why we took our chances in the woods. First opportunity, we ran." Billy looked around the table. All eyes were on him. "It was clear to me she didn't want to leave any witnesses."

"You're right. Group moves around frequently, just when we get a line on them. That clusterfuck her people caused when they shot down your plane meant they'd have to head out again. So you were on borrowed time. Good thing you got away."

"They chased us for miles. Shot at us too." Billy reached for the pitcher of water in the center of the table, poured a glass then gulped it down, proud that his hand didn't shake. But his insides were shaking. Shit. He and Shannon could have ended up in a shallow grave in those woods. That water sloshed in his stomach and he swallowed again. He was determined to keep it together in front of these men who took serious to a whole new level.

"Why were you flying so low that they could shoot you down?" The head agent turned the tablet so Billy could see a map. "According to the scouts that found your plane, you were here." He used his fingertips to enlarge a spot on the map. "That's still miles from the reservation. There's no landing field anywhere near here. You told your local airport that you were just going to fly over here and then come back to home base. Trip shouldn't have lasted more than a couple of hours."

"That's right. I flew low because I wanted to show the area to my lady. I spent many summers on the reservation, exploring the Big Thicket. I wanted Shannon to see how rough it was. I was taught survival skills in those woods when I was a kid. I got a text and let her take the wheel. Mistake, I admit it. The plane dipped and that's when we were hit the first time." He sounded like an idiot. Couldn't be helped.

"Really?" The agent just kept staring at him, waiting.

"We weren't *that* far from the reservation. It was just a buzz over what I thought was an uninhabited area. Then we were going to take a look at some Calhoun oil wells on reservation property. We had a map with us, binoculars, and a camera with a telephoto lens. Shannon works in marketing and public relations for the company. Thought maybe photos might be good in a brochure someday. But that paraphernalia made the people who shot us down suspicious. Thought we had to be government agents, spying on them."

"That was a tough break. But you obviously handled yourselves well to get away." The agent smiled. "Those survival skills came in handy." His phone buzzed and he listened for a moment. "We've got tread marks that gave us the type of vehicles they're driving. And they don't have much of a head start. How many people did you see in the compound, what kinds of weapons?" The agent tossed more questions at Billy.

He spent the next hour answering with as much detail as he could. They wanted to question Shannon too but decided that could wait since they were happy with the information Billy had given them and eager to get in on the chase. When another call came in, they left.

Feeling drained, Billy finally got out of the conference room. He'd had to turn off his cell phone when he walked into that room. Now, when he turned it on, he saw texts from Shannon and a call from the chief. Before he could do anything about either of those, Daniel stopped him in the hall.

"Chief wants to see you."

"I left Shannon in the cabin with no way to get breakfast." Billy wanted to at least send her a quick text.

"I sent someone over there with food an hour ago." Daniel smiled and gestured toward the chief's office. "He's waiting. It's important."

"All right. And thanks for taking care of Shannon. I was trapped in there." He sent her a quick text saying he'd be there soon.

"I figured." Daniel followed him into the office.

Billy took a breath. The Chief looked solemn and had a pile of papers in front of him. "Yes, sir? Sorry if you had to wait for me."

"I hope the FBI was satisfied with your report."

"They had to be. I told them all I knew. Jacob and his trackers ran the location down pretty quick." Billy sat when the chief gestured.

"Yes. They did a good job. They say your plane looks in decent shape. Of course, it has bullet holes, a busted fuel tank, and will need repairs. But the big problem will be getting it out of there. The roads are too narrow to haul it out on a flatbed truck." He frowned. "Unless you take the wings off. An expensive proposition."

"I'll leave that to an insurance adjuster. I'll call them later." Billy really couldn't get too excited about stuff like that now. He was still shaken by the idea that he and Shannon had had such a close call.

"I had Daniel pull our records on the Calhoun oil wells. You reminded me about our dealings with Conrad Calhoun. I should have said something last night to Ms. Shannon." The chief picked up a paper and passed it across the desk. "Take a look."

"What is it?" Billy got up and took it. "An agreement? With Calhoun Oil. This is dated two years ago."

"Yes. We have an agreement that should explain your numbers. Our lawyer here drafted it and you can see that Conrad Calhoun signed it. Right after we got permission for the casino, I had to find financing to build the casino and to enhance the grounds around it. We knew we had to make the entire experience here look inviting. It would be expensive." The chief tented his fingers. "Income has always been an issue for the tribe and tourism at the campgrounds doesn't bring in enough to sustain the programs we wish to provide for our people. What did provide a steady cash flow were our oil wells. Though the price of oil has declined in recent years."

"So you thought about asking for more wells to be drilled." Billy could see that the contract was favorable to Calhoun. If his uncle had brought it to him, he'd have tried to get better terms. He glanced at his cousin Daniel, the accountant. "What did you think about this?"

"I advised against it. There weren't enough safeguards there to keep wells from being drilled where we might not want them. You know we have lands we wish to remain untouched because of the wildlife and the lake. Oil drilling is noisy, messy, and not always kind to the environment." Daniel glanced at the chief. "But Conrad Calhoun offered to advance us the money we needed with little interest. The best part, as you can see, was that he would take payments out of future royalties, which he has done. The new wells are near the old and so far have not caused any problems that we can't live with. The price of oil is coming up, so we are able to pay back the loan faster than we anticipated."

Billy felt one worry fall off his shoulders. "Then any discrepancies in the paperwork on the Calhoun end might be because Conrad didn't file the paperwork at Calhoun headquarters or tell anyone how he'd handled this."

"He liked to make deals on his own. He grumbled about having a board of directors that tried to tie his hands." The chief frowned. "I knew how he felt. I have the Tribal Council looking over my shoulder. Budget, always budget." He threw a pen across his desk.

"Billy doesn't want to hear about our issues, Chief." Daniel got to his feet. "Remember, he has just survived a plane crash and a rough time in the woods. He's a city dweller. I'm sure this has taken its toll."

"Yes, this has been a hard twenty-four hours. And I'm anxious to get back to the cabin and check on Shannon."

"Of course. You will wish to go home soon, I'm sure." The chief stood and walked around the desk. "I understand."

"I have clients in Houston to deal with, and I know Shannon is anxious to get home too." Billy shook hands with the two men. "I'm glad things seem to be going well here. The casino, the grounds, everything looks good. I hope you will consider the advertising Shannon mentioned. For the restaurant. I had two excellent meals there."

"It will be done." The chief nodded to Daniel. "Tell Shannon that I remember her father well. It is thanks to Conrad Calhoun that we were able to open and become successful here so quickly." He sat behind his desk again. "Tell the person checking the numbers at the oil company that we will continue to pay off our loan the way it was arranged. I can e-mail you a copy of this contract if you need it." The chief opened his laptop.

"Please do. I don't think Conrad turned one in at Calhoun headquarters." Billy couldn't wait to tell Shannon and Ethan that this time their father hadn't pulled a fast one.

"One of our security people will drive you home. In about an hour?" Daniel walked him out to the golf cart.

"Thanks. That's perfect." Billy looked around and saw that the casino was still going strong. The rumble of big motors warned him a moment before the Blue Star Brotherhood came roaring down the road out of the woods where the cabins were located. They didn't stop, just drove past. Many of the men saluted him before they were down the road and out of sight.

"Friends of yours?" Daniel looked amused.

"Yes. Be glad. I think they dropped some serious cash here last night." Billy settled into the golf cart. "What do you think about the casino business?"

"It helps where we need income. I can say no more."

"And if someone has a gambling problem?" Billy realized there was still one motorcycle parked in front of the casino. Was it Simon?

"We post signs with telephone numbers for a helpline." Daniel was clearly uncomfortable with the subject.

"I guess that's all you can do." None of his business. "I'll be in touch. Tell Jacob thanks for tracking down my plane. I'll call him later and thank him personally." He took off, eager to see Shannon. His phone buzzed. He had a text from Mai. Shit. Court later today. They needed to get back to town in a hurry.

* * * *

"Are you and Billy taking a break? After what you went through together?" Cassidy had invited her out to lunch and Shannon had been happy to take her new sister up on the invitation.

"Not exactly a break. He's had a busy schedule the past three weeks. He has a big client list plus his aunt has a court date coming up. Then I needed to get work done here." Shannon heard herself making excuses. She twisted her napkin. "Honestly, Cass, he doesn't sleep. When I stay over there, I don't get any rest." She ignored Cass's raised eyebrows." Oh, come on, you know what I mean. Billy takes insomnia to a whole new level. Sometimes I just need a good night's sleep. You know?"

"I certainly do." Cass flushed. "Mason won't let me out of his sight when we're not at work, even though… Well, I'm not in danger now but he likes me next to him. Every night. Sometimes I wish I could have my own bedroom again." She sighed. "But I'm getting used to sharing a bed. And enjoying it." She picked up her water glass. "You and Billy aren't at that point?"

"We haven't broken up or anything." Shannon played with her wine glass. She'd automatically ordered a glass with lunch. Bad habit. Now she finished it then shook her head when the waiter asked if she wanted another. She'd promised herself she wouldn't keep drinking. Billy wasn't here and he wouldn't know. But she would. If only this vague craving would go away.

"I'd think that harrowing experience in the woods would have brought you two closer." Cass toyed with her salad. "You made Billy sound like a hero when you were telling me about it."

"He was. I didn't exaggerate the things he did. But then later that night we had a long talk. About our breakup back in college. It opened old wounds for him." Shannon pushed her plate away. She wasn't about to tell Cass about the drinking issue. It was nice to have someone in her life who didn't know what a lush she'd been most of her adult life. "I dumped him in the worst way possible back then. He hasn't forgotten."

"But he still wants you. I've seen you two together. He can't take his eyes off you." Cass pointed her fork at Shannon's bracelet. "He gave you that. I think that means almost as much as a ring." She waved her own ring finger with the large diamond on it. "Okay, maybe not as much." She smiled.

"Quit glowing. Have you set a date?" Shannon decided a subject change was for the best. She could analyze the slight chill with Billy all day long and it would do no good at all. It hurt her and puzzled her. And there was no quick fix that she could discover.

"Do you think it would ruin everyone's Christmas if we got married on Christmas Eve?" Cass laid down her fork and waited.

Shannon thought about it. It would be the first Christmas without Daddy. It had been his favorite time of year and he'd always made it special. Filling the holiday with a wedding might be just what she and her siblings needed to get past the pain of losing him. Cass had never had a father. Neither had Billy. Shannon couldn't imagine what her life would have been like without big, bluff, always larger than life, Conrad Calhoun. Yes, he'd worked too much, but when he was around, you knew it.

She studied Cass, who looked more like him than any of them. He'd never gotten the chance to spoil her, take her to a carnival or throw lavish birthday parties for her. So she'd do whatever she could to make Cass feel like she was part of their family now.

Shannon nodded. "Christmas Eve sounds perfect."

"Great." Cass smiled then touched Shannon's hand. "Having you and Megan as bridesmaids will make it even more perfect."

"Are you sure? You hardly know me." She blinked as tears filled her eyes.

"You're my sisters. You need to pick out your own dresses. Red or green, your choice. None of that hideous over the top frou-frou stuff." Cass grinned. "Though if you'd love to look like a fifties' cake topper, be my guest."

Shannon jumped up and pulled Cass into a hug. "That sounds wonderful. Megan was traumatized once by a green dress that made her, in her words, look like a bowl of guacamole. So let's say red dresses. Will that work for you? Is your best pal Ellie going to be your maid of honor?"

"Maybe my matron of honor. She and Manny are planning to tie the knot in Cancun at Thanksgiving." Cass sat back down and gestured to the waiter. "A bottle of your finest champagne. We're celebrating."

"Oh, I shouldn't. I have to go back and write a press release. The Ballet Ball is this weekend." Shannon did pick up the crystal flute though when it was set in front of her and laugh when the cork popped. She did love that sound.

"I've read some of your press releases. You're a natural. I'm sure you can do them even if you are a little buzzed." Cass clinked her glass against Shannon's. "Here's to a Christmas wedding. I hope you'll be planning your own very soon." She grinned and took a gulp of her champagne. "Oh, that's good." Her cheeks were pink with her happiness. "You know the board of directors approved my move to CEO. So it's a double celebration. Holly's moving me up to our father's old office right now."

"That's incredible! Congratulations!" Shannon tapped her glass against Cassidy's then sipped and savored. Oh, it was delicious. So much better than what they'd served at the reservation. She finished it too fast and let the waiter refill her glass. Before she knew it, they'd polished off the bottle then were headed back to the office arm in arm.

Sisters. It was nice having a new one. Cassidy was smart and pretty and had some great ideas for saving their father's company. No, *their* company. No wonder the board had let her take over the leadership. Saving Calhoun wasn't going to be easy and no one outside the family needed to know what they were dealing with anyway. Cassidy was a lot like Billy, coming up poor and determined to become successful. Shannon told her how much she admired her in the elevator on the way up to her cube. She knew it was all she deserved now but maybe, if she worked hard, she could prove to everyone, even a frowning Caroline Wilson, that she could handle her job, do more, even move up in the company herself. Hah!

By the time Shannon settled at her desk, she realized she was too buzzed to start proving much of anything. She was reaching for her purse when she got a text. Billy. Was she in the office? Could they meet? They'd gone two days without seeing each other. That had worried her. But she couldn't see him now. Not when she'd been drinking. She let it go unanswered and got up. Coffee. Where?

"Shannon, did you get that press release done?" Her boss loomed in front of her just when she'd almost made it to the elevator.

"Soon. I need to clear my head. Sorry about that." Shannon leaned against the panel next to the elevator. "Where's the coffee bar?"

Caroline Wilson shook her head. "Are you drunk?"

"Not even close." Shannon straightened her shoulders. Of course, she wasn't drunk. Three drinks or had it been four?

"Go home. You're useless in this state." Caroline turned on her heel, muttering about Calhouns and their entitlement.

"I'll be back!" Shannon poked the air, then the down button, breaking one of her last decent fingernails in the process. "Well, damn." Coffee in the lobby. Oops, her purse. She headed back to her desk, smacking her knee on the corner of the wood. "Shit."

By the time she got back to the elevator, the doors had shut. She hit the button again and waited, leaning against the doors. When they opened, she fell inside, right into strong arms. She looked up. Just her luck. Of course, he'd come up to see her anyway. She smiled but knew she'd blown it. He'd hate seeing her like this. Why hadn't she popped a breath mint? Too late.

"Billy. I was just going down for coffee. Come with me?" She scooted around him and hit the button for the lobby. She couldn't look at him. Instead, she dug in her purse for that mint. Not too late. Maybe.

He didn't say a word. The ride down to the lobby lasted forever with three stops so four people could get into the car. Shannon let the man and three women separate her from Billy as they rode down. She chewed her mint and reapplied lipstick using the mirror on the wall. Hair okay. Lipstick, check. Cheeks flushed. Eyes bright. One glance. He knew. She was in trouble and she resented it. So she stomped off the elevator and over to the coffee shop.

At least the ride and the mint, not to mention her anger, had taken care of most of her buzz. But not all. She swayed as she stared up at the menu above the counter. The barista was waiting for her order. Shannon couldn't for the life of her think of what she wanted.

"She'll take a regular, black." His deep voice was right next to her ear. "Better put a tight lid on it. Not sure she can carry it back upstairs without spilling."

Shannon whirled to face him. "Seriously? What's your problem?"

"I don't have one. Do you?" He took the coffee and handed the woman a ten-dollar bill. "Keep the change." Then he grabbed Shannon's elbow. "Do you need to go back upstairs or can you come with me?"

"Why would I want to come with you?" She heard herself and hated the tone. Picking a fight. When had she become an obnoxious drunk? "Are you going to lecture me?"

"No." He handed her the coffee and walked away. Just like that.

"Billy, wait!" She realized her hands were trembling and set the coffee on a nearby table.

He stopped a few feet away. But he didn't turn around. His shoulders were rigid and he waited. Like she'd asked him to.

She walked around him, faced him. "I'm sorry. Cass was celebrating at lunch. I, uh, helped. It won't happen again."

"Don't make promises you can't keep, Shannon. Not to me." He stared at her, his eyes searching hers.

What was he looking for? Commitment? Truth? She couldn't stand it.

"I know this is an issue for you. Believe me. I know." She walked back to the table and grabbed her coffee. Took a deep swallow. When she looked back, he was gone.

Chapter 12

Shannon ran to the glass doors that led out to the street. Thank God she'd given up those heels. She pushed outside and looked both ways. There he was, striding down the sidewalk like the hounds of hell—or his drunk girlfriend—might be after him.

"Billy! Stop!" It didn't work a second time. She ran flat out and luck was with her. He was a law-abiding citizen and the light held him at the corner along with a half dozen others waiting to cross the street. She got there in time to grab his arm before he could step off the curb.

"What do you want, Shannon?" He didn't pull away. That was something.

"I'm not going to apologize. Shit happens. But I want to know why you were coming to see me. You're freaked out and I don't think it's all about me getting tipsy." She managed to get them out of the flow of pedestrians. Where the hell were all these people going at two in the afternoon?

"I just came from court. Something happened." He leaned against the corner of the building. Billy looked tired. His sleepless nights were catching up with him and there was something else. She knew him, he was barely holding himself together.

"Tell me." She moved in and slid her arms under his suit coat. "Did you lose an important case?"

"You could say that." He rested his chin on top of her head. "I'm sorry if I overreacted. Seeing you under the influence just then made me crazy. After what happened in court, I couldn't handle it."

"I'm sorry. I don't drink at lunch anymore. Or at least hardly ever. Special occasion. Cass and Mason set a date. I'm a bridesmaid. And she's the new CEO at Calhoun. She ordered champagne." Shannon realized she was babbling.

"You don't have to make excuses, Shan. We already discussed this. I have an issue with alcohol. That issue just got a hell of a lot worse." He let her go. Shannon had no choice but to step back. "What happened?"

"I'd worked out a plea bargain for Aunt Sally. Today we went before the judge. Sally wasn't there, thank God. It was just the assistant DA and the lawyers. The DA had hammered out seven possible deals she presented to the judge. So we wouldn't have to go to trial." He ran a hand over his face. He looked tired, discouraged, and so sad it made Shannon want to pull his face to her breast and just hold him. "He's running for reelection. The judge, I mean. So he decided to play hard ball. He threw out all the plea deals for the DUI. There have been some deaths on the highways recently because of drunk drivers. Made the news."

"I know. I hate to watch the local news. So sad."

He just looked at her. "Well, it's had an impact. Voters are up in arms. And when he saw Sally's third strike? It wouldn't fly. I argued. Forget probation. House arrest and an ankle monitor weren't good enough. Judge insisted. Sally has to serve time, Shannon. She's to report to the county jail tomorrow. She got a year. It could have been much worse. With luck and overcrowding, she'll be out with good behavior in months." Billy's mouth quirked. "The judge considered that a light sentence. If Sally had so much as dented someone's fender, she'd be looking at eight to ten."

"Years?" When he nodded, Shannon swallowed, not sure she wasn't going to be sick.

"Now I have to go tell her." He gripped Shannon's hands. "Tell my grandmother too. I failed them both."

"No, stop that." She held onto him. "This is not your fault. The judge…" She shook her head then fought a wave of dizziness. Shit. She was still a little drunk. No way was she driving herself home after this. "I meant to say it was your aunt's fault. For drinking and driving. I totally get that."

"I doubt she'll think that way." Billy glanced toward the entrance to Calhoun headquarters. "Do you have to get back to work?"

"I should. That's why I was going down for coffee. I have to send out a press release about the Ballet Ball this weekend." Shannon hoped he didn't want her to go with him to see his grandmother. That old woman would take one look and realize she'd been drinking. It would be the final nail in her coffin. Call in the gang boys on the corner.

"Oh, yeah. That." He ran a hand over his face, straightened his tie. "Life goes on. Right? So Friday night. I'll pick you up. Will it look bad if we don't stay too long?" He walked her back to the double doors. It was clear that every word required an effort. How on earth did Billy keep going on so little sleep and under so much pressure? Sally was just one of his cases.

"Relax, Billy. This will be easier than you think, I promise. I'll text you the details. Black tie." Shannon promised herself she would not add to his stress. He would find out that the Ballet Ball was her element. She knew everyone, had grown up helping make those kinds of events a success. He would see the woman he loved there and they would get their relationship back on track. "I have a beautiful dress. I hope you like it."

"You're always beautiful. I have a tux." He ran a hand down her arm. "Drink your coffee. I'm sorry I can't see you tonight. Family drama will last quite a while. I'm sure Gran will want to go with me to break the news to Sally." He rubbed his eyes. "I'm glad you don't have to be part of that."

"Good luck." She reached up to kiss his solemn lips. "I'm so sorry, Billy. Remember, you did the best you could. You're the number one lawyer in Houston. No one could have done better."

"I doubt Sally will agree with you." His shoulders sagged as he walked away.

* * * *

Sally had cried so much she'd made herself sick. A physician on staff finally came in with a sedative and orderlies took her away.

"Billy, don't look so sad. I know there wasn't anything else you could do." Gran patted his shoulder. "Take me home, boy. I just want to go to bed."

"I'm sorry." He steered her out to the car.

She settled into the passenger seat and waited for him to start the car then put her hand over his before he could pull out of the parking lot. "Wait. I have something to say."

Billy leaned back. "Do we have to do this now? I'm beat. I can't sleep, not sure when I ate last, and I have files to go over before an important meeting tomorrow."

"You work too hard." She patted his hand. "Yes, we're doing this now. Maybe I should drive. I know you're not sleeping. Driving without sleep is almost as dangerous as Sally driving drunk."

"Stop it. You won't compare me to a damned drunk driver. I'm perfectly fine." He threw the car into gear and backed out of the spot. "I really don't need a lecture right now."

"Don't you?" She buckled her seat belt. "Driving angry isn't a good idea either, young man."

He choked out a laugh. Young? He felt about a hundred years old. Why couldn't he shut down his mind? It kept running. Got worse when he lay in his bed at night and stared at the ceiling. Working out didn't help. The few hours of decent sleep he got always came after he made love to Shannon. But lately he'd denied himself that pleasure. Because he worried that she'd do it again. Pull him in with her beauty and charm and then lose interest and cast him aside.

He knew he wasn't an easy man to live with. When he'd tried with other women, it had always ended the same way. He was a workaholic—pushing constantly to be the best, get more clients, always be available. It was how he'd become successful and he was proud of how far he'd come. Work had filled his life for a long damned time. It wasn't poisoning his liver, but it was becoming clear to him that it was taking a toll. God. Had he turned into an addict and not realized it?

His car beeped and he realized he'd almost mowed down a traffic barrel. Like Sally had done just before a cop pulled her over. Gran was right. He was dead on his feet and shouldn't be driving. But he knew she couldn't see well at night and he didn't trust her to drive either. He exited the freeway and hit a drive-thru.

"Coffee at this time of night? No wonder you can't sleep." She complained the entire time they were sitting in line but did accept an ice cream cone.

"I could fuss at you. Didn't the doctor say you should lay off the sugar?" She had a sweet tooth and it made him smile to watch her savor the treat.

"Hah! At my age, I'll do what I want. What's the point of living a long time if you have to deny yourself small pleasures like ice cream?" She licked the cone and winked at him. "What gives you pleasure, my Billy?"

"You don't want to hear it." He grinned. "Adult things."

"Ah. Your woman then." She shook her head. "You're right. I don't want to hear it. Wrong woman. Is that one of the things that keeps you up at night?"

"Maybe. But I won't discuss Shannon with you." Billy wished he could talk this out with his grandmother. Seeing Shannon drunk in the middle of the day had rocked him. Celebrating. How many times had his mother thrown out that word as an excuse to get sloshed? She'd celebrate a Friday, a new job, a pretty haircut. Shit. She'd celebrate a good grade he brought home on a test. Then he wouldn't see her for three days straight while she went out on a bender and he'd think it was his fault.

"I warned that girl not to break your heart." Gran crunched the last of the cone then wiped her mouth with a napkin. "If she's giving you pain, I'll see that she's sorry."

"Gran! You leave Shannon the hell alone." Billy set his empty cup in the center console. "I love her. I'll decide if she's worth my time or the pain." He realized he'd said too much already.

His grandmother leaned back and closed her eyes. "I knew it. Shannon

Calhoun is wrong for you. Please let her go." She turned her head away. So he wouldn't see her tears?

"We'll work it out. You stay out of it. I hope to marry her. Have children with her. Your great grandchildren. If you ever hope to see them, you'll become reconciled to this." It wasn't until he'd said it out loud that Billy knew it as the truth. When he'd run to Shannon after that judge tossed out Sally's plea bargain, it had been pure instinct. She was his comfort. The one place besides at his grandmother's knee where he knew he would find acceptance and no judgment. He had to reach deep inside himself and do that for her too. Otherwise he'd be doing her no favors if he wanted this relationship to work.

"Marriage. So this is it. You're committed to her?" Her cheeks were damp when Gran faced him across the dark car.

"In my heart, yes. I haven't proposed yet, but I'm planning on it. If you want to be part of our lives, begin to accept her. She's not perfect but, God knows, neither am I." He reached for his grandmother's hand. It was bony and spotted with signs of her age but surprisingly strong as she gripped his. She'd moved on from orange to a deep violet hair color that made her blue eyes vivid. They were his mother's eyes. His eyes too.

"You will always be perfect to me, Billy boy. I have loved you all your life and will love you until I draw my last breath. If this woman is your choice, I will shut my mouth and say no more." She shook his hand until it hit the gear shift. "Smart boy. Why do you have to be so stupid sometimes?" She pulled away. "There. My last word on the subject."

"Hey. At least I picked someone stylish. You saw her in a work suit. Wait till you see her dolled up for the Ballet Ball. I'll bring her by. You can take pictures. Friday night. What do you say? The ladies at church and bingo will love it." He heard her chuckle.

"Yes, she does come from that rich family. I bet she has some beautiful clothes. Not my size. Too bad." It was quiet for a few minutes then he heard a sob. "Billy, Billy, what's going to happen to my Sally in that jail?"

Billy had nothing to say to that. He'd tried not to think about it. Was there anything else he could do to keep his aunt out of there? A doctor's note? Sally had not looked well. Nervous breakdown? He didn't mention that. With the sound of his grandmother's crying filling the car and breaking his heart, he drove on. He had less than twenty-four hours to figure out something. Everyone counted on him to be a hero. But at what cost? His eyes were gritty and the coffee had done nothing but make his stomach acid burn.

Think. Yeah. That was all he did. But he was getting nowhere. By the time he'd helped his suddenly frail grandmother into her house, he wondered if it was time to call in help. But who? He was supposed to be such a hotshot lawyer. Was there anyone else who could take Sally's case and handle it better?

* * * *

Shannon knew Billy would need her when he got through with Sally and his grandmother. She didn't know how to cook, had lived with a fantastic housekeeper all her life. But she could order food and had decided to have a meal waiting for him. He liked Chinese and it was easy to reheat. She hoped this had been a good idea.

Billy didn't take good care of himself. He'd called it family drama. That was too light a word for what he must have endured at the rehab facility. Shannon could only imagine how Sally had taken the news that she was going to jail. The idea was terrifying. And his relatives might blame Billy. So unfair.

As soon as she heard the garage door open, Shannon stuck his plate in the microwave. When he walked through the door, she got to see him, unguarded. It was a shock. He looked totally exhausted and defeated. Not her strong confident Billy at all.

"Surprise!"

"Shit. You almost got a briefcase tossed in your face." He dropped it on the floor and opened his arms. "How did you know I was hoping to see you tonight?"

"Were you? I took a chance." She walked into those arms and leaned against him. "A cab dropped me off." She rubbed his back.

"Something smells good. I haven't eaten since—" he stopped. "Maybe breakfast?"

"Sit. I ordered pepper steak. I know you like it." She pulled out the plate and set it in front of him, then got each of them a bottle of water. "Eat. When you feel like it, tell me how it went tonight."

"Depressing as hell. As you can imagine." He stirred the rice into the beef then started eating. "This is good. I guess you found the drawer with all the delivery and take out menus."

"Yep. Give me a menu and I'm good to go." She waited while he ate. "There's nothing you can do for Sally?"

"I've been asking myself that question all the way home." He drank some water then pushed away his empty plate. "I'm so damned tired my mind is blank. Oh, I may have an idea rolling around in there, but I have to wait until morning to do anything about it."

"Then take a shower and let's go to bed." Shannon pulled him to his feet. "I'll help with that." She rinsed off his plate and stuck it in the dishwasher while he watched.

"You'll help? With the shower?" He grinned. "I'm waiting."

"You have to promise me something." She grabbed his hand and pulled him toward the master bathroom.

"Anything." He unbuttoned her blouse as they walked.

"You have to sleep tonight. You look like hell." She stopped in the doorway and let her blouse drop to the floor.

"You know I can't promise that." He unclipped her bra and threw it down on top of her blouse. "It's not as if I don't *want* to sleep. It's my brain. I can't seem to turn it off."

"Let's test that. What are you thinking, right now?" She pulled off his tie and draped it over the doorknob, then went to work on his shirt buttons.

"That we both have on too many clothes and that I want you." He opened her pants and slid them down her legs along with her panties. "Step out of these." He groaned when she did. "That's better. Naked. Exactly the way I like you."

"But that's not your problem when you're trying to go to sleep." She'd managed to get him naked too. It wasn't difficult. He was always eager to strip off.

"Shannon, a guy is always thinking about sex. When he can have it, how it is when he's having it, how it was afterwards, and then when can he have it again." He laughed and pulled her against him. "Men are dogs. We proudly acknowledge that. Dogs and men. Best friends. Kindred spirits." He cupped her buns, his erection touching her where he fit so perfectly.

He wasn't a tall man, just tall enough. They were almost eye to eye but he was big because of his incessant workouts. He'd defined his body, honed it. His shoulders were broad, his abs tight, and his waist lean. Shannon had told him before that she found his body beautiful and she hadn't been flattering him. She loved every inch of it. She ran her hands over his back and down to his firm butt. Perfect.

"Okay, so we'll make sure you get plenty of mind-blowing sex. Then what do you think will keep you awake? What thoughts will run through your mind?" Shannon saw him frown. "Oh, I know. Sally's situation."

"Of course. I've got to figure out a way to keep her out of jail. You should have seen her reaction. I really don't think she can handle it."

"Do you think you can do her any good if you're dead on your feet?" She kissed his chin. "Honestly, Billy. Didn't you tell me you hurt a client recently because you'd been tired in court and let a witness get away with testimony that was prejudicial to his case? That you should have objected and didn't because you almost dozed off?"

"Thanks for paying attention." He looked pissed but thoughtful. "Yeah. That happened. And now I realize I told you that and shouldn't have. What the fuck? I'm not operating at full capacity. Maybe I need a sleeping pill or something."

"Some people would say that or a stiff drink. I know better." Shannon felt him react to that. Body language. Yes, he'd die before he'd drink himself to sleep. And she didn't blame him. "I did research. While a drink might make you sleepy initially, it'll wake you up in a few hours and you won't get good rest anyway."

"No kidding. Research on drinking. You surprise me." He let his hands wander to her shoulders then her breasts. "Do we really have to have this conversation before the mind-blowing sex?"

"Yes, you are a dog. And I love you." She laughed when he barked and picked her up to carry her into the bathroom.

He turned on the shower and waited until she pronounced the temperature perfect. "I had Mai get you a shower cap." He nodded toward a basket on the counter. "Even a dog wants his mate to be happy."

"Thanks. At least you didn't call me your bitch." Shannon slipped it over her hair, then dragged him inside the glass enclosure. She was determined to find a way to help him. Was this love? This need to take care of him? To make him happy? He was certainly trying for her. He hadn't mentioned this afternoon and her "condition." His attitude was playful as they made love until the water cooled and he swore he was calling in a plumber to install a larger hot water heater.

"You're insatiable." Shannon kissed him as he dried her with a towel and pulled off her shower cap. "I don't know about you, but I'm totally relaxed now. I'll sleep like a baby." But Billy just seemed to be revved up. He stalked out to the kitchen and grabbed his briefcase, pulling out his laptop.

"What are you doing?" She couldn't believe it when he fired it up.

"I just thought of something. Maybe a way to get Sally some time before she has to appear at the jail." He was busy typing.

Shannon pulled on a nightgown and crawled into bed. Then she hopped up again and turned off lights—all except the lamp on his side of the bed. She lay next to him and watched him work. He frowned and typed, frowned and typed some more. Finally, he slammed the laptop closed.

"Fuck. That won't do it. I was hoping there was a loophole. Sally's a quarter Indian. Maybe she could ask for counsel from the Tribe. Seek asylum. I don't know. But there's nothing."

"I can see your brain going. No wonder you can't sleep." She settled on her pillow and yawned. "It's two in the morning, Billy."

"I know. Go to sleep. Maybe I'll work out for a while. Unless…" He lifted the sheet and looked her over. "Nice gown. But I like you better naked."

"I don't think I have another round in me, lover." She kissed him then gently pushed him away. "I have work tomorrow. You do too. What time are you picking up Sally?"

"Ten. Out there. It's a two-hour drive round trip." He slipped out of bed.

"You've got to get some sleep." She could barely keep her own eyes open. How did he do it? "I think you need to see a doctor. This isn't normal."

"Thanks for your professional opinion." He grabbed his pillow and laptop and left the room.

Shannon sighed and stared at the ceiling. Should she go after him? But what was the point? This *wasn't* normal. At least he wasn't tossing and turning beside her. He'd left the lamp on. She pulled the comforter over her face and closed her eyes. She'd wanted to help but maybe this was something he had to figure out for himself. Too bad.

* * * *

His phone went off at seven. He'd set the alarm when he'd finally given up and climbed into bed beside Shannon at four. Three hours of sleep. He felt drugged. Water running in the bathroom. Obviously, Shannon was already up. She'd be tired too. This had to stop. For both of them. Maybe she was right and he needed to see a doctor about his insomnia. But pills? He looked at those like he did alcohol. An addiction just waiting to happen. God help him.

She came out of the bathroom with that fresh scrubbed look he loved and smelling of mint toothpaste. He wanted to pull her back to bed and make slow love to her. She smiled and walked over to kiss him.

"If you keep looking at me like that, we'll never get to work." She pulled off her nightgown and slid into bed next to him. "How do you feel?"

"Like shit. But I'm about to feel much better." He groaned when she touched him, her hand circling his erection. "Good morning to you. What can I do for you?"

"I want you to quit feeling so responsible for Sally's situation. Is that at all possible?" Her fingers moved in a way designed to make him agree to anything.

"I know. She did the crime, she does the time. That's what they say, isn't it?"

"Yes." She climbed on top of him, her breasts swaying close to his mouth as she guided him inside her. "Keep that in mind when you're enduring what is sure to be a hell of a day, my lover." She moved, sighing when he captured a nipple in his lips. "I'll have a reward for you when your day is over. I promise. Now be a good boy and move. Harder, faster. We don't have a lot of time and I, um, oh, yes." She held his head against her breast and hummed that sweet little sound she made when her orgasm was close.

Billy held her hips and pumped into her. Yes, she was right. You make your own fate. Suffer your own consequences.

He would be happy to die like this. In Shannon's arms. Sally fucked up. She'd have to pay. He was sorry about that. But not so sorry that he was going to lose another night's sleep over it. His head hit his pillow, Shannon's name coming just as he did. He let it all go, the guilt and the pain, and took in the pleasure.

When she dropped on top of him, breathing hard, he held her tight. This was what he wanted. Not just the sex but the knowledge that he had someone who knew him, cared about him, and wanted him to be whole. He had to trust her, this. That it would last. Yes, it would. It had to. He didn't want to see *this* go. Ever again.

His phone buzzed and he reached for it automatically.

"Seriously? When we're together like this? Still connected?" Shannon rolled off him. "Oh, go ahead, counselor. I guess you're on call twenty-four/seven."

"Sorry." Billy glanced at the number. "It's Sally's rehab hospital. I'd better take this." Dread convinced him this couldn't be anything good.

"Mr. Pagan?" The voice on the other end was professional.

"Yes. This is Billy Pagan. What is it? Something about my aunt, Sally Winthrop?"

"Yes, sir. I have some bad news. She listed you as her emergency contact person." Deep breath on the other end of the line. "We are very careful here, sir. I want to assure you—"

"Spit it out! What the hell has happened to Sally?" Billy couldn't just lie there. He jumped to his feet.

"Sir, she tried to commit suicide an hour ago." The man rushed on. "She survived but is in bad shape. We took her by ambulance to Woodlands Memorial Hospital. She's in intensive care there."

"How did that happen? I knew she was upset when I left, the doctor on staff had to sedate her. Don't you people monitor your patients? How did she do it? What did she have access to that could harm her?" Billy's mind raced. Shannon's arm came around his waist and he barely stopped himself from shrugging it off. He wasn't used to having anyone to lean on. She meant well but all he wanted now was… He mouthed the word and she raced away.

"She slashed her wrists, sir. Got hold of a knife at breakfast. That was early this morning. She obviously sneaked it back to her room. We didn't have her on suicide watch. Apparently, you told a staff member that she was leaving today. That she had to report to the Harris County Jail, but we had no idea—"

"You had no idea that going to jail might make her suicidal?" Fuck. Fuck. Fuck. This was his fault. He'd known how hard Sally was taking this. How terrified she was. The attendants who'd taken her away in hysterics should have notified someone, too, about her state of mind.

"Sir, she was sedated last night. We were closing out her file. No one could have predicted—"

"You'll be hearing from me about this later. I'm Ms. Winthrop's attorney as well as her nephew. You've been negligent. I hope you at least informed the hospital that she should be on suicide watch now." He slammed down the phone and ran to the bathroom. After taking care of business and using a toothbrush, he came out to the bedroom to take the steaming cup of coffee Shannon handed him. "Thanks." He took a deep drink, cursing when he burned his tongue.

"Sally?"

He told her what had happened. "I'll head to the hospital as soon as I'm dressed."

"What can I do?" She ran to his closet and pulled out a fresh shirt and suit. She laid out a matching tie and socks on his bed before he could even thank her. "Boxers or briefs?"

"I hate to ask you this." He snatched the briefs out of her hand and stepped into them.

"Go ahead." She held out his shirt and he slipped into it.

"Gran. I'll call her but I don't want her driving when she's upset. Plus, I don't think she could find that hospital. You have GPS, right?"

"Yes. I'll take a cab home, get my car and pick her up. You're calling her now? Or do you want me to tell her when I get there. That might be better, Billy. Otherwise she could just take off in her car." Shannon looked calm except she was wringing her hands.

"You'd do that? I know you two aren't pals. Gran confessed she let you have it when we went by there before. I had a talk with her though. Told her she had to accept you. She promised to try." Billy stuffed his wallet into his back pocket and picked up his cell phone.

"That's progress." Shannon ran his tie under his shirt collar, tied it like a pro.

"But, you're right. That's the way to handle it. Gran gets a slow start in the mornings. Usually doesn't go anywhere until after nine. She'll be home and in her recliner when you get there."

"Then that's what I'll do. Go on out to the hospital. I guess you'll call the jail. Explain why she can't report today." She followed him to the kitchen.

"Look at you, thinking like a lawyer. Yeah, I'll do that or they'll issue a warrant for failure to appear." He filled his travel cup from the pot on the counter then stopped at the door into the garage, trying to decide what he was forgetting. Shannon handed him his briefcase with his laptop inside. God, he was braindead.

"Go. Don't worry about us. I'll call in to work then take care of Grandmother." She kissed him at the door. "Maybe I'll call her that. Should freak her out."

"Yes. Do that." He hunted for his car keys then realized they were already in his hand. "I hope to hell Sally makes it. Don't know what Gran would do if she lost her other daughter."

"Let's pray she doesn't have to face that." Shannon gave him one more hug then opened the door behind him.

"Do you pray?" He stopped next to his car.

"Sure." She nodded, looking so right there in the kitchen door. "Don't you?"

"Maybe. Sometimes. Guess I'd better try this time. Thanks, baby. I love you." He got in the car and almost drove into his own damned garage door. He hit the button to run it open then backed out.

He heard her say she loved him too. All right then. Praying. It wasn't something he was in the habit of doing. Church. He'd lost track of that too, though his grandmother had dragged him there until he'd rebelled as a teen. But praying. It was a start.

God, are you there? Talk some sense into Sally. She just needs to get past this. Figure out something worth living for.

Hey, what do you know? That had actually turned out to be kind of a prayer. Billy joined the gridlock that passed for morning traffic on Houston's freeways and added more to the conversation. Sleep. Why couldn't he sleep?

God, have any ideas on that?

At least the coffee had jolted him wide awake. That and the news about Sally. Now he had an angle for keeping her out of jail. Doctor's testimony. Psychiatric issues. What a hell of a way to avoid punishment. He'd never have wanted this to happen.

Chapter 13

Shannon had to psych herself up before she got out of the car in front of Billy's grandmother's house. First, delivering this bad news was going to be a nightmare. And to a woman who hated her? Even worse. Second, there were people on the corner again. Teenagers who should have been in school stared at her. She didn't think they were waiting for a bus. In fact, when a big yellow school bus went past, they made signs and shouted obscenities.

She clutched her purse to her chest and made a run for it. Two girls detached themselves from the pack and strolled toward her. She didn't wait to see what they wanted, even after they shouted at her to "Wait up!"

On Mrs. Pagan's porch Shannon hit the doorbell repeatedly. The girls were on the sidewalk now, but didn't mount the steps. They looked her over, smoking and flicking ashes into the flower beds. They were obviously waiting to see if she was going to be allowed inside.

"Who is it?" The voice inside was reassuring. At least Billy's grandmother didn't open the door to just anyone.

"It's me, Mrs. Pagan. Shannon Calhoun. Billy sent me. I have important news. About Sally." Shannon ignored the girls blowing smoke rings in her direction. She could feel all eyes on her. Their boyfriends must be watching too. Deadbolts turned, then the wooden door swung open and she could see Billy's grandmother through the iron burglar bars.

"Why didn't Billy call me? Or come himself?" His granny's purple hair stuck up like she'd just got out of bed and she wore a brightly colored house coat. "Shannon? What's wrong?"

"You want us to get rid of her, Mrs. P.?" one of the teen girls shouted. "Is she hassling you? One of those social services bitches?"

"Run along, Tasha. She's my grandson's girlfriend. I've got this. But thanks." Gran pulled a key from her pocket and stuck it in the lock.

Tissues fell to the floor. "Come in, come in." She stepped back. "Tell me what's going on."

Shannon handed her the wad of clean tissues, then took the key from her and turned to relock the door. Thank God the two girls took off, butts twitching in tight jeans as they headed back to the corner.

"Sit down, Mrs. Pagan. I have some bad news." Shannon jumped when the elderly woman gripped her arm, her fingers sinking in like an eagle's talons. It freaking hurt. She endured and helped her over to her recliner.

"Bad news? Tell me." Gran's lips trembled and she finally let go to put the tissues to her mouth. "Sally?"

A game show was on the TV and Shannon grabbed the remote, turning it off. "Billy said she was upset when he told her she was to report to jail this morning."

"Yes, yes. She fell apart. She didn't try to escape, did she?" Gran leaned forward. "That girl. Headstrong. Has a half-dozen old boyfriends. No accounts she met in some bar. One of them would come if she asked him to pick her up. Oh, no, tell me she didn't try that."

"It's worse than that, I'm afraid." Shannon couldn't just stand there, looking down. She pulled up an ottoman and it clanked. What was the thing made of, metal juice cans? Anyway, it was better to sit facing the lady.

"No! What could be… Oh, God! Is she…dead?" Tears trickled down her wrinkled cheeks. She hadn't put on her makeup yet and looked every bit her advanced age.

"No. But Sally did try to commit suicide. She didn't succeed but she's in intensive care. I've come to take you to the hospital. So you can see her." Shannon laid her hands on the woman's knees.

"Suicide!" The cry came straight from the elderly woman's heart. "How could she do such a thing?" She bowed her head and sobbed into her tissues. Finally, after several long moments and gasps for breath, she looked up and into Shannon's eyes. "You sure she's all right?"

"That's what they told Billy. But it's serious. We should go."

"Yes, yes." She shook her head and plucked at the snaps on her house coat. "I can't believe she would give up hope like that. How did she…?"

"I don't know. Billy didn't say. But I know she was scared. I would be. Sometimes fear makes us do crazy things."

"Where's Billy?" Gran was struggling to get out of her chair and Shannon rushed to help her.

"He went to the hospital. It's out by the rehab facility. He didn't want you driving when you're upset so he sent me. If you're up to it, I'll take you there." Shannon held onto the woman's elbow when she swayed. She didn't look well. "Are you on medication? Have you taken what you need yet today? You won't do Sally any good if you become ill."

"Give me some time to pull myself together, girl. Of course, I'm going out there." But she did look around then pick up a pill bottle from the table next to her recliner. "I take this on a full stomach. After breakfast. Haven't had it yet."

"Why don't I fix you something while you get dressed? You can eat, then take your pills before we get on the road." Shannon prayed that all the old lady wanted was a bowl of cereal. She could handle that.

"Quit looking at me like I'm going to fall over. I won't. But I will take my cereal with a banana cut up in it and some of that two percent in the icebox." Her hands fluttered around her face. "Look at me. I can't go anywhere like this. I have to fix my hair and my face. Seeing me like this would scare Sally for sure."

Shannon had nothing to say to that.

"Come on now, help me get into the bedroom. Foolish, but I feel a little unsteady." Gran used that talon grip again, holding onto Shannon as she shuffled down the hall in her pink fuzzy slippers. "You did say Sally was going to be all right, didn't you?"

Shannon figured she'd have bruises from that grip. "We'll know more when we get out there. But let's take it as a good sign that she made it to the hospital. Okay?"

Gran's lips trembled but she quickly firmed them. "Yes, you're right. Now sit me down at my dressing table then go to the kitchen. I think you can figure out where everything is."

Shannon obeyed orders, careful not to bump the old-fashioned dressing table that was loaded with makeup, perfumes, and hair products. The bedroom itself was centered by a queen-sized bed that had been neatly made. The bedspread was a beautiful quilt that someone had done by hand. The colors were vibrant and suited the lady who reached for moisturizer as soon as she was settled on the vanity stool.

"Did you make this quilt? It's gorgeous." Shannon left Gran's side to smooth her hands over it. Velvet pattern blocks. It felt as good as it looked.

"Play your cards right and I'll make one for you and Billy. Wedding present." Gran ran a brush through her hair. "Oh, don't look surprised. He told me. Wants to marry you. Give you children. I have to accept it and *you* if I want to see the great grands. So there. Peace offering." She took a watery breath. "By God, Sally better live through this. If she doesn't…"

"I've been praying for her, Gran." Shannon went down on her knees beside the old lady. She put her arms around her. "Billy is praying too. I love him. I promise I'll do my best to make him happy." She inhaled the sweet scent of baby powder. It was comforting and she knew she'd never smell it again without thinking of this strong, sassy woman who'd raised the man she loved.

"That's all I ask, girl." Gran laid her head on Shannon's shoulder for a moment then sniffed and straightened. "Don't dawdle now. I have to get to that hospital. See Sally for myself." She took a breath that sounded almost like a wheeze but quickly got it under control. She eyed Shannon's reflection in the mirror. "Coco Charms. Lots of milk. Half a banana. Now scoot." She picked up purple eye shadow. "Hope that girl's awake. I'm going to let her know what I think of this stunt she pulled."

Shannon got up and hurried into the kitchen. Chocolate cereal? But she had to admit there'd been a breakthrough moment there. Gran was going to try to accept her. And Billy had told her he planned to propose! She hugged that thought close—a wedding, a life with Billy—then got to work. She found the banana, frowning at the brown spots, then carefully cut around them.

She had the cereal ready when Gran called for her to come help her into the kitchen. The woman needed to lean on her to walk again. That was a worry she'd have to share with Billy. But not until they got to the hospital. She texted him when they were in the car to let him know they were on the way. His text said Sally was stable. Stable. Not very encouraging but not a death sentence either. The long ride out to the hospital was fairly quiet with Gran muttering prayers. Over and over again. Couldn't hurt.

* * * *

"Thanks for bringing Gran out here." Billy and Shannon were in the waiting room while his grandmother sat with Sally. His aunt had finally opened her eyes. Just in time to listen to her mother give her hell for trying to end her life. Billy had tried to calm them both with the hope that he could postpone jail, maybe get it off the table altogether, if he could get a psychiatrist on board.

Suicide. He still couldn't believe Sally had tried to kill herself. She'd come close to succeeding too. The doctor had been clear about that. She'd needed transfusions and Billy had given blood, glad he'd been able to donate. Of course, now he was a little light-headed. He'd had juice in the lab but the temporary boost seemed to be wearing off. He decided to keep all of that to himself. Shannon was already giving him a narrow look, like maybe she suspected something. He kept the subject on the miracle of seeing her help Gran down the hall.

"You and Gran looked like buddies when you arrived outside the ICU. What did you do?" He smiled for the first time since he'd gotten to the hospital. "Turn that famous Shannon charm on her?"

"Hah! As if that would work. But we've called a truce. She told me some interesting things." Shannon smiled back and ran her hand down his lapel before straightening his tie. "I admired the velvet quilt on her bed."

"She's quite a quilter. Doesn't do it much anymore. But I'm sure the compliment meant a lot to her. See? Charm. You've got it in spades." Billy pulled out his phone when it vibrated. He wasn't taking the call but it reminded him of all the things he had to do later. "I have an important meeting this afternoon. Now that I know Sally is going to be okay, I've got to go. I think we can safely leave Gran out here and both take off."

"Really? How is she going to get home?" Shannon glanced at the intensive care unit. "She didn't look well this morning, Billy."

"Do we need to get her to a doctor?" He hated that he was pulled in two different directions. But clients put their lives in his hands. Rupert Billingsley was counting on him and right now, Rupert was in danger of spending the rest of his life in prison. He needed to ask him some serious questions today.

"She's on medication. Do you know what it's for?" Shannon frowned.

"Blood pressure. She took it, didn't she?" He walked over to the coffee pot in the waiting room and got a refill. "Quit frowning. What's wrong?"

"How many cups have you had so far this morning? Have you eaten anything?" She took the cup from him. "We should find the cafeteria."

"I don't have time, Shannon." He slung his arm around her. "But I appreciate the thought. I'll drive through somewhere and get one of those breakfast sandwiches. Promise."

"Billy. I'm worried about you." She pulled his face down to study it. "Your eyes are bloodshot and you have bags under them. You're thirty-two years old and look fifty."

"Thanks a lot." He kissed her lips then pulled away. "And here I thought I missed having a mother."

He stuck his phone in his pocket and went inside the unit to say good-bye to his grandmother and Sally. "I'll check in with you later, Gran. I have work to do. Will you be okay?"

"We're fine." Gran patted Sally's hand. "She won't do this again. Will you, Sally?"

"No, Mama." Sally looked terrible, an IV in her arm and monitors keeping track of her heart rate and pressure. She was pale and her cheeks were sunken. The bandages on her thin wrists wouldn't let him forget how she'd rather die than go to jail.

"I hope you mean that, Aunt Sally."

She stared up at him. "Promise me I won't have to go to jail, Billy."

"Sorry, no promises." He realized he'd been too quick to claim he could work wonders for his clients. Sometimes, he wasn't going to win. It sucked but there it was.

Sally closed her eyes and turned to face the wall but not before he saw the tears that ran down her cheeks.

"Sally, you know Billy will do all he can." His grandmother glared at him. "You're just tired." She grabbed Billy's hand and pulled him to the door, leaning heavily on her cane. Once outside with the door closed, she wagged a finger in his face. "Shame on you. The girl needs hope right now. What's wrong with you?"

Billy grabbed that finger and held on. "I couldn't lie to her. I'll do what I can but—"

Gran threw off his hold. "Stop! I don't want to hear it. Fix this. I know you can." She glanced at the door to ICU. "I'm staying here until I talk to her doctor. I don't like the way she looks, so pale and listless."

"She lost a lot of blood, Gran. Give her time." Billy tried to put his arm around her but she shrugged it away. "Call when you need a ride home. I'll arrange something."

"No. I'll get one of my friends to come get me." She frowned at him. "Giving up isn't like you, Billy boy. Obviously, you need rest. And maybe time with Shannon. She wants to take care of you. Let her." She thumped her cane. "Don't get me wrong. I'm still not sure I trust her. But she was good to me this morning. Even made me bring this thing." She held on to the door frame and thumped that cane again. It was a fancy one with pink and purple stripes that he'd bought her but she never used. "It was the right thing to do but makes me feel old."

"She likes to take care of people." Billy kissed her wrinkled cheek. "Like someone else I know." He held the door for her to go back into the ICU then looked for Shannon. For a moment he thought she'd left. He wouldn't blame her. He'd been an asshole.

The elevator doors opened and there she was. She walked up and handed him a sack. "A breakfast sandwich. Try not to drive one-handed. Eat it when you're stopped at a light."

"I love you and I'm sorry." He took it then pulled her in for a hungry kiss. He gave her points for not hitting him. He probably tasted like that horrible hospital coffee.

She tugged at his hair and he let her go. "I love you too. But don't compare me to your mother again. I was just trying to help."

"I hear you and I appreciate that." He ran a hand over his face and realized he'd forgotten to shave. "I've got to go."

"I'll follow you as far as the turnoff for your office."

"Did *you* eat anything?" He had to start this caring thing. She always looked good to him, but obviously her own rough morning had taken a toll. Her hair was pulled back in a ponytail and she had on yesterday's clothes.

"Coco Charms. At your grandmother's." She grinned. "They were a rare treat."

"She needs a doctor's appointment. Next week. To get her blood sugar checked among other things." He rode down in the elevator with her then held her hand all the way out to the parking lot.

"She told me she has a sugar addiction. She's not apologizing for it or giving up sweets. Stubborn lady." Shannon stopped next to her car. "I'm going home. I need fresh clothes. And a nap. I may head into the office later. Or not." She kissed him again. "I wish *you* could take a nap."

"No chance." He glanced at his phone. Albert had e-mailed him with some files attached. "I just got some new information I have to look over before my meeting this afternoon. I'll be in the office all day. Dinner tonight?"

"Sure. If you think that's possible. You won't be coming back out here?" She glanced at the hospital.

"No. They'll be moving Sally out of intensive care later today. I got that from her doctor. Then I'll have her transported to a hospital in the Texas Medical Center. Closer to Gran. It'll be more convenient for both of us. I'm arranging an independent psychiatric evaluation too." He shook his head when Shannon pressed her hand to his heart. "I know. Sounds bad. But it may be what keeps her out of jail. We'll see."

"I'm sorry, Billy." She opened her car door. "If it's one less worry for you, though, then this was a good thing."

"Maybe. Don't wait to follow me. Go ahead. I'm going to sit here and read my email while I eat." He kissed her one more time then watched her drive away. He sat in his car and devoured the breakfast sandwich. It helped. He had a long drive ahead of him and some thinking to do after he read the file Albert had sent him.

Background information on Rupert and financials for Evelyn. He hadn't thought to look at the woman's money trail but Albert had. It made for interesting reading. What he did with it depended on how his meeting with Rupert went this afternoon.

It made him crazy that things in this case hadn't come together yet.

Usually he was more confident when putting together a defense. He never went into court without the knowledge that he had right on his side. It helped him face a jury convincingly. Without it? Well, Rupert wouldn't have a snowball's chance.

* * * *

"Rupert, how are you doing?" Billy had offered the man a drink and they both settled into chairs with bottles of water. He figured they could probably compare notes on how to deal with insomnia. The grieving widower had bags under his eyes too and seemed to have aged since they'd last met.

"How the hell do you think I'm doing? I'm facing a murder charge. Unless you've got good news for me, I'm ready to hire myself another lawyer. One who earns the fortune I'm paying him." Rupert twisted the cap off the water and drank half of it down.

"I've had my investigator working on your case nonstop since the hearing. He's been digging into financials for the Greenes who I considered the most likely suspects." Billy set his bottle on the corner of the desk. "But then that digging brought out some interesting information we hadn't expected."

"What? Did they do it? Hire a hitman?" Rupert's eyes filled. "I can't believe it."

"Calm down, Rupert. We need to concentrate today." Billy got up and walked around to sit behind his desk. "Let's start over. Where did you meet Evelyn Greene?"

"What?" Rupert grabbed a tissue and blew his nose. "What the fuck does that have to do with anything?"

"Humor me." Billy opened the file Mai had printed for him. "Give me a timeline. When and where you met for starters."

"I think you must already know." Rupert drank more water. "I was working at M.D. Anderson. Evelyn was a patient. She was taking chemo treatments in my unit. It's a long, drawn-out process. I admired her spirit and she…" He sighed. "Well, she hit on me. I was young, flattered, and it didn't hurt that she was rich and beautiful. When she made me an offer, I accepted. I moved in as her private nurse. One thing led to another and we got married. That was almost ten years ago."

"And did you know her cancer had come back recently?" Billy had double-checked that autopsy report. The medical examiner had estimated Evelyn had only a few more months to live at most when that bullet had killed her.

"Of course I did!" Rupert burst into tears. "I know you think I was just using her, but I loved her. We were planning that cruise as our final trip. I promised to give her the meds she'd need to keep her comfortable." He bowed his head. "She decided not to have treatment this time. It wouldn't have done much to prolong her life anyway. Chemo is so harsh. The side effects." He shuddered. "She refused to go through it again."

Billy gave Rupert time to pull himself together. His grief seemed genuine. The man was a caregiver. Maybe he'd taken advantage of a rich older woman, but she'd used him too. Evelyn had enjoyed Rupert's handsome looks and adventurous spirit. He'd looked good on her arm and satisfied her needs. Then, near the end of her life, she had a companion who would take care of her. Billy had just learned that knowing someone cared could enrich your life in ways he'd never expected.

"What about Evelyn's will? Did you know she was changing it?" Billy threw this question at Rupert when he reached for another tissue.

"She told me. She wanted to leave most of her money to the cancer center. They gave her ten years more than she might have gotten otherwise. She was grateful. It was the right thing to do. And she hated the Greenes. Didn't want them to run her late husband's company into the ground—her words." Rupert mopped his face. "It was complicated, arranging that new endowment. It was large enough that I hoped we could get a wing or maybe an oncology suite named for her after her death." He sighed.

"She didn't sign it before she died." Billy had prepared a subpoena and Mai was messengering it over to the court today. But he'd seen the new will, thanks to Albert's snooping.

"Oh, no! Then those awful Greenes will get their way." Rupert was up on his feet. "Do you see how this could be their motive for murder?"

"Yes, of course." Billy shook his head. "But, Rupert, she was supposed to meet with the lawyer and sign it days before. It was on their calendar, but she cancelled at the last minute. Do you know why?"

"She had good days and bad. Pain would come and go. Honestly, she wasn't always thinking clearly then. So she cancelled many appointments. Hair, nails. I guess seeing her lawyer was one of them." He studied his own nails. "Truth be told, the Greenes would have had grounds for challenging the new will if they got wind of her condition at the end. I'm not saying she wasn't right for changing her will, just that the cancer had moved to her brain too. It did affect her judgment at times."

"That's interesting. But maybe Evelyn's idea that the Greenes were ruining the company was also caused by her illness. So far my investigator hasn't found solid evidence that they've done anything wrong at Greenespace." Billy made a note. Not that he had to help another attorney. But if the Greenes were charged with Evelyn's murder, their lawyer might be interested in what Albert had found or not found.

"Paranoia. Well, it's possible. But she convinced me those two were up to something. And I'm sorry she didn't get to sign that new will." Rupert seemed genuinely sad.

"You come out well in both wills. Better in the first one though." Billy tossed his copy of that one on the desk. "The house is yours too. You can move back in now if you wish. The police have released the crime scene."

"Wait. That sounded almost like you're accusing me, your own client, of killing Evelyn." Rupert was on his feet. "I need to know. Right now. Do you think I did it?"

"I have a theory." Billy walked around to face Rupert. "You say you loved Evelyn and I believe you. What I find hard to believe is that there was a hitman who tied you up. That you managed to get free but not in time to save your wife."

"I explained that." Rupert glared at Billy, his face red. "You son of a bitch. What kind of lawyer are you?"

"The kind who likes to have all the answers before I'll defend a client in court." Billy laid his hand on Rupert's shoulder. As usual, the man was in an expensive suit and looked like an ad in *GQ*. "If the woman I loved was in horrific pain and had nothing but more suffering ahead, I might be tempted to help her."

"Help? You mean end her life?" Rupert reared back. "You think I participated in a mercy killing? Because she was dying anyway?" Tears ran down his cheeks. "No! I wanted every day I could get with that woman. I knew how to ease her pain. I was her nurse, by God. I took care of her." He sank back into his chair.

"Had she asked you to help her die?" Billy stood there, waiting.

"I wouldn't listen to such talk and she knew it." He stared at the wall as if seeing his life with Evelyn. "And shoot her?" He looked back at Billy, his eyes very focused. "If I'd wanted to kill her, there were plenty of drugs in the house that would have provided a much kinder, gentler way for her to die than a fucking bullet." He grabbed Billy's hand and squeezed. "You've got to believe me."

"You know? I do." Billy held Rupert's hand then released it. "I finally do." He picked up a paper. "I think you took such good care of Evelyn that you wouldn't let her go. Even though she was ready to die."

"Shut the fuck up! What do you know about it?" Rupert jumped up, both fists on the desk. "Evelyn was a fighter. Okay, she said something to me. She was tired, that's all. I knew she wasn't serious, but I kept the pain meds locked away anyway. Just to be safe. Depression is to be expected in a terminal patient." He wiped away a tear. "Listen to me, Pagan. She'd never really give up, not if she was thinking straight. My Evie? Ready to die? No way in hell."

"Then how do you explain her cash withdrawal of fifty thousand dollars the week before her murder?" Billy handed the paper to Rupert. "Looks like a payoff to me. Unless you remember seeing 50K lying around somewhere."

Rupert stared at it. "What are you saying? That she hired her own hitman?"

"That's exactly what I'm saying. Now all we have to do is prove it." Billy sat behind his desk again. "But that's the problem. Tracing a cash transaction is a bitch. I have my man on it, but it's going to be tough to prove. We need evidence, Rupert. So you're going to have to think. How would Evelyn go about hiring a hitman? Where would she go? Who could she ask about it?"

"I can't imagine." Rupert looked stunned. But it was clear he was thinking. "Do you put an ad on Craigslist? How the fuck should I know?"

"She was your wife for almost ten years. Think about her habits and if there's anything she did in those last days that might help us figure this out." Billy sent a text to Albert. "We need to talk to your housekeeper. I know she's a hostile witness, but the key word here is witness. She knew Evelyn better than almost anyone. Maybe she can help us."

"Help me? I wouldn't count on it." Rupert pulled out his own phone. "But I'll give it a try. Maybe we can set up a meeting."

"That's a start. Let me know when it will be. I have to be there." Billy got up, ready to walk Rupert to the door.

"What else can I do?" He frowned at his phone. "I'll let you set that up. She won't answer my call. Thinks I'm a murderer."

"Okay, leave it to me. Give Mai the number." Billy squeezed Rupert's shoulder. "And prepare to be your own star witness. You just convinced me you loved Evelyn and would never hurt her. I want you to do the same to a jury if it comes to that."

* * * *

Shannon usually looked forward to the Ballet Ball all year long. With everything that had been going on, she realized she'd given it little thought this time. Yes, she'd arranged the large donation from the Calhoun Petroleum and Pagan Law Firm alliance that had helped sponsor the event, but the actual details had been left to a committee she had resigned from once she discovered the company was in trouble. Her friends had been shocked that she'd given up the chairmanship that was her right. She'd worked her way up to that senior position. But now that she had a day job, she'd realized devoting hours every week to a volunteer position just wasn't practical.

Of course, the real reason she'd dropped her committee memberships for all the charities and volunteer organizations she supported was that she knew once word of her father's double dealing came to light, she'd be asked to resign anyway. She'd seen it happen before when scandals broke. Shannon Calhoun, volunteer of the year, head of this committee, founder of that outreach program, would be whispered about, maybe pitied because her daddy had been a cheat and a liar.

Shannon looked longingly at the decanter of bourbon sitting on her dressing table. When had she gotten so dependent on the booze that she'd moved it in here? A bad sign. She refused to give in to the urge to splash some into a glass and ease this tension that was giving her the start of a headache.

Stop it. No one knew yet that Calhoun was on the brink of collapse. Letters had gone out to the injured parties, Billy called them, and they were going to work on settlements. As long as they could keep things quiet and the price of oil kept going up, why things might just come out all right. She should try to stay positive. Certainly her job tonight was to keep the Calhoun name shiny and bright.

So she and Billy would go to the ball. Dance. Yes, he'd said he could tango, hadn't he? Okay, then. They'd have fun. Act like sponsors who had the money and prestige to support the arts in Houston generously. It was one of her favorite causes. Time enough to worry about the company and the future later.

She dressed carefully in the dress her mother had sent her. Last year she'd had her personal hairdresser and a makeup artist come to the house the day of the ball. No way could she afford that now. So she did her hair and makeup herself. Looking in the mirror at the end of her huge closet, she had to admit she looked pretty damned good. Billy liked her hair down anyway and he'd have hated the airbrushed makeup guaranteed to last through a wind storm or crying jag. Not that she was anticipating either of those tonight.

She practically flew downstairs when Janie called and told her Billy was waiting. Sky high stilettos tonight, so when she walked into his arms, they were almost eye to eye.

"Wow. You are gorgeous." He pecked her on the cheek. "Guess I'd better not mess up your lipstick."

She picked up her jeweled clutch from the table in the entry. "Go ahead. I can fix it in the car." She raised her lips and pulled down his head. "You look pretty gorgeous yourself."

A wolf whistle broke them apart. Shannon laughed and faced her brother in the living room doorway.

"You clean up well." She approved of his tux. She couldn't remember that he'd ever worn one before.

"It's Dad's. I sneaked it out of his closet before you donated his things. Just fit." Ethan looked a little sheepish. "Was it stupid of me?"

"No, I think it was the right thing to do." She walked up to him and straightened his black satin bow tie.

"You two are getting an early start. We have a couple of hours yet before we have to be there." He held a glass of bourbon in his hand, and it was all Shannon could do not to snatch it and take a drink. First, he looked like Daddy and now he smelled like him too.

She shook her head, clearing it. No, her daddy might have sponsored the Ballet Ball, just for her, but she'd never seen him this young or, hmm, excited about going.

"Command performance. We're stopping at my grandmother's first. She wants to take pictures of us. To show to her friends," Billy answered when it became obvious Shannon wasn't going to.

"Yes, that's right." She took Billy's hand. "What about you? Need a ride? We can take you with us."

"No, I've got a date. I'll pick her up in a little while." He stared down at his drink, not meeting Shannon's eyes.

"Who is it? Do I know her?" His usual dates were women who would look good in a ball gown but had boob measurements bigger than their IQs.

"You'll meet her at the ball. We'll be sitting at the Calhoun table." He set down his drink. "Guess you two had better take off." He opened the front door. "Nice night anyway."

"A mystery lady." Shannon punched him on the arm as she grabbed her silk wrap then breezed past him. "Now I can't wait."

"Good luck, Ethan. This woman can be dangerous when she decides to focus her attention on you. I can vouch for that." Billy almost bumped into her when she stopped short at the sight of the limo waiting in front of the house. A chauffer jumped out to hold open the passenger door for them.

"What's this?" She gave him a raised eyebrow.

"We should arrive in style. We're sponsors after all." He grinned at her. "Stan is our chauffer this evening. We went to high school together. He actually owns a fleet of these. Stan, Shannon Calhoun."

Stan doffed his cap. "Good evening, Ms. Calhoun. Enjoy your evening."

"Thanks, Stan. I'm sure I will. I like your style, Mr. Pagan." She let the chauffer help her into the car, then scooted over so she could make room for Billy. Once the door was closed, she turned to him. "I see there's a divider that can give us total privacy." She ran a hand over Billy's smooth jaw. He'd had a recent and very close shave and smelled deliciously like something subtle and spicy. "After the ball, I can imagine a celebration here. What do you think? Will Stan be scandalized?"

"I bet Stan has seen everything. He's driving us tonight personally as a favor, right, Stan?" Billy looked at the driver who had just put the car in gear.

"I make it a policy to be deaf when I'm driving. Didn't hear a word you said, Billy." The privacy screen buzzed up, closing with a click.

"A good friend, I think." Shannon smiled.

"You just made this event worth my while, Ms. Calhoun. And here I'd been dreading it." He slid his hand over her bare shoulder. "I'd like for us to slip out of there as early as possible."

"Excellent idea." She leaned back as the driver put the car in motion. "Can you imagine the stir this limo will cause in your grandmother's neighborhood?"

"Yes, I can. So I told Stan to bring his handgun. He's ready for anything."

Shannon gripped Billy's leg. "You did not!"

Billy laughed and picked up her hand. "Relax, Shannon. We'll be fine. But, yes, I did."

Chapter 14

"I can't believe you had her committed." His grandmother was furious with him.

Billy tried to distract her. "Gran, look at Shannon. Isn't she beautiful?" He pulled her inside the house and slammed the burglar bars behind him.

"Yes, yes." Gran stopped fussing long enough to glance at Shannon. "Red. Now that's a color that looks good on you, girl. Much better than all that black you wear. High heels too. Shows off your legs through the slit in your long skirt. Very pretty."

"Thanks, Gran." Shannon looked uncomfortable. "Maybe I should wait in the car. If you two need to discuss something."

"No, stay put. I had to do it, Gran. It's part of the strategy to keep Sally out of jail. She was going to have to be on suicide watch anyway. Did you want that to be in the jail? How closely do you think they could watch her there? The place is notoriously overcrowded." Billy helped his grandmother into her recliner. Her lipstick was bitten off and she looked pale. There were dark circles under her eyes that some kind of white makeup hadn't been able to hide. Damn it, Gran looked older than she had even a few weeks ago. Sally and her drunk driving had done this. If it wouldn't kill his grandmother, he'd let his aunt rot in jail.

"They won't let me see her, Billy. She's locked in. Like a crazy person." Gran pulled out a wad of tissues and pressed them to her eyes. "I hate this!"

"I had no choice. I'm trying to get her help. You saw how depressed she was. She needed to be evaluated. I called it a strategy but I think—" Billy hated to say it, "Hell, she may really be sick. Might try to kill herself again. She's not thinking straight." Shannon's hand slipped into his and he held on.

"You're right. I saw it. She doesn't care about anything. Just lays there. Won't talk, eat, nothing." Gran wiped her eyes. "I have to trust you on this. You're trying. That's all I can ask." She pushed herself out of her chair. "Now let me look at you two. My, oh, my but you make a handsome couple." She picked up her phone. "Show me again, Billy, how to take a picture with this fancy thing."

"It's easy." Billy punched it on. "See? The icon that looks like a little camera? Touch it to turn it on. Then a button appears on the bottom. When you want to show your friends the picture, you just hit *photos* next to the camera icon."

"So complicated. What's wrong with using a real camera?" She aimed her phone at them, pressing it to her eye. "I can't see a dadgummed thing."

"Hold it out a little, Gran. Then you can see us." Billy tried not to laugh at her. "A real camera uses film and then you'd have to make a trip to the drugstore, get it developed. How long would that take? Now you'll have the picture instantly."

"All right. Let me try." She stabbed her phone with a fingernail. "You moved. Let me do it again."

"Maybe you shouldn't hit it so hard, Gran." Shannon bit her lip, also holding back a laugh. "And warn us when you're going to take it. So we can pose, put on our best smiles." She slipped her arm around Billy's waist. "Can we stand somewhere else? I don't like those bars behind me. Like I'm in jail."

"Oh, child." Gran's voice quavered. "Yes, move. In front of the drapes." She waved them over. "That's better. If I ever get to see Sally, I'll want to show her. Not with you looking like jailbirds either." She aimed the phone, gently poking the glass several times. "Billy, come show me what I've got now. If the pictures took."

"They took. But they might be blurry." He stood behind her. "Hey, these are all right. I'm sending them to my phone. I'll get Mai to make some prints for you. You'd like that, wouldn't you?"

"Yes!" Gran smiled when he scrolled through the photos with her. "Shannon, come see. You two look so pretty. A perfect couple."

Shannon looked over her shoulder. "I'd like a copy too, Billy." She smiled up at him. "I'll put one on my desk at the office."

"Consider it done." He put his phone away. "We'd better go." He kissed Gran on the cheek. "I'll let you know how things move along with Sally. She has to stay in the hospital for a while. She'll see a psychiatrist, maybe be put on some medication, whatever they recommend. If we're lucky, it'll be enough to convince a judge that rehab is a better option than jail. At the least, she'll have time to heal, in mind and body."

"It's just so hard." Gran followed them to the door. "But I know we have no choice." She managed a smile when she saw the limo. "Look at that. Showing off for your girl, Billy?" She stepped out on the porch. "You young'uns move along now. Scoot!" She waved her hands at the group of teens who'd gathered around the front of the car.

Billy saw Stan talking to them, apparently not bothered by the crowd of boys and girls who waved at Gran. The boys bowed and tipped their ball caps before they all strolled back toward their usual corner.

"You've got them trained." Billy gave her a hug. Damn it, she felt fragile, bony.

"I told you. I feel sorry for them. A couple of them used to live in those apartments down the street. Some developer bought them and the warehouse next door. Evicted every family. Now they're either homeless or doubling up in the rent houses while they try to find something else." She shook her head. "I slip them cookies and a few dollars now and then."

"Gran, that's not a good idea." Billy frowned as an expensive black SUV drove slowly down the street. The tinted windows kept whoever was inside hidden, but it had all the trappings—fancy hubcaps, sound system that vibrated the pavement—that the kids on the corner admired. It wasn't the first of its type he'd seen in the neighborhood. The teens tried to get it to stop, waving and shouting at it, but it turned the corner and sped away. That was a relief at least. Drug dealer? Pimp? Or just a local kid who'd made good? Any of those was a possibility.

"Leave me alone, Billy. I'll do what I please. You two run along." She waved them away this time. "I guess there will be dancing. A ball, you said."

"Yes, Gran. Billy's a good dancer." Shannon held onto his arm.

"He is. Runs in the family. His granddad could cut quite a rug. We loved to go out on a Saturday night." She looked wistful. "Big band music. That was our favorite. Can't find it anymore. No partner anyway with his grandpa gone."

"So what are you going to do tonight, Gran?" Billy felt guilty, leaving her alone in this sketchy neighborhood.

"Don't worry about me. Fran is coming over, bringing a pot of her famous spaghetti and a couple of DVDs. Girls' night." Gran shook her head. "Didn't I say run along?" She stepped back inside the house and locked the burglar bars. "Have fun. Make him dance every dance, Shannon."

"I will." She pulled him down the steps. "We're going to be late if we don't get moving. There's the dinner first and they'll put us at a table near the front. The chairman should invite us to the podium to say a few words. Don't worry, I'll handle it. You can just stand and be acknowledged as a sponsor."

"I'm sure you will handle it. Rubber chicken, I guess." He thanked

Stan when he held the door for them to get in the limo. "Kids bother you?"

"Naw. I remember what it was like growing up here. They're bored. Need something to do and a way to make money that's legal. I told them to get back in school. Not that they'll listen to a geezer like me." Stan laughed. He and Billy were the same age. "You know how it is. When you're sixteen, you know everything."

"Yeah. Until some shithead comes along and proves that you don't." He and Stan bumped fists before the driver slammed the door shut. "This area needs a community center, someplace for those kids to hang out. Outreach and job training too." He turned to Shannon. "Maybe we can work on that together."

Her eyes lit up. "I'd love that."

Billy sat back and listened to her talk. She'd worked for years as a volunteer helping others and was full of ideas on how to provide options for these kids and the neighborhood. Maybe that developer would consider donating a unit that could be turned into a rec room for the cause. He'd get Albert on it. Find out who'd purchased the property. Convince them that helping the community could be a win-win, improving the area along with property values and maybe get a tax write-off.

Shannon had a good heart. It was great to see more evidence of that. Instead of worrying about Gran in this place, he should start doing something to make it better. They pulled out from the curb and Billy asked Stan to stop next to the kids. He ran down his window.

"Hey, thanks for looking out for my grandmother."

One of the boys, the obvious leader, hitched up his jeans and walked over. "She's cool."

"Yeah, she is. My man Stan says you guys might be looking for work."

"Oh, yeah? Well, he be wrong." The kid sniffed. "We got plenty to do. Right here."

"Oh, I get it. Neighborhood Watch." Billy pulled out his card. "Well, I know things can change. So if you decide you want to do something that pays a little better, call me. I might be able to hook you up."

"What are you? Some kind of do-gooder?" The kid leaned in. "A rich one for sure. Pretty lady wid ya."

"Yes, she is. She likes to help people. So maybe I want to do some good." Billy smiled. "Makes me look good to *her*, know what I mean?"

The kid cackled. "Hell, yeah." He glanced back at one of the girls who wore shorts so tiny they should have been illegal. "I sure do." He glanced down at the card. "If you're throwin' money around, maybe I'll check this out."

"You do that." Billy felt Shannon's tug on his sleeve. "Got to go. Keep those eyes open, Watchman." He pressed a large bill into the boy's hand. "Call me if anyone hassles my grandma. Got it?"

"Uh-huh. We'll be on the job, rich guy."

The last thing Billy saw as he buzzed up the window was the tip of the boy's cap.

"Neighborhood Watch?" Shannon smiled at him.

"Hey, it's a start. Can't hurt to have them on my side." Billy frowned. "I didn't like the looks of that SUV that drove past. Did you notice it?"

"No." She'd pulled out her lipstick and compact. "I'm thinking about the ball. This will be our first public outing as a couple. Will you mind if we get publicity? The gossip columnist for the newspaper will link us, take a picture."

"Great. I want to put the other men in town on notice." He slung his arm around her shoulders. "Shannon Calhoun is mine." He laughed when she pursed her lips. But he couldn't help himself. He glanced back. Was that the same black SUV behind them? Stan merged them into the downtown traffic. Now there were so many cars, so many dark SUVs for that matter, he couldn't tell. Maybe he was getting paranoid. Like those crazy Exiles. But he was glad he'd put the word out to watch Gran. He just hoped those kids took him seriously and called before anything went down.

* * * *

Shannon remembered why she'd looked forward to the ball as soon as they walked into the enormous ballroom in the luxurious downtown hotel. The committee had outdone itself with the decorations. This year's theme was taken from one of the ballet's most popular offerings, *Swan Lake*. The ballroom had been turned into a pink, silver, and white fairyland. There were swans everywhere. Table decorations were white and silver with mirrored "lakes" and miniature swans floating across them. Some members of the ballet corps wore their feathered costumes and directed guests toward the silent auction items along one wall. The ball was obviously a sellout, judging by the size of the crowd.

Before dinner was served, a popular band played. Shannon and Billy went straight to the dance floor. They fit together so perfectly that she couldn't resist letting him hold her too close. They swayed to the music, moving as one. Their relationship was certainly out in the open now. Anyone who saw them dancing like that would be able to tell they were more than lawyer and client. She was glad. In her own way, she was claiming Billy Pagan.

Dinner was accompanied by full wine glasses. No rubber chicken for this well-heeled crowd. Not when tables cost five figures. Tender medallions of beef, roasted vegetables, and a chocolate soufflé were delicious. A hovering waiter was eager to keep the wine flowing, but Shannon just sipped and shook her head when offered a refill even though it was a decent red. She was having a wonderful time and didn't need the buzz.

Ethan and his date sat on one side of them. When Shannon found out that the beautiful woman was his boss at Calhoun, she was tempted to razz him about it. But it was a relief to see her little brother with an intelligent woman for a change. Didn't matter that Amanda was almost Shannon's age. Ethan could use the steadying influence.

Mason and Cassidy were on their other side. They'd arrived just as dinner was served and were full of plans. The Christmas Eve wedding was going on, despite some pushback from the church where Mason's family had been members for decades. They had to work around holiday services. Shannon liked how the two glowed with happiness. When Billy's hand reached for hers, she turned to look at him. Was he wondering if she was ready for something like that? A dream wedding? She touched his lip, wiping away a bit of chocolate, and he smiled. Her breath caught. There was nothing she wanted more at this moment than to spend the rest of her life with him.

The clang of spoons hitting water glasses broke the spell. The chairwoman of the event, Mindy Foster, glowing in a vivid pink and silver designer gown, stood at the head table. She paused dramatically to scan the room before thanking the crowd for their generosity. She reminded them to hit the silent auction while the band played again after dinner for their dancing pleasure. Then she focused on the Calhoun table.

"Underwriting the expenses of the evening allows us to support the arts even more generously. When the price of oil dropped, we were worried we'd lose our sponsors, but, here they are again, dipping into their wallets for the cause. How about some applause for the Calhoun family from Calhoun Petroleum and their new friend, attorney William P. Pagan? Thanks to them, we can truthfully say that every dollar we raise here tonight will go to the programs the ballet will be putting on in the coming year. Isn't that wonderful?" Mindy waved toward their table.

Shannon and Billy, along with Ethan and Cassidy, stood to wild applause and waved to the crowd. Then Mindy invited everyone to enjoy the dancing as the band began to play.

Wait. What? Where was the invitation to speak to the crowd? Shannon had prepared remarks and had been ready to drag Billy toward the podium. But it was clear that was all they were getting. That wave. At the very least there should have been a gracious speech about the many good works Calhoun Petroleum did for the city of Houston. And, damn it, accolades for Billy as the leading criminal lawyer in Houston.

Shannon couldn't believe Mindy had let her personal feelings influence the way she'd handled their sponsorship. But then why should she be surprised? Mindy had taken what used to be a close friendship and decided Shannon was her bitter enemy years ago. Their rivalry went back to their days as young debutantes, both eager to lead the pack in Houston society. When Shannon had resigned from the chairmanship, she was sure Mindy had felt like she'd won the volunteer lottery as she'd stepped in to take charge of the ball. Well, she'd done a great job, no surprise there. Mindy was a ruthless perfectionist, everyone who'd ever worked with her knew that.

As soon as the band started again and everyone left the dinner tables to dance or hit the silent auction, she saw Mindy, flushed with success, accepting congratulations on what had proved to be a wonderful evening. If she got the chance, she would compliment Mindy too.

"So no speech after all." Billy smiled as he led her toward the silent auction items.

"No." Shannon wasn't about to whine about it. But she might let Mindy know what she thought if she got the chance.

"What do you think?" Billy was eyeing the offerings at the auction table. "A guided hiking trip up Machu Picchu? Or a luxury cruise on a private yacht in the Mediterranean?"

"What?" Shannon watched him sign his name on one of the bid sheets.

"For a honeymoon." He grinned when her mouth dropped open.

"If that was a proposal, I think you'd better try again, Pagan. In a much more romantic setting than a crowded ballroom with, oh, about nine hundred people around us. And it had better not have been the hike you bid on. My feet still hurt from the last one." She stumbled when someone bumped into her on their way to check a bid sheet. Billy caught her and pulled her close.

"I'll take that as a yes." He kissed her, breaking it off when she gave him a gentle shove.

"There you are. A little late, weren't you? I noticed that you didn't arrive until cocktail hour was almost over. I was shocked, Shannon. That was always your favorite part of any party." Mindy Foster stared down at the sheet on the table. "Goodness. You must really want that cruise, Mr. Pagan."

"Billy." He held out his hand. "Mrs. Foster. I hear you organized this shindig. Everything looks great. Makes me proud to be a co-sponsor with Calhoun Petroleum."

"Why, thank you." She smiled and looked pointedly to where he still had his arms around Shannon. "Are you two an item? Is this co-sponsor thing more than just a business arrangement?"

"The room looks beautiful, Mindy. Good job." Shannon put a few inches between herself and Billy. "Yes, Billy and I are dating. But Billy decided to be generous to the ballet and some other good causes Calhoun supports because he believes in them too. It would have been nice to have the opportunity to tell the crowd that."

"You know no one wants to hear boring speeches after dinner, Shannon." Mindy scanned the room. "Besides, starting tomorrow everyone will know why Calhoun Petroleum hired a *criminal* attorney to represent it."

"What do you mean?" Shannon didn't like Mindy's smirk.

"I'll tell you in a minute." Mindy waved an elegant hand at a man across the room. "I bet you know my date, Billy. Rand Pierce? Of Phester, Meinie, and Pierce. Top oil and gas attorneys in the state." She smiled. "Oh, good. He's coming over." She smoothed her low-cut bodice, the silver beading sparkling under the lights. "Too bad you dropped off the committee, Shannon. Did you notice? We're all wearing shades of pink tonight. So pretty with the theme. Your red? Unfortunate."

"Shannon looks beautiful in red. And of course, I know Rand." Billy wore his alligator smile. "The fact that I'm a criminal lawyer is immaterial. I represent Calhoun because I'm a friend of the family."

"Yes, I guess you'd like to spin it that way. Though clearly you and Shannon are *very* friendly." Mindy couldn't quit smiling. "But when my housekeeper showed me a letter she got from Calhoun Petroleum, I realized there was something going on at Calhoun that no one had suspected."

Shannon felt her breath freeze in her lungs. "Oh?"

"You know, I've been running Jake's business since he died. That's R & F Pipeline, Billy. Oil and Gas is not new to me." She shook a finger. "So when I saw that letter, I could tell there was something peculiar about this situation with the mineral rights. I took Edith to Rand right away. He did some investigating." She reached out and pulled a tall man to her side. "Here he is. I'll let him tell you."

"Billy, how's it going?" Rand was clearly comfortable in his tux, handsome and smiling as he extended his hand to Billy. He wore his blond hair short and had the tanned and toned look of a man who probably played a lot of outdoor tennis or golf.

"Pretty well, I thought. Do you know Shannon Calhoun?" Billy shook hands with him.

"A pleasure, ma'am." He took Shannon's hand in his and squeezed it gently.

Billy pulled Shannon close again. "Mrs. Foster suggested you had something to tell us. About a letter from Calhoun?"

"Now, Mindy, that isn't a subject we need to get into at this kind of event. Billy and I can make an appointment. Sit down in my office." Rand graced Shannon with a dazzling smile. Obviously, he'd had his teeth whitened recently. "Ms. Calhoun is paying him to take such worries off her pretty shoulders."

"Don't be silly, Rand. Shannon is tough enough to handle the bad news." Mindy was obviously eager to be the bearer. "Starting tomorrow Rand's law firm is running an ad. On TV. We've already found out that Edith isn't the only one who got a letter. She's from a little town south of Houston. Some of her mother's neighbors got the same letter. A half dozen so far that she knows of. Can you believe it?" She shook her head. "But of course you do. I'm sure you have a list."

"Don't suppose you'd share that with me, Billy." Rand laughed. "Unless I had a court order, right?" He quit smiling. "Don't worry. It's in the works."

"It's only right that all the people who got that letter should get together. File suit for compensation and such. Thirty years' worth." Mindy fanned her face with her hand then rested her fingertips on Shannon's arm. Anyone watching would think she was being kind. But her eyes told another story. "Can you imagine how the damages would add up over time?"

"Seriously, Rand? You're using the media? Like one of those ambulance chasers?" Billy was clearly not pleased.

"Don't jump on your high horse with me, Pagan. Our junior associates have been hip-deep in research. Clearly Conrad Calhoun pulled a fast one on Edith Perry and her neighbors. Didn't take long for me to realize this was when Calhoun was just getting started. There must be dozens, maybe hundreds of people who are owed what will probably be millions for the crimes he committed back then." Rand shook his head. "Sorry, Ms. Calhoun, but facts are facts."

Shannon felt the warning squeeze of Billy's hand on hers. He was clearly signaling her to keep quiet. God, but she wanted to wipe that self-satisfied smirk off Mindy's face. But what could she say? She stood there while Billy handed Rand his card and told the lawyer to call and make an appointment with *him*. She guessed that was a sort of victory. Make Rand come to them, not the other way around.

"I'll wait a while on an appointment, Billy. Have to see how many people respond to the TV ad. I'm seeing a class action suit here." Rand smiled. "Mindy, I think they're playing our song." He steered Mindy away but not before the woman hissed in Shannon's ear.

"How's it feel, girlfriend? You told everyone at our come-out that I had to show up with my cousin Mike 'cause I couldn't get a date." She sniffed in Billy's direction. "Humiliation's a bitch, but payback? Sweet."

Shannon just stood there. Payback? She'd never told anyone anything about Mindy. It had been Mike himself who'd let drop that he'd been called by Mindy's doting parents. After that ball, Mindy had gotten a nose job and her boobs enhanced to a double D. Then she'd started her campaign to marry the richest single man in town. She'd gotten her man—Jake Foster, owner of R & F Pipeline. He'd been decades older and something of a bore, but Mindy had walked down the aisle like a conquering hero. Rumor had it that both her kids had her unfortunate nose. Talk about payback.

"You ready to get out of here?" Billy hadn't let go of her arm since Mindy's attack. Yes, that was what Shannon was calling it.

"Please." She waited while he called Stan to bring the limo around. "Put your phone number next to your bid on the cruise. Sounds like a perfect honeymoon. They'll call you if you're the winning bidder."

He whooped, turning heads. "I'll definitely take that as a yes." He gave her a kiss to seal the deal.

Shannon leaned into it, not caring that they were garnering attention. She loved him. He was going to do whatever he could to help them save Calhoun. And if they couldn't save it? A life with the man she loved was not a bad thing to look forward to. When she pulled back, she heard a smattering of applause. A couple of her friends raised champagne glasses in a mock toast. Yep, it was pretty clear she was in love and making some kind of commitment. She smiled and nodded, happy to leave the ball and get into the limo as soon as Stan texted he was outside at the curb.

The privacy screen was still firmly in place. "I believe, Mr. Pagan, that we have something to celebrate."

"You sure? That woman seemed determined to bring your family's company down." Billy studied her with concern.

Shannon reached for the zipper on Billy's tux pants. "Let her try. I have you on my side." She smiled when she found him ready and willing. "Now relax and enjoy the ride." With that she leaned over and showed him how much she loved him. His groan of pleasure was all she needed to make her realize she'd meant every word. No matter what happened with the company, it was just that—a company. And her father was dead. He couldn't be hurt anymore. Or hurt anyone else.

Billy wouldn't just let her please *him*. He slid his hands under her long dress and found that she'd left her underwear at home. It would have ruined the lines of the clingy dress.

"Woman, what are you doing going out in public like this?" He laid her back on the seat and let his fingers drift over her with his usual expert touch. "Am I going to have to check you before we leave the house from now on?"

"Maybe." Shannon smiled up at him. "That feels good." When he leaned down and pushed aside her bodice to take a nipple into his mouth, she sighed. "That too."

"I'm figuring out what you like." His thumb found that special spot inside her and she jerked. "Yeah, there I think."

"God, yes." She grabbed his hair. "You could press a little harder. Even bite me if you felt the urge." He didn't hesitate and she hit the seat to keep from screaming her pleasure.

He looked up and grinned. "I like it when you give me directions. Anything else?"

"We don't have that far to go. So give it to me, big boy. Now. Fast and hard." She raised her hips so he could push her dress up and out of the way. When he was inside her, she held onto him, digging her fingernails into his shirt under his jacket. A quickie. Ridiculous. Yet he could still make her lose her mind. Her heart? Long gone.

He leaned down to kiss her, pounding into her while he cradled her head, apparently afraid she'd bump it into the door handle. Caring, always thinking of her. Shannon's last thought before she couldn't think at all was that she couldn't marry him in the middle of a scandal. It would taint everything. He deserved a wonderful church wedding with his grandmother proudly showing him and his bride off to her friends.

Oh, Billy. I should let you go. Instead, she held tighter. He was hers, damn it. Forever.

Chapter 15

"Family meeting in my office. Now."

Shannon hung up the phone and got to her feet. Monday morning. No surprise that Cassidy wanted to meet. The ad had been running all weekend but she'd refused to watch it. Billy had, of course, and cursed when he'd seen it. A quick check told him it was appearing all over the state. She felt sure that Rand Pierce's law firm had received dozens of calls already.

Ambulance chaser. That's what Billy had called him. If only they could brush this off as a nuisance. A powerful firm had taken the case against Calhoun Petroleum. Billy was a one-man office. Had they made a mistake letting him handle this? Was she disloyal for even thinking that?

She stopped at the office down the hall. "I have to meet with Cassidy. I don't know when I'll be back."

Caroline Wilson dropped her reading glasses onto her desk. "Go. But good job on the Ballet Ball sponsorship. Nice article in the *Chronicle* about you and Pagan. Made the company look generous, community-minded."

"I saw it. Considering we got hardly any recognition from the podium, thanks to Mindy Foster, it came out well." There had also been a nice photo in the lifestyle section.

"Take care of your family business." Caroline waved her away and put her glasses back on. "Oh, Shannon?" She looked over the top of the stylish tortoise rims. "I hope while you're up there you figure out some kind of statement to give the press about that TV ad running this weekend. Your sister's 'No comment' coming into the building won't cut it."

Shannon leaned against the desk. "She was ambushed?"

"Of course. And my phone's been ringing off the hook. I had any calls from the press diverted to me. We need a formal statement from the family." She looked grim. "I don't know what's going on. Maybe I don't want to know. I've had stock options over the years and used them. So I have a lot invested in this company." She picked up her smart phone. "They've lost too much value just this morning. Please tell your family that we, the stockholders, need some kind of reassurance that this is a greedy lawyer going after a big corporation and it's being handled. No need to panic." She set the phone down gently. "If it's not? Heaven help us all."

"Amen to that." Shannon sighed. She and Caroline would obviously never be drinking buddies, but she'd like to tell her the truth. And start a sell-off? Couldn't do it. She just shook her head, already trying to compose something that would appease the fact-hungry media.

She rode the elevator up to Cassidy's floor and stepped out into another world. No cubes here. These were the executive suites where the power players reigned. Cass now occupied Daddy's old office. It was a corner with a view of Houston stretching out toward the southwest. No oil derricks in sight, of course. But there was the bayou meandering through Memorial Park and a cluster of high rises near the Galleria shopping mall where the rich and famous loved to drop big bucks. A traffic snarl on one of the many freeways looked bad, even from up here. Cass wasn't noticing. She leaned forward as she stood behind her huge desk, Daddy's marble-topped import from Italy, and talked seriously to the three men in front of her.

"We've got to figure out a way to get ahead of this, Dylan. If we can get a judge to put a cap on the payouts, that'll save us." She waved Shannon in. "We need you."

"To come up with a statement to the press." Shannon had thought to pick up her laptop, and she settled on the couch and opened it. "Tell me what we can safely say and I'll try to spin it for us."

"My woman." Billy sat next to her and kissed her cheek. "You read our minds."

"It wasn't hard. Plus, my boss said Cass had to fight her way through the press this morning. I parked in the garage and missed that."

"Mason dropped me at the front door. Big mistake." Cass walked around her desk and put her arm around her fiancé. "I forgive him but I'm going to have to start driving my own car again and go straight into the parking garage where there's security."

"All right. I give in." He rubbed her shoulders. "Dylan, what do you think? Can we get this in front of a judge?"

"Hi, Shannon." His brother Dylan nodded. "It's a solid idea. If they're really going to make this a class action suit, we need to see if there's a way to get ahead of it. Show that we've put a settlement fund together. Cass has been working to give us a figure, Billy. Here comes Ethan. He should have a better idea of what we need at a minimum."

Ethan came through the door with his own laptop under his arm. "Looks like a wake. For good reason. Have you seen that ad?" When Shannon and Cass shook their heads, he set his computer on Cassidy's desk and opened it. "Take a look."

"Mineral rights to your property can be worth thousands, even millions of dollars. Big oil knows this and has even gone so far as to steal those rights from unsuspecting land owners. If you or a family member has received a letter recently from Calhoun Petroleum about mineral rights for land you own or have sold in the last thirty years, you could be eligible for compensation. Call—-" Ethan hit the pause button. "You get the drift. The pictures of the granny knitting on her front porch with pumping wells in the background was a nice touch. Did you notice the peeling paint and sagging shutters? They know how to get the public stirred up. Big bad oil cheating little old ladies."

"And they wouldn't be lying." Cass's words hung in the silent room before Mason cleared his throat.

"Baby, you didn't know him. Stop feeling guilty." He kept his arm around her and swept the room with his bright blue eyes. "None of you had any part in making this mess."

"I don't feel guilty personally. But we need to make this right." Cass looked at Shannon, then Ethan.

"We're with you, Cassidy." Shannon had cried herself to sleep when she'd first learned what her parents had done.

"Cass, we can't fix what Daddy did, but we want to help you show our family's remorse." Ethan shook his head. "To most people, that means more than an apology. They want to hit us where it hurts. In the pocketbook."

"Thanks. I know it's going to cost you all most of your inheritance. When I met you, I didn't know what to expect." She gave each of them a tremulous smile. "It wasn't to be welcomed into such a great family."

Shannon jumped up and hugged Cassidy. Of course, her new half-sister might be having doubts about them. She and Ethan had lived under Conrad's influence. All Cass knew about her father was that he'd disappeared before she was born and signed away his parental rights. Her mother had blackmailed him with the proof of his double dealing. As a thirtieth birthday present, Elizabeth Calhoun, Cassidy's mother, had made sure Cass found out the bitter truth. Now they were having to deal with the fall out.

Shannon let Cass go and looked into her eyes. "Hey, Mason's right. If this company goes under, then that's what was meant to be. No one is going to blame you, Cass. No one."

Cass swiped at a tear. Sunlight sparkled off her diamond engagement ring. No matter what, she'd come out all right married to Mason MacKenzie, CEO of Texas Star. They'd have a good life and she'd be happy with the man she loved. Shannon patted her shoulder and sat down.

"Thanks, Shannon. You know it still feels strange to sit here in Conrad Calhoun's office and call the shots. Now I've got all this power. Budget in the billions. Controlling the lives of thousands of workers." Cass put a hand to her forehead. "Surreal."

"You've been doing great." Mason took her elbow and eased her into a chair in front of the desk. "Jumped right into a job without any background in oil. You're amazing."

"Thanks, but you're not exactly objective." She gave him a weak smile and squeezed his hand. "That ad." She straightened. "It said some might be owed millions. Is that true, Ethan? Are any of those people going to be entitled to that much?"

"It's been damned complicated." Ethan walked around and sat in the leather chair behind her desk to work his computer. "Here's the thing. Some wells never paid off. Others went dry or were shut down when they started petering out. Then there are the lucrative fields, with wells still pumping today." He looked up and frowned. "Just wait till Megan and Rowdy get here. Rowdy's family had a field that should have set them up for life. Daddy had Rowdy's grandmother sign away their rights completely without any royalties coming to them."

Cassidy's pained cry echoed in the room. "She had Alzheimer's, Ethan." Her hands were shaking as she looked at her sister and brother. "How could he do that?"

Shannon leaned against Billy, tears in her eyes. "The Daddy I knew? I can't imagine."

"Baby, are you okay?" Billy held her tight, his warm comfort seeping into her. "You are not your parents. You know that, don't you? None of you are." He looked at each one of them. "I've defended people who grew up hard. With parents who were little more than animals. But those men and women were innocent, I made sure of that before I took their cases. Just because you come from a rotten tree doesn't mean the fruit is spoiled." He rubbed Shannon's arm, a habit of his when he wanted to comfort her.

"We're fruit, seriously?" Shannon fought what was probably hysteria.

"Okay, blame that on courtroom rhetoric." He rubbed her cheek where a tear must have escaped. "Your father managed to keep his past from you. He was damned clever."

"Billy's right. Stop beating yourselves up about what Conrad and, yes,

Missy, did back then. They covered their tracks well once they made their millions." Mason had Cass in his arms and looked into her eyes. "Cass, even your mother isn't blameless, keeping this shit a secret. All these folks could have gotten justice a long time ago if Elizabeth had stepped up."

"I know that." She blinked, like she was doing all she could not to cry on his shoulder.

Mason glanced back at Ethan. "I'm proud of all of you. This could have been swept under the rug. You didn't do that."

"Because, despite the sociopaths who raised us, we developed a conscience." Ethan laughed but it was strained.

Shannon figured her little brother might be fighting tears too. This mess might have been hardest on him. He'd trailed their daddy around as a kid, desperate for his approval. Conrad hadn't given it. He'd wanted his only son to get his head out of his computers and "get his hands dirty." When he'd tried and failed at things Conrad considered important, Ethan had started doing stupid stunts to get their father's attention. She wanted to get up and give Ethan a hug but was afraid that would make him lose his cool.

Ethan hit a button. "About Rowdy. His family is one that's owed millions. Can you imagine how those oil royalties would have changed his life?"

"You have no idea." Cass was pale but quickly pulled herself together. "So bottom line for all of the claims?"

Ethan nodded. "We're looking at ninety to a hundred million for our total liability. That's still an estimate."

Dylan had walked over to look over his shoulder. "In actual damages."

Ethan stared at Cass. "Can we get that kind of money together?"

"Sell off the pipeline division and we have that covered. I've got a buyer in mind." She stepped away from Mason and looked encouraged.

"If that was all we were looking at, I'd say you're in good shape." Billy scanned the room. "Dylan and I have been talking. I brought him on board, Shannon, because the MacKenzie firm specializes in oil and gas. He can talk their language when we meet with Rand Pierce."

"That's fine, Billy. I knew our problem was outside your comfort zone." She smiled at him. She could tell he was disappointed that he couldn't ride to her rescue all by himself. "But what do you mean, if that was all we were looking at?"

"Punitive damages, Shannon." Dylan sat on the couch with them. "Of course these people are owed something for the deception. We'll have to wait and see what Rand uses as his arguments, but I fully expect him to ask for a hell of a lot of money in punitive, even for those with dry wells. A judge will be happy to award it. Big companies like Calhoun are favorite targets, crowd pleasers, when it comes to making us pay."

Billy nodded. "He's right. We really don't want to get this in front of a jury. That ad they're running is already poisoning a potential jury pool. The best thing would be to settle this well before it gets to court. Dylan and I will jump on this. Ethan, you and Cassidy need to come up with a figure you can live with. One that leaves this family with something to keep the company going after all is said and done. There are a lot of people who work here who hope for the same thing, not to mention the stockholders."

"Punitive damages. Of course. When I think of how just Rowdy's life was affected... Not that money can make things right." Cass ran a hand over her eyes.

"Of course you feel bad for Rowdy, but you can't get hung up on each individual case." Mason kept his arm around her. "The best way to help these people, Cass, is to do what you do best—deal with the numbers. Squeeze out as much as you can for them."

Mason must have said what she needed to hear because Cass straightened her shoulders then walked over to look out the window. "Okay, so we've got that new field in West Texas. It's going to bring in plenty once we get it going. The price of oil is up. Of course, the expense of getting that field started is going to be horrendous. Even with Texas Star partnering on it." Cass sighed and faced the room again. "Give me some time. I can sell equipment but that's small change when we're talking millions."

"No bank is going to loan you money to work that West Texas field either, Cass. Not with this lawsuit hanging over your head." Mason stayed close. "I have to answer to my own stockholders. If you can't hold up your end, I'll have to pull Texas Star out of our partnership on West Texas."

Cass took his hand. "I understand."

Shannon glanced down at her computer and the cursor mocking her.

"Hey, Caroline Wilson said our stock is tanking. So I guess we don't dare raise money by selling some of our own." Shannon got five shocked stares. "Oh, knock off the death rays. I know better. That would really make the price go down. So help me figure out something reassuring to tell the press. Can we call Pierce a liar?"

"I've been telling people who've called that the letters were part of an internal audit. That we fully intend to make things right. Calhoun Petroleum has always stood for, um," Cass looked around the room. "Come on, people, you know I'm late to this party. What in the heck does Calhoun stand for?"

"Right now? Making money no matter what it takes." The voice from the doorway had them all turning toward it. The door had been closed. None of them had heard it open, they'd been so focused on figuring out what to do.

"Megan! And Rowdy!" Cass jumped to her feet. "I knew you were coming but didn't think you'd get here today."

"We finished out west and landed in Houston last night. No reason to waste time. Janie told us about the TV ad running this weekend. We figured we'd better come see if we could help." Megan looked tanned and content despite the serious situation in the office. The way she clung to Rowdy's hand, it was clear that more than inspecting oil rigs had gone on in West Texas.

Shannon ran to hug her. "Welcome back, sis! I'm glad you survived the field. Hey, Rowdy. We were just talking about you."

"Not surprised. My mother got one of those letters from Calhoun." He never let go of Megan's hand. "I hope like hell the plan is to compensate every one of the people cheated by Conrad Calhoun."

"Rowdy, please. That's my daddy you're talking about." Megan looked distressed. "I'm sure that's exactly what they plan to do."

"Yes, of course. You must be Rowdy Baker. Please sit down. I'm Dylan MacKenzie, one of the lawyers handling this mess." Dylan held out his hand and offered a chair. "I think you know everyone else here. Billy Pagan and I are going to see to it that the settlements will be fair." He glanced at Billy. When Rowdy did reluctantly shake Dylan's hand, Dylan visibly relaxed.

"Rowdy, I know you're pissed. Can't blame you. I have no idea how this affected your family personally, but there's no doubt that what happened back then was wrong. We're not hiding it or denying it." Billy was on his feet, taking his turn to shake Rowdy's hand and give Megan a hug like the friend of the family that he was.

"That's good." Rowdy took the chair Dylan indicated, making sure Megan had one right next to him.

Billy paced in front of Rowdy like he was addressing a jury in the courtroom. "You seem to have gotten to know Megan pretty well. The family is trying like hell to make things right. What we're asking now is that you and all those taken advantage of by Conrad Calhoun have a little patience. Let us run the numbers and see what we can do for you. You work in the oil industry so I'm sure you can imagine that figuring out the damages is complicated."

"Complicated, but not impossible." Rowdy scanned the room as if looking for someone to blame. He saw Ethan at his computer. "I'm sure there are records you can access. Even from thirty years ago."

"Yes. It's all computerized now, Rowdy. I've been working on it." Ethan didn't get up. "You and my sister look tight. Do I need to whip your ass?"

"You could try. But I wouldn't advise it." Rowdy smiled for the first time since he'd come into the room.

"Stop it. You don't need to protect me, Ethan. Rowdy's naturally worried about what's been going on here at headquarters. Not for himself, but for his mother." Megan pulled her chair closer to Rowdy and wouldn't let go of his hand.

"I read the papers. Another oil services company declared bankruptcy just this morning to get out from under their debt." Rowdy leaned forward and looked at Billy who still stood in front of him.

Megan spoke up. "We swore we would never declare bankruptcy."

"Bankruptcy is not on the table." Billy glanced at Cass. "I've not heard that word in this room yet and that's the God's honest truth."

"All right then. That's what I wanted to hear." Rowdy relaxed and focused on Cass. "Congratulations, I hear you and Mason set a date."

"Christmas Eve." She walked over to him. "Maybe we should put it off. With this mess going on at the company, it seems wrong to celebrate anything right now."

Mason put a proprietary hand on her shoulder. "We're not putting it off, Cass. Court cases can drag on for years. Billy and Dylan can tell you that. The church is booked. We're doing this."

Rowdy set Megan's hand in his lap, staking his own claim. "He's right, Cass. When you find the one person you know is it for you, don't waste time. I know now what it feels like with the right woman. So I wish you and Mason luck." He turned to Megan and kissed her.

Shannon sighed. It was good to see Megan with a man so ready to stake his claim like that. Rowdy was kissing her like he couldn't get enough. Wow.

He finally let Megan go and smiled with satisfaction. "We'll be at your wedding. Right, sweetheart?"

Megan flushed but didn't deny it. "Gee, put it right out there, Rowdy."

"No reason not to." He nodded at Mason then made eye contact with Cassidy. "You're the numbers expert, Cass. So where do we stand with this company? Is there going to be anything left once you pay all the claims that will be coming in?"

"That's what I'm trying to figure out." Cass headed back to her desk. If Rowdy's declaration about his relationship with Megan had bothered her, she didn't show it. She gestured and Ethan cleared his things off her desk and settled into a chair next to Megan.

"Hey, sis. Looks like the field agreed with you. Or was it the field engineer?" Ethan grinned then winced when Megan popped him on the arm.

"You have no idea what we went through out there. I had more than one near-death experience." She glanced at Rowdy. "But there were some good times too."

"We can't afford to keep you two in the field. Our insurance company is threatening to cancel us after the way you two went through RVs." Cass shook her head.

Shannon saw Megan and Rowdy exchange smiles. Whatever they'd been through must have been very interesting.

Cass tapped her desk with the engraved brass oil derrick Daddy had been given when he'd been declared Oilman of the Year at the Petroleum Club in 1998. "Shannon, you get on that press release. I'm sure you'll figure out what to say. Billy and Dylan will handle the claims. I'm going to be working up the bottom line number with Ethan. Rowdy, I'm hearing from people inside the company that you've proved you know how to run our rigs efficiently. I need you to look over expenses in the field and see where we can trim. Also, I'm thinking we may need to sell some of our fields. Oklahoma? You've worked there. What do you think?"

Shannon got busy. She wanted to show the group what she had before they broke up the meeting. The two lawyers had their heads together. To her surprise, Megan was just as interested in discussing costs in the engineering department as Rowdy and Cassidy were. Mason took a call from his own company.

Family. She was surrounded by it and it felt amazing. Could they save Calhoun? Only time would tell.

* * * *

"I've got that housekeeper coming in an hour. She was reluctant but I told her you had a copy of Evelyn's will and that she was named in it. She wants to know what she'll get, but I explained we couldn't discuss it over the phone." Mai handed Billy the photos she'd printed from Friday night. "You and Shannon look good. I wish I could get Albert to take me to something fancy like that ball."

"Say the word, doll. You got some place in mind?" Albert loomed in the doorway. "I can dig up a tux."

"To fit you?" Mai laughed. "No, I like you in your suit just fine. Next Saturday night. We'll go to a nice restaurant downtown. I hear they have a piano bar. Good dance music."

"How's your dancing, Albert?" Billy tried to imagine the big man with Mai in his arms on the dance floor. It would be like a polar bear waltzing a porcelain doll.

"I can hold my own. Don't suppose it's country music." He looked hopeful.

"Not a chance." Mai grinned. "Brush up on your foxtrot, big boy." She hummed as she left the room and closed the door.

"I'm doomed." Albert settled into a chair and pulled out his tablet.

"Hey, you can fake it. Just hold her close and keep off her toes. She won't care what other moves you make."

Billy had spent so much time on the Calhoun issues the past few weeks, he'd almost forgotten about his plan to work on Gran's neighborhood. But he knew Albert. Give him a problem and he rushed to find a solution.

"That apartment complex. Interesting getting into it. A developer paid cash for it about three years ago. Cleared out the families then let it sit. A shame really. There's not much affordable housing in that neighborhood. Some of the kids were squatting there until a week or so ago. I interviewed a couple of them. The dudes who ran them off were pretty rough—showed off guns, made some threats. Kids figured they might be setting up to deal drugs out of there. Now a group of men and women have moved in and started working on the place." Albert frowned. "They also bought the adjacent warehouse. Could be a meth lab. There's suspicious activity night and day."

"Well, shit. I was hoping to clean up that neighborhood. Seems like this is going to make it harder." Billy picked up a pen. "Got a name for me?"

"It's a company name, though it's not registered anywhere that I can find. Alamo. Of course, in Texas you can find a hundred Alamos, everything from rental cars to taco stands. But this company is into rehabbing apartments. I looked hard but couldn't find a paper trail."

"Paper trail." Billy shook his head. "Those crazies who wanted to kill Shannon and me were obsessed with avoiding a paper trail. Funny coincidence. But the last place they'd come would be near downtown Houston."

"Right." Albert checked his phone. "Speaking of trails, I've been trying to find a path from Evelyn Billingsley to a hitman. I know she hired pretty boys for her fun times with Rupert. I wonder if one of them might have been interested in making some bigger bucks to do the deed."

"That's a possibility. Do you know where she found them? Her sex toys?" Billy still couldn't imagine that kind of threesome. But then he didn't like to share. He sure as hell wouldn't invite another man into his bed with Shannon.

"There's a website. I'm contacting Rupert. Evelyn must have had her own computer. Where the hell is it?" Albert got up. "One more thing. Simon's been after me to ask if you'll sell Gertrude back to him. He won big at the casino. He has the money now."

"I like that bike." Billy thought about it. "Tell you what. If he'll give up gambling, hold onto his winnings and invest them and bring me proof he did that? Sure, I'll sell him Gertrude. Same price. Then you can find me another bike. I did enjoy the rides."

"I like it. We'll see how motivated he is to get that bike back." Albert laughed. "Now I've got to see about dance lessons. Say what you will, I don't want to disappoint my lady. Foxtrot? What the fuck is that?" He left the office, the door closing behind him.

Billy hit his own paperwork until Mai buzzed him. The housekeeper was here. He knew she was going to balk once she recognized him as Rupert's attorney and he was right.

"What is this? You were in court with that murderer." She shook her head and refused to sit down. She was a short woman in her fifties, maybe sixty. She had dark hair and a comfortable figure dressed in a knit pantsuit. Her sensible shoes were a brand Billy recognized. His grandmother had several pairs in bright colors. Maria's were navy to match her pants.

"Now, Maria. Calm down. I'm sure you still want to know what Evelyn Billingsley left you in her will. I have a copy right here." Billy walked around his desk, the will in his hand. Of course, he didn't bother to tell her that Evelyn's attorney would be contacting the housekeeper as soon as Rupert's trial was over. If Evelyn's husband was found guilty, he would forfeit his own part of the estate. If innocent, Rupert would stand to inherit millions. It was only natural that the reading of the will was being put on hold.

"I'm really in her will? Mrs. Greene's will?" She stopped with her hand on the doorknob. "I would never call her Billingsley. She knew that."

"I'm sure you were a valuable and loyal employee. So she put up with your attitude." Billy held out a chair. "Please, sit. We need to talk."

"Just tell me what I want to know. That's all I came here for." But she dropped into the chair and set her large designer handbag in her lap. "See this? Very expensive. Mrs. Greene gave it to me. A Christmas present. She was good to me. Then that silly man came into her life. Things changed. Not for the better."

"Did you know she was sick again?" Billy sat behind his desk and opened a file.

"Her cancer. How could I not know? She was a brave lady. I was so sad to see her suffering." Maria reached for a tissue from the box on the corner of the desk. "She fought that cancer. We thought it was gone. I think she married that boy because he could take care of her. It was a mistake."

"But he did care for her." Billy shut the folder. "I've talked to Rupert. He's convinced me that he really loved Evelyn. He was a nurse, able to give her pain medicine to help her deal with her illness."

"He didn't give her enough!" Maria dabbed at her eyes. "She had days when she didn't get out of bed because she felt so bad. But would he give her more for her pain? No. He said the medicine was bad for her. He kept it locked away. I begged him to give her more." She gripped her purse handle, her knuckles white. "Why didn't that stupid man die instead of my sweet lady?"

"Sweet lady?" Billy got up and pulled a chair next to Maria. "But you testified that Evelyn was mean to Rupert. Called him names, even in public. That doesn't sound sweet to me."

"Oh, yes, she had her ways." Maria sniffed. "Personality, I call it. Rupert laughed at her. Thought it was funny when she called him a dumb shit." She faced Billy, her eyes hard. "Not so dumb, I think. He married a rich woman and was letting her suffer. I think he was making her pay at the end for that name calling. She made him look a fool in front of her rich friends."

"Maria, is it possible that Evelyn *wanted* to die?" Billy asked that in the soft, persuasive voice he used when he was close to worming the truth out of a reluctant witness.

"Of course she did!" Maria sobbed. "She was ready to go. God was calling her." She bent her head and took the handkerchief Billy pressed into her hand. "So much pain, so many years of fighting that disease. She was tired."

Billy had to lean closer to hear this last word. "But you say Rupert wouldn't help her. He let her suffer. Why?"

"He said he wanted her awake. So she could know him. Talk to him. If she was too doped up, she was as good as dead." Maria dried her eyes and blew her nose.

"Does it make sense then that he would shoot her?" Billy had to hide his satisfaction. He'd just turned Maria into a witness for the defense. He should have asked her permission to record this. But he saw the light of awareness in Maria's eyes. She got it. There was no going back now.

"No, it doesn't." She said this as if to herself. She grabbed his hand. "I was wrong, wasn't I? Rupert wanted Mrs. Greene to live longer. They played these bad games. Sex." She shuddered. "The police told me he claimed he was tied up in the bathroom. I believe it. That was something they liked." She couldn't seem to stop shaking and Billy picked up the throw Mai made him keep on the couch and put it across Maria's shoulders. She hugged it around her.

He gave her time to calm down. "So you believe that a masked man might have come in and tied up Rupert? Left him in the bathroom? That it's possible he would have thought it part of their usual games? Gone along with it?"

"Yes, I suppose so." She stared down at that expensive purse before she let it slide from her lap to fall to the floor.

"Would Evelyn have been up to that then?"

Maria's breath hitched. "She'd been having a good day. Several good days in a row. I was happy for her. She'd gone to get her hair done. I was hopeful that this was a turning point. The doctors, so negative. They could have been wrong!" She clutched the throw. "Of course it was foolish. She was going to die. She'd lost weight, her hair dull, even with fresh color on it."

"Could she have felt good enough to arrange a surprise for Rupert? Maybe called a man to come in for one of their games that night?" Billy reached for his tablet. "I need to record the rest of our conversation. Do you mind?"

"No, go ahead." She watched him start it on the computer. "Mrs. Greene would do that. Set up games for them. I didn't understand it, but she loved Rupert. Adored him. Those were her words. She wanted to make him happy. So bringing in handsome young men was something she did from time to time." Maria crossed herself. "I cannot understand such sins. But I had to keep my thoughts to myself. She paid me well and, since she was so sick, I did what I was told without complaint."

"What did she tell you to do the night of the murder, Maria?"

"I was to turn off the security system that night before I went to my room. I knew to ignore any sounds I heard. In the years Rupert had been with us, I knew what would be happening."

"But then you heard the gunshot." Billy took her hand. It was ice-cold.

"Yes. I'd never heard that before. I ran. It is a long way from my apartment over the garage to the master suite. But I ran to see what had happened. When I got there, I saw Rupert holding her in his arms. He was covered with her blood. I called 911."

"Did he tell you to call an ambulance?"

"No. He was crying and rocking her. I think he knew it was too late. That she was dead. The gun was on the floor next to them. The police said it had been wiped clean of fingerprints." She stared at the floor. "I also called Mrs. Greene's stepchildren. They paid me each month to tell them what was happening in the house. So I had to report." She looked up. "You may think this is wrong, but I was worried about Mrs. Greene. Now I see I was right to worry."

Billy patted her hand. "Do you know how Evelyn arranged for the men who came to play those sex games?"

"What?" Her eyes widened. "I just told you about her death and you ask that?"

"What if the man who came to play was the one who killed her? What if Evelyn paid him to put her out of her misery? To end her suffering? Do you think that's possible?" Billy dropped her hand.

Maria's lips trembled.

"How did Evelyn find the men she hired to play their sex games? Do you know?" Billy pressed the point even though Maria looked close to losing it, her eyes brimming with tears again.

"Computer. She told me you could find anything on the Internet. It was a joke to her." Maria had shredded his handkerchief with restless fingers. "She made me promise that after she was gone I would destroy it. Because she didn't want the Greenes to see how bad she had been with Rupert."

Billy hated to hear that. "Did you? Destroy it?"

"I couldn't do it. But I hid it. The police came in and searched the house, but not my rooms over the garage. They had no reason to go there. So I put her computer away, before they had a chance to see it." Maria grabbed Billy's arm. "I had to honor her last wishes. She was a lady with many friends. Wanted to leave money to the hospital. A generous lady. I couldn't let her be remembered as someone who played sex games with her young husband, could I?"

"I understand, Maria. But I need that computer." Billy stood. "You were being loyal. That's a good thing. But would Evelyn really want the husband she loved to spend the rest of his life behind bars for a murder he didn't commit? I have to prove his innocence. If I can show that she hired a hitman to end her own suffering, I can help Rupert go free. Evelyn would want that."

"Yes, she loved Rupert. But for everyone to know—"

"I promise that if what I need is on that computer, I'll keep this as quiet as possible. Hiring a hitman and hiring a sex partner are two different things. I can take evidence to the DA and make sure it's not made public knowledge." Billy hoped he could keep that promise.

"You must swear it. I never liked Rupert. If he sits in jail, it will be for his sins."

"But Evelyn loved him. Think of her." Billy helped Maria to her feet.

"What are you doing?" She glanced at his desk. "What about the will?"

"I want you to take me to the house now and give me that computer." Billy picked up the will. "Do it for Evelyn. Because, Maria, she left you a million dollars in her will. Wisely invested, that will keep you in comfort for the rest of your life. You will never have to work again. Don't you think that's reason enough now to help me save the man Evelyn loved?"

Chapter 16

"I think we've caught a break on Sally's case." Billy had stopped by Gran's house on his way home.

"What do you mean, Billy?" Gran paused the TV even though it was time for *Wheel of Fortune.*

"The judge who came down so hard on her was just appointed to the state Supreme Court. Which means he won't be hearing Sally's case now. I think I can work with this new judge. You ever hear the term 'wet reckless'?"

"Watch your mouth, boy." Gran frowned at him. "I'm pretty sure that's how you were conceived."

Billy laughed, couldn't help it. "Why, if I didn't know better, I'd think my eighty-five-year-old grandmother had a dirty mind."

"Quit laughing and explain yourself." Her cheeks were pink and she couldn't look at him. "And I won't be eighty-five until the end of November."

"Wet reckless is what they call reckless driving while under the influence of alcohol. Sally didn't hit anyone and was just a block from home. I think this lesser offense will fly with the new judge." Billy dropped down onto Gran's old print couch and got poked in the butt with a loose spring. The damned thing had to go. He was buying her a new couch this year for Christmas. Or maybe that birthday.

"A lesser offense. So not DUI or DWI, whatever they're calling it these days? What will that mean for her?" Gran leaned forward, her eyes alive again. It had been a while since he'd seen that.

Billy realized he was exhausted. He'd hardly stopped running the last few weeks. What with the Calhoun thing coming to a head and access to Evelyn's computer giving them a line on a possible hitman, he'd had so much on his plate, he hardly had time to breathe, much less just chill with Shannon like he wanted to. The good news? He'd won that cruise for them. Now all he had to do was get the proposal right, buy a ring worthy of the woman, and set a date. He realized Gran was on the edge of her seat and he'd zoned out.

"Billy? Boy, you are somewhere else. Come back here and answer me."

"Sorry, Gran. Okay, here's what I've been working on. Sally's psychiatrist has her on some anti-anxiety meds. He says she's better but needs a stay in a facility. Maybe rehab, maybe something like a mental hospital to treat her depression. The judge will like that."

"Oh, Billy." Gran pulled out the tissues. "What did I do wrong? Both of my daughters never did find the happiness I thought they deserved or amount to a hill of beans."

"Don't beat yourself up, Gran. I don't think I turned out so bad and I give you full credit." Billy heaved himself out of that pit in the old couch, knelt in front of her, and took her hands. "What do you think?"

"Yes, I'm proud of you, Billy boy." She leaned her head on his shoulder. "But my girls… I just don't understand."

"I don't either. But there's not much we can do about it now. Sally was right about one thing. She's got a disease. Alcoholism. Withdrawal has left her depressed. Therapy has helped her pull out of it some, but it'll take time for her to be able to stand on her own two feet again."

"Shoot. That girl has never stood on her own." Gran sat up and sniffed. "But nice try, Billy. So what do you think? Will this keep her out of jail? That's the best I can hope for now."

"Then that's what I'm going to make happen." Billy was glad he could say that with some confidence. It was already in the works or he wouldn't have mentioned it tonight.

"You *do* make me proud." She kissed him on the cheek.

"Now help me out. I kind of proposed to Shannon at the Ballet Ball but I made a mess of it. I need to do it again. Right. Make it romantic. Give her a nice ring at the same time. Something worthy of her." He pulled out his phone. "What do you think of these?" He'd downloaded a few pictures from the Internet but none of them struck him as quite right.

"You sure she's the one? What about her drinking?" Gran gripped his hand.

"She's just about given it up because she knows what it means to me. And, yes, I'm sure. You going along with this or will we have a problem?" Billy didn't look away. "I love her. I'm marrying her. You can accept that or take the consequences."

"You know I only want you to be happy." Her eyes filled.

"She makes me happy. She's not going to turn into an alcoholic, I promise you." Billy held onto her frail shoulders. "Trust my judgment?"

"I guess I have to." She glanced at the phone he'd dropped in her lap. "Those rings aren't good enough. If you're bound and determined to do this, wait here. I've got something I think might work." Gran let him help pull her up.

To his surprise, she grabbed her cane and thumped down the hall toward her bedroom. What could she have that Shannon would like? Yes, Shan enjoyed vintage jewelry, but as far as he knew the Great Depression had wiped out anything of value in this family except for that bracelet he'd already given her.

He heard Gran coming and met her halfway. "What have you got there?"

She had a small velvet pouch in her hand.

"It was your great grandmother's. I think you could put a new sparkler in the middle." She opened the pouch and let the ring drop into his palm.

Billy stared down at the old-fashioned engagement ring. He knew at once that Shannon would fall in love with it. "White gold?"

"No, platinum. Your great granddaddy's restaurant was a hit in the twenties. He always wanted the best for Mama. That's what I called her. She was like a mother to me after I married your grandpa. Anyway, she told me he came home with this one night. Flashy, she called it. She was almost embarrassed to wear it to church. But she never took it off. Not until…" She smiled and shook her head. "This is art deco, Billy, the style back then. I watch the shopping channel. They're making reproductions of this now. All it needs is a new diamond where the center stone is missing."

"Yes, she likes old pieces." Billy studied the delicate ring. "Gran! Are those real diamonds?"

"Sure are. The ones around where the center stone should be were too small to sell. Broke Mama's heart to part with that big diamond, but times were hard after the restaurant went under." Gran sighed. "She did it behind Great Granddaddy's back. He wanted to throw a fit, but they needed the money. So he just took it and never said a word." She handed him the velvet bag. "I'm sure they'd be happy to see it used in the family again. Polished up, it'll make a real nice ring for Shannon." Gran held onto his wrist. "It needs a big stone for the wife of the best criminal lawyer in Houston. You take it to a reputable jeweler. Don't let some crook set one of those fake diamonds in there."

"No, of course not. Only the best for my girl." Billy hugged Gran then kissed her wrinkled cheek. She always smelled so clean and sweet. "I love you, Gran. And Shannon will love this. I guess I should let her pick out a wedding band to go with it. Something from the same time period."

"Yes. We buried Mama in her wedding ring." Gran patted his cheek. "I always wondered if that undertaker let it stay or if he slipped it off before she went in the ground."

"Now, Gran, always so suspicious." Billy figured living with alcoholics had done that to her. His mother had lied about everything. She'd say she'd given up drinking then sneak around to do it. Or claim she'd been laid off from a job, then they'd find out she'd been fired for coming back late from boozy lunches. He'd told Shannon's family that good fruit could come from a rotten tree. Gran proved damaged fruit could come from a strong and honest tree. He still didn't know why he'd been able to resist going down the wrong path.

"I don't think it matters how you propose to Shannon, Billy. Just tell her you love her. That's what a woman wants." Gran looked wistful. "I know you'll treat her right."

"I tell her all the time. I never left for school that I didn't hear you say it." Billy smiled at her then handed her the remote control. Damn it, he was getting a little choked up. Gran couldn't live forever and he didn't know what he'd do once she was gone. "Now turn on *Wheel*. I'll watch with you for a while."

"Sweet boy. I bet Shannon's waiting for you now." But she did get the show started.

"No, she and her sisters are having a girls' night. Like you enjoy with your lady friends." Billy lay on the couch and kicked off his shoes. "Okay, let's see if you've still got it. What do you think the solution to that puzzle is?" He laughed when she guessed it immediately. Sharp as a tack, she would say. He studied the ring she'd given him then slipped it back into the pouch before tucking it safely into his pants pocket. Tomorrow he'd go to a former client who was a jeweler. They'd find the perfect stone. Then he'd have to work out when and where to propose. Gran might be right, but he wanted to make sure Shannon had a good story to tell their kids someday. He closed his eyes, imagining a little girl with Shannon's pretty face.

"Billy, it's late." Gran shook his shoulder.

He stretched and hit the china lamp on the end table next to the couch. Luckily, he caught it before it hit the floor. "What time is it?"

"Midnight. You slept for five hours." She took his hand as if to pull him up. "You needed it."

"Yes, I did. I hope I didn't keep you up." He was careful not to use her as leverage when he sat up.

"No, this is my usual bedtime. I like those late-night talk shows. Karaoke in a car. So funny." She laughed. "But, Billy, maybe you should just sleep in my guest room. I hate for you to drive this late."

"I'll be fine." He slipped on his shoes then picked up his tie and suit coat. He checked his pocket. "Thanks for the ring, Gran. And the nap. I don't sleep worth a damn most nights. I feel like a new man."

"I like the old one just fine." She followed him to the door and unlocked her burglar bars. "You be careful. Why don't you sleep?"

"My mind keeps going. Shannon's been on me about it. Bought some kind of herbal remedy. I keep meaning to try it, but haven't yet." He kissed Gran's cheek.

"That girl likes taking care of you. So maybe she'll turn out to be a blessing after all." Gran patted his back as he stepped out on the porch. "See? I'm trying."

"I had to get over our history. So it's no wonder you're having a hard time with it. Shannon and I have both grown up since college. We're different people. She respects how I feel about drinking so I'm not worried she'll end up like Mama or Aunt Sally." Billy yawned, still tired but awake enough to make the drive home. "I was too intense back then. Way too driven to succeed at all costs. I thought I had to control everything and everyone around me, including Shannon. Guess watching Mama so out of control all the time did that to me." He paused. Damn if that wasn't hitting the nail on the head.

"I'm sorry, Billy. Your childhood was rough. If Jeannie had ever managed to pull herself together..."

"Gran, my childhood wasn't all bad, thanks to you. I always knew Mama loved me. But she was as sick as Sally is. I've been pushing hard for a long time. In a way, I got as addicted to work as Mama and Sally were to the alcohol. When I did let someone into my life, I thought I had to be in charge, call all the shots, control everything or it would all fall apart. That sure didn't help me make a relationship work either." He shook his head. "I'm finally ready to let go of the reins to make this relationship with Shannon stick. As for work? It's cold comfort at night."

"That's good, Billy. If Shannon taught you that, then maybe she is the right woman for you." Gran gently shut the bars and locked them. "Take care. Let me know how the proposal goes and what she thinks of that ring."

"I will." Billy checked the corner but the usual gang had obviously found beds for the night. He'd tried to contact the owners of that apartment complex, but they dodged his calls. He decided to drive by and see what was going on. Albert had said there was action in the warehouse day and night. He got in the car and picked up his phone. He had a text from Shannon. She was staying at home with her sisters and would see him tomorrow night. Damn, he missed her. Maybe he'd sleep some more tonight, take that herbal thing.

He drove down the street and saw lights on in several apartments. There were quite a few vehicles parked in the slots behind them—jeeps, a few motorcycles, and a couple of SUVs. One of those SUVs was black with fancy hubcaps. It could be the one he'd seen the night of the Ballet Ball. Of course, if it belonged in the neighborhood, then there was no reason to think it had anything to do with him.

He turned the corner and checked out the nearby warehouse. Lights on inside and a pair of pickup trucks parked by the garage doors. He was tempted to get out and see if he could get a glimpse inside. No, without backup, that would be stupid. Especially if these were drug dealers.

Instead, he got on the phone to one of his connections in the Houston Police Department. It wouldn't hurt to give a buddy a head's up about this new bit of action. He let the car idle at the curb while he made the call.

"Yo, Pagan. A little late for you, isn't it?"

"Buchman, you should know I never sleep. You running the streets tonight?" Billy was using his hands-free option so when he saw movement at the garage doors, he put the car in gear and drove on down the street. Once he got around the corner, he stopped again. He still had a view of the apartment building's parking lot. Lucky for him but unlucky for the neighborhood, the street light was burned out and he sat in the dark. He turned off his headlights to blend in.

"Yeah. What are you up to?"

"I'm in my grandmother's neighborhood. You remember where that is?"

"Sure do. My auntie still lives a few blocks over. Did you know they're getting ready to tear down some of those old places and put up fancy townhomes? Bet they run a couple of hundred grand each. Ugly shit."

"I've seen them. Three stories and they look like shoe boxes standing on one end." Billy couldn't imagine living in one of those. "They take a decent-sized lot and cram four of them on it until there's no yard left."

"Man, it's a shame. Soon there's going to be no place downtown where the working poor can rent a decent home."

"I'm sitting near some apartments that are getting gentrified right now. But there's something going on here. Owner bought a warehouse too. Action this time of night. Seem strange to you?" Billy gave him the address.

"After midnight? I'd say so." Buchman said something to someone, probably his partner. "You be careful. Don't play detective, Billy."

"I hear you. But if you get a chance, you might swing by, take a look. I was thinking drugs. We sure don't need that moving in here." Billy thought he heard a door slam and slipped down in his seat.

"Hell, no. I'll check it out. Knock on a few doors. Got a young cousin who dropped out of school and runs with a crowd of kids that are just looking for trouble near that location. He told me you gave one of the punks your card."

"Yeah. I'd like to do something for the neighborhood. Put up a place for those kids and offer job training or a rec center. Maybe tutoring for a GED, you know what I mean?"

"I sure do. Sounds like a great idea. Count me in. You need security, I'll hook you up. No charge. About time we pushed for positive change in the inner city. All those bulldozers coming in so that rich folks can build McMansions? It makes me sick."

"Thanks, Buchman. I'll be in touch. And you have my number. If this apartment owner will cooperate, I'd like to see it become the start of something. We could use a unit, I'd pay for it, to begin the outreach. Now if they're thinking to do something illegal out of there, then I'm counting on you to run them off. You hear me?"

"Sure do. Shit, got to go. Call's coming in on a robbery. Not near your grandma. Go to bed, Billy. Leave the night to those of us who have to cover it." He ended the call.

Billy watched that black SUV roll out from the parking lot. Where were they going at this time of night? He waited until it was almost out of sight and then followed. But the streets were almost empty. Damn it, he was going to be made if he kept trailing the car. When it stopped at a red light, Billy decided he'd better make a turn and go on home.

What did he hope to see? A drug deal? Then what? He wasn't going to pull out his gun and make a citizen's arrest. Besides, those damned Exiles had his gun and he hadn't had time to replace it yet. He'd been focused on his call and didn't have any idea how many people were in the SUV either. He would probably be outnumbered *and* outgunned.

Don't play detective. Good advice.

He yawned again and concentrated on his driving when his eyelids felt heavy. Almost zero traffic. Then he saw lights behind him. Was *he* being followed now? He made a couple of turns to test it. Still lights. So he stopped at a McDonalds and went inside. He needed to eat, had forgotten to earlier, and hadn't wanted to bother Gran about it. He filled up on fries, a shake, and a Big Mac. No big black vehicles pulled into the lot while he ate. Finally, he walked out to the car and looked around. He was alone except for a couple of workers power-washing the lot. Good. It must have been a false alarm. Time to go home. With a full stomach he thought he just might sleep.

* * * *

"Come on, I want to see clean plates. I didn't get up and make my famous pecan waffles so you could just drink coffee and ignore them." Janie had her hands on her hips and looked ready to start swatting each Calhoun with her wooden spoon. She'd been good at that when they were growing up.

Shannon picked up her fork. They looked delicious. "You did go to a lot of trouble. Thanks, Janie." She tried, she really did, but it was hard to swallow past the lump in her throat.

"Hey, I'm eating. I'll take another one." Ethan held out his empty plate. "No one cooks like you, Janie."

"I may need you as a reference, boy. Since my Calhoun stock doesn't seem to be holding up like I planned." She headed back to the waffle iron and poured in more batter, sprinkling in a liberal amount of chopped pecans. "I may move to Fredericksburg and find I have to get a job in a diner to make ends meet after I retire."

"We're working on a plan, Janie. Don't give up on us." Megan sat next to Shannon at the kitchen counter. She'd managed to eat half of her waffle. Now she got up to refill her coffee cup. "I know the dividends were your pension plan. Daddy gave you stock every year as a bonus."

"Now I realize that was to avoid paying me cash." Janie stared at the waffle iron like she could make it hurry. "I thought I could trust him. Now I'm questioning everything Conrad ever did for me."

"I know." Megan hugged the housekeeper and looked back at Shannon. "Say something," she silently mouthed.

"He loved you, Janie. I'm sure Daddy thought he was doing the right thing, giving you that stock. When oil was at its peak, the stock price was through the roof. I know your dividends were good then. Just wait. When we get the company back on its feet, you'll have a comfortable retirement." Shannon glanced at Ethan.

"Cassidy's doing a fantastic job. I wish she'd stayed over so she could explain her plans." Ethan sipped his coffee. "Trust us. We'll make sure you don't have to work in some coffee shop in Fredericksburg."

"Boy, if I do, you'd better come see me there and order an expensive breakfast. I expect big tips too." Janie sniffed and returned Megan's hug. "Oops, waffle's ready." She opened the appliance and used a fork to pull out a perfectly browned masterpiece. "Now tell me why you're all so upset." She dropped the waffle on Ethan's plate. "You think I can't see there's something bothering all of you this morning? Besides the usual Calhoun thing?"

"We're going to see Mama today." Shannon pushed her plate away. The smell of the maple syrup was making her a little nauseated. "Her doctor called me. She's getting really agitated and insists she has to see us. All three of us. We've been putting it off, but this is the one day this month she's allowed visitors. The doctor says we have to come if at all possible."

"She *is* your mama." Janie settled on a stool with her own cup of coffee. "I know she's done some bad things, but…"

"Some bad things?" Megan slammed her cup on the counter so hard it cracked. "Shit!" She mopped up spilled coffee with a towel then threw the cup into the trash compacter.

"Calm down, sis." Ethan got up and found her a new cup, filling it at the pot. "Here." He put an arm around her and led her back to her own stool. "Janie, we've all had to face the fact that both our parents weren't who we thought they were. They lied, cheated and, in Mama's case, tried to physically hurt people."

"I know. It's been hard to take in for me and I don't carry their blood." Janie wiped tears from her eyes. "Kids, you have to know that I never saw it. Oh, we all knew your mama had her spells. Mental illness is just that, a sickness. So I cut her some slack. When she took her medicine, she was a fine and loving mother."

"That doesn't excuse what she and Daddy did to those people when they started Calhoun Petroleum, Janie. They hurt so many lives." Shannon needed fresh air. She got up and walked to the French doors and threw one open. It was a cool morning and she just breathed, trying to get the nauseatingly sweet maple smell out of her lungs. What was wrong with her?

"Okay, so they were crooks. Mama's in what amounts to a cushy jail and Daddy's dead. So we're trying to clean up their mess." Megan walked over to put her arm around Shannon. "That's all we can do, Shan. We'll go out there and see Mama and tell her we're done with her until she can show some remorse. I don't care what she wants. This will be our last visit for a long time."

"You can cut ties with her? Just like that?" Ethan stood on Shannon's other side. "She wasn't all bad. I remember special birthdays. She brought ponies out here to this very yard. We had great times." He chuckled. "Ice skating in the Galleria. The four of us had the rink all to ourselves. She bought out the whole place so you could practice your twirls, Shan."

"Yeah. When she was up, she was way up." Shannon leaned against Ethan when he put his arm around her too. She loved her brother and her sister. But her mother? She never knew what she'd find when she saw her. The laughing lady who would do anything for her? Or the screaming banshee who couldn't be pleased no matter what her daughter tried? Ballet had been a refuge for her. She'd spent most of her summers away at camp because she couldn't stand being in this house. As the oldest, she'd tried to shield these two and made sure they'd had their own summer camps. Ethan had always loved computers, Megan riding.

"Stop remembering the bad times. I can feel the tension in your body." Megan shook her a little. "We'll get this over with and that's that. Mama's getting therapy and medication while she serves her sentence. That's a good thing. Maybe someday we can have a rational talk with her. I wouldn't count on that today, though." Megan hugged her, then looked her over. "Now tell me about you and Billy. Is it serious?"

Shannon faced her. Billy. He was her anchor, steady and always there, loving her. No uncertainty with him. She was about to tell Megan how much she loved him when the fresh air quit working. She was going to be sick. She ran for the bathroom.

Later in the car, she sat with an ice pack on her forehead. Ethan was giving her looks, Megan had decided she knew what was wrong.

"Could you be pregnant?"

"I don't know. I had this implant, oh, years ago. It's supposed to be really effective. But maybe... I need to check and see how long that thing was supposed to last." She thought about it. She and Billy were so exclusive they'd given up condoms a while ago. She'd stopped the pill in her mid-twenties because it made her occasional migraines worse. When had she last had a regular check-up?

"Would it be a disaster or a blessing if you were?" Megan was driving. They'd stuck Ethan in the back seat. Youngest always had to ride there.

"He's already proposed and I sort of said yes. I love him. He loves me. So a blessing." Shannon leaned against the door and closed her eyes, thinking. "I want his children. He'll make a wonderful father." She sniffled and looked at Megan. Her sister always acted tough but looked a little teary too.

"Auntie Megan. That's awesome, Shan." Megan grinned.

"Are you kidding me? How can I be a decent mother? Look at our role model." Shannon's stomach lurched.

"Shut the fuck up. You'll be great. You sure know what *not* to do." Megan patted her hand.

Ethan, who'd refused to wear a seatbelt, reached forward to hit her lightly on the back of the head. "Megan's right. You'll be great. And Billy's a hell of a guy. A lawyer in the family. You couldn't do better. Tell Megan about the reservation. You know he's part Indian, Meg. And Shan got chased by crazies through the piney woods. Awesome."

"Not so awesome. I had to be interviewed by the FBI recently. Those crazies tried to kill us. The only reason they didn't finish the job was because they stopped to harvest their marijuana and take it with them."

"No shit. You didn't tell me that part." Ethan leaned between the seats. "They were drug dealers?"

"Dealers, dopers, tax evaders. All of the above. The FBI is hot on their trail except it's grown cold. I talked to them last week. They grilled me for hours, hoping I'd remember seeing something in the cabin where they held us that would give them a lead." Shannon put the ice on the back of her neck when a wave of nausea hit her. "Convenience store coming up. I need a Coke to settle my stomach. Can we stop?"

Megan exited the freeway. "I could use a drink too. Ethan?"

"Sure." He leaned back. "You both have had adventures lately, and all I'm doing is sitting in front of a computer all day. Life is not fair."

Megan and Shannon exchanged looks.

"Really, little brother, the kinds of adventures we've had? You don't want." Shannon clutched the door handle. "Hurry, Meg, I think I'm going to throw up again. Shit. I may be pregnant. I wonder how Billy feels about eloping?"

* * *

When Shannon, Megan, and Ethan walked into the conference room, Missy was already there. She jumped up from a wing chair as soon as she saw them and rushed to embrace Ethan.

"My baby!" She clasped him to her bosom with tears of joy. When she moved on to Megan, she was met with a stony look and hands held out to block her.

"Forget it, Mama. I'm not feeling the love."

"Megan!" Mama pulled back her hand like she was going to slap her. The muscular guard at the door took a step forward and she let it drop. "Shannon, are you going to be mean to me too?"

"Afraid so, Mama. Sit down. Tell us why you wanted us to come out here." Shannon couldn't believe that her mother looked exactly the same. You'd think that being in a mental hospital would show on the surface, but it didn't. Apparently, this facility had a beauty salon. Hair and makeup were freshly done. Too bad those tears had made her mascara run. A good daughter would send her waterproof. Shannon decided not to mention it.

"Ethan, come sit next to me." Missy sat on a velvet loveseat and patted a spot next to her. "At least one of my children still loves me."

"No, thank you, Mama." He took the wing chair she'd vacated. "You hurt all of us with what you and Daddy did. We've done nothing but work to try to clean up your mess ever since we learned the truth. If you think we can just forgive and forget, you're wrong."

Her lips quivered. "That mess, as you call it, paid for everything you've enjoyed all of your lives." She lifted her toned chin. She'd had a facelift right after the divorce from their father. Alexandra, the woman Daddy married after her, had taunted her about waiting too late for it. Now she looked years younger than her fifty odd years. If she ever got out of this place, she'd probably hunt for a new husband. Shannon felt sorry for whoever got stuck with her.

"Why did you want us to come out here?" Megan was determined to get to the point.

"Why do you think? What in the hell are you doing at Calhoun? I have stock in that company. It was part of my settlement from your father. I can't sell it yet because that was a condition in the divorce decree. So I have to live off the dividends. The lower the stock price, the lower the dividends." Her face flushed and she jumped up. A glance at the alert guard and she sat again. "I need you to stop ruining that company!"

"First, we're trying to save that company from what you and Daddy did." Shannon stood and the room swirled around her. She held onto the back of the chair until it steadied. "You tried to stop her, but Cass sent out those letters to the people you cheated and got the ball rolling. Now we're getting the money together to pay them what they're owed."

"More than they're owed. Now that they've got a hell of a legal team on their side." Missy laughed wildly and the guard shifted his feet. "You think I don't keep up with the news? I've seen the ads on TV. Those are the best oil and gas lawyers in the state. They won't rest until they bankrupt Calhoun. Then what will any of us have? You'll be out on the street and I'll end up in a state facility."

"Cut the drama." Megan wasn't sympathetic.

"Drama?" The word was a shriek. "You have any idea what those places are like? I've heard all about them. People in here who've been there can't wait to share the horrors. Screams coming down the hall, locked cells. Shock treatments. Group showers." She swayed and pulled at her highlighted hair like she was caught up in a nightmare.

"Calm down, Mama. You're exaggerating." Ethan watched her warily. Just like all of them, he knew the signs that one of her manic episodes was coming. "Are you taking your medications?"

"You think I have a choice here?" She moaned but at least stopped pulling her hair.

The hairdo shifted and Shannon realized her mother was wearing a wig. Had she ripped out her real hair in one of her frenzies? Weren't they watching her carefully? No, she didn't care. Mama could be bald and it would serve her right. There'd been so many times when she'd run from the house to avoid her mother's scenes and taken Meg and Ethan with her. Dodged things thrown at her. Found her room torn up because her mother didn't like something she'd done or had imagined a transgression.

Okay, so Mama was sick. But she was also a liar and a thief. Shannon looked away and took even breaths. Underlying the subtle scent of the air freshener she could see plugged into the wall was antiseptic. A hospital. More breaths. More nausea. Pregnant. And this woman would be her child's grandmother.

"I'm in a mental hospital, son. But it's the same as a prison. Court ordered. If I can't afford to stay in this one, I'll have to serve out my time in one owned by the state." Missy shuddered and ran a hand down her stylish green pantsuit. "Wear, God help me, orange jumpsuits like on that TV show. You know the one. Become someone's bitch." She started to cry. "You have to save the company or what's to become of me?"

Ethan grabbed the box of tissues and gave it to her. "I'm helping with the numbers, Mama. We're doing all we can to make sure the company survives." He sat beside her and put his arm around her. "Don't carry on so. It'll be all right."

"That was quite a performance, Mama." Megan slowly clapped. "Get away from her, Ethan. Next thing you know you'll be sending her flowers on her birthday."

Missy glared at Megan, her tears gone. "Would that be so bad?" She gripped Ethan's arm until he winced. "At least one of my children still shows me a little sympathy."

"Let go of him, Mama." Shannon walked over and grabbed her mother's hand. "Do I have to call for help?" Missy wasn't going to release him until that guard moved toward her.

"I wasn't doing anything." Missy whined but freed Ethan before the guard reached Shannon's side. "Ethan?"

"You hurt me, Mama." Ethan hurried to sit in the chair again. "And it's not the first time. Shannon, get away from her."

"I have something to say." Shannon stayed put. "We're not coming back here until you've admitted what you did was wrong, Mama. To Cassidy and to those people when you and Daddy started Calhoun." She glanced at Ethan. He nodded.

"She's right." Megan looked determined and had gone to stand behind Ethan, her hand on his shoulder.

"If I could, I'd make sure you never got one damned dime from the company. Calhoun was built on lies, yours and Daddy's. You're right about one thing—our cushy life was built on them too. You think it makes me happy knowing that I danced and played the rich socialite while other people suffered? No, it makes me sick." She took a breath and thought how lovely it would be to throw up in her mother's lap. "You've never even said you're sorry."

"Stupid people like that don't deserve your pity, Shannon." Her mother frowned at each of them. "Why are you wasting Calhoun's money on them?" She reached out with perfectly manicured nails and Shannon took a quick step back. "I thought I raised you all better than that! Why are *you* being so damned stupid?" She raked the air where Shannon had been a moment before.

The guard stepped in front of her.

"Leave me alone! These are my children. I'm talking to them. Trying to set them straight." Missy slapped at his broad chest.

"Mrs. Calhoun, if you don't settle down, I'm going to have to take you out of here." The guard stood calmly in front of her. "Sit now." He made it into a command.

"Fuck you. I've got to make these kids listen to me." She screeched when he caught her in a hold that pinned her arms to her sides. "You see how these animals treat me here? Help me! Ethan! Shannon! Megan!" She continued screaming as he picked her up and carried her out of the room.

Shannon collapsed on the loveseat, her hands shaking so hard she couldn't pull a tissue from the box next to her. There it was again, that swirling room, turning and turning until the spots in front of her eyes became a kaleidoscope of colors.

"Shannon, are you all right?"

That was the last thing she heard before the room went dark.

Chapter 17

"Rupert, we've got an appointment with the district attorney this afternoon. I think I can get the charges dropped." Billy had thought long and hard about this, and he was pretty sure he had enough to pull it off.

"You're serious? This nightmare might be over?" Rupert paced the office. "What did you find out? What made you decide to set it up today?"

Billy opened his laptop and pulled up a page with a photograph. "Come here, since you refuse to sit down. Look at this guy and tell me if you recognize him."

Rupert came to peer over his shoulder. He didn't seem to know boundaries and rested his hand on Billy's neck, rubbing lightly. "Sure. That's Sean. He came to our house twice." Rupert sighed. "Evelyn liked him, but he was a little rough for my tastes. I told her not to hire him again." He sat on the edge of Billy's desk. "Why? Do you think he…" He leaned even closer. "Billy! Do you think he's the one who shot Evelyn?" He peered at the photo. "Where's one of his whole body? There has to be a full body shot. Evelyn liked a muscular build."

Billy hit the keys until a photo array came up. There was one with Sean in jeans and a tight muscle shirt. It was an outfit similar to the one Rupert had told the police the murderer had worn.

"Dear God! That could be him! Of course, there was the ski mask. Let me think." Rupert was on the move again, pacing. "Tattoos. The murderer had one on his arm. Was it a snake? No, a dragon! Look in the police report. I told them about it that night. I'm sure they wrote it down, though they didn't believe a word I said."

Billy smiled. "Yes, you claimed he had a dragon tattoo on his right bicep." He zoomed in on the hooker's right arm. Did you call them hookers when they were male prostitutes? He didn't know or care. "Look at that."

"Holy shit! That's it. Red with yellow eyes. Exactly the right place too." Rupert screamed and hugged Billy, kissing his cheek. "You found him. Will the D.A. believe us? Will the police pick him up? Is there an address there?"

"You know they're not going to just take your word for it, Rupert." Billy hated to bring him down. Rupert was actually dancing around the room. He'd picked up Billy's golf trophy and was playing it like a guitar.

"What?" He stopped in mid-strum. "Then why are we going in today?"

"Because I have more evidence to tie Sean Crockett to the crime. There were emails to him on Evelyn's computer. The two before, when she'd obviously arranged for him to come to the house for your sex games. Then another, three days before the murder. Evelyn was too smart to put anything incriminating in an email, but she arranged to meet Sean in person." Billy saw Rupert's face go white and got up to grab the trophy before it hit the floor.

"Sit before you fall down."

"What else? What makes you think Evelyn hired Sean for anything more than a fuck?" Rupert stared up at him.

"Fifty thousand dollars. I doubt that's the going rate for a threesome." Billy sighed when Rupert just shook his head. "Lucky for us, Sean is as dumb as a box of rocks. He obviously took that money from Evelyn and deposited forty of it into his personal checking account the day before the murder. He spent another five thousand in cash at Nordstrom's on red leather jeans and expensive shoes. Even posted a picture of himself in his new pants on Facebook, bragging about where he'd bought them. My investigator was able to score video of him forking over the cash in the men's department." Billy flinched when Rupert grabbed his hand. "Rupert?"

"That son of a bitch!" Rupert was shaking and tears filled his eyes. "He let Evelyn pay him to kill her."

"Looks that way. And I think this is strong enough to convince the D.A." Billy let Rupert hold on. "I'm really sorry. I'm glad this will probably clear you but sorry that Evelyn arranged her own death."

"My fault." Rupert gulped. "If I'd known how desperate she was …" He leaned against Billy's leg and sobbed.

Billy just let him cry. He extricated his hand, patted his back, and pulled out yet another handkerchief. It took a while before Rupert calmed down enough to take it.

"She loved you, adored you. She told Maria that. I'm sure she never meant for you to take the fall for her murder." Billy pulled up a chair. "I studied the medical examiner's report again. There was gunshot residue on Evelyn's hand. I think Sean had second thoughts and Evelyn might have pulled the trigger herself at the last minute. Of course, the police figured she was fighting to get the gun away from her killer and it went off. Sean obviously wiped their fingerprints off the gun."

Rupert looked up at Billy. "But even if it happened that way, he took the money. He should go to jail."

"Oh, he will. My investigator has a recent address and has given it to a police detective I know. Sean will be picked up today and confronted with the evidence. By the time we meet with the D.A., I'm hoping that dumb piece of shit has confessed."

Rupert wiped his eyes. "You know, now that I think about it, I wasn't supposed to be home that night. Evie would never have wanted me to be there and end up accused of her murder. I had tickets to a play. She begged me to go on without her, even got upset when I wouldn't. I gave the tickets away at the last minute because I didn't want to leave her. Not when she had so little time left." He sighed. "I guess she'd arranged it and it was too late to stop it. When I saw the man in the ski mask come in that night, I thought she'd decided to surprise me, to make up for me missing the play."

"Well, that answers the last question I had. Give me the name of the friends, details about the play, and when you gave away the tickets. It will help with the D.A." Billy pulled back and picked up his tablet again.

Rupert watched him take notes with reddened eyes. "You are so good at this. I owe you my life, Billy. I'm sorry I ever doubted you."

"And I'm sorry I ever doubted *you*, Rupert. When I first took your case, I had a hunch you were innocent or I wouldn't have agreed to represent you." Billy patted Rupert's shoulder. "Then somehow we got crossways with each other."

"My fault. I was impatient. I didn't trust you to do your job." Rupert looked down at the crumpled handkerchief. "I owe you a box of these. I'll have some sent when I pay your bill. You're worth every penny." He smiled. "That is, if we get this settled this afternoon like you think we will."

"We should. I noticed they never checked you for GSR that night. Do you know why?" Billy couldn't blame Rupert for having doubts about him after that first fuck-up in court. He'd been too tired to do a decent job preparing the defense. That's why he'd finally gone to a sleep specialist. He felt strange doing it, but he'd started classes in meditation and it was helping.

"My hands were covered in Evelyn's blood." Rupert sighed. "They said something about that being all the proof they needed."

"Well, it helps our case for dismissal." Billy stood and checked his watch. "Appointment's at three thirty. I'll pick you up. You back at the house?"

"Yes. Believe it or not, Maria's agreed to stay on. She and I worked out a truce and she *is* an excellent housekeeper." Rupert walked to the door. "Of course, as soon as the will is read, she'll be worth a cool million. She told me that right away."

"But she'll still work for you?" Billy couldn't believe it.

"I agreed to hire some help for her. She can order around someone else. It's her dream job. And she says she likes her apartment above the garage. It's been her home for twenty years." Rupert laughed. "Hey, maybe I can take that cruise after all. It doesn't leave until November twenty-first." He sighed. "But it won't be the same without Evie."

"I have a feeling we'll be done well before then. But you have a double room booked." Billy held the door open. "You have someone to go with you?" He had always wondered if Rupert was as true to his wife as he claimed.

"Don't look at me like that." Rupert straightened Billy's tie. "I'd ask you along but Mai tells me you're as good as engaged. Too bad."

"I like you, Rupert, but I'm very into women. One woman in particular." Billy saw that one woman sitting in his reception area. "Here she is."

He introduced Shannon to Rupert.

"Why, Billy, I know Shannon Calhoun. Look at you, scoring one of the beauties of Houston's social scene." Rupert kissed her on the cheek. "How are you, honey?"

"I'm great. But I'm so sorry for your loss, Rupert. Poor Evelyn. She was always so generous for a good cause." Shannon put her arm around Billy's waist. "I hope my man here is helping you."

"Helping me? We're pretty sure he just managed to clear my name! I love him." Rupert waved at Mai. "I love you too, Mai! See you later, Billy." He rushed out the door.

"Well, that's good news. I know you were working hard on his case." Shannon pulled Billy into his office. "Mai, it was great to meet you in person after talking to you on the phone so many times. Can you give us a few minutes, undisturbed?"

"You've got it, Shannon." Mai winked at Billy. "He hasn't eaten lunch yet. You should make him go out somewhere. He doesn't take care of himself. Next appointment in two hours."

"Thanks for telling me." Shannon smiled at Mai. "I'll take care of him." She closed the door and leaned against it then turned the lock.

Billy pulled her close and kissed her. "Are we having a nooner?"

"I have news." She looked like she did have something she was bursting to tell him. "But I could be persuaded."

"Is it something with Calhoun? Or did those Feds bother you again?

I can whip some ass if I have to. But now you're smiling. So maybe it's good news." He ran his hands up and down her sides. She felt so good to him. A nooner. An afternoon delight but sooner, he'd heard someone say.

"The FBI hasn't bothered me again. Calhoun is the same as always, teetering on the brink of disaster." She pulled him over to his leather couch. "Sit."

He sat then pulled her into his lap. "What's up?"

"I've been having some symptoms. Dizziness, nausea." She leaned against his shoulder.

"My God!" He'd just been talking to Rupert about terminal cancer. And his mother...

"Have you seen a doctor?" He moved her until she was lying down, her head on the arm of the sofa. "Baby, tell me. Whatever it is, we'll get through it together."

"That's right." She pulled his face down and kissed his lips.

"You're not making any sense. Are you dizzy now? Can I get you some water?" He jumped up and pulled a bottle of water from the mini-fridge.

"Okay. Not dizzy but cold water helps settle my stomach." She sat up to take a sip. "I saw my doctor this morning."

"Good." Billy took a steadying breath. What would he do if she was seriously ill? "Who did you see? You know the best doctors are in the Texas Medical Center. Was it a specialist? If you went to some G.P., I'm going to have to insist—"

"Billy, would you listen to me for a moment?" She put her finger over his lips. "I'm not sick. My symptoms are your fault."

"What? Are you allergic to something in my house? I had the carpet ripped out when I remodeled. My hardwoods are the real deal. I've heard laminates can have chemicals ..." He shook his head. What else? Lead paint? Asbestos? "I know the house is over ten years old, but the pipes are sound. I had the air conditioning ducts cleaned out last summer. But—"

"For God's sake, will you shut up and listen?" Shannon grabbed his shoulders. "I'm pregnant!"

"I thought you were, uh, taking care of birth control." Billy heard himself but couldn't seem to stop. Why didn't he just say what he felt? That he couldn't imagine anything better than her carrying his child.

"I thought I was too." She still held his shoulders. "It seems time ran out on my contraceptive implant. It quit working. And we do enjoy our lovemaking. Frequently. Without any stops for my monthly cycle or hadn't you noticed?"

"I thought women were supposed to keep track of those things." Why couldn't he shut the fuck up?

"Keep talking, Pagan. You get any more insensitive and I'm going to dump you on your ass." Her mouth had tightened.

"Oh, hell, Shannon. I love you. You're going to have our baby?" He pulled her into his arms. "Just wait till I tell Gran. She's going to be thrilled."

"And what about you, Daddy?" She felt stiff, not exactly relaxing into his embrace.

"I can't wait. We made something together. A little person. Can you believe it?" He leaned back so he could look into her eyes. So she could see that, shit, he'd teared up.

"I sure can. Especially when I'm hugging the toilet bowl." She finally smiled again. "So you're okay with it?"

"Baby, I can't imagine anything better than starting a family with you." He smoothed his hand over her stomach, still flat. But soon …

"All right then. Now you can have your nooner. Doctor says it can't hurt Billy junior or baby Brianna."

"Brianna? What the hell kind of name is that?" But he went to work on her buttons. One of those office blouses. White. Gran would hate it. He loved it for its easy access. Hook front bra. There they were. Her pretty breasts. Had they gotten bigger yet? He was going to google this pregnancy thing first chance he got.

"I always thought I'd name a little girl Brianna. What about you? Any ideas for names?" She had his tie off and on the floor. She was quick with buttons too.

"I never thought about it. But Billy Junior is a nonstarter. A kid needs his own name, not mine."

"Mmm. Yes, right there." She pressed his head against her. "I think they're getting tender. No biting this time." Her hand was inside his pants. "Hormones. The doctor explained I might be really horny now. Isn't that great?"

"Baby, you've been horny ever since I met you. Ouch!" She'd tugged a little too hard. "Keep in mind I don't want to have an only child, Shannon."

"Really? Can we get the first one out before we make those kinds of pronouncements?" She laughed and moved under him. "Hurry, lover, I'm starving and Mai said I needed to feed you. You need to feed me too. I'm craving a burrito with extra chili and cheese."

"I live to serve." Billy was very careful as he set about pleasing the woman he loved. He was as happy as he could ever remember being. And tomorrow night was the big proposal he had planned. Good timing if he said so himself.

* * * *

"I never had grandparents."

"What?" Billy had been tracing circles around Shannon's belly button, an innie, and worrying about logistics. They'd need a bigger house. He'd turned one bedroom into his home gym, another into an office. That left one full of junk he should probably throw away. He could cook, Shannon didn't pretend to. They couldn't raise a kid on Chinese takeout. His schedule was so crazy they'd obviously need help, though he should take fewer clients. He could afford that now. Too bad Janie was talking about retiring. He liked her motherly vibe.

"Are you listening to me?" She swatted away his hand and covered herself with the throw.

"No grandparents. Why not?"

"Mama said she ran away from home as a teenager. Claimed her parents were abusive." Shannon frowned. "Now I wonder if they kicked her out."

"What about your father?" Billy didn't know what he'd have done without Gran. And there had been the Chief too. He'd been a grandfather figure, making sure Billy had a strong male role model in his life.

"Daddy said he was an orphan, raised in a boy's home. He wouldn't talk about it. Obviously, it made him determined to succeed, no matter what he had to do." She sat up and reached for her bra. "This is depressing. I'm hungry. Let's get dressed."

"Wait a minute." Billy pulled her close. "Our child will have plenty of love, if that's what's on your mind." He smoothed her hair, glad she didn't go for one of those hard, sprayed and fussy hairdos. She'd run a brush through it when they got ready to leave and look great.

"I know that. Auntie Megan showed up at the office this morning with two little outfits, one pink and one blue." Tears filled her eyes. "Oh, crap. I'm an emotional wreck."

"I love you, Shannon Calhoun." Billy kissed the tears from her cheeks. "You wreck *me*."

She threw her bra across the room. "You have such a way with words. No wonder juries love you. So do I." Shannon pulled him on top of her. "It's going to be a very late lunch, counselor."

* * * *

"Shannon, they need you in your sister's office." Caroline stopped in front of her desk. "I don't know why you don't just move up there."

"I'm sorry, Caroline." Shannon had just gotten off the phone with a reporter from the *Wall Street Journal*. She pulled a bag of saltines from her desk drawer and stuffed one into her mouth. The nausea was back and heartburn from a drive-thru taco wasn't helping. She'd spent way too much time playing in Billy's office so that had been the best they could do for lunch. Now she was suffering for it. She gulped water and brushed cracker crumbs off her blouse.

"I heard some of what you said to that reporter. You're getting really good at handling those calls." Caroline smiled as Shannon stuck the crackers in her purse and tried to juggle her laptop, water, and purse on the way to the elevator. "Are you feeling all right?"

"A little heartburn. I'm swearing off tacos." Shannon closed her lips over a burp. "Thanks, Caroline. Clearly you know about the claims against the company now. We got a break with the judge and now we know how much money we have to come up with." She punched the up button with her elbow. "Hopefully I can spin things so the stock doesn't take a tumble."

"I'm all for that. Good luck." Caroline grabbed the water bottle when it started to slip. "I'll put this back on your desk. I feel sure your sister will give you a new one up there in the executive suite."

"Okay, thanks." Shannon stepped into the elevator. What now? She'd like nothing more than to go home and take a nap. The doctor had given her something for nausea, but it had warnings about causing drowsiness so she hadn't dared take it yet. She had too much work to do. The lurch when the elevator stopped wasn't kind to her stomach. She held on to the door and breathed, finally stepping out when the doors almost closed on her.

"Shannon, are you all right? You're pale." Holly Rogers, Cassidy's executive assistant, hurried forward to take her computer.

"A little woozy. Let me sit for a minute." Shannon collapsed into a chair.

"I'll get you some water." Holly set the computer on the chair next to her and rushed away. She was back in a minute with a glass of cold water. "Here."

"Thanks, Holly." Shannon sipped, then dug out a saltine. "I'm pregnant. Still early but it's hitting me with all those symptoms you read about."

"Oh, congratulations! Cass didn't tell me!" Holly sat on the other side of her. "When are you due?"

"July. Not sure of the exact date. We're still working on that." Shannon sipped some more water and finally felt the nausea and dizziness pass. "I guess Cass is waiting for me."

"Cass and someone else." Holly glanced at the closed office door. "I think it means trouble, Shannon. When they asked for you, I wondered why."

"Who's in there?" Shannon knew Holly was sharp and not much went on at Calhoun that she didn't know about. Cass trusted her and she was one of the few people outside the family who knew the truth about Conrad and his dealings.

"Mindy Foster. Cass hopes to sell her our pipeline division." Holly stood. "Ms. Foster doesn't like to be kept waiting."

"Oh, I know that, believe me. But why am I here?" Shannon picked up her laptop.

"Ms. Foster asked for you." Holly took the empty water glass. "You sure you feel up to this? Nothing that woman does is easy. I got that vibe from her."

"Anyone else in there?" Shannon stood. Thank God the room didn't move.

"Lawyers. Dylan MacKenzie and Rand Pierce. They're trying to hammer out the terms of the sale." Holly heard her phone buzz. "Bet that's them wondering what the holdup is." She hurried to her desk and picked up her phone. "Yes, she just got here. I'm sending her in now."

"How do I look?" Shannon wished she'd had time to freshen her lipstick.

"Pale, but okay. I like your hair like that." Holly was trying to be nice.

Shannon straightened her shoulders. Her hair was pulled back in a twist because she'd made a mess of it with Billy. The less seen of it the better. Maybe pale was okay. Not that she'd get pity from Mindy. That shark had no pity for anyone. If Mindy got joy from sticking it to Calhoun in front of her former friend, Shannon would be damned if she let her see how much it hurt. She'd keep smiling no matter what Mindy tried to pull in there.

Holly threw open the door. "Shannon Calhoun." She stepped back, closing the door softly behind Shannon.

"You took your sweet time getting here." Mindy Foster sat on the leather couch, one Louboutin high heel dangling from her foot where she'd crossed her legs. She wore a red power suit that matched the soles of those shoes. Shannon had to admire her look.

"I was on the phone with the *Wall Street Journal*. I was happy to tell them about our progress in making Calhoun a strong and profitable company again." Shannon carefully set her laptop on the coffee table then settled next to Mindy. Why not? She was just as important here.

"Shannon really is great with the press." Cass had moved out from behind her desk for this meeting and was in a chair beside the two lawyers. They all had stacks of paper in their laps the size of a small phone book.

"Did you call me here to write a press release? About the pipeline deal?" Shannon smiled at Mindy. "You do love your pipelines."

"Yes, I do. Especially when I can get them at fire sale prices." She leaned back and stared at Cass. "I was just telling your, um, sister, that I won't pay what she's asking. I know Calhoun is hard up for cash. Fifty million.

That's my offer." Her smile gave Shannon the shivers.

"It's worth one-fifty, Mindy." Cass wasn't smiling. "The connections it will give you in Louisiana and Oklahoma more than make up for any of the issues you and Rand pointed out earlier."

"Some of those pipes are old and need replacing. Pumping stations are out of date. Though I do like those right-of-ways." Mindy glanced at Shannon. "I'm sure this is way over Shannon's head. Don't let us bore you. I got you in here to ask about your house. Is the family selling that place in River Oaks? I always did like the mansion's location."

"You want to buy our house?" Shannon reared back, thinking about the home where she'd grown up.

"Why not? It's on a prime piece of real estate, right down the street from the country club. Of course, I'd tear it down and build something more to my tastes. Modern, not a *Gone With the Wind* knock-off." Mindy patted Shannon's knee. "Remember when we were in junior high school and you showed me your daddy's circus-themed bedroom?" She laughed. "My God! We should have figured out then and there the man was cracked."

Shannon jumped up, knocking her laptop to the floor. "What's wrong with you, Mindy? Junior high? We were best friends then. Daddy took us to the circus and we rode the roller coaster together at the carnival there." She stomped around the table to face Mindy. Damn it, she was setting this bitch straight once and for all.

"Listen to me and listen good. I never said a word about your damned date at our come-out. It was your idiot cousin who told everyone that he'd been *paid* to take you to the dance."

Mindy flushed.

"Oh, you didn't know that, did you? Instead, you blamed me. Made me into your enemy. I, I didn't deserve it!" Shannon fought tears. Oh, no. She couldn't cry. Stupid hormones.

Mindy stared up at her. "Why should I believe you? Your daddy was a liar. Look what he did to those poor people he robbed."

"Mindy, I never lied to you. I'm not like my daddy. None of us are." Shannon looked over at Cass who was by her side suddenly, taking her hand. "We're ashamed of Daddy. And so, so sorry for what he did. We're doing our best to make things right."

"Shannon, don't waste your breath." Dylan stood on her other side. "I've known Mindy as long as you have. She's here to do business, not travel down memory lane."

"MacKenzie is right. Maybe Shannon should leave. She looks a little unsteady. Been drinking at lunch? Mindy tells me you have a habit of that." Rand Pierce had moved closer to his client. "Why are we talking about what happened decades ago? I thought we were here to do business."

Mindy dropped both feet to the floor. "Shut up, Rand."

"I've given up drinking. I'm not drunk, I'm sick." Shannon held onto Dylan and Cass. She wasn't going to fall down now. "Mindy, I'm sorry. We won't be selling the house. Not to you, anyway. I don't want it torn down. It's full of memories. Some bad, I admit it. But there were good ones too." She wished Megan was here, Ethan too. They'd back her up. Would Billy want that house? Oh, she wasn't thinking straight. "I need to get out of here."

"Wait!" Mindy stood, brushing off Rand's hand when he offered it. "You really didn't tell the world that night about my cousin? My parents *paid* him?"

"Why would I tell anyone? We were friends. *I* don't hurt my friends, Mindy." Shannon looked around and saw a pitcher of water on the bar against one wall. Water. No, she already needed to pee. But that damned nausea was back. The room was too hot, no, cold. She breathed and clutched Dylan and Cassidy, glad for their support. How was she going to survive seven more months of this?

"All right. One-ten, best and final." Mindy held out her hand to Cassidy.

"I can live with that." Cass let go of Shannon and reached out to shake Mindy's hand. "Gentlemen, draw up the contract."

"What's wrong with you, Shannon? You look like hell." Mindy shoved the laptop out of her way and walked over to look into her eyes.

"Gee, thanks, Mindy. I'm pregnant." Shannon sighed. "Now get out of my way. I'm afraid I'm fixing to lose my lunch." She saw a trash can and grabbed it, falling onto the couch with it between her legs. Thank God, she breathed through the nausea. "False alarm."

"Pregnant. Been there, done that. Twice. Besides, wouldn't have been the first time I've seen you throw up, girlfriend." Mindy settled beside her again and patted her back. "Remember the time…"

Shannon accepted a glass of water from Cassidy and listened to Mindy reminisce. It was about good times for once, though Mindy had to dig deep. They hadn't been friends since that debutante ball when Mindy had jumped to the wrong conclusion. Obviously, Mindy had decided to mend fences. Shannon would allow it because the woman made a bitter enemy. Mindy's experience with her two children meant she might also have some good advice—about schools, nannies, all the things Shannon would need to know soon.

At least now the pipeline sale would go through and help them save the company. She should call Billy. No, he was in a meeting with Rupert and the D.A. He would call her when he got out of there.

What about the house? She was supposed to finish out the year living there, according to Daddy's will. But Dylan had figured out a loophole for Cass and she'd already moved out. He'd surely find one for her if she wanted to move in with Billy. That would leave Ethan alone there. Unless... Would it be terrible if she asked Billy to consider living in the mansion with her? They'd have Janie for the rest of the year. Shannon would love her help, especially after the baby came.

Tonight they planned to tell Billy's grandmother the big news. Would the old lady expect them to get married right away? Set a wedding date? Shannon wouldn't mind it. She sure didn't want to waltz down the aisle with a bowling ball for a stomach. Or carrying a screaming baby. She'd been to weddings featuring both.

She looked down at her boring work outfit. She should change into something colorful. Gran still wasn't entirely happy with Billy hooking up again with the woman who'd dumped him years ago. Shannon figured the least she could do was dress to please the lady. At least now she knew it would be a long time before she'd take another drink. In fact, just the thought of champagne made her pull that garbage can closer. God, would she ever feel right again?

* * * *

"Congratulations. It took some work but Mai says Rupert is a free man." Albert had come by Billy's office to pick up his lady. "You got a minute?"

"Yep. I'm supposed to pick up Shannon in a while but wanted to clear up this paperwork first. Did Mai tell you? I'm going to be a daddy." Billy couldn't quit smiling.

"No, she didn't tell me." Albert came around the desk and pulled Billy up into a bear hug. "Man, that's awesome." He squeezed so hard Billy asked for mercy. "Sorry. I get carried away sometimes." He wiped his eyes. "You don't have to tell me how you feel. It's written all over your face."

"I've got the engagement ring ready to go. Now I'm worried my house is too small." Billy walked over to sprawl on the couch while Albert took a chair. "You know real estate. Help me find a bigger place. One with quarters. We'll need someone to live in. Maybe a nanny, maybe a housekeeper. I'll talk it over with Shannon."

"I'll start looking right away. You know the style she likes?" Albert pulled out his tablet.

"She likes vintage stuff. But a house? It had better have modern upgrades." Billy liked to imagine their life together. A growing family.

"Hate to bring this up, but I finally got a meeting with the head of Alamo today. You know, that company rehabbing those apartments you were interested in?" Albert frowned. "I can't say it went well. Woman in charge didn't want to cooperate. She said all the units were rented. Can't spare one for community outreach. When I gave her your card, in case she changed her mind? Well, I got a feeling she recognized your name and didn't like it."

"I have been in the news with the Billingsley case. Criminal lawyer. Maybe she's afraid I'll bring some possible felons into the neighborhood. I could call her, reassure her." Billy got up and stretched. He'd been sleeping a little better but work was killing him. He had trouble saying no to new clients, especially when he knew they were charged with a crime they didn't commit. Now that he was going to be a father, he'd need to examine his priorities. Family first, then work. It wouldn't be easy after so many years of hard charging toward success. But it would be more than worth it.

"Bill, are you still with me?" Albert snapped his fingers in front of his face. "I swear you're in a haze. Get your shit together, man. You're taking on a big responsibility." He gripped Billy's shoulder. "My old man flaked out. Never knew him. I ever have kids, they'll get sick of me, because I'll be around so much."

"I know what you mean. I never had a dad either. I plan to be there for mine too. Little League, ballet lessons, whatever they want." He nodded then did the fist bump that was Albert's signature move. "Thanks for checking into that apartment complex. You got a phone number for me?" He picked up a pen and paper.

"I'll give it to you, but I don't think you're going to have any luck. She was also pissed that cops are making regular drive-bys now. One of them is a pal of yours. I hope she doesn't get wind of that." Albert read the number off his tablet.

"No reason to if everything is legit there." He settled behind his desk again. "Any word on Simon? He taking our challenge on the money?"

"I meant to tell you. Get ready to sell Gertrude. He showed me that he opened a brokerage account. I sent him to my guy." Albert chuckled. "You know the stock market is a little like gambling. So he's all into it now. I told him he'd better not start day-trading but of course he won't listen. So far he's ahead."

"Gertrude probably needs to go anyway. I can't see hauling around a pregnant woman on the back of a bike. Maybe later I can get back into it." Billy figured he was facing lots of changes.

"If you're getting married, you might want a bike so you can escape the old lady. That's what a lot of the boys claim riding does for them. Gives them an excuse to take off alone. Think about it."

"I heard that." Mai walked through the open door. "Albert! I thought we were making progress. Now I hear you say you need to escape from an 'old lady.' Is that what I am to you?"

Albert rushed to her side. "Didn't I learn the foxtrot for you? I'm going to learn the rumba next. How would you like that?"

"I don't. Who teaches these classes? Some hoochie mama in a mini-skirt and high heels? No! You stay out of those dance classes. I'll teach you, Albert." She grabbed him by the arm and headed for the door. "We are leaving for the night, Billy. You go home too. Take Shannon out for a nice dinner. I saw the bag from Taco Delight. What kind of lunch is that?"

"Good luck, Albert. Mai, be nice to him. He's invaluable to my clients." Billy heard her lock the front door. He leaned back and closed his eyes. Just for a minute. When he heard the doorknob rattle, he opened them again. Was someone trying to break in?

Chapter 18

"Who is it?" Billy pulled the gun he'd finally remembered to buy out of his desk drawer and walked to the door.

"Simon Davis. I ran into Albert outside and he said you were willing to sell Gertrude back to me." He rattled the doorknob again. "Will you let me in?"

"Just a minute." Billy unlocked the deadbolt then threw open the door. "Come on in. Did you bring your proof?"

"You're shittin' me. You really need to see my brokerage account?" Simon walked inside and looked around. "Nice office." He pulled out a checkbook. "Look, this is a checkbook from the firm. You don't get one of these unless you have money invested there."

Billy laughed. "You think I'd take a check from a gambler?" He walked back into his office. "Have a seat. Let's talk."

"I'm reformed. Haven't been back to the casino since I hit it big there. I figured out that a lucky streak can end. When Albert told me you were willing to deal, I jumped on it." Simon settled into a chair across from Billy's desk. "I took what I'd won, after I paid taxes on it, and invested." He made a face. "Would you believe the Feds were right there, making me give a percentage to the IRS immediately?"

"You did win big, didn't you?" Billy was impressed.

"I told you. Now that I'm studying the stock market, I can see there's money to be made, and I like it. It's giving me the same, I don't know, rush that winning at the slots or the blackjack table did. And it takes some smarts."

"It does that." Billy realized Simon was eyeing his gun warily so he slid it into his briefcase. "Sorry about that. Can't be too careful. I've defended a lot of people who were innocent, but when they come back guilty as hell of something else, I won't handle their case."

"They take it hard?" Simon looked behind him at the door Billy had forgotten to lock.

"Sometimes. That's how I got to know Albert. He intervened when a former client tried to push it with a shotgun in my face. I know the Blue Star Brotherhood is a tight group and Slash is something of an expert on PTSD. But he can't always control the men who run with him. I was happy to defend the Brotherhood when they were targeted because of profiling."

"I remember. Bogus charges were brought against us in that little town northeast of here." Simon smiled. "You set those fuckers straight."

"I was happy to do it. But later, when one of his men almost beat his girlfriend to death, I told him to forget it." Billy shook his head. "I couldn't represent him, no matter what he claimed she did that made him lose his shit."

"I can see that." Simon slouched in his chair. "Me? I had some rough times in Iraq, but I don't use that as an excuse to act like an asshole here."

"Good." Billy got up. "I have someplace I have to be in a little while. Bring me cash tomorrow at the bank and I'll hand over the title to Gertrude. Tonight, I want to ride her for the last time."

"Hey, you be careful." Simon stood and followed him to the door. "We agreed, same price. But if there's damage…"

"I've only had that baby out twice. You're lucky I don't jack up the price. My lady said that bike was awfully pretty." Billy turned off the lights. "See you tomorrow? Give me your number and I'll text you the best time."

"Yeah, yeah. Just be damned careful with Gertrude." Simon got on the elevator with him. "Don't suppose you'd tell me where you live. I might want to follow you, make sure you don't mess up my bike."

"Feel free. I'm going to a neighborhood where I could use a bodyguard." Billy laughed and stepped out into the lobby. He handed Simon his phone and waited for him to put in his number.

"What do you mean, a bodyguard?" Simon stopped what he was doing. "Where are you taking Gertrude?"

"Relax, Simon. I'm going to visit my grandma. Surely you can understand." Billy slapped him on the back. "Guess if I buy a different bike, I should name her Diana, after *my* grandma."

Simon grinned. "You do that. Go. I'll protect you and Gertrude. Got a gun in my saddle bag. Meet you there."

"I was kidding." Billy realized Simon wasn't when the biker's gaze hardened again. Yes, this man had seen war and come out alive. He noticed scars among the tattoos on his arms and decided to humor him. So he told him Gran's address and the time he expected to be there. "We're having dinner first. Don't bother my grandmother. But feel free to cruise around. There's an apartment complex near her that worries me. I think they might be dealing drugs out of there."

"I'll check it out. I don't do drugs. Had enough of that shit in the hospital." Simon got on his bike, a silver and black Harley and started it with a roar. He blew out of the parking lot before Billy had even found his car keys.

Billy wondered if he'd done the right thing. But then again, what could it hurt to have a little extra protection in that neighborhood? He drove home thinking ahead. He needed to warn Shannon they'd be going to dinner at Gran's on the back of a motorcycle. She'd want to dress right for it.

* * * *

"Why sell it now? This is the first time you've taken me for a ride on this pretty bike." Shannon decided to give Billy a hard time about this. He was already treating her like spun glass. If this continued, it was going to be a long seven months.

"I can't see us riding around on a bike when you're far along. Besides, the guy was desperate to get it back. He named it Gertrude, after his late grandmother. I took pity on him." Billy handed her the special helmet he'd bought her, complete with bug shield. "I can buy another one later, maybe after the baby is born."

"Okay. That's a nice story. But I'm not breakable, Billy." She shrugged his hand away. "I could ride behind you for a few more months yet."

"I don't think so. I want you to be careful. You're carrying precious cargo." He smiled and pulled her in. "Let me take care of you and our baby."

"Don't smother me, Billy." She gave him a warning look, but it didn't seem to faze him.

"Get used to it." He helped her onto the back of the bike. "I have a special dinner planned."

"Good, I'm starved." She decided to let it go. Mood swings. Great. Her hormones were in free fall. He was going to get sick of her if she didn't rein them in. "Where are we going?"

"I want to surprise you." He patted her leg. "I like the outfit. Gran will too. You must have figured out by now that purple is her favorite color."

"This month. Last month it seemed to be orange." Shannon had dug out black skinny jeans and a soft purple shirt to go over it. She figured this would be the last time for a while that she could wear the jeans that didn't stretch. The jacket she'd tossed over the outfit was from her rodeo days—black with purple and red stars in a fancy design with sparkles. If she ever got big money again, she'd pick up a jacket like it for Gran. Billy had told her Gran's birthday was coming up at the end of the month.

"You look great." He snapped her chin strap before climbing on in front of her.

The roar of the motorcycle startled her, just like it always did. And got her blood pumping. Shannon leaned against him and held on when they took off. Was this what she had to look forward to with Billy? One adventure after another? They rode for a while until they reached an empty parking lot. Had Billy made a mistake? The restaurant was closed tonight. He turned off the engine and reached to help her off.

"What's going on? I love this place but it's obviously not open." Shannon looked around. She hadn't been here in a while but knew it was one of the most romantic restaurants in Houston. The grounds were wooded with a small lake in back where swans made their homes.

"It's open. Just for us. Come on." Billy pulled her up the wooden ramp to the porch and front door. It opened before they got there.

"Mr. Pagan, all is ready for you. Please come this way."

Shannon recognized the world famous chef. Billy called him by name, shook his hand, and thanked him as they were led through the empty dining room toward the patio dining area that faced the lake. It was getting dark and lights twinkled among the trees. A candlelit table was set for two and a waiter hurried forward to pull out Shannon's chair and set a snowy napkin in her lap.

"No wine tonight, Evan, just sparkling water." Billy sat next to her and took her hand.

"It's beautiful. What's going on?" Shannon breathed in the fresh air and was happy to realize she wasn't nauseated. She'd come home from work and taken one of those pills and a nap. Now she was refreshed and curious.

"I really wanted to take you to the reservation. To the woods again." Billy pulled her hand to his lips.

"Seriously?" Shannon laughed. "Not that it isn't beautiful there with its own lake and trees."

"We got closer there. That's where I knew we were meant to be together. I think you knew it too. We survived as a team, a couple. You said you admired the way I got us through the woods. Hell, Shannon, you were awesome. You never gave up. I can't imagine another woman with your background handling an experience like that with so much courage." He smiled. "You blew me away."

"Billy!" Shannon leaned forward and kissed him, short and sweet. "Thank you. I didn't want to disappoint you. I never want you to regret taking a chance on me again."

"I don't, I won't." He slid down to his knees. "So I'm trying to do this right this time." He pulled out an old-fashioned ring box. "Shannon Calhoun, I love you. I want us to spend the rest of our lives together, making a family and a home with each other. Will you marry me?" He snapped open the lid and she could see his hand shaking.

She dropped to her knees in front of him and took that shaking hand in hers. "Yes, you know I will! What is that...? Billy, it's beautiful." She pulled the ring out of the box. "Where did you get this?"

"It was my great grandmother's. Gran gave it to me. Try it on." Billy helped her fit it onto her ring finger. "Janie told me your ring size. That woman is a treasure."

"Yes, she is. But so is Gran. She actually let you have this for me?" Shannon stared at the ring which was perfect. It was just what she would have picked if he'd taken her shopping. Vintage, exquisite. She grabbed Billy's shoulders and pulled him in for a long kiss. "I love you. Did I forget to say that?"

"You were stunned into silence by the ring. I'll have to tell Gran that. She'll be tickled." He pulled Shannon up and helped her settle into her chair again. "Can we eat now? I ordered some of their specialties and I know it's all going to be delicious."

Shannon admired the sparkle of a really big diamond, glad she'd done her nails. "Oh, food. Yes, of course. Bring it on." She grabbed Billy's hand, loving the way he couldn't stop grinning. He was looking at the ring too. "You did good, Pagan. Much better than in the ballroom. Did you win the bid on the cruise?"

"I did. We can book it when we're ready. So we need to set a date." He leaned back when a waiter set a salad in front of him. "Soon. I want you locked down before this baby is born."

"I'm all for that." She forked up perfectly seasoned greens with bacon. "Mmm. Did you get your plane back yet? We could fly to Vegas."

"Gran would have a fit. A church wedding in her neighborhood would make her happy, but we'd have to have heavy security." Billy waved his fork. "Do you have a church you've gone to all your life?"

"Not steadily. Can you imagine my mother working with the ladies in the altar guild?" Shannon frowned. "I'm sorry, Billy. I want my family there, but I'm not very religious."

"That's okay, I have an idea. There's a nice chapel at the reservation. What if we get married there? I have a cousin who's the preacher. Would that be all right? It's close enough for your family to drive up. I can call and find out what dates are open then clear my calendar for the honeymoon. Three weeks sailing the Mediterranean, just the two of us and a discreet crew. What do you think?" He studied her with those little frown lines he got when he was anxious.

Shannon knew this actually would mean a lot to him. And she would get married barefoot next to that crooked creek as long as he was there to say "I do."

"I love it. All of it. We can tell Gran our plans when we tell her about the baby. Maybe she'll forgive me a little for breaking your heart all those years ago." She grabbed Billy's hand. "Make it soon. I don't want to be showing when I walk down the aisle." She glanced down at the Steak Diane that had been put in front of her.

"The sooner the better." He leaned over to kiss her then gestured toward her plate. "I can't wait for you to get a tummy. Eat every bite, woman."

Shannon laughed and picked up her steak knife. Things were falling into place. It was almost too good to be true.

* * * *

Billy helped Shannon down the steps at his grandmother's house. He really should install hand rails here. Why hadn't he done it years ago? The visit with Gran had gone better than he'd expected. Of course, his grandmother still had reservations about Shannon. Old wounds took a long time to heal. But now that Shannon was carrying her great grandchild? Well, they would be bound together forever. Gran got that. She'd already started a quilt for them and now was talking about making a baby quilt with an airplane theme.

"You be careful now. Riding around on a motorcycle with Shannon expecting? Boy, I think you've lost what sense you had." Gran had the last word as she clanged the bars shut and locked them. "Good night!" Her smile could have lit up the neighborhood. Which needed it. Didn't they ever replace the burned-out street lights?

Shannon laughed. "She's making us a velvet quilt. Those things are gorgeous."

"I think so, but you don't have to use it if you don't want to. It's just her way of showing you she's trying." Billy heard a loud motor coming. As he'd expected, it was Simon making the rounds. He glanced toward the corner and saw the gang there, juking and jiving, calling out to Simon on his Harley. The biker stopped and said something to them.

"Well, I'm tired, full of delicious food, and ready for bed." Shannon held onto his arm as they stepped into the street where he'd left Gertrude next to the curb. She dangled the helmet from one hand. "Of course, I also feel the need to celebrate when we get to your house." She stopped him before he could help her onto the bike. "Speaking of houses. There's something we need to discuss. About where we're going to live."

"I've already asked Albert to start looking for places. I know my house is too small for our growing family." Billy heard the thump of heavy metal music coming closer. He glanced down the street and there was that same black SUV, moving fast, too fast. Right toward them. He grabbed Shannon's arm.

"What?" She staggered when he shoved her toward the house. "Billy!"

"Run!" He heard a thump as the car jumped the curb. Was the asshole nuts? He wrapped his arms around Shannon, carrying her as he dove for the house. He rolled both of them, coming up hard against the concrete porch supports.

The roar of a Harley came from behind him. A squeal of brakes, the screech of metal meeting metal. The heat and smell of exhaust blew over them, all hell breaking loose when the car took out the wooden porch steps then kept going. Gunshots. Glass shattering. Billy held a trembling Shannon under him and prayed like he'd never prayed in his goddamned life.

"Stay inside." That was for Gran.

"Go the hell away." That was for those insane assholes who must have a grudge against him. No idea why.

"Protect my woman and my baby." That was straight to God.

Billy finally snapped to the fact that the only sound he heard was his own harsh breathing and Shannon whimpering underneath him. He raised his head cautiously.

Shannon clutched his jacket. "Billy?"

"Don't move." He got slowly to his hands and knees and surveyed the scene. Deep ruts and tire tracks where the SUV had taken out the steps and his grandma's garden. A shiny black fender cast aside on the grass. Gertrude overturned and knocked to the center of the street. No sign of Simon on his hog. Shit. It was a war zone but at least he didn't see bodies or blood.

The kids! He saw them lying on their stomachs, hands over their heads. Good idea with gunfire. Watchman held his phone to his ear. Distant sirens might mean the kid had actually called the cops. Billy felt Shannon's hand on his face.

"Are you all right? What just happened?" She gasped when she saw the front of Gran's house.

Gran peeked out from behind her bars. "Billy! Are you two okay? I called the police. They said officers are already on the way." She rattled her key in the lock. "You two get in here. I'll lock us in."

"Shannon, how do you feel? Are you all right?" He ran his hands over her.

"I'm fine. Come on. Let's get inside." She tugged him toward the mangled porch.

"You go. Let me help you." Billy wasn't about to cower behind the bars. He boosted Shannon up. He'd have to rig some temporary steps or Gran would be trapped there. Shit. He wanted her out of this fucking neighborhood. "Lock yourselves in. Do it now."

"No! Come with us." Shannon reached out. "They might come back."

"Listen. I hear sirens. They won't come back now. I need to see what's going on. Talk to the police." He took her hand and held it. She was pale, trembling. "You sure you're okay? Did I hurt you when I grabbed you?"

"Not at all." She pulled, frowning when he shook his head and stayed where he was. "Be careful." She slipped inside then locked the door. Billy saw her put her arm around Gran.

"Close the wooden door too." He strode out to Gertrude and pulled his handgun out of the saddle bag. Son of a bitch. Who had tried to kill him? And when he was with Shannon? He wanted to hurt someone. Beat them bloody. Slam that gun against their motherfucking heads. He stalked down to where the kids were back on their feet, talking and gesturing as they rehashed what had just gone down.

"We got the license number, boss. Told it to the cops." Watchman spoke for the group. He held out his hand, palm up, not about to miss an opportunity.

"You kids okay? Everyone here all right?" Billy saw them nod as he dug for a large bill and slapped it into the boy's hand. "Did you see the driver? Any idea who did this?"

"It was a woman drivin'. Didn't you see? She leaned out and shot at your friend on the other bike when he came at her and tried to steer her away from the house." Watchman was clearly excited now that the coast was clear. He glanced at Billy's gun. "You don't think they'll come back, do ya?"

"Doubt it. Since you called the cops." Billy hoped he was right. "I didn't see what happened. I was protecting my lady." Billy glanced back at the house. Pieces of lumber, potential murder weapons with jagged edges, were scattered inches from where he and Shannon had been.

"Your guy? He mighta got hit but he kept goin'. Chased that big car. Never stopped. I told the cops which way they went."

Billy dug out another bill. "You did good, Watchman. Be careful." He turned when he saw a police car pull up next to Gertrude. "Stick around. Talk to the cops. I'll make sure none of you get into trouble. You hear me?"

"Yes, sir." Watchman grabbed one of his posse by the back of his shirt when he tried to make a run for it. "You heard the man. We wait, we're witnesses."

There was some grumbling but they all held their places. Billy strode over to meet the police. The cop and his partner were out of the car, looking around. It took a while to explain what had happened. The tread marks and damage to the porch told most of the story. Then a call came in over the scanner. The SUV had crashed not far from their location after more police cars had joined the chase.

"Did they say if the man on the Harley was still with them? The kids over there said he was following the SUV." Billy was worried about Simon. Two more police cars drove up. One of them was driven by his friend Buchman.

"What's this I hear about you playing dodge the SUV in your grandma's front yard?" Buchman and his partner got out of their car and walked over. He whistled when he saw the mess.

"Not a game I'd ever want to play again, my friend. My fiancée was with me at the time." Billy nodded toward the house. Now that the cops had arrived, he saw Gran and Shannon looking out through the bars. "You see what they did to Gran's porch steps? A nightmare."

"You got that right. She all right, your fiancée?" Buchman frowned as he studied the damage. "Engaged? That's new. Congratulations."

"Thanks. Yes, she's fine. Tell me you arrested the assholes who did this."

"Yeah, my pal Jimbo did. Thanks to some guy named Simon Davis who pursued them on his hog. He wouldn't let them get away. He called in on his cell and gave his location so we could follow his cell phone signal. Pretty smart. And those kids on the corner? One of them is my nephew. They stepped up and gave us the license number." Buchman waved and a tall youth shrugged and looked away. Being related to a cop must not help his street cred.

"I want to talk to the perps. Find out why this happened. What it was all about." Billy wanted to do more than talk, but he tried to rein in his temper.

"Here's your chance. I asked them to bring the two people in the car here. To see if you could identify them. They clammed up right away. Wouldn't say a word and carried no ID, though they had some fire power. I thought we were going to have a bloody shootout on our hands, but when they saw they were surrounded, they gave up and threw out their guns."

"I'm glad of that." Billy remembered those gunshots. Right in his grandmother's front yard. Shit, if one had gone through her window… It happened all the time. An innocent bystander hit by a stray bullet.

Buchman pulled out his notebook. "Funny thing, Billy. Car's registered to a company. Alamo Apartments. Didn't you tell me that's the outfit a block over? Why the hell would they be trying to run you down? You didn't play detective when I told you not to, did you?"

"No, I left it alone." Billy followed him to the police car that had pulled up. "You were going to check…"

"I did. Drove by but had no probable cause to search the warehouse or any of the apartments. Questioned a few of the residents I met in the parking lot about the late-night action. Got nothing useful. Me coming around might have made them nervous. I sure never mentioned your name." Buchman waved at the driver of the car that stopped next to them. "Hey, Jimbo, this is the guy who needs to look at your perps. He's the one they tried to run down. Let him see if he can give us an ID."

"You read them their rights, didn't you?" Billy made sure his gun was covered by his jacket. He was grass-stained and clearly had been through a hard night.

"Sure. Did it at the scene of the crash. Don't want this to come back because of a screw-up." The cop gave him a sympathetic look before he opened the back door and reached inside. His partner did the same on the other side of the car. Billy froze when he saw who emerged and was shoved against the back of the police car.

At first, the handcuffed woman and man didn't look up, just stood hostile and silent, staring at the ground.

"Take a look, Billy. Do you know them?" Buchman stepped aside.

Billy breathed through the roaring in his head. If he wasn't sworn to uphold the law… *Calm. Hold your shit together.* God, but he wanted to pull out his gun and slap it across the woman's sullen face. Like she'd slapped Shannon that day. He kept staring at them and the woman must have felt something in the air. She lifted her chin and looked back at him defiantly.

"Call the FBI, Buchman. She's Margaret aka Maggie Lioni, leader of the Exiles. She's wanted by the Feds on a multitude of charges." Billy looked at her sidekick. "This one's name is Charlie. I never heard his last name. For some reason, he wasn't in the photo array the FBI showed me, but he's facing charges now." He walked up to Charlie and poked him in the chest. "Good luck, asshole. I see attempted murder in your future. Maybe if you sing loud enough to the Feds about your lady friend and the Exiles you can cut a deal."

"You just couldn't leave us alone, could you, Pagan?" Maggie spit at him. She missed, which seemed to infuriate her. "We were settling in. The last place the Feds would look for us is downtown Houston. Then you come sniffing around." She was practically screaming. "How did you know? How did you fucking know?" She jerked away from the cop holding her arm and tried to head butt him. Buchman stepped between them and did what

Billy longed to do. He used his nightstick to slam her back against the car.

"Paranoid, Maggie? I didn't know you were living there. I just wanted to find a place for the local kids to hang out. Something better than a street corner." Billy glanced at the group with shifting feet on the corner who were talking to a cop taking notes.

"You're a lawyer, right?" Charlie spoke up. "You really think I could cut a deal with those Feds?"

"Shut your fucking mouth, Charlie. It was your stupid idea to fit in, to buy a car that made it look like we're part of the neighborhood." Maggie kicked him so hard he almost fell over. "Dumb shit."

"Get me away from her. I'll talk to the Feds. I want to make a deal." He sobbed and huddled next to the cop who had his arm in a strong grip. That policeman looked at Charlie scornfully.

"Called the Feds earlier. This woman popped up as wanted when we ran her prints." Jimbo grinned when the telltale big black SUVs pulled up to the crime scene.

"So much for loyalty, Maggie." Billy saw more of the black cars the Feds drove pull up. He walked over and told the agents where the Exiles headquarters were located. The man in charge was eager to "clear out the nest" and got on his phone. Charlie was talking to an agent, eager to make a deal.

"Buchman, where's the guy who chased them? Simon Davis?" Billy asked once Maggie was led away. He bent down to examine the damage to Gertrude. He'd have to call his insurance agent and have it towed to a repair shop.

"They wanted to take him to an emergency room. He had a minor gunshot wound. Ambulance driver called to the scene cleaned him up and said the man was good to go. Then Davis demanded to be given his bike back. He needed to make a statement then he'll be let go." Buchman turned. "I think he's coming now."

Billy heard the powerful motor. Yep, Simon turned the corner and ran straight into a crime scene. He convinced the cop at the yellow tape to let him park and Buchman waved him in.

"Look at her." Simon knelt next to Gertrude. "She'll need new paint, pipes. It's a crime. Where are the fuckers who did this?" He was on his feet, his gun in his hand.

"Settle down, Mr. Davis. They're in federal custody." Buchman put his hand on Simon's shoulder. "I assume you have a permit to carry that weapon."

"Uh. Billy?" Simon's eyes darted around the area. "I may have left it at home. On my dresser."

"Cut him some slack, Buchman. He was a hero tonight." Billy nudged Simon and he put his weapon out of sight behind his back. "My client here has a permit. I'll vouch for him."

"This one time." The policeman frowned. "But if I catch you carrying again without the proper paperwork on your person, you're going downtown, Davis."

"Yes, sir. It should be in my wallet. Careless of me." Simon couldn't take his eyes off Gertrude. "I still want her. I'll do the restoration myself."

"Are you sure? She's insured." Billy had never seen such devotion to a machine.

"No one touches my baby but me." Simon nodded when a tow truck pulled up next to the yellow tape. "A buddy of mine is here. If you'll trust me to pay you tomorrow, I'll have him take it to my garage tonight."

"Go ahead. After what you did tonight, you can have her. Half price." Billy realized Simon's interference had probably saved his life and Shannon's. Maybe he should just give the man his bike. He'd definitely helped capture Maggie and her crew.

"Thanks, man." Simon fist bumped then turned to Buchman. "Can I take her out of here?"

"Yeah, go ahead. Crime scene photos are done and we need to clear this street." He smiled as Simon lovingly righted the motorcycle and rolled it away. "Hey, Billy, it's time for my break. You want some help building temporary steps? Looks like you have two ladies dying to get out here." He nodded toward Gran's porch where they could see Shannon and Gran watching them.

"Yeah. Thanks. I think there's some lumber in the garage." Billy followed him and thought about that close call. He'd thrown Shannon beneath him and prayed. It had definitely shown him what he was willing to die for. Her and his child. He took a deep breath and felt the knot of tonight's tension release a little. Taking on a family was a heavy load. But he could and would handle it. Gladly.

Epilogue

It was one of those perfect fall days in the piney woods, cool enough for the long sleeves on her wedding dress and not a cloud in the sky. Shannon was glad they'd decided to hold the wedding here. The chapel hadn't been big enough to hold her family and Billy's many cousins. It seemed he was related to half the Tribe and they all wanted to attend the wedding.

She breathed in fresh air and pine and thanked God her stomach was cooperating. She wasn't showing yet, thank goodness. Megan's good friend who ran a boutique had found the perfect dress for her at a bargain price. Or at least that's what her sister had told her. Now that Rowdy was worth millions, it was possible he'd footed the bill. Shannon had said "Thanks" and let it go because it was gorgeous and made her feel like a princess.

"Are you ready, big sister?" Ethan was taking his job of walking her down the aisle seriously. He had on Daddy's tux again and looked great. The photographer had made her pose for a picture with her sisters and brother before the bridesmaids had walked down the aisle. The Calhouns. None of them was allowed to cry, it would ruin the girls' makeup and Ethan was too manly.

It seemed a little silly for all of them to be so dressed up when the wedding was outside next to a lake, but Billy had insisted. He had found out from Megan, who'd snooped and read her diary when they were growing up, what Shannon thought would be a perfect wedding. He'd become determined to make it happen. So there were six bridesmaids, including her sisters, wearing an array of pastels, each holding single white roses. It was just like she'd written when she was sixteen. She held a bouquet of orchids and roses. Perfect.

Shannon took her brother's arm. "Billy's waiting for me. I'd better make him mine before one of those single bridesmaids gets her hooks in him. Did you see them all over him last night?"

"You've got nothing to worry about, sis. That man has eyes only for you." Ethan kissed her cheek. "You look beautiful." He smiled, then led her out of the cabin and down the porch steps.

The music swelled and she saw Billy at the end of the aisle looking like he'd just won a case in front of the Supreme Court. White folding chairs were in rows on either side of an aisle lined with satin streamers tied with more roses. Every seat was filled and the congregation stood as the keyboard, played by yet another of Billy's cousins, broke into the wedding march. Traditional. She loved it.

Ethan squeezed her arm as they set off slowly down the aisle. It seemed to take forever yet no time at all before she stood beside Billy and said her vows. How far they'd come since the night she'd first seen him. One thing in her diary wouldn't be at this wedding. Champagne. She wouldn't miss it either.

When the minister pronounced them husband and wife, Billy kissed her until someone started whistling. That set off a chorus of whistles until she flushed and pushed him away.

"Save it for the honeymoon, cuz." Jacob, the best man, poked Billy in the side before they started back down the aisle.

"I still have plenty left, don't you worry about it." Billy's quip got the crowd roaring.

Shannon stopped next to Gran sitting in the front row and handed her a white rose from her bouquet. She got a kiss on the cheek as a thank you. Their relationship was coming along. Having the wedding on Gran's birthday had been a good idea on Billy's part and they'd enjoyed birthday cake last night at the rehearsal dinner.

Since Billy had decided they could try living in the Calhoun mansion for a while, Gran had agreed to stay in the pool house. The promise of a great grandchild had persuaded her that it might be time to make a move. Gran and Janie had already found plenty to talk about over *Wheel of Fortune* and their morning coffee.

At the reception, the chief came up to them and gave them his blessing. "May you have many happy years together." The chief gently laid his hands on their heads. "And be blessed with a houseful of children."

"Already working on it, Chief." Billy patted Shannon on her stomach.

"Billy!" She flushed and saw the chief raise his eyebrows. "Thank you, sir. We appreciate your allowing us to get married here."

"Please come visit anytime. And bring your little ones." The chief walked away, then turned around and winked at Billy. "Good job, son."

"Now look what you've done. Soon everyone in the tribe will know you knocked me up." Shannon decided it was time to cut the cake and pulled Billy toward it. "Did I see Stan's limo outside?"

"Yes, you did. He was at the wedding, didn't you see him? He's driving us back to Houston so we can go straight to the airport." Billy waved Mai over. "Tell Shannon I cleared my calendar. We're good to go for the honeymoon."

"Yes. His calendar is clear. Mine is overflowing. He is trying to cut back his workload. Even talking about bringing in another lawyer. Can you believe it?" Mai kissed Shannon, then Billy. "Albert promised me he would help me at the office. We're waiting for the federal auction so he can buy those apartments in your grandmother's neighborhood, Billy. It might happen while you're gone."

"Albert's buying them?" Shannon was surprised.

"Yes, I am. They're a good investment." Albert walked up with a big piece of chocolate cake on a plate. "You people are too slow cutting the cake. I went into business for myself."

"Oh, you are too bad. They're supposed to cut the cakes in front of the photographer." Mai slapped his hand, then took his fork and tasted the cake herself. "Delicious."

"Did you know they baked the cakes here on the reservation? You should try their restaurant sometime." Shannon was too happy to worry about cake cutting or photos. "Now about those apartments... We were hoping to start a youth center in that neighborhood."

"I'm on it." Albert slapped Mai's hand when she tried to eat more of his cake. "You can have a unit or two for your project. Stan might help out too. He's interested in the warehouse for his limo company. He grew up in that neighborhood and likes the idea of bringing commerce to it. There may be some jobs in it for the kids you work with."

"That's good. The Feds found a ton or more of marijuana inside that warehouse. The Exiles had brought it with them and were about to start growing more as soon as they got settled." Shannon realized the crowd was forming around that wedding cake so Albert wasn't the only one ready to eat. "It would have been horrible if that had hit the neighborhood."

Billy pulled Shannon toward the cake. "Excuse us. We have wedding business now. Baby, are we going to shove cake in each other's faces like some people do? Or can we eat a little then get out of here?"

"Don't shove it in my face if you know what's good for you. And how can we skip the dancing?" Shannon grinned. "You hired the DJ. You know he's booked for three hours of nonstop music."

Billy gestured at the large crowd. "Look, everyone here is having a good time. They can dance, eat cake, and even go over to the casino if they want to. What do they need us for?" He pulled Shannon against him. "Me? All *I* want is that long limo ride with my new wife back to Houston. I seem to remember that back seat is a lot of fun. Then…"

Shannon put a finger over his lips. "Say no more. Let's cut that freaking cake then get out of here."

Billy laughed and twirled her around. "Now you're talking, Mrs. Pagan."

Shannon grabbed his hand and led him to the table. Yes, she was taking his name and proud of it. A camera flashed and she smiled until her face hurt. But it was fine. Because she had what she wanted now. More than she could have ever imagined when she'd been writing in her diary so long ago.

Of course, they couldn't just slip away. Billy pulled her onto the dance floor at his cousin's urging and they swayed to a love song. He whispered promises of a honeymoon to remember, making her shiver. It seemed that they really had moved on from the past toward a bright future. Together, forever.

TEXAS HEAT

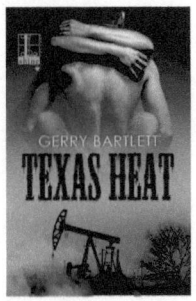

A surprise inheritance. A family of strangers. And a man she can't avoid . . .

Cassidy Calhoun can't believe she's the secret daughter of an oil billionaire. This small-town Texas girl with student loans by the barrel has never gotten a thing she didn't earn for herself.

The terms of her late father's will say Cassidy—and her newfound spoiled half-siblings—must work a year at the family's floundering business before they inherit a dime. Too bad the only thing Cass knows about oil is that it makes the junker she drives go.

Mason MacKenzie, the evaluator for their test, will help her get up to speed. Or will he? Mason is a boot-wearing, truck-driving Houston hottie who runs Calhoun Petroleum's biggest rival. The sparks between him and Cassidy could combust any minute. But the closer they get, the more strange near-accidents Cassidy seems to be having. And Mason has plenty of reasons to play up their attraction for his own benefit.

If she can trust him, the two of them working together might save a crumbling dynasty. But if she can't, Cass might just lose both her fortune and her heart . . .

TEXAS FIRE

Her father's dream. Her crossroads. And a man who sees just her . . .

Megan Calhoun doesn't stick with anything long. She's the daughter of a billionaire—why pretend to be somebody else?

Until she finds out her father's will says she has to. She has to last a year in the oil patch, in the dust and heat of West Texas, working for her daddy's company. Otherwise she's cut off without a cent—and no way to earn one.

The only upside is her new pal Rowdy Baker, ex-football star, Calhoun engineer, and grade-A stud. If she has to live in a trailer, his doesn't sound so bad.

Rowdy knows the roughnecks running the rigs won't take kindly to a smartass blonde rookie whose last name matches their paychecks. He can't control his attraction to her. And with everyone from the foremen to the stockholders spitting mad at the Calhouns, he expects trouble ahead.

But Megan has never been scared in her life. And with Rowdy to help her plot, she has the chance of a lifetime: to find her calling, to fix her company, and, if she doesn't screw it up—to capture a heart . . .

Meet the Author

A nationally best-selling author, Gerry Bartlett is a native Texan who lives halfway between Houston and Galveston. She freely admits to a shopping addiction which is why she has an antiques business on the historic Strand on Galveston Island. She used to be a gourmet cook but has decided it's more fun to indulge in gourmet eating instead. You can visit Gerry on Facebook, twitter or Instagram. You can also check out her latest releases on her website at http://gerrybartlett.com where you can sign up for her newsletter or read her articles with advice for aspiring writers, The Perils of Publishing.